PRAISE FOR THE *POLIZEI BI*

"For aficionados of fine police detection and procedure, it doesn't get better than Kim Hays's Linder and Donatelli series. Puzzling mysteries, artful prose, and engaging characters abound in these Swiss-based treats for mystery fans of all tastes."

—GEORGE EASTER, Editor,
Deadly Pleasures Mystery Magazine

PRAISE FOR *SPLINTERED JUSTICE*

"...A twisty, humane procedural bringing the urgent darkness of Scandinavian noir to Bern.... The suspense is richly layered, [and]... for all the novel's heft, Hays keeps the pages turning with urgent personal stakes, twists that make logical sense, and a deep humanity."

—*BookLife Reviews*

"Kim Hays proves once again that her Linder and Donatelli books have joined the ranks of top-notch police procedurals. In this expertly paced and crafted novel, the vivid Bernese setting and her relatable, engaging protagonists will have readers hooked from first page to last. *Splintered Justice* should shoot straight to the top of this year's mystery must-read lists—Renzo Donatelli and Guiliana Linder have certainly joined my list of favorite detectives!"

DEBORAH CROMBIE, bestselling author of
the award-winning Kincaid and James series

"The author has lived in Switzerland for decades, so readers can expect vivid portraits of its locales...[along with]...humor and rich descriptions...A page-turner [that]...can also be enjoyed slowly, like a delicious Swiss chocolate."

—*Kirkus Reviews*

"Hays makes sure the historical aspects of the story are as compelling as the murder mystery at its heart. . . . A smart Swiss procedural that keeps its mystery ticking."

—*Kirkus Reviews*

"The second outing of Linder and Donatelli is as crisp and skilled as the first. . . . Brisk plot, depth of character, great setting–what's not to love?"

—LAURIE R. KING,
Edgar Award-winning author

PRAISE FOR *A FONDNESS FOR TRUTH*

". . . Hays remains . . . consistently focused on current affairs, international cultures, and hot topics. . . . A brisk, smoothly written police procedural from an author engaged with contemporary social issues."

—*Kirkus Reviews*

". . . Offers readers an utterly compelling and elegantly written police procedural . . . [with] a glimpse of Switzerland . . . [T]he perfect elements for an absolutely riveting mystery."

—WILLIAM KENT KRUEGER,
Edgar Award-winning author of
the Cork O'Connor mysteries

"Hays's empathetic, entertaining, smartly plotted mystery will keep readers guessing . . . [in this] stellar series procedural with compelling detectives."

—Editor's Pick, *BookLife Reviews*

Splintered
Justice

Splintered Justice

A LINDER AND DONATELLI MYSTERY

KIM HAYS

SEVENTH
STREET
BOOKS®

Published 2025 by Seventh Street Books®

Cover image: shutterstock / jorisvo
Cover design by Paula Guran
Cover design © Start Science Fiction
Layout and Design: Westchester Publishing Services

This is a work of fiction. Characters, organizations, products, locales, and events portrayed in this novel either are products of the author's imagination or are used fictitiously. Any similarities to real persons, living or dead, are coincidental and not intended by the author.

Inquiries should be addressed to
Start Science Fiction
221 River Street, 9th Floor
Hoboken, New Jersey 07030
PHONE: 212-431-5454
WWW.SEVENTHSTREETBOOKS.COM

10 9 8 7 6 5 4 3 2 1

978-1-64506-094-9 (paperback)
978-1-64506-104-5 (ebook)

Printed in the United States of America

For my father

Thomas Raymond Hays
1928–2004

Novelists need insight into people
and the ability to tell good stories.
You had those gifts in abundance, Papa.
I miss you.

Foreword

Croatian Names

After three Polizei Bern books, I imagine my characters' German names and Bernese nicknames have started to make sense to many readers. If not, the forewords in *Pesticide* and *Sons and Brothers* may prove helpful. This fourth book introduces six Croatian Swiss, and I thought you might like to know how to pronounce their names. The men are Lovro and Goran Horvat, and the women are Katica and Zora Horvat, Ivana Pavić, and Jelena Tomić.

Vowel sounds are always crucial to pronunciation, and in Croatian, they are similar to Spanish, French, and German: a = ah, e = eh, i = Tina, o = roll, and u = moon.

"c" versus "ć" The letter c is pronounced ts, while ć is pronounced ch. So, Katica is pronounced *Kátitsa*, with an accent on the first syllable, and Pavić is pronounced *Pávich*. The suffix ić means "son of" and is used to form last names in Croatia, Serbia, Bosnia, and Montenegro.

"j" Like Germans, Croatians pronounce the letter j as a y. So, Jelena is pronounced *Yélena,* and the word majka (which means "mother") is *Mah-ee-kah.*

Croatians call their country *Hrvatska*. Horvat is a common Croatian surname that means "person from Croatia." The accent is on the first syllable.

1
Before

"In a moment, I'll show you the choir's sixteenth-century vaulted ceiling, decorated by Bern's most famous painter, Niklaus Manuel, who died in 1530. But before that, let's stop at this stained-glass window. It's a modern copy of Manuel's *Dance of Death*. Notice how Death is . . ."

". . . portrayed in each panel as a mocking skeleton." Denis whispered along with Frau Fischer's words. He'd been tracking the guide and her group as they straggled through the Bern Münster, and no one had spotted him—yet. In the nave, he could wriggle on his stomach between the side pews to stay hidden. But if he followed the tourists into the choir, he'd be seen before he could take cover. The best he could do was tiptoe around the sanctuary, crouch behind the big statues of Jesus and Mary, and wait for the tourists to come out on the other side of the choir so he could stalk them as they moved down the nave's north aisle.

He wondered if Frau Fischer knew he was here today. She was his favorite of the church ladies because even when she caught sight of him inching along on his belly—a Lakota creeping up on a fort's sentries or a Celt closing in on Roman soldiers—she never gave him away. She had three children and five grandchildren, she'd told him. She hadn't forgotten about playing.

Frau Arnold had kids, too, but she was mean. She fussed at him no matter what he did, like when he was sitting with his back against the fence around the dead Jesus to read the names on the war memorials or lying on the chancel floor counting the beards on the ceiling's saints. Frau Arnold complained about him to his grandparents and got him into trouble with the sexton. He didn't need help making the sexton mad at him; he managed that often enough on his own.

"... portrayed *himself* with Death in this last panel," Denis heard Frau Fischer say. Motionless on the wooden floor, he waited for the cameras to finish clicking and the footsteps to creak up the ramp into the choir. He peered over the back of the pew to make sure no one was left in front of the *Dance of Death*. Then he bolted out from between the benches and dashed across the church toward the Jesus and Mary statues. About two-thirds of the way there, he stopped.

A girl sat in the pew closest to the altar, hands folded in her lap, watching him. She didn't smile, but she didn't look cross, either, simply curious. "What are you doing here?"

"I live here," he told her. She frowned, but before she could ask another question, he continued, "So, why are *you* here?"

"I came with my mother."

Denis looked around. Far down the nave, two women with white hair stared up at the ceiling, but neither looked the right age to be the girl's mother.

"Where is she?"

The girl shrugged and made a face. "Who knows? She tells me to wait on this seat and do my homework till she comes back."

Now he noticed that her schoolbag, a briefcase-shaped backpack, was next to her on the pew. "I never saw you here before."

She shrugged again. "This is only the third time."

She looked about his age, which was almost ten. Like him, she had blue eyes, and they both had brown hair, although hers was much darker, a great mass of it pulled into a big, puffy ponytail.

"If you aren't going to do your homework, I could show you stuff," he told her.

"Like what?"

Suddenly, it seemed important to make her want to see all his favorite carvings in the cathedral. But he didn't know how to win her interest. "Things I look at," he mumbled.

She gazed at him a moment longer. Then she got up—she was taller than him, like most of the girls in his class—and swung the straps of her bag over both shoulders. Denis could still hear Frau Fischer's tourists, but he was done stalking them. This girl was much more interesting. "You don't have to carry that around," he told her. "We'll hide it."

Denis led her across the nave to a dark, straight-backed wooden bench separated into individual seats by carved panels. He lifted one of the folding seats and showed her the man with a big mustache and a forked beard that was carved underneath it. He knew from his grandfather that the carving was a misericord, but he didn't want her to think he was a show-off. "This is the shaggy man; it's one of the oldest stalls in the whole church. Here." He held out his hand for the bag.

She passed it to him, and he slid it under the seat. "There's a woman, too. Look." He raised the hinged seat next to the shaggy man to display a woman with fat round cheeks and a band of cloth running over her ears and under her chin. "I like the man better, though."

The tall girl—he noticed she had small gold rings in her earlobes—stared critically at the woman. "I do, too. Are there other interesting people?"

Denis grinned at her. "Are you kidding? There are tons. The windows are full of them, and there are saints on the ceiling behind the altar, but the best faces are on the choir stalls. Come on!" They loped down the south aisle and ran up the ramp into the choir.

Denis hoped she'd like the man shearing the lamb as much as he did, but before they approached the rows of seats with their carved figures, he stopped. So did she, right next to him, and turned to give him an eager, questioning look.

"What's your name?" he asked.

"Zora." She smiled at him, her lips parting, her blue eyes shining, and her cheeks making dimples.

"Mine's Denis."

He found himself wanting to tell her more than just his name. "My mother leaves me here in the Münster, too. That's why I live with my grandparents," he confided. "In a tiny apartment in the tower."

"Does your mother come back?" She sounded upset, and Denis hoped it wasn't with him. Without waiting for him to answer, she added, "Mine always does." Before he could decide what to say, she added, "You're lucky to be with your grandparents. I barely remember mine. They live in Istria."

"Where's that?"

"It's a piece of Croatia that hangs down into the sea. You take a boat from Venice." She glanced at him. "That's in Italy," she added, in case he was too stupid to know where Venice was. "And Croatia is a country."

"I know *that*," he said, relieved that he actually did—he'd had to list all the EU countries on a quiz a few weeks earlier. "Look." At last, he gestured at the high-backed choir stalls. "It's like people are coming out of the wood."

She stared up at a carving of Moses, then smiled her big smile at him again. "Yeah. Like they've woken up!"

He grinned back, feeling happier than he had in a long time.

2

Over fifteen years later
Bern's Old City, Tuesday afternoon, June 25

Walking up Junkergasse from the dentist's office, Renzo felt like he'd been conned. Redo one of his fillings? It was misery enough to have a tooth filled, but no one had warned him that old cavities might have to be drilled out and replaced.

Thinking dark thoughts about his dentist, he reached the entrance to the park that ran along the southern side of the Münster and paused at the ornate gate. Most Bernese called the park the *Pläfe*, short for *Plattform*. Formerly a graveyard, it was now a rectangle of land with gravel paths, manicured patches of grass and shrubbery, comfortable green benches, a tiny playground, an outdoor café, and rows of pollarded trees. The Pläfe's sides bordered land belonging to Old City mansions, where terraced gardens sloped down a long, steep hill to the Aare River. Along the river was the Matte, a neighborhood that had housed Bern's medieval leather workers and still wasn't totally gentrified. It pleased Renzo to think of the tanners' stink drifting up centuries earlier into the noses of the patricians who'd lived high above them.

He glanced over at the café, thinking he'd have a quick espresso before returning to work. He'd just joined an investigation that had been transferred to Giuliana Linder a few days earlier when the detective who'd previously worked the case had gone on an emergency leave of absence. Now Giuliana was speed-reading files to determine what state the case was in and what still needed doing. As always, he was thrilled that she'd gotten him assigned to help her, but the case itself... Right now, it was nothing but desk work; he was stuck checking timelines for the weeks before the wife had poisoned her husband.

He was still hovering by the entrance to the park, trying to decide about coffee, when a slight figure in a gray hoodie crashed into him. Renzo staggered, grabbed at the edge of the gate, and kept his balance, but the kid ricocheted off his chest and fell backward onto the gravel path. It was a boy—about fourteen, maybe?—his brown eyes wide, struggling to breathe. He'd only had the wind knocked out of him, but that could be frightening to someone who'd never experienced it. Renzo knelt on the gravel and put a hand on the boy's shoulder. The kid was starting to gasp now. Good.

"Should I call an ambulance?" called a woman with a baby and a toddler in a double stroller who'd stopped her progress through the Pläfe when the boy hit the ground.

"Thanks," Renzo answered, "but he'll be fine in a minute." He looked down at the boy, who was frozen, his face twisted in fright. Renzo's lightweight jacket had flapped open, and the kid's eyes were on his gun in its holster. Then his gaze shifted to Renzo's face, and something panicky in his expression made Renzo tighten his grip on the youngster's shoulder.

The boy exploded into action, wrenching his body back and to the side, and was on his feet running, all in what felt like a single movement. He sprang through the gate and turned right and right again to plunge down the flights of stone stairs leading to the neighborhood spread out along the river.

For a moment, Renzo stayed where he was, listening to the thump of the boy's feet as he took a group of stairs in a single leap and began clattering down the next flight. Then Renzo was off and running, too. It wasn't rational, but the cop in him had taken over.

Reaching the foot of the long, steep staircase, Renzo saw the boy run toward the river—and right into the path of a car. Renzo's heart clenched, but with a screech of brakes, the driver stopped in time. Sprinting past the car, Renzo heard the white-haired driver cursing and gave him a nod of commiseration. When he turned to look for the boy again, Renzo cursed, too—in those few seconds, he'd lost his quarry. He stood on the sidewalk, wondering what to do.

Two rows of low buildings ran along either side of the Matte's single main street. One row backed onto the Aare; behind the other, the ground ran up steeply toward the ornate buildings flanking the Münster. Small as the Matte was, it offered great hiding places: countless little shops and cafés, buildings with dark recessed doorways, narrow alleyways, a big parking lot with cars to crouch behind, and shady stone arcades that extended out from the half-timbered buildings to provide a roof for the sidewalk. Renzo was already overdue at the police station, he had no idea where the kid had gone, and he didn't even know if a crime had been committed. Still, he spent ten minutes walking down the street in the direction the boy had run, looking carefully right and left until he reached the Untertor Bridge and then strolling back, eyes and brain on alert until he reached the foot of the staircase. He saw no sign of the youngster.

He shook his head, as much at his own foolishness in following the boy as his failure to catch him, and moved toward the steps. There was an elevator next to them that would carry him up to the Pläfe, but he'd have to be old and gray before he'd take it. Instead, he ran up the steps fast—but not as fast as he could—putting on a burst of speed for the last two flights: a good exercise in pacing himself. When he arrived at the top, he found he could walk on without panting.

When he got to the paved Münsterplatz that opened off the front doors of the cathedral, he didn't go straight back to work. Instead, recalling the boy's expression as he'd stared at Renzo's gun, Renzo called the dispatcher to ask if anyone had reported a crime in the Old City during the past half hour, especially near the cathedral.

"Not near it—in it," the woman answered. "Somebody knocked a man off a scaffold. I got an ambulance for him and sent a patrol over."

"It wasn't an accident?"

"Apparently not," she told him. "Sounded like it was on purpose."

No wonder the kid had looked at Renzo with terror. He must have seemed like the world's speediest cop, arriving seconds after the attack. He thanked the dispatcher and texted Giuliana. *Sorry I'm late. Sidetracked by possible crime. Back ASAP.* Then he headed for the Münster's double doors.

He couldn't remember the last time he'd been inside Bern's most famous church. Probably as a child, dragged along on some sightseeing tour with relatives visiting from Italy. Of course, he was—nominally—a Catholic, and the church was Protestant, at least since the Reformation. He tried to remember when Martin Luther had nailed his piece of paper to the church door in . . . some German town. Whenever it was, Bern had switched religions shortly afterward.

He gave up his struggle with history and walked into the gift shop just inside the doors. Two women over sixty stood behind a glass counter that displayed small stuffed bears and red mugs with white Swiss crosses; their voices sounded hushed and worried.

He removed his police ID from his pocket and held it out. "Donatelli, *Kantonspolizei*," he told them. "You had a workman hurt. I believe my colleagues are here?"

The older looking of the two women nodded. "Thank you for coming. Yes, I think there's a policeman still in the nave. Please go on inside." She gestured toward a turnstile that led into the shadowy church.

The second woman was almost quivering with excitement, like a dog that has spotted a squirrel. "Yes, he was just here asking us what we knew, the policeman. It started when we heard the most terrible noise. There's nothing worse than the sound of breaking glass in a church. And it was one of the really old windows. Denis shouldn't have been allowed to work on it; he shouldn't be here at all if you ask me. I bet it's something to do with drugs, the whole thing."

Drugs? Renzo glanced back at the woman who'd spoken first. Unobserved by her colleague, she raised her eyebrows and shook her head before putting a hand on the shorter woman's arm. "Why don't we let the policeman do his job?"

Renzo smiled at them both and walked on into the church, coming to a halt as the great nave opened before him and tilting his head back to gaze up at the vaulted ceiling. His breath caught at the beauty of it. The long stems of stone were like vines that had been woven into a basket; his eyes followed the pattern from column to column until they rested on the tall stained-glass windows at the eastern end of the church, behind the altar. Patches of blue light from more windows fell across the pale gray walls of the nave, high above the pews. Renzo drank in the colors.

Quickly, he pulled himself together and spotted the man he'd been looking for: a uniformed policeman standing in a side aisle, half hidden by a thick pillar. Renzo strode over. The man was young, and Renzo vaguely recognized him, although he couldn't be sure what case they'd worked on together. Was his name Tinu? Till—that was it. Till Messerli.

The cop was talking to a large, plump man with gray hair slicked back from his forehead, whose hands were clasped at his waist. Or rather, the man was talking. Till listened, but something about his posture said he'd had enough. Relief filled his face when he saw Renzo.

"Sorry to interrupt," Renzo said.

The two men were standing next to a workman's scaffold, which had been erected among the side pews in one of the former chapels. The top platform was level with a panel of stained glass where one small round window, elaborately patterned with lions and curlicues, had a hole in it that let in a sharp beam of clear light.

Till seized the opportunity to turn away from the speaker, his hand outstretched.

"Ciao, Till." Renzo shook Till's hand. "Looks like you're getting some background on the accident." Turning to the gray-haired man, he held out his hand a second time. "Renzo Donatelli, Kantonspolizei."

Till said, "This is Klaus Friedli, the sexton. He's in charge of the church."

The older man unclasped his hands to offer one to Renzo. "Well, God's in charge. He's helped by the parish council, followed by the lady minister. I come a poor fourth, but I do my best." Renzo smiled before realizing the man was not trying to be funny. "Unfortunately, as I was telling your colleague, I didn't have a say when it came to hiring this disaster-prone young man. And now this!" He gestured theatrically up at the window with the hole in it. "That panel with the Diesbach coat of arms dates back to 1550!"

They all seemed very concerned about the window, Renzo thought; didn't anybody care about the glassworker? "Herr Friedli, I appreciate your sharing this information, but right now, I need to talk to my colleague . . . if you'll excuse us?"

"Certainly," the man said, reclasping his hands and bowing slightly. "I'll be here until six this evening if you need me again. My office is over there"—the sexton pointed to a door at one side of the chancel—"although I'm rarely behind my desk." With that, he turned and walked briskly away.

"Let's go outside," Renzo suggested to Till. They left through the shop, where Renzo raised his hand to the two saleswomen, and walked out onto the Münsterplatz.

Unlike the Pläfe, this square to the west of the church was paved with stone and surrounded by buildings. Since the space had no benches, the city had scattered a group of red metal chairs around it. When they'd first been delivered, not only here but in other parks and squares downtown, Renzo had expected them to disappear within days, but most had managed to survive without being stolen or vandalized. He and Till dragged two chairs together and sat.

"Tell me everything," Renzo said. "But, first—was a boy involved, maybe fourteen, gray hoodie, black training pants with a red stripe, red running shoes?"

Till's eyebrows drew together. "Gray hoodie, small size. That's all I got from either of the women in the shop. How the hell . . . ?"

"He ran right into me and fell. I almost went over, too. Picked himself up and legged it downstairs to the Matte. Seemed suspicious, but I didn't know what he'd done. So, tell me." Renzo leaned toward Till, who got out his phone and opened his notes.

"A twenty-five-year-old glassmaker named Denis Kellenberger was standing on that scaffold, which was pushed up against the wall but not attached to it. He was cleaning an old window and planning to fill in some cracked glass with . . . solder, I think. Someone grabbed the lower bars of the scaffold and started shaking it, swearing at him."

"Swearing," Renzo echoed. "What was he saying?"

Till looked at his screen. "The glassmaker said it was, 'You fucking murderer, I hope you bust your head open.'"

Renzo raised his eyebrows. "Murderer, huh? The guy on the scaffold's okay, then, if he was able to tell you this?"

"Kellenberger, yeah. He fell off the scaffolding, hit the backs of the pews, and landed on the floor. Thank God the floor's wood where he fell and not stone. My partner went with him to the hospital. They think his worst injury is a broken wrist. Which is amazingly lucky, considering."

"Maybe not for a man who works with his hands," Renzo pointed out.

"Yes, but it was a long way down—he could have split his head open like the kid said. Or broken his back. We were really worried about him, but all they kept going on about was the damn window." He put on a busybody voice. "'He put his fist through five-hundred-year-old glass!' I told the sexton they should be glad Kellenberger didn't cut open a major artery on that glass and bleed to death."

Renzo appreciated Till's outrage. "Did Kellenberger know his attacker? Did he even see him?"

Till shook his head. "While we were waiting for the ambulance, my partner asked. He was in a lot of pain, so he wasn't too clear about exactly what happened, but he said the voice wasn't a man's—which I thought meant a woman, but I guess would fit the boy you saw. And he had no idea why someone would call him a murderer. At least, so he says."

"Okay. Anything else?"

Till scrolled through his notes. "The woman in the shop—the small one—she talked about Kellenberger like he was some kind of delinquent. She seemed determined to blame him for something, although *he* was the one who got attacked. Why's she so down on the poor guy? And you heard Friedli—he disapproved of him *being* there."

Renzo remembered the woman behind the counter mentioning drugs. Maybe it hadn't been overexcited babble after all. "First, we need to take care of the scene," he told Till. "The boy probably left his fingerprints on the scaffold. Put some police tape around it, and I'll call the station and ask for a tech. If the sexton or anyone else gives you trouble you can't handle, hold on and wait for me. I'll be back in there in five minutes."

Renzo got out his phone while Till disappeared up Münstergasse. Two minutes later, he was jogging back toward the cathedral entrance, a roll of yellow plastic tape in his hand. Renzo smiled at the younger cop's energy while he reported in and waited to be connected to forensics. Then he called Giuliana.

"There you are," she answered. "On your way back?"

"Not yet." He summarized what had been going on during the last—he looked at his watch—twenty-five minutes since he'd left the dentist's office. It felt longer. "Forensics is on the way to work the scene, and I'll see if I can find out anything else. That okay with you? Am I holding you up by not getting on with the case?"

"No, I'm fine," Giuliana told him. "I like your new tactics, by the way—chasing the criminal before you know there's been a crime."

"Yeah, well, that would've worked better if I'd actually caught him. Thanks, Giule. See you as soon as I can."

"Good luck."

Renzo took his time walking back to the crime scene. He was torn between guilt at abandoning Giuliana to deal with the Allemann case alone and delight at having something more interesting to do. It wasn't merely boredom motivating him; now that he and Fränzi were lurching toward a divorce, he needed money, and the best way to get it was a promotion to homicide detective. He needed visibility on some good cases, and this one, an attempted murder involving a criminal whom Renzo had actually witnessed, might prove interesting.

By the time Renzo joined him, Till had wound tape around both the scaffold and the place where the man had fallen among the pews. Renzo noticed a woman in a striped shirtwaist dress and navy blazer coming toward them down the south aisle, heels tapping on the floor. She was in her early forties, he judged, with short, neat blonde hair and reading glasses on a chain around her neck. She looked like a person of some authority, and Renzo guessed she was the *Pfarrerin*, the "lady minister" the sexton had mentioned. He got out his ID.

She glanced at his badge and gave him a brisk handshake. "I'm Selina Zehnder. I just got in from a meeting and heard there'd been some kind of . . . well, accident or crime; I'm not sure. Could you fill me in?"

Renzo let Till tell the story; he included Renzo's encounter with the boy in the Pläfe and his disappearance in the Matte. The woman's face grew graver with every word.

"I must call the hospital. Who knows what internal injuries Denis may have?"

At last, Renzo thought, someone was concerned about the young glassworker. He broke in before the minister could say anything else. "There weren't any witnesses, and Herr Kellenberger had no idea why he'd been attacked. One of your shop ladies and the sexton seemed to think that Kellenberger himself must have been to blame. Herr Friedli said he was disaster-prone—something like that. Can you . . . ?"

She was shaking her head. "Our sexton has been here for over twenty years, and he has . . . strong feelings about some things. Frau Arnold in the shop is a great fan of his with a long memory; she also has a—" The minister paused and sighed. "A love of drama." Renzo thought she'd been about to say something else, and he wondered what. "I've known Denis for four years now while he has been assisting the glass master, who is one of the cathedral's most respected craftsmen and restorers. I've had only positive experiences with Denis."

"Frau Arnold said something about drugs . . ." Renzo put in.

The minister's eyebrows shot up. "I imagine you could fit what Frau Arnold knows about illegal drugs into a thimble," she said acidly. "As far as I'm concerned, you can assume anything Denis tells you is the truth."

"That's good to know," said Renzo.

"If you don't need me anymore, I want to phone the hospital. Here's my card." She reached into her blazer pocket. "I've written my cell phone number on it, so you can let me know how this develops."

"Thank you." As Frau Zehnder hurried down the south aisle to the front of the church, Renzo turned to Till. "The woman from forensics will be here soon. I know her, and she's good." The younger cop was chewing on his lower lip. "What's bothering you?"

"I should have done the crime scene stuff right away," Till burst out. "My partner, she wanted to get the tape from the car, but I . . ." He looked down at his feet.

Renzo saved him. "It's always hard to judge how serious an incident is. If you overreact, you get in trouble for wasting time, but when you don't do every little thing by the book, you get your ass chewed if you miss something important. Best advice I can give you is to pass the buck. If you think something might be worth looking into, call your boss or a general investigator like me who handles different types of cases and ask for advice."

"Well, luckily, I got you without calling," said Till. "So, what should I do now?"

Renzo spent a few minutes taking the uniformed man through what he thought would be the best way to get information out of the two women in the shop, who might have heard or seen more than they realized; the sexton, Herr Friedli; and the minister, whose opinion on the other people could be useful. All of them would need to be pinned down on their whereabouts during the attack.

Till listened, his lips pressed together in concentration. Then he said, "I think I should talk to the minister first. She's probably the busiest, so I should grab her while she's in the church."

Renzo nodded. "Good thinking. Sounds like you're okay to handle this alone, at least until your partner gets back from the hospital. Or do you want me to get someone over here to help you?" "Are you kidding?" Till grinned. "How often do you think I get to interview witnesses to an attempted murder? I know it's simply preliminary stuff, but still!"

"Okay, then," Renzo said, smiling back. "Go find the Pfarrerin, and I'll guard your crime scene until forensics gets here. Have fun!"

Till gave him a thumbs-up and took off after the minister while Renzo sat down on the end of the pew to wait for the forensic techs.

Would it be possible to get himself officially assigned to this case when he was already working for Giuliana? Would she understand? For at least two years, he'd fought to insert himself into her investigations, both to learn from her and . . . to be near her. And now he was trying to figure out how to get away from her, at least for the rest of the week. But he needed more independence, more responsibility. How else would he get a promotion to homicide? Wanting to work on his own wasn't just about Giuliana. Except . . . except that in another way, it was. Since he and Fränzi had split up, the sexual tension between him and Giuliana seemed more stressful than exhilarating. He needed distance in more ways than one.

He shoved his thoughts about Giuliana aside and mulled over what the sexton, Friedli, had said about Denis Kellenberger. Disaster-prone: that could mean so many things. Unless it was a case of mistaken identity, the boy in the hoodie hated Kellenberger enough to try to kill him. And yet, Kellenberger said he had no idea who he could be. Somehow, Renzo found that hard to believe.

3

D enis Kellenberger had been grateful to have the policewoman with him in the ambulance. A stern-looking woman of about fifty, she'd turned out to be a softy, wincing along with him as the paramedics applied antiseptic and a bandage to the cut on his head, which had bled all over his coveralls. The cop had even taken his hand—his *other* hand—while they manipulated his left wrist. He'd screamed then, all right. Thank God he was right-handed, he thought. But he still felt a jolt of fear at the thought of how the wrist might heal—or not.

By the time the ambulance arrived at the hospital, they'd prodded and poked most of his front, treated a few more cuts, tutted over his knees and hip bones, then told him that they thought his wrist was broken, but his ribs weren't.

"You'll have some spectacular bruising," the older of the two EMTs pronounced, resting a gentle hand on Denis's good arm, "but you'll be okay."

The policewoman let out a breath. "That scaffold must have been twelve feet high, maybe fifteen," she told him. "When I saw you lying there in a pool of blood, I was sure you were dead."

Now Denis lay on a gurney in an emergency room cubicle. A young doctor had gone over him again, more thoroughly. She'd stitched a cut on his face and another on the hand that had gone through the window; something cool and numbing had been applied to his bruises, and he was waiting to be X-rayed. They'd check for other fractures at the same time, the doctor had told him—cracked ribs were still a possibility.

He decided that he must have been given a sedative along with painkillers because he felt pleasantly detached from his aching body. Detached, too, from the anxiety he'd felt in the ambulance that the damage to his wrist might end his glassmaking. *If* Grospaps *were still trying to turn me into a violinist,* he thought, *I'd be happy about breaking my wrist.* At that, he gave a laugh that made his whole chest hurt. But even *that* pain felt muffled. He was vaguely aware that he should have called someone to explain where he was. But it was all too much to deal with.

The policewoman had tried hard to get him to remember details about what happened before and after he fell off the scaffolding, but there was nothing more he could say. No, he hadn't heard anyone approaching, and once he'd hit the floor, he'd thought only about how much he hurt—he hadn't tried to lift his head. But he did remember what the voice had said. A child's voice. "You fucking murderer."

He'd told the cop he had no idea who would call him that. But he knew exactly who it was. It was Zora.

Right now, though, the well-worn grooves of grief and guilt that his mind always followed when these thoughts came to him seemed to be clogged by the drugs. He drifted away from them, first into childhood memories of playing in the cathedral and then, at last, into sleep.

4

"Our poor father. Married to a murderess."

Tamara Hofstetter's head was bowed, and, with her hands covering her face, her words were muffled. Detective Giuliana Linder, sitting across the table from her, understood what she'd said but restated it for the policewoman in the corner taking everything down.

Sebastian Allemann, sitting next to his sister, rolled his eyes at Giuliana before putting a hand on his sister's shoulder. "I know you're upset. We both are. But could you stop covering your mouth when you talk so Frau Linder doesn't have to repeat everything you say?"

Tamara might be genuinely distressed—she had reason to be—but it was clear that she was milking the situation for drama. Her younger brother was the opposite: a natural downplayer of crises. At least, that was Giuliana's impression so far.

At Sebastian's words, Tamara straightened up and dried her eyes on a tissue from her handbag, leaving the pack on the table. "Sorry," she said, with a pout that rather spoiled the apology.

The room's one dusty window faced away from the sun, which was a blessing. The afternoon was growing warmer, and the space stuffy. If they opened the window, though, the noise from the street would make the notetaker's task even harder.

Giuliana shifted in her seat. "We'll come back to what made you suspect that your stepmother had poisoned your father. But first, I'd like to ask a few general questions and try to get the order of events straight." She glanced up at them, eyebrows raised.

They both nodded, so she looked back at her notebook. "Your mother and father separated permanently twenty-seven years ago, Frau Hofstetter, when you were twenty-two and already at university." Tamara nodded again, and Giuliana turned her gaze to Sebastian. "And you were twenty, Herr Allemann." That made him forty-seven, which was her age. "Your father stayed in Bern, and your mother went to live in Zürich, where she became involved with a man she'd known as a teenager."

"Became *more* involved," broke in Tamara with a short, bitter laugh. "I'm sure they were already having an affair before she left Paps."

"All right," said Giuliana, writing in her notebook. "Four years later, your father started seeing Frau Seiler, and two years after that, they got married. When your father died—"

"When she killed him!" Tamara put in hotly. Sebastian frowned and put a hand on her arm.

Giuliana noted that but carried on with her summary. "When he died in February, they'd been married twenty-one years. Did either of you ever live with your father and Frau Seiler?"

"No," Sebastian answered. "We've never called her or thought of her as our stepmother. By the time they got together, we were living on our own. Tamara had already moved in with her future husband, and I was living in an apartment with four other students."

"Frau Seiler has no children, so did you get the impression, at least at the beginning of her relationship with your father, that she wanted to become close to you?" Giuliana asked the two siblings. "Not necessarily as a mother but . . . in some way?"

There was a long silence before Sebastian answered. "Looking back, it's hard to know what . . . attempts she made and how I responded. I think during the first few years, she *did* try to be nice to me, but I just . . .

well, at that point in my life, I couldn't be bothered. Then I got a job in Hamburg, and I've lived in Germany ever since." He paused. "Having Tamara always going on about how awful Ruth was didn't help." He gave his sister a look that reminded Giuliana of the way her younger brother Paolo sometimes looked at her, a look conveying the mixture of love and exasperation that was so much a part of family relationships.

"I *tried*," Tamara said. She directed her words to Sebastian; to Giuliana, it sounded like she was genuinely seeking his understanding. "I knew how much Paps wanted me to like her. But that was part of what made things so weird. All of a sudden, there was this strange woman in our house that I was supposed to grow fond of in order to make Paps happy. I hated it. I didn't *want* her in my family. It made every minute together stressful."

Yes, it would be stressful. And not just for the brother and sister. Giuliana wondered what the Allemann family holidays had been like.

Tamara seemed to read her mind. "I did my best to see him at Christmas, but once I was married, it was easier to go to my in-laws' house. My mother came regularly from Zürich to visit us in Zug, so she got to know my kids pretty well. But my father . . ." Her voice trailed away.

Giuliana leaned back in her chair and clasped her hands in front of her, nodding as if all this was perfectly normal. "It sounds like neither of you is really in a position to tell me about Frau Seiler and your father's marriage." She intentionally didn't pause there; she didn't want them to get defensive and derail her. "When did you realize that your father had developed dementia?"

"Last fall," said Sebastian. "I came to Bern for a wedding, and I went to see Paps. It had been . . . quite a while since I'd seen him. By then, he . . . he didn't know who I was. He pretended for a while, but . . ." His lips tightened. "I was so upset with Ruth for not telling me sooner that I . . . well, I was very sharp with her. When I got home, I called Tamara—she had no idea about Paps, either."

Tamara clenched her fists where they rested on the table. "That woman kept us completely in the dark."

Giuliana tapped her pen on the table. Dementia didn't develop overnight. Werner Allemann could have contacted his children himself long before the disease progressed so far if he'd wanted them to know about his illness. "Did she explain why she hadn't said anything?"

"She said Paps asked her not to." Tamara shook her head. "As if he was in a position to make that kind of decision. And that's assuming what she says is true." Sebastian stared at his hands and seemed to have nothing to add.

"You've talked to me today about what happened next," Giuliana said. "You decided you wanted professional care for your father and got him onto the waiting list at a home specializing in patients with dementia near where he and Ruth lived. But she was against it."

"Imagine," Tamara said, "Ruth had a twenty-four-hour job looking after our father by that time—diapers and everything." Her mouth puckered in distaste. "Okay, a carer sometimes came in to help her, but still . . ." She shook her head. "We thought she would be grateful, but she was upset—can you believe it? She didn't want us to spend his savings on residential care for him. She wanted his money for herself!"

Sebastian stirred in his chair. "It's our money, too." He glanced at his sister's angry face. "I'm just pointing that out, to be fair."

Tamara shrugged as if to say, so what? Maybe she really didn't care about the money: Tamara and her husband, who was in finance, were extremely wealthy. Sebastian, although not so rich, was a high-level exec with a multinational firm in Hamburg and must live very comfortably. Still, this apparent indifference to their father's money was odd. The older couple had saved around one-and-a-quarter million Swiss francs; Allemann's will left half to his children. The house and its contents already belonged to them, with the legal provision that Ruth be allowed to use them until her death. The other half of the money went to Ruth with no restrictions.

But how much money would have been left if Allemann, who'd been eighty-two when he died, had lived on for another ten years in a care facility?

This was the heart of the accusation made by Tamara against Ruth Seiler: that she had poisoned their father with insulin six weeks before he was due to enter a home in order to preserve her half of his money. It had led to Seiler's arrest.

"I still don't really understand why our answering these questions is necessary," Sebastian said. "The autopsy found the insulin overdose in Paps's system, and Ruth admitted she gave him the shot, so . . ."

Both the Allemann children had received a registered letter from the district attorney's office explaining what was requested of them and why they were being interviewed, but Giuliana was prepared to go over it again.

Before she could answer, Tamara rolled her eyes at her brother. "Come on, Basti. Just because someone confesses to a crime doesn't mean they can conduct a trial without evidence. The police still need to check off all their boxes, even when everyone knows what the result is going to be."

Giuliana's eyebrows rose. *She* wouldn't have made the investigation sound like a pointless waste of taxpayers' money. But essentially, Tamara was right. "As Frau Hofstetter says, we're continuing to collect evidence. The police have checked your alibis for the time of your father's death, so we're now getting your version of the events leading up to it. Your statements today will be written up; you'll read and sign them, and they'll be given to the defense lawyer, prosecution team, and judges. After this, you should be able to respond to questions remotely instead of having to come to Bern. Unless there's something else you want to tell me, something relevant to your case against Frau Seiler, then I think we're done."

Tamara seemed taken aback. Then she frowned. "Well, I do have more. I want to state for the record that I'd like my father's doctor investigated. Maybe he wasn't in league with Ruth, but he had no intention of ordering tests. He was talking about the death being a blessing! I had to threaten him with a lawsuit to make him alter his death certificate to say the death looked suspicious so an inquiry could be opened and an autopsy performed."

Sebastian closed his eyes and gave a tiny shake of his head, perhaps implying that *he* wished Tamara had left things alone. Giuliana wondered why he'd supported his sister's schemes.

"The police are looking thoroughly into everything and everyone connected with your father's death," she said.

She half expected Tamara to demand the final word; Sebastian's hand was once again resting on his sister's arm as though he was anticipating more drama, too. But Tamara only nodded curtly.

Giuliana ended the interview, thanked them, and stood to shake hands. As they were gathering their belongings, she threw the window open. Sunlight and air, smelling slightly of exhaust, poured into the room. Giuliana took a deep breath and thanked the colleague who'd been taking notes; then she escorted Allemann's children to the elevator.

After she'd arranged to review the final write-ups of the interviews before she sent them to Tamara and Sebastian for their signatures, she went back to her own corridor and made herself a cup of coffee in the tiny kitchen area, thinking all the while about something that still wasn't clear to her but which could become an important argument for defense *or* prosecution, depending on the answer.

Werner Allemann had been due to enter a home at the end of March, and his wife had given him a lethal dose of insulin in mid-February. But what quality of life had Allemann had by then?

She carried her coffee down to a small room near the end of the hall. The window here was already open, and it faced away from the main street. A tall fan stood in front of it, blowing in fresh air—it was Giuliana's private fan, which she guarded jealously. This was the space she used when she wanted to escape from the bustling open-plan office shared by the homicide detectives.

At the only other desk in the room was Renzo, his cell phone to his ear, his back to her. The mere set of his shoulders told her he was impatient. "No one is accusing you of a crime. All I need you to do is confirm the date and time that you sold the insulin to Ruth Seiler." As he listened, he typed notes into his laptop. "Thank you. Now I'd like you to scan the paperwork that shows Frau Seiler's purchase and email that to me. By the end of the day, please." He paused to listen. "Yes, you can fax it." He dictated his email address and homicide's fax number, said goodbye, and spun his chair to face her.

"Still faxing!" He shook his head, then gave her one of the ravishing smiles that crinkled his hazel eyes. "Sorry I went AWOL. I'll tell you all about it as soon as you have time. But you just came from the Allemann interview, so you go first. How was it? Anything new?" He rolled his desk chair forward and leaned back with his hands locked behind his head, his legs stretched out, grinning up at her and looking like . . . As usual, none of the clichés her brain came up with fit. He looked too mischievous to be an angel and not arrogant enough to be a model. He was just . . . as preposterously beautiful now at thirty-five as he'd been when she'd first met him eight years earlier, long before she'd started working with him on homicide cases and discovered that he wasn't the mindless blob of beefcake she'd expected. And long before he'd tried to start an affair with her.

It said a lot for how much they enjoyed working together that their friendship had survived all the . . . all the what, exactly? The affair had never happened, but she'd never rejected him either. She'd been hopelessly ambivalent and indecisive because of how she felt about him. In fact, she'd been stringing him along for over a year now.

She perched on the edge of her desk, pushing these shameful thoughts away. "No new facts, although I'd like you to have a look at the interview and see if you pick up on anything I missed. But talking to the pair of them made me wish I could interview their father. Maybe then I'd be able to understand their relationship with him—their lack of relationship, I mean."

Renzo raised an eyebrow. "Not much contact, huh?"

Giuliana snorted. "They made me decide to call my father tonight. If *he* were Seiler's defense lawyer, he'd get those two to write down the number of days they've spent with their dad since they left the family home almost thirty years ago. No, not days. Hours! That minuscule number would be something to show the panel of judges at the trial."

"Here I am, laboring to set up our case against Seiler, and you're planning her defense."

"Nothing justifies killing your husband for money," she said. "But I can understand why the couple didn't tell the kids about his dementia. They'd made no effort to stay close to Allemann, and he wanted to keep his illness private as long as possible."

Renzo's brows furrowed. "That makes sense. Think of your mother-in-law this past March, refusing to talk about her colon cancer. My father wanted to keep his first set of cancer treatments secret from us kids, too. Thank God my mother would have none of that bullshit—she realized we'd want to spend as much time with him as possible, in case . . ." Renzo fell silent.

Giuliana knew how much he still mourned his father's death from lung cancer less than three years earlier. She was quiet for a moment, then she said, "Yes. Seiler had no reason to think Allemann's kids would come dashing home to be with him. And she had no loyalty to them, only to him. When he asked her not to tell them, naturally she went along with it. That's what she said in her statement, and it rings true."

"I hate cases where everything depends on who said what, when, and there are no records or witnesses. When are you interviewing her?"

"Probably not for another week. Her lawyer told me she has pneumonia. She's out of the hospital, but I'll leave her alone until I can't be accused of badgering a sick old woman. It'd be good if you could join me when I do speak with her. I'll let you know."

"Okay." Renzo seemed to be lacking his usual enthusiasm. She tried not to take it personally; after all, this case had been thrust on them—they hadn't done the original work—and, as Renzo'd said, it was very short on evidence.

But then he got up and walked over to the window. The fingers of his left hand tapped on the sill. "Look, I . . . I have a favor to ask. I'd like to follow up on this attack I got involved with at the Münster today. I want to go to the hospital and talk to the man who was hurt. I feel like . . . well, it's one of those stories I'd like to see to the end. Can you . . . ?" He paused and then said in a rush, "Do you think you could clear the paperwork so I could investigate officially? I promise not to let it interfere with our other work."

Ah. This was why he suddenly seemed so lukewarm about the Seiler poisoning. Relieved that it had nothing to do with her, Giuliana looked at her watch and saw it was almost four thirty. "Do you know the names of the cops who were at the scene?"

"I know one—Till Messerli."

She wrote it down. "Give me what you've got on the pharmacists and get as far as you can with Allemann's timeline of medical visits and treatments by . . . let's say six? Send me that and the financial stuff you were working on earlier. I'll find out who Till reports to, ask what's happening with this Münster case, and see what I can do. In the meantime, you might as well go ahead and question the man in the hospital. If anyone complains, which they won't, we'll say it was my mistake."

Renzo came close to her, his face full of warmth. Of *love*—there was no other way she could read it. "Thank you," he said. He met her eyes and cupped her cheek with his palm. She heard herself inhale sharply and, unthinking, reached up to cover his hand. They stood that way for the briefest moment, out of sight behind the half-open door. Then she let her hand fall to her side, and Renzo did the same.

He stepped back, dropped into his desk chair, and whirled it around to face his keyboard, pulling his phone out of his pocket. "I have to call Till to find out what hospital Kellenberger's in, so I'll ask him about his boss, which'll save you having to do that. Then I'll work on the timeline." His voice was shaking slightly.

Not trusting herself to speak either, Giuliana took her time sitting down and fussing with some papers on her desk. "Good," she said eventually and was pleased to hear that her voice was steady.

"Tomorrow, after our workout," Renzo said as he stared down at his phone, "I'll tell you all about it. I'll know more after I talk to the glassmaker in the hospital."

Glassmaker? But before she could form a question, he was on his call, and she was struggling to focus on Ruth Seiler. She could still feel his fingers on her skin, and the memory came to her, as it too often did, of that time on the bank of the Aare when she hadn't held him at a distance. That had been almost exactly a year ago, and they—no, she—hadn't resolved . . . anything.

The rush she'd experienced with Renzo's palm on her cheek and hand under hers vanished, and contempt for her behavior seeped in to take its place. Facing risks was normal in her job, but the chance of ravaging her own marriage was not a risk she wanted to take.

She opened an already hefty file on the Allemann siblings and began typing in new information. When Renzo murmured a goodbye and left, she answered without glancing up from her computer.

5

" **I** 've got your dinner here if you want it."

Denis opened his eyes. A brown-skinned man in a pale green uniform was holding a tray with a covered plate in the middle of it, surrounded by other small dishes. When the orderly saw Denis was awake, he slid the tray onto the narrow table along one side of the bed, helped him sit up against his pillows, and then swung the table over the bed so that the tray was in front of him. Denis looked around the ward at the other three men he shared it with; they were already eating.

He felt groggy; his left forearm was numb. Had the wrist been set? He could remember lying on the Münster floor perfectly well, but his time in the hospital was murkier. Slowly, it came back to him that they'd decided to put plates in his wrist, but the operation wasn't until the following morning. Now they were trying to reduce the swelling in the arm, so it had been wrapped and immobilized against his body. His brain was awash in drugs; he could feel that. Still, his body appeared to be hungry.

He thought about phoning his mother, recognizing dimly that he'd had this thought before—maybe several times. But if he called her, she might visit. Plus, she'd call his grandparents, and *they'd* want to visit, too. Mam might even decide she had a responsibility to let his father know, and then the calls from Fort Lauderdale would start. He pictured having to deal with his family's worries and questions and decided he'd wait until after the operation to contact anyone. Until six months earlier, he'd shared a ramshackle apartment with five friends, but the beauty of living alone in his new place on Herrengasse was that no one knew what he was doing or where he was supposed to be. Which meant perfect freedom—like now.

He looked down at his tray: some sort of salad with chickpeas, pieces of fresh fruit for dessert, a brown roll, butter, and—he removed the cover over the main plate—a chicken stew with vegetables and rice. His drink was a bottle of mineral water. Not bad, although he wished he had a beer. He started on the stew before it could get cold.

When he finished his food, he got a nurse to help him walk to the toilet; it was a relief to know he could move around. His ribs were taped, and his body felt like one giant bruise, but he sensed that he was going to be okay. There was still the open question of how his wrist would heal, but he pushed that thought away again.

He was wondering what the nurse had done with his phone when a guy walked into the ward and came straight to his bed. One of his doctors? No white coat, and he didn't remember seeing him before, but maybe . . .

"Hello," his visitor said. "The nurse told me you're Denis Kellenberger, the man who got shaken off the scaffolding at the cathedral."

"That's me," said Denis. "Nice of you not to say 'the idiot who fell off.'"

The man gave an easy smile. "Can I sit down and talk to you?"

Denis didn't mind a bit of company. "Pull up a chair," he said, waving his bottle of water toward a table in the corner with four straight-backed chairs around it. "Sorry I can't offer you a beer. Also, I have to warn you that I might fall asleep in the middle of a sentence. I'm crammed full of painkillers."

The man fetched a chair and set it close to Denis's head. Before he sat down, he pulled the curtains around the bed, and Denis felt a stab of unease. "What the hell—?" he began.

Pulling a leather wallet out of his pocket, the guy handed it to Denis with his ID card showing. "My name's Donatelli. I'm from the Kantonspolizei."

Okay, he was a cop. Was that good or bad? Denis read the name again to be sure of remembering it and handed the wallet back.

The man went on, "I walked into the Münster right after the ambulance took you away. I've talked to the cops who showed up, so I know about the boy who shook the scaffold."

"A boy?" Denis considered what he wanted to say next. It was complicated. "I thought it was a girl."

Donatelli looked at him closely before asking, "Do you think you *know* who it was?"

"Right after it happened, I thought I did. But now I realize it can't be because . . ." Denis trailed off. There was no way he was going to get Zora in trouble. A piece of him was still mad at her all these years later. But he figured a much larger piece of *her* would still be mad at him.

Like a mind reader, the cop said, "You told the policewoman in the ambulance you had no idea why anyone would call you a murderer or why they'd hope you'd 'bust your head open.' But I get the impression that isn't true. I think you do know." He paused.

Denis sat in silence, chewing his lip.

"Look, I'm not going to dash out the door and drag whoever you tell me about off to the police station. I promise. Sure, I'll look into it, but this isn't a TV show that has to end in forty-nine minutes with an arrest."

Denis couldn't help smiling at that, especially when Donatelli was looking at him with so much sympathy. But he had to think this through. He took a sip of water, playing for time, then set the bottle down on his tray. Finally, he said, "Okay, I guess. If I don't tell you this now, someone else will—Frau Arnold at the cathedral shop for a start."

The cop flashed him a mischievous grin. "Is she the short, round one who never stops talking?"

Denis laughed, then groaned at the ache in his ribs. "Ah, I see you've met her. Yeah, she's known me since I was a little kid, and she's always hated me. She thinks I'm kin to one of those devils over the Münster's front door."

"Which is why I'd rather hear the story from you," said Donatelli, leaning back and crossing his arms.

"Right." Denis wished he could cross *his* arms, but he settled for reaching around with his good hand to adjust his pillow. "Well, it's a long one. So . . . where to start? Growing up, I mostly lived with my grandparents. When I was eight, they got jobs as tower guards at the Münster, and we all moved into the apartment at the top of the bell tower. I spent a lot of time playing in the church. I made noise and didn't behave respectfully or . . . reverently. That offended Frau Arnold. But I *did* respect the place. I loved it. For me, as a kid, it was glorious. I still love it. That's part of why I became a glassmaker, so I could work there. I live near the Münster, too."

For the first time, a memory flashed into his head: of trying to keep his balance on the scaffold, flailing with his arms, feeling one hand go through the window, lurching back in alarm, losing his footing, and seeing the pews and the floor loom beneath him as he fell. He closed his eyes and heard how shaky his breath sounded.

Donatelli leaned toward him. "Do you want me to call a nurse?"

Opening his eyes, Denis shook his head and scrambled for his place in the story. "Anyway, when I was ten, I had a friend who came to the Münster to play with me—a girl called Zora Horvat."

"Horvat," the cop repeated.

"Yeah, it's a Croatian name, but Zora and her brother were born in Bern. Their parents kept that corner grocery shop in the Matte, the Golden Goat."

"Do they still work there?" The man looked interested, as though this might mean something to him.

"I think so." Actually, he'd passed the shop a few weeks before and seen Zora's father behind the counter, but he wanted to keep that to himself. Why? He had no idea. "They used to live above the shop, too. Maybe they still do." Suddenly, he didn't want to continue. Perhaps he'd simply go to sleep. He slid down against his pillows until he was lying almost flat.

"Okay," the cop said, clasping his hands on one knee as if he was forcing himself to be patient. "Go on." When Denis didn't speak, Donatelli unclasped his hands, lifted a black box that must have been hanging from the side of the bed, and started to fiddle with it. Something whirred; the top half of the bed went flat; then it rose until it was almost vertical.

Denis found himself forced to sit up straighter than before. His ribs throbbed. "Hey," he grumbled. "Don't mess with that thing."

Donatelli raised an eyebrow. "You aren't allowed to go to sleep yet, man. You haven't gotten to the important part."

Denis glared at the guy and, forgetting about his wrist, tried to cross his arms. Pain swallowed him. He closed his eyes and pressed his lips together.

"Did moving your bed make it worse? What can I do? Shall I change your position back?"

Denis opened his eyes to see Donatelli standing, reaching toward him. "I'm okay," he said. His words sounded distant, as though he wasn't quite inside his body. "It wasn't you. I tried to move my bad arm, and it . . . hurt. I'll be fine. Right, the important part. I'm getting there." He took a deep breath and tried to focus. "As a child, Zora came to the Münster after school while her mother ran errands in town. I guess she thought it was a safe place for Zora to sit and do her homework. Sometimes Zora was there for a couple of hours."

"Did you know her mother, then? Her father?" Donatelli was sounding more like a cop now, Denis thought. Why was he asking about the parents? It was Zora who hated him, Zora who'd screamed at him. She had to be the one who'd tried to kill him. Except, if he was twenty-five, how could she still be a child?

"Herr Kellenberger. Denis. Are you still with me?"

Denis managed to drag his attention back to Donatelli. "Zora's parents were Lovro and Katica Horvat. I knew Katica, her mother, better. I saw her when she came to pick up Zora. My grandparents met her, too. Sometimes Zora had dinner with us. My grandparents and I always walked Zora home to their shop in the Matte. I met her father there . . ." Denis remembered thinking Lovro was a good father. In those days, he'd paid a lot of attention to other people's mothers and fathers—still did, he supposed. Gathering data.

"Katica and Lovro Horvat." Donatelli was typing this into his phone. "So, what happened?"

Denis gave a deep, heavy sigh. He had to get on with it. But he was so tired now. "One of my jobs was to go down the tower stairs and check that everywhere was empty and all the doors were locked. Especially the doors along the north and south sides of the church and the one at the bottom of the tower staircase. This started after I turned ten when my grandparents decided I was responsible enough."

The fingers of his good right hand twitched against his thigh, and he made them stop. His eyes were trying to shut. But he forced himself to keep talking. "One Friday night around eight, I checked that the church was locked. I checked the doors in the nave and then locked the door to the tower behind me when I went back up the stairs. At least . . . I was sure it was all closed up." He swallowed, his mouth and tongue dry. Where was his water? He took a swig, and the rest of his words came out in a rush. "But in the middle of the night, Zora's mother came into the church and through the tower door. She climbed the staircase, jumped off the tower, and died. She killed herself."

The cop sat back in his chair. "That must have been . . ."

"The sexton woke my grandparents in the morning. The head of the parish council and the police talked to them. I had to go to school." It was taking all his energy simply to push his voice out. "The sexton said I'd left the doors open, that it was my fault. Other people started to blame us, too—me and my grandparents. I was banned from the cathedral until I was eighteen, and my grandparents lost their jobs and the tower apartment. I felt terrible." The word was inadequate, but it was all he had; he was just about done for today.

He thought Donatelli would grow impatient, but the cop sat silent, waiting.

"My grandmother went down to the shop in the Matte to tell Zora and her father what had happened—Goran, her brother, was only a little baby. Later . . ." He could hear his voice speeding up again, and he looked down at the duvet as he spoke. "Later, after the funeral, Zora told me she hated me and didn't ever want to see me again. She called me a murderer in front of everyone. She hit me, too, although the grown-ups kept her from really hurting me." He stared at his knees. "She was my best friend."

"Which is why, when you heard that voice say, 'You fucking murderer, I hope you bust your head open,' you thought of Zora. But she's not a child anymore, right?"

Denis snapped, "I *know* that," like a petulant little kid. "But I have no clue what she looks and sounds like. I've only caught a few glimpses of her since we were kids. Maybe . . . maybe she has a high voice."

It wasn't quite true that he didn't know what Zora looked like. In fact, he'd tracked her down a couple of times, and he knew she'd stayed tall. But that didn't mean she couldn't be the person who'd shaken the scaffold.

An older nurse, not the young one who'd helped him to the bathroom, jerked open the bed curtains and said, "This is a five-minute warning, Herr Donatelli. We need you to go so we can get Herr Kellenberger ready." *Ready for what?* Denis thought.

The policeman gave the nurse a big smile. Once she'd left, he stood up. "I'm going to leave you with a couple of things to think about, Herr Kellenberger, and we'll talk more about this tomorrow or the next day, depending on how you're feeling. First, you've told me that Zora had a baby brother—how old would he be now?"

Goran? Why would that matter? "I guess . . . about fifteen."

Donatelli nodded. "And second, I was standing at the Pläfe gate right after you fell, and a teenage boy with dark hair came pelting through the gate and crashed into me. I followed him down the steps to the Matte and lost sight of him racing in the direction of the Horvats' store."

So that was it. Denis had been squinting at the cop's face, but now he closed his eyes. "Oh, no," he said, and then, more forcefully, "Oh, shit! Not Goran. After all this time? Surely he wouldn't . . ." He felt tears threatening and squeezed his eyes shut tighter. "Jesus, it's hopeless. Everybody hates me. Even my boss is going to hate me now that I've put my hand through that fucking window."

Donatelli sat back down. "It wasn't your fault that piece of glass shattered—it's just lucky you weren't badly hurt by it. And it's absolutely not your fault that Zora and Goran's mother died, even if you did accidentally leave a door unlocked. Believe me, people who are determined to kill themselves will do it no matter what." Donatelli put his hand very carefully on Denis's right shoulder. "Try not to feel upset. I doubt anyone has *any* reason to hate you. I'm sure there's an explanation for what happened, and I'm going to find out what it is." He patted the shoulder gently. "Good luck with your wrist tomorrow."

"Wait!" Denis grabbed the cop's sleeve with his right hand. "You're not going to do anything to Goran, are you? Arrest him or—?"

"Or drag him into a dark corner and beat him up?" Denis felt a rush of shock before he realized Donatelli was joking. "We don't usually do stuff like that, especially not to children, so don't worry." He gave Denis a thoughtful look. "Tell you what. I won't go after Goran until you and I have talked again. It's just . . . we need to make that soon."

"Right after the operation," promised Denis. But he was reeling. What did this mean about Zora—did she still hate him, too? He resolved to be there in person when this man confronted Zora's brother. Maybe if Denis spoke to him face-to-face—

"Look," Donatelli said, "we don't know that the boy you heard and I saw *is* Goran Horvat, not for sure—even if he called you a murderer and disappeared in the Matte next to the shop where your friend Zora used to live. The first thing I'll do when I get home is find his photograph online and make sure it's the same boy."

"It's him," mumbled Denis.

Eyes closed again, Denis heard rather than saw Donatelli exchange a few words with the nurse as he left. She came back, supported him to the toilet, checked his various cuts, helped him get his long hair brushed and back into a ponytail, and gave him something to help him sleep, although it was only seven thirty. His first instinct had been to refuse more drugs; wasn't he stoned enough? But with his mind now full of Goran, Zora, and accusations of murder, he accepted the pill gratefully.

As he felt himself slipping away, a picture of Zora came into his mind, now mysteriously both child and adult at the same time. The young-old Zora watched him mournfully, tears streaming down her cheeks. He tried to speak to her and tell her he was sorry, but nothing came out.

6

Giuliana used the drive home to chew over the case against Ruth Seiler. Because she hadn't been the original investigator, taking it on had made her feel as if she had to run just to stay in place. Now, though, she was starting to make progress. It helped that she'd known the prosecutor, Rosmarie Bolliger, for years; Rosmarie had done a lot to bring her up to speed.

In her official statement, Seiler explained that her husband's mild type 2 diabetes had meant she already had some of the insulin she'd used to kill him. Since then, everything about how Seiler had acquired enough of the hormone for an overdose, when she'd injected it, and what she'd done afterward had been more or less verified. As Giuliana drove up Muristalden, she was considering how to get reliable information from Seiler's employer and her best friend, both of whom were witnesses for the defense, not the prosecution.

Gradually, she found her mind drifting from the case to her home life, and the closer she got to the apartment, the more her concentration frayed. Her daughter Isabelle was such a worry at the moment that Giuliana had begun to dread seeing her, which wasn't fair. The problem was that Quentin, Isabelle's boyfriend of almost a year, had broken up with her. Saturday night, she'd come home from a dinner with him that she'd been looking forward to for weeks with her face swollen from crying. Since then, she'd shut herself in her room and barely come out, except to eat an occasional meal or go for long, lonely walks.

Giuliana found a parking space on Alpenstrasse, walked up the hill, and opened her door, forcing a cheerful grin onto her face. "Hello?" she called, stepping into the foyer.

There was no answer, although the apartment smelled slightly cabbage-y. She kicked off her shoes and hung up the lightweight jacket that she wore, even in summer, to keep the gun on her hip out of sight. Isabelle's door was still firmly closed. Eleven-year-old Lukas had recently decided that running to greet his mother when she walked in from work was babyish, but he usually emerged to say hi, so his silence meant he was probably out. A whole cauliflower in a steaming basket on the stove hinted that Ueli wasn't far away—and also explained the smell. There were pieces of chicken and a box of rice on the counter, too.

She was in the bedroom changing out of her work clothes when she heard the front door. Still pulling a purple T-shirt over her head, she came out and saw Ueli, also in a T-shirt and jeans, running a hand through his pumpkin-colored hair. The bottle of white wine in his other hand meant he was just coming up from the cellar. "Hey," they said simultaneously, grinning at each other. He spread his arms to get the bottle out of the way, and she stepped close and kissed him, his beard brushing her chin.

"I see you're going for white-on-white," she said, following him into the kitchen.

He put the wine into the freezer. "Don't let me forget it's there," he said with his back to her, then turned. "White-on-white?"

"I was admiring your artistic palette," she said with mock seriousness. "White plates filled with cauliflower, rice, and chicken served with white wine."

Ueli raised an eyebrow at her. "Parsley on the cauliflower, pine nuts and currants in the rice, and mustard on the chicken. Not exactly a rainbow, but ..." He bent to wash his freckled hands at the kitchen sink under the window while she stood behind him, gazing over his shoulder at the enormous copper beech in their neighbor's front yard. The sight of it always soothed her.

"How's Isabelle?" she asked in a low voice. It was like poking at a bruise—she couldn't leave it alone.

"Still acting like the world has ended." Ueli began flattening four pieces of boneless chicken breast with a mallet.

Giuliana got herself a glass of water from the tap, drank half in one go, and sat at the kitchen table. "Do you think she's being theatrical?"

Ueli took a jar of Dijon mustard from the fridge. "I think she's honestly miserable."

Privately, Giuliana and Ueli both thought the break-up made perfect sense. Quentin had been away a lot, doing his army service as a *Durchdiener*, which meant serving ten months in one stretch instead of an initial eighteen weeks. Why should either of these youngsters—Quentin was just twenty and Isabelle nearly seventeen—be tied to each other while they were apart for almost a year?

"If she hadn't finished all her exams, I'd never indulge her like this," Giuliana said. "Three solid days of mourning. Did you ever do anything like this? Didn't you go out with a girl named ... something beginning with E? She broke up with you, right?"

Ueli was at the stove sautéing pine nuts in olive oil. "You're thinking of Eva," he said over his shoulder. "Actually, by the time you and I started going out, I'd had four girls tell me they didn't want to see me anymore."

"Four! That many? What happened? You must have been heartbroken over and over." Giuliana couldn't remember Ueli telling her about any tragic romances.

Ueli glanced over his shoulder sheepishly. "Early on, I decided I was always going to let girls break up with me so I'd never have to be the bad guy."

"You mean you engineered four breakups?"

"Well, three. One was a surprise, but it hurt my pride more than my feelings. As for the others, well ... I deliberately called them less and less, and when we were together, I just spaced out, and they eventually ended it."

Giuliana frowned. "Those poor girls must have tried desperately to figure out what they'd done wrong."

Ueli shrugged, the side of his mouth turning up. "I can see *now* how manipulative it was, but thirty years ago, I thought I was being considerate." He turned back to the stove and added rice to the nuts and oil in the pot, stirred it, and poured in boiling water from an electric kettle. Then he got out a large frying pan, covered the bottom with more olive oil, and turned on the burner.

"So, you've had girls break up with you and never had your heart broken," Giuliana said, "and I've never been dumped by anyone and *still* had my heart broken a couple of times. Once by unrequited love . . ."

"Lars at the riding school?"

"Right. The other two were guys I was crazy about, but as soon as I felt them drawing away, I broke it off. I still ended up feeling sad and rejected, but at least I hadn't let anyone dump me."

Ueli laughed. "Those poor guys. They were probably distracted by a D in chemistry or a bad week on the soccer field, and you gave them the boot. To this day, they're still wondering if they were lousy in bed or . . ."

"I was a kid," Giuliana protested. "I wasn't sleeping with them. Well, not the first one." She shrugged. "But you're right. What I did was as stupid as what you did. Do you notice what's missing in both our stories? Conversation! No explanations, no discussions, nothing. I guess at that age, you simply aren't capable of it. Thank God I never have to be a teenager again." She pointed at the pan. "Watch out, your oil is smoking."

"Whoops." Ueli added the four mustard-slathered chicken breasts to the pan. "Well," he said, "Quentin seems to have discussed things with Isabelle, which makes him more mature than we were at his age."

"Maybe," Giuliana said. "But if that's true, why is she so devastated?"

"I think we should sit down with her," Ueli said. "I know we said we'd give her space, but I'm getting worried." He glanced at Giuliana. "Is this a mother-daughter thing?"

Giuliana considered. "Let's give it a little longer and see if she can shake this mood on her own. No matter what, though, tomorrow she goes back to school."

It was Lukas's job to set the table, but he wasn't home, so Giuliana got out glasses, plates, and cutlery. As she was finishing, Lukas burst through the front door and, without a word of greeting, began to complain that he'd raced all the way home just to set the table. "You did it so you could fuss at me," he ranted, which was so ridiculous she almost laughed.

"Maybe I should have given you more time to get here, but that's no reason to shout at me. Go wash your hands, and be sure you come back polite."

Isabelle crept out of her room to the table, as silent as Lukas had been loud. She wore an oversized T-shirt with baggy sweatpants and looked as if she'd been lying in bed all day, her thick red hair all over the place. Giuliana almost sent her back to brush it but didn't.

They sat down to eat. As promised, the food didn't look so uniformly white after all. Ueli remembered to get the wine out of the freezer and poured himself and Giuliana "each" a glass while Lukas fetched water for everyone and milk for himself without being asked. Giuliana and Ueli met eyes across the table and clinked wine glasses. Here we are again, their toast said, having a family dinner. Let's enjoy this moment of peace since who knows what will be going on in two minutes?

"The man with Alzheimer's whose wife killed him—anything new going on with that?" asked Ueli after he'd taken a sip of wine.

"Chicken's good," said Giuliana, swallowing. "Well, I haven't had a chance to talk to the wife yet, so . . ."

Lukas looked up from shoveling in rice. "Are you sure she did it?"

"Pretty sure," Giuliana answered and decided it was all right to tell Lukas a bit more. "At first, the man's doctor assumed the death was natural. Then his grown-up daughter made the doctor report a suspicious death, and when the pathologist checked, the husband had too much of a hormone called insulin in his body, so the police were called. The daughter wanted her father's wife to get into trouble, so she made sure the newspapers got hold of the story. That's when the—"

Isabelle finished her sentence. "That's when the shit hit the fan."

Delighted that Isabelle had joined the conversation yet determined not to make a big deal of it, Giuliana gave her daughter a mock punch on the arm. "Hey, you! I was going to find a more delicate way of saying that."

"I only said what you were thinking!" Isabelle was actually smiling at her. "But why didn't the old man sign up for Exit or Dignitas? It would have been legal and wouldn't have caused all this trouble."

"More rice or cauliflower, anyone?" asked Ueli, and Lukas, as usual, held out his plate. As Ueli filled it, he said, "That's not quite true, Isa. Assisted suicide is only allowed for people who know exactly what they're doing. Maybe this man was already too confused to state his wishes clearly and hadn't written anything down earlier to explain what he wanted."

Lukas was listening intently. One of his grandmothers had already had cancer, Giuliana reflected. He was no stranger to the reality of death.

Isabelle was frowning, pushing a last piece of cauliflower around her plate. "So, he couldn't sign anything because he was already gaga. But we know he wanted to die. I mean, who'd want to live like that? People in comas are taken off life support when their brains are kaput, right? So why not this guy?"

Giuliana said, "It's a legal problem, love. *I* wouldn't want to live like that, nor would *Vati*. We've discussed it and filled out end-of-life documents. But we don't know if this man felt the same way. Maybe he believed it was up to God. Or that being alive was worthwhile no matter what. If people haven't left instructions and can't explain their wishes, how does the law know what they want?"

Isabelle tossed her head. "I understand that. I just don't agree with it. I bet his wife knew what he wanted, all right."

That was exactly what Ruth Seiler had told the police, but Giuliana didn't say that. "Maybe. But suppose she wanted to live with another man and needed their money? Or what if she was simply fed up looking after him?"

Isabelle's frown was deepening, and Ueli caught Giuliana's eye, so she shut up. She didn't want to drive Isabelle back into a dark mood.

But Isabelle wasn't finished. "Keeping people's bodies alive when their minds are useless—I think it's like keeping them in prison. It's . . . it's like torture."

"I don't think that," Lukas said. With a dramatic flourish, he drained his glass of milk and set it on the table. "What about tiny babies?" he said. Ueli and Isabelle looked puzzled. "Their minds are useless—they can't explain what they want; they don't *know* what they want, right? So there have to be laws to say what happens to them. You can't let people do whatever they like with a baby. Someone might . . . throw one in the garbage or something."

Isabelle smiled at her brother. "That's interesting, Lüki-boy," she told him. "*Your* mind certainly isn't useless."

Lukas looked pleased with himself, and Giuliana patted his shoulder. She was not going to tell him how often newborn babies *did* end up in the garbage. Nor was she going to launch into a speech about how, over the centuries, the law had judged not merely babies but people with perfectly good minds to be incapable of making decisions about their own welfare: women and children, slaves, the poor, the deaf, the physically disabled. The list went on and on. Still, that was another conversation for another time.

Later, when she was getting ready for bed, she thought about what her children had said and was struck again by how complicated Ruth Seiler's case was, morally if not legally. The law had accused the woman of homicide because it had to protect her husband's right to life, whatever the state of his mind. It was up to Giuliana to make damn sure that, this time, at least, the law was in the right.

7

Renzo Donatelli set his pizza on the island that separated his tiny kitchen from the rest of the room. Then he turned the oven on low and transferred the pizza, box and all, to the middle rack to keep it warm while he changed clothes.

Barefoot, in shorts and a T-shirt, he sat under the striped awning on his balcony, drinking an Eichhof lager and taking in the view of the apartment buildings across the street and *their* balconies. On one, an older couple half hidden by red geraniums sat in folding chairs drinking from espresso cups; the man noticed Renzo and waved. Renzo waved back and felt, at that moment, deeply content. He had warm sunshine and cold beer, and tomorrow he'd tackle the case with the young glassmaker. Tonight, as soon as he finished his pizza, he planned to have a look for the boy Goran Horvat online.

He took a bite. The pizza was excellent: a crispy crust but not too dry, its *prosciutto crudo* and porcini topping salty and fragrant. He ate and drank slowly in the shade of the awning. Except for occasional noises from the narrow side street below, it was quiet.

He sighed. Quiet was the problem.

He ought to appreciate it, especially after last week. He and Fränzi had decided the kids would continue to live full time in the family apartment in Wabern, while they would take turns living in this one-bedroom flat on Blumenweg. A week with the kids, followed by a week alone. So last Tuesday, for example, he'd galloped out of the police station, leaving several tasks undone, and driven over the speed limit to reach Angelo and Antonietta's daycare at five forty-five. He'd packed the kids into the car, unpacked them at home—or, rather, at what was now *their* home, but not his—bathed them, gotten them into their pj's, and made them pasta primavera. He'd changed Antonietta into clean pajamas after she'd lifted her half-eaten bowl of farfalle and, locking eyes with him, poured it deliberately into her lap. Angelo then started crying for his mother—or, Renzo suspected, because he thought his sister was getting too much attention. Eventually, he'd gotten them into bed, read to them, sung to them, and turned out the lights at eight thirty. Every day of the week with them had been just as hectic.

Fränzi had been gleeful about the arrangement. "I already know what it's like to take care of the children alone because you were barely here. Now you'll find out what I've been going through all these years, and I'll get a week off twice a month and have time to . . . see friends."

By which Renzo knew she meant see men. Whenever his colleagues at the station teased him about his newly single status, he played innocent, but *of course* he thought of the little apartment in terms of its sexual potential. Knowing that Fränzi saw it exactly the same way upset him, but he knew he was ridiculous. You couldn't tell your wife you didn't want to be with her anymore and then feel jealous at the thought of her sleeping with other men. It was irrational and—well, primitive. But knowing that didn't change the way he felt.

That wasn't the main problem with the Lorraine apartment, however. The trouble was that in spite of how chaotic life was with the kids, he missed them fiercely when he wasn't with them. No matter what Fränzi might say, he'd never gone seven full days without his babies. Yes, he *had* spent too little time with his children, he knew that, and as a result, every minute with them had become precious.

Had he really done the right thing to leave Fränzi just because they didn't like each other anymore? The sex between them had never stopped working, and at least they'd been a family. He'd put up for years with her telling him what a bad father and husband he was. Maybe he should have kept putting up with it for another ten years or so, at least until the kids were teenagers. A divorce would be easier to organize with older kids who could ride their bikes to after-school sports or take public transport. Maybe by then—

His cell rang: Fränzi. He hoped she was calling to put the kids on the line to say good night to him, although that wasn't part of their arrangement. No, it was after nine, too late for the kids to be awake. He answered cautiously. "Hi, Fränzi. How was your—?"

She interrupted; her voice high-pitched and fast. "My day was lousy, and it didn't get any better when Angelo told me you'd said he could stay up until eight thirty every night, whether you were there or not. What were you thinking?"

Renzo did what he always did when Fränzi was angry with him: he spoke slowly and calmly. It not only gave him the upper hand, but it drove her wild and made her feel he was treating her like a child. In his deliberate voice of reason, he said, "You *know* I didn't tell him that; he's trying his luck. We agreed we'd each have our own set of rules and make them clear to the kids. Last week I made a point of telling both of them that with Mama, they'd have to go to bed at seven thirty, like always."

"But why *do* you have to let them stay up so late? It's bad for them."

Oh, God. He was not going to start this discussion again. "For over six years I've let you make decisions for our kids. Now, every other week, I can do things my way. We agreed to this."

This time, when she spoke, her voice was low and throaty. "Oh, Renzo, let's not . . ."

Aha! She was resorting to her sexy voice. And it worked; he felt the response in his groin just as he always did. Like one of that Russian guy's dogs, he thought, slavering at the dinner bell. He refused to let himself be manipulated. His tone impassive, he asked, "Was there anything else? Otherwise, my dinner's getting cold."

Back she went to her angry voice. "I can't imagine—"

Now it was his turn to interrupt. "Fränzi, if you're having a problem with the way we decided to handle the separation, call the mediator. Not me. Good night!" He hung up.

He breathed in and out a couple of times to calm himself. Then he finished his beer. His last quarter of pizza was almost cold.

Had he actually been wondering if he'd done the right thing leaving Fränzi? There was no way he could have handled ten more years of conversations like the one they'd just had. Well, he could stop feeling guilty. He had *not* made a mistake. And if it seemed like the kids weren't getting enough sleep during their weeks with him, he'd put them to bed earlier. Or at least see what his mother thought.

Thank God for his mother. For his whole family, in fact. His two sisters, his brother, and all three in-laws had promised to help with childcare, especially if he had a work emergency. Even his older nieces and nephews were pitching in, offering to babysit. He got tears in his eyes thinking of them all.

As he took the empty beer bottle and pizza box inside, his mind wandered from his own family to the two boys he'd encountered that day: Goran and Denis. According to Denis, Goran had lost his mother so young he probably didn't remember her. Had his older sister raised him? And what about Denis? He hadn't mentioned his mother at all. Did he have one? Grandparents could do as good a job of childrearing as parents, but it would be a bit of an odd coincidence if both Denis and Goran were motherless.

Assuming Renzo got assigned the attempted murder as his own case, he'd see if he could find out something about Katica Horvat's suicide before he tracked down Goran. The Pläfe—where he'd been planning to have an espresso before Goran crashed into him—was infamous for suicides. Jutting out above the Matte neighborhood, it used to attract lots of jumpers aiming for the pavement ninety feet below until the city had strung nets under the wall and put a stop to it. By contrast, the Münster Tower was not known for suicides—it was closed at night, and there were members of the staff on the watch there during the day. Renzo couldn't remember anyone jumping from the cathedral's tower in the thirteen years he'd been a policeman. But fifteen years ago, Katica Horvat had done it. How? Why?

A police investigation into a suicide didn't have to be kept on file, but he hoped he'd find something about the case anyway. If not, there must be someone who could give him a first-hand account. He thought of Denis Kellenberger's grandparents, who'd known the woman whose death had had so much impact on them and their grandson. Maybe they had ideas about why she'd killed herself. They might even give him insight into what had made the dead woman's son, Goran, so angry. It was too late to call them tonight, but he'd do it first thing in the morning.

If it *was* Goran.

Grabbing his laptop off the sofa, he took it out onto the balcony with an espresso. He hadn't bothered to buy a desk for the new flat—it didn't even have a proper table yet, just the kitchen bar with three stools, a coffee table in front of the sofa, and the bistro table on the balcony. But, in the long summer twilight, the balcony seemed like an ideal place for doing research.

He'd tried a quick Google search for "Goran Horvat" earlier and had found photos of a great many Croatian men but no teenagers. Now he thought about social media platforms where the kid might have posted something. Not Facebook or Twitter, not a fifteen-year-old boy. Maybe something on YouTube or Snapchat?

First, though, he tried googling the sports clubs for teenagers in the Matte neighborhood and found lots of photos: boys and girls running around a track, playing basketball and volleyball, kicking a soccer ball around a field. Team photos, too, with names under them. He had to enlarge lots of faces, but even so, it only took twenty minutes to find the terrified boy who'd run into him just inside the platform gate. There he was, grinning, an arm around one of his soccer teammates. And below the photo were names, including Goran's. *Gotcha*, thought Renzo. But there was still so much he didn't know.

He began with the website for the Berner Münster. He learned that it was Gothic, begun in 1421 and finished in the mid-fifteen hundreds, except for the last third of the tower. That extravagant stone filigree cap, which brought the tower to its full hundred-meter height and made it the tallest in Switzerland—*that* part had been added in the eighteen nineties. Sneaky, he reflected, shaking his head. But none of this was relevant: he wanted to know more about the tower guards, who'd kept watch from the large viewing balcony since the fifteen hundreds, ringing the fire bells if they saw any part of the city burning. And, in more recent times, keeping an eye out for possible jumpers.

In 1826, the guardroom had apparently been turned into living quarters so the chief watchman and his wife could move in. From then on, there had always been families at the top of the narrow spiral staircase, two hundred fifty-four steps up. The last occupants, said the write-up, were Hans-Peter and Ursula Kellenberger. Excellent! And their landline and address were online: thank God for the internet. Renzo typed the Kellenbergers' contact information into his phone. The couple lived in Kirchenfeld, the same neighborhood as Giuliana, but a posher section of it.

Giuliana. He thought about the moment in the case room when he'd touched her cheek, and she'd put her hand on his. He leaned his head back until he was gazing up at the underside of the yellow-and-white-striped balcony awning and closed his eyes. When they were together, she always made him feel that if he couldn't have what he wanted, he was willing to settle for close companionship and the occasional sparks between them. But when they were apart, the game they were playing—if that was what it was—made him feel tired and depressed. Something, he knew, was going to have to change.

8

Lorraine, Wednesday morning, June 26

For two years, Giuliana had been working out with Renzo most weeks at the gym across from the police station, either Monday or Wednesday morning. Officially, hers was a desk job: reading and digesting reports, deciding what new information was needed, and sending *Fahnder*—general investigators like Renzo—out to get it. But much as she enjoyed being a homicide detective, she missed fieldwork, so she tried to slip as much action into her job as she could. Action didn't just mean interviews; it could mean chasing suspects. Over high walls, too, she reminded herself as she groaned through her last two chin-ups and crossed the room to lie face down on a leg curl machine. In her younger days, she'd stayed fit thanks to hiking, riding her bike, and taking combat classes, and she always did regular target shooting. Now, at forty-seven, she had to do more.

She lifted her head to see Renzo, ten feet away, holding a handstand on a bright blue mat. Now *that* was a sight. Panting, she stared at his upside-down face, hoping it would start to show the strain, and he gave her a slow wink. She laughed out loud and then concentrated on getting her breath back.

Later, in the bakery café next door, Renzo fetched their croissants and hot milk coffees from the counter while she skimmed through the notes he'd written the night before. As Renzo set down the tray, she looked up. "I remember this suicide!" she said. "It made a big impression on me. It was only my second year in homicide."

He passed her her usual whole wheat croissant and hot milk coffee and unloaded his own food. "Tell me."

She took a cautious sip from the full cup. "I was called out early in the morning. The body of a young woman was lying on the paving stones in front of the cathedral. I can still see her." She closed her eyes, the image sharp in her mind. "She had a lot of long dark hair. It was soaked . . . absolutely *drenched* in blood, and I had to push it aside to see her face, which looked . . ." She stopped and took a deep breath, ". . . as if she'd died in agony. Her body was completely distorted, too. She was just . . . mangled."

"A really bad one," Renzo mumbled through his bite of almond croissant. He wiped his mouth. "It's great that you were there, though. I'm planning to track down anything left from the case before I talk to the couple who lived in the tower. Maybe you saw them at the scene? A man and woman of about sixty?"

Giuliana drank more coffee, calling to mind the Münsterplatz on that cold, dark November morning. "I don't know," she admitted. "Everything was chaos. It was a Tuesday—market day, you know." Renzo nodded. "So, although it was early, there were people everywhere setting up their stands—it was one of them who found the body." She searched her memory. "A butcher, I think, who'd arrived before six and was getting fresh water from the Moses fountain when he saw her."

Renzo swallowed another mouthful. "Who else worked the case?"

"There were four uniformed men on the scene when the homicide team arrived—which was me and Samuel Grossenbacher," Giuliana said. "He was way before your time, already close to retiring then. I never really got to know him. He acted quite detached around me, even when we were at lunch or getting coffee. Believe me, that was better than flirtatious, which I got from a lot of other male colleagues in those days, so I'm not complaining. But I always had the feeling . . ." She trailed off.

"And he was in charge of the investigation?" Renzo asked.

"Yes, I was there to assist, and it was a nightmare. We couldn't keep either the market folks or the Münster officials out of the way. Worst of all, someone had fetched the dead woman's husband before Grossenbacher and I got there, and he'd called a Catholic priest, who turned up in full regalia at the same time as the police doctor. We ended up having to remove the husband and priest from the scene, although by then they'd already tracked all over it. They were very upset, and I felt bad, but it had to be done. I mean, the woman had been dead for hours; she was long past receiving the last rites." She gulped down the rest of the coffee and bit into her croissant with a pleasing crunch.

Renzo cradled his cup and frowned in thought. "According to the young glassmaker Denis Kellenberger, his grandmother was the person who went to fetch the husband. She must have been there in the crowd." He stared at his empty plate. "What do you remember about the investigation?"

It was exactly what she'd been asking herself. "It's weird," she told him. "I have such strong memories of that morning and how upsetting it was. But the aftermath is a blank. Fifteen years isn't so long ago, and it was early in my homicide career—you'd think I'd remember. I suppose since Grossenbacher was the primary detective and I was very junior, he just took it over and didn't need me anymore. But I feel as if the death vanished from homicide's radar quickly. Anyway . . ." She leaned down to pick up her handbag—it was time to get to work, even if there wasn't the usual eight o'clock staff meeting for the Seiler case since she and Renzo were pretty much holding the fort alone for the moment.

She smiled to herself as Renzo tidied their plates and cups into the center of the table. He'd never paid any attention to their breakfast things before, yet this was the second week in a row that he'd stacked the dishes. And the third week in his new place. Not a coincidence, she was sure. A few weeks of being responsible for meals, and he was already becoming house-trained.

"Giule," Renzo called as she left the café a few steps in front of him. "Have you found out anything about . . . about me working the Münster case?" He paused. "I'm pretty sure what happened yesterday connects with Frau Horvat's suicide, so I guess I'd be looking into *both* cases. Am I cleared to do that?"

They waited at the yellow-painted crosswalk for the cars to stop, and Giuliana moved closer to Renzo as they crossed. "I'm sorry I didn't keep you posted. I did phone around to find out where the fall-off-the-scaffold case was going, and it was in limbo. So before things went any further, I thought I would talk to Rolf." When Renzo frowned, she added, "I think it's a good idea for him to know you're taking on the case. That gives you his tacit approval. Plus, you never know when you might need a recommendation from him—if you were looking for a promotion to specialist detective in the homicide department, say."

His frown dissolved into a smile. "You know me so well," he told her. "I know I've only talked about it as a long-term goal, but with the divorce and everything, it suddenly feels more urgent."

He was probably hurting for money now, she thought. But that wasn't something she'd ever mention unless he brought it up. "Do you want me to get someone else for the Seiler case?"

"No, no," he said quickly. "I can handle both." As they reached the door of their case room, he put his hand on her arm. "Thanks for thinking of Rolf," he said softly, and then, in his normal voice, "Want another coffee? I'm getting myself one." She shook her head, and he jogged off to the little kitchen down the hall.

An hour later, Giuliana was puzzling over the Seiler case again, skimming the interviews that had been conducted before she and Renzo had taken over. The Fahnderin who'd worked it before had talked with six of the couple's neighbors and three sets of their close friends, trying to learn more about the husband and wife's characters and their relationship with each other. Unfortunately, the interviews had generated almost nothing.

Or rather, they'd turned up little that would be useful to the prosecution. The reports were full of words and phrases like "always helpful," "quiet but not standoffish," "somewhat in her husband's shadow, but certainly pleasant," and "not that easy to get to know." Giuliana was struggling to form any real picture of Ruth Seiler.

The reports revealed more about Seiler's husband, Werner Allemann, than about her. He emerged as a sociable though occasionally overpowering talker, a convivial drinker who sometimes took a glass too much but was not a drunk, and a man with strong opinions who was still willing to listen to people who disagreed with him. His friends had watched with horror and pity as he'd succumbed to dementia, first with a brave front, then with confusion and increasing silence, and finally by retreating from social life, which they'd accepted sadly but with a certain amount of relief.

The wife of one of Allemann's oldest friends provided the most insight into the couple. "I was very fond of Werner," she'd told the policewoman. "He was warm and friendly. He told funny stories, too, and I liked that he made *himself* the butt of his jokes, not other people. There was something simple about him. At least, once he got rid of that first wife." At this point, the interviewer, a woman called Mädi, had added: "Subject rolled eyes and made gagging noise re: first wife." This was followed by a vomiting emoji. Giuliana smiled. Mädi's reports were thorough and professional but never dreary.

She kept reading. "Werner's wife left *him*, but it was the best thing that could have happened. One of her complaints about him was his tightness with money—he *was* a bit too careful with it. But he could joke about his miserliness, and he always paid for his round."

The information about Werner's attitude toward money was useful, although again, not for the prosecution, since it suggested that Allemann might not have wanted their money spent on care for himself. This matched what Ruth Seiler had told the police.

At that point in the interview, Mädi had skillfully brought the woman around to talking in more detail about Seiler, and she'd reproduced the friend's words as faithfully as possible. "Ruth is more complicated than Werner," the woman had said. "She thought about everything she did. I got the impression that it was important to her—because it was important to Werner—that he be the life of the party. But secretly, I think he was quite dependent on her. I liked her. I can't believe she'd cold-bloodedly murder him. But her coming up with some sort of... *scheme* to deal with his dementia—that wouldn't surprise me. She was always a planner, and what's the difference between a planner and a schemer except in the eye of the beholder?"

The prosecution's official view of Seiler was that she'd committed murder to inherit money, as Allemann's daughter Tamara kept insisting. That meant the investigators' agenda had been to find out if Seiler either lusted after luxury or was afraid for her financial future. Here, their questions had backfired. Coworkers from Seiler's office at the cantonal tax department had scoffed—one had actually laughed—at the idea. The laugher had said, "I've known Ruth for thirty-five years, and her idea of luxury is to get a good quality pair of shoes and then look after them religiously until they literally fall apart. And her work handbag— I'll bet she's had that thing for fifteen years—maybe more!"

Yet it was Seiler herself who'd stated that one of the reasons she'd killed her husband was to "save his money." Her confession—she insisted on calling the killing an assisted *suicide*, although he hadn't given himself the insulin—was written and signed.

Giuliana read and reread the documents. Whatever Tamara Allemann thought, Giuliana saw no evidence that her stepmother had been grasping for money. But it was quite possible that a woman widowed young—as Ruth had been when her first husband died of cancer—and now facing a second widowhood might have been afraid of being left in poverty if her husband's and her own savings were devoured by the costs of his care.

She made a note to ask the prosecutor, Rosmarie Bolliger, if someone had looked into the couple's financial affairs. The prosecution might not think they needed to with such a lovely, watertight confession. But Giuliana's father had been a brilliant defense lawyer, and her brother was following in his footsteps—and it often helped Giuliana to anticipate the other side's approach to a case. In this instance, she thought the defense would try to prove that Ruth didn't need to kill her husband for his inheritance because she'd have enough to live on no matter what his care situation turned out to be. But was that true?

As she was thinking about this, Renzo walked into the little office and became Italian. This was how Giuliana labeled it when his entire presence seemed to broadcast his feelings. With raised eyebrows, wide eyes, and pleading hands, he demonstrated the depth and magnificence of his outrage. "Nothing," he lamented. "Can you believe it? Not a single file—paper *or* computer—on the investigation into Katica Horvat's death."

"What did you expect?" she asked. "It was fifteen years ago, and no one here keeps records unless they're required to, which, in this case, they weren't."

"So, I'll just have to start over." Renzo sighed loudly, and then his extravagant *italianità* vanished as he said, "I've gotten everything cleared on my end to take on the Münster case. Have you heard anything official?"

At least she could give him some good news. "I spoke to Rolf. Denis Kellenberger's fall and anything you decide to investigate in relation to it is yours. So . . . good luck."

To her surprise, there was no fist pump or blazing grin. Nodding his thanks, his face serious, he sat down at his desk and logged on. "That's great," he said, pulling his phone out of his back pocket. "Time to talk to Denis's grandparents. And the first thing I want to know is how Katica Horvat could have jumped off a balcony completely surrounding their tower apartment without either of them hearing a thing."

9

"Kellenberger." The strength of the man's voice on the phone surprised Renzo. Then he remembered that Denis was only twenty-five, so his grandparents didn't have to be ancient.

Renzo didn't get past "your grandson's fall" before the older man interrupted. "What fall?"

They didn't know? But why? He couldn't remember Denis asking him to keep what had happened at the Münster secret.

Before Renzo could answer, Kellenberger went on. "Are you saying that you're investigating an injury sustained by Denis because of a fall? Is Denis . . . is he still alive?"

Renzo rushed to reassure the man, all the while marveling at someone using the phrase "sustain an injury" in normal speech. "He was alive and well when I saw him last night at the *Inselspital*. He looks pretty messed up, but the only thing that's serious is a broken left wrist. He's having it operated on this morning. In fact, he may already be out of surgery."

Kellenberger sounded hesitant. "Denis wasn't doing something illegal when he fell?"

"Not at all," Renzo said. "He was on a scaffold, fixing a stained-glass window in the Münster, and someone deliberately knocked him off and ran away. It happened yesterday afternoon, and I interviewed him in the hospital last night. I'd like to speak with you and your wife, too—this afternoon or evening, if possible."

There was silence as if Herr Kellenberger's brain were rebooting to process this new set of data. When he spoke again, he didn't sound so starchy. "I see. We would be glad to talk to you. My wife is away today until after five this evening. Would it be acceptable for us to meet you at the police station at eight o'clock tonight?"

"If it wouldn't be an intrusion," Renzo said—now *he* was talking like a book, for Chrissake—"I'd be glad to come to your house instead." During the pause that followed, he added, "If you'd like to check that I am who I say I am, I suggest you call the main number of the cantonal police and ask for Renzo Donatelli, and they'll connect you to me. But . . . look, why don't you phone the hospital first? I'll be here for the next half hour at least."

"Thank you," said Kellenberger. "I'll do that."

As Renzo waited, he looked up Hans-Peter Kellenberger online and discovered that he was a professor of medieval and early modern European history at the University of Bern, specializing in the Protestant Reformation. One of his books was called *Creative Destruction: The Reformation in Germany and Switzerland*. Well, thought Renzo, the Berner Münster had certainly seen a lot of destruction. In the nineteen eighties, hundreds of pieces of medieval statuary, hauled down and broken when the church had switched from Catholic to Protestant, were found buried in the Pläfe. Although Kellenberger probably didn't mean destruction quite so literally, Renzo decided.

Then he typed Denis's grandmother's name into Google, along with "Bern." Ursula Kellenberger, he discovered, worked in textile conservation at the Abegg Foundation, which he'd never heard of. The organization was housed in a country mansion about half an hour from Bern and had its own museum. A museum that showed ratty bits of old cloth? Or rugs and tapestries, maybe? He did a bit more searching and learned that in her fifties, Ursula Kellenberger had transitioned from restoring cloth to making it; she'd become a weaver. He was about to click on a gallery where she exhibited when his desk phone rang.

"This is Donatelli."

"Herr Donatelli. Greetings again," said Denis's grandfather. "My grandson isn't out of surgery yet, and I have confirmed that you are a policeman. You are welcome to come to our home tonight. What about eight thirty?"

"Thanks. I'll be there." Renzo hung up, wondering again why Denis had kept his injury to himself. Even as he mulled this over, he acknowledged the advantages of such a silence. When he'd almost been killed on a case the previous summer, so many visitors appeared at his bedside that he'd asked the nurses to throw most of them out after fifteen minutes.

He was starting to think about coffee and wondering why Giuliana wasn't at her desk when his office phone rang again. The caller, Nathan Winter, came straight to the point.

"Have I got this right—that you're looking into what happened to Denis Kellenberger? I only just heard about his fall from his grandfather. None of those fools at the Münster had the sense to call me, and I'm his boss. Before that, he was my apprentice, and I'm friends with his grandparents, too, so I've known him since he was a baby. I'd like some information."

Renzo interrupted. "I'm in charge of the case, yes. Can we talk?"

"Great," Winter said. "I'm already on my way to the School of Design, so I can be at the police station in less than ten minutes."

Denis's boss was bigger than Renzo had expected. Perhaps the delicacy of glass had led him to picture a delicate man. Winter was mid-fifties, Renzo guessed, with very short dark hair, brown eyes surrounded by laugh lines, prominent features, and a muscled body starting to thicken. When they shook hands, Renzo felt the roughness of the man's palms.

"Thanks for letting me come right away," said Winter. Once they were both settled at the oval table in the meeting room at the end of the hall, coffee mugs in hand, he picked up where he'd left off. "Denis didn't contact me, and neither did anyone at the church, as I said. I was working in my studio all day yesterday and earlier this morning. About half an hour ago, I went by the cathedral to see how Denis was getting on with the windows, and—no Denis. The sexton told me what happened to him but didn't know where he was, so I called Hampi Kellenberger, who said Denis was in surgery but generally okay and gave me your number."

Renzo related some of what Denis had told him the evening before. He mentioned that Denis believed his attacker was a teenager but left out his own encounter with the panicky boy in the Münster park.

Winter tapped the tabletop, shaking his head. "I blame myself," he said. "I knew that scaffold wasn't as stable as it should have been, but I decided not to request more work on it when Denis was only going to be doing some cleaning and a few simple repairs."

"The attacker shook the whole structure as hard as he could," Renzo reminded him.

"No teenager should be able to budge a decent scaffold." Winter's eyes were troubled. "Have you found out who he was?"

Renzo wasn't sure he should say anything about how the attack on Denis might relate to Katica Horvat's suicide. After all, he hadn't yet talked to Goran or his parents. And then there was a bigger question that had been growing in the back of his mind: since he didn't know anything about the investigation, could he be sure that Katica's death *was* a suicide?

Winter waited, watching Renzo's face.

I have to start somewhere, thought Renzo. "We don't know for sure, but it's possible he's the son of a woman named Katica Horvat. She died falling from the Münster tower fifteen—"

"I remember that," Winter interrupted. "I wasn't working in the church then, but Denis had started hanging out in my glass workshop after school. I heard the talk, the Kellenbergers being evicted from their apartment, all that. They were going to be kicked out anyway a year later because there was restoration work due on the tower, and the apartment was needed by the builders. But it was . . . a distressing overreaction."

"Denis told me about getting in trouble for leaving the tower door unlocked. But he was only ten. How could anyone blame him?" Winter rolled his eyes. "That was the sexton, Klaus Friedli. He's not an easy man to like, but I do have some sympathy. Denis used the church as a playground, and it drove Friedli mad. He'd been looking for an excuse to get the Kellenbergers out since the day they moved in. Nobody I knew really blamed Denis. But the kid took it to heart—I think he feels guilty even now. It's ridiculous, but . . ." He broke off.

"Why put a child in charge of checking the doors in the first place?" Renzo pressed.

"Oh, that was only one of Denis's little jobs." Winter smiled. "It's an old tradition. Frau Kormann, who was the tower guard for almost sixty years, paid a boy to sweep the steps and help sell tickets. That was in the fifties, I think."

Renzo was fascinated by the whole idea of generations of people living at the top of the tower. "You can't possibly remember back then."

Winter grinned. "Well, not personally, no. But my memories of the Münster do go back fifty years, and before that, I have my father's stories."

"Of course. I think of the place as a monument, but for your family, it must have been a parish church."

Winter, still smiling, shook his head. "My family didn't worship there—we're Jewish. Not that we spent much time in the synagogue either. But as a boy, I was in the Münster learning my father's trade. He was responsible for taking care of the stained-glass windows before me." He rubbed his hand through his short hair. "Didn't *you* ever go to work with your father?" He seemed genuinely curious.

"My father was a fireman," Renzo told him. "We were four kids, two boys and two girls, and we loved visiting the fire station. But it didn't happen often. They didn't want kids around in case they were called out to a fire. It was different for you, huh?"

Winter leaned back in his chair, both hands holding his mug so that it rested against his chest. His eyes looked as if they were seeing the past, not the plain cream walls of the meeting room.

"I started working with him in the studio when I was seven. By thirteen, I could do almost everything he could do—just badly." Winter's eyes refocused, and he smiled again. "I wasted so much material—dyes, lead, copper wire, glass. He got cross sometimes, but he never made me feel like an idiot."

Renzo had only one childhood friend who'd taken over the family business and stuck to it—a plumber, and he regularly complained about the pressure of his father's expectations. "You never thought of doing something else?"

"Oh, sure," Winter said. "I wanted to be an artist. A *real* artist, not an artisan. But at some point, I had to recognize that the world was full of young people trying to be artists, whereas I already had a profession that let me draw and paint and sculpt. Then I got married and had kids, which gave me a new perspective on money. Besides, restoration work is only a small part of what I do. I produce a lot of stained-glass coats of arms for families and businesses, which is boring, but I also make windows, room dividers, and sculptures, which I get to design. I love that side of it."

"You took Denis on as an apprentice, so presumably, he's no longer banned from the church?"

"The current parish council members are a much more tolerant bunch than the ones in charge fifteen, twenty years ago."

"One of the older ladies working in the Münster shop didn't sound like she approved of Denis at all."

"Frau Arnold. The old bi—biddy is constantly after Denis. She's never liked him."

Renzo frowned. "Yeah, we have exactly that type of 'old biddy'"—he made air quotes around the words—"on our corridor." He meant the building he'd moved out of because of the separation, but that was irrelevant. "If one of my kids even squeaks in the hall, she's hanging out her door growling. Imagine having nothing better to do than terrorize little kids."

Winter nodded sympathetically, then drained his coffee and leaned forward, palms open on his thighs. "I've got a class at the Design School, so I'd better go. Thanks for filling me in. Let me know if I can give you any more help."

As they stood and headed for the door, Renzo thought of something. It had nothing to do with his investigation, but still... "This piece of glass Denis broke—is it a big deal?"

"The fashion now is to salvage everything that can possibly be kept in place by painstakingly repairing it. But fifty years ago, anything that looked worn was knocked out and replaced wholesale. In those days, new pieces of colored glass and new lead were added to all the old windows as needed."

"Are you saying it does matter, or...?"

Winter flattened one hand in the air and wiggled it back and forth between yes and no. "I believe in restoring as much as possible, sure. But honestly, some restorers treat everything like a holy relic. There are small sections of old glass in some of the windows whose cracks are mended with so much soldered-in copper foil that... well, new glass would make more sense, and it wouldn't look any different, at least not if I did it. The glass Denis broke can easily be replaced, and it won't be the only modern piece in that window."

Renzo held out his hand. "Thanks for explaining—and for coming by." As they shook hands, another question came to him. "Denis told me he was raised by his grandparents. Are his parents dead?"

Winter raised his eyebrows. "Not at all. His father's an American who lives in Florida with a wife and kids, and his mother has an apartment outside Bern and works in the city. His grandparents brought him up, yes, and there's a bit of a story behind that; maybe Denis can tell you. But there's no big estrangement. He sees both parents regularly. Got to run," he added, looking at his watch, and he set off at a trot, raising a hand to Renzo over his shoulder.

It was one in the afternoon, and Renzo was hungry, so he made for the cafeteria in the basement. He grabbed a tray and chatted with the middle-aged server while she filled his plate with rice and a Thai curry that she claimed contained five vegetables in addition to pork. So, better for him than pizza. With the divorce making life more expensive, he'd given up buying mineral water for lunch, so the woman filled a beer mug with tap water instead.

Balancing his tray, he scanned the room and was about to join the nearest group of uniformed men when he spotted Madeleine Trachsel sitting alone at a small table by the wall, reading something on her iPad. Like him, she was a general investigator—a Fahnderin. She'd been promoted about six months before, so he'd only worked with her on one case. But that had been enough time to notice she was sexy—well, it only took a second to see that—and smart. She had a sense of humor, too.

"Hi, Mädi. Can I join you?"

Her eyes widened in surprise before she beamed at him. "Hi! You know I did interviews to get background on Ruth Seiler and her husband. But I've been off the case for a while now. I'd love to get an update."

He smiled down at her—something he couldn't do when she was standing since she was slightly taller than he was. Her dyed white-blonde hair was shorter and spikier than he remembered.

He didn't want to talk shop; he'd been hoping to find out more about her. Still . . . "Sure, I can give you the latest news." He set his tray down and took the chair across from her. "First, though, tell me what's going on with you?"

"Let's see," she said. As he took a bite of curry, she held up a thumb. "One, I'm working with Sabine Jost on a domestic abuse case where a man killed his wife, and it looks like we're going to be able to put that bastard away for a long time." Her forefinger joined her thumb. "Two, I just became an aunt. My older sister had a boy, and they named him Elvis." She grimaced. "What a choice! Still, he's cute." She held up the next finger. "I turned thirty last week, and I've decided it's time to look for my own place instead of sharing an apartment—*if* I can afford the rent."

Renzo started to tell her that *he* had his own apartment now. But given the way gossip traveled around the police station, she probably knew that already. Instead, he said, "That all sounds positive. How are things going with Sabine?"

Mädi thought before she answered. Eventually, she said, "I was a little intimidated by her at first—I mean, she was the first woman ever on the homicide team. Plus, her style's different from Giuliana's. Quieter, drier. But now that I've gotten to know her, I like working with her. She's very clear about what she needs me to do, but she gives me space to make decisions." She finished her wedge of rhubarb pie and wiped her mouth with a napkin. "Now, tell me your opinion of Ruth Seiler. Greedy monster or mercy killer?"

Renzo did a mock double take. "Quoting newspaper headlines at me, huh?"

Her expression turned sheepish. "I guess I am, but still, I want to know what *you* think. I mean, from what I heard, her husband wasn't in terrible pain. But none of my grandparents ever had dementia, so I can't imagine . . ." She trailed off.

"I haven't had to look after anyone with dementia, either. But if I try to picture it—slowly becoming like a lost child and then a vegetable in a diaper . . ." He shuddered. "I think I'd rather be dead."

Mädi swallowed a laugh. "I don't think it's woke to refer to people with dementia as vegetables."

"I know, but I guess you won't rat on me. And, truly, that's how I feel about it. As for Ruth Seiler, she has pneumonia, so we haven't been able to interview her. All we can do right now is read your interview notes and the other background stuff and verify all the details, although Giuliana had a productive talk with her stepchildren, too. What do I think? At this point in the investigation, I see her as brave."

"Brave?" Mädi pushed her tray away and leaned forward, elbows on the table, her chin on her hands.

Renzo inhaled with pleasure the scent of whatever mixture of creams, soaps, and perfumes Mädi used. Nothing heady. Just . . . appealing. "She absolutely knew she'd committed a crime and that there might be trouble. She tried to get away with it, but as soon as it became clear she couldn't, she explained what she'd done and why it was what her husband had wanted. She appears utterly convinced that she did the right thing."

"But there's nothing in writing?"

"Nope," Renzo confirmed. "So far, we have only her word."

Mädi sat back and folded her arms. *"Äs huere puff!"* she exclaimed. Renzo nodded—yes, it *was* turning out to be a huge mess.

She was much skinnier than his usual type. Probably not obsessed about her weight, he decided, just a naturally thin person who stayed in shape. Not much in the way of breasts . . . Quickly, he lowered his eyes to his plate, although it was empty, in case she'd think he was staring. Which he was. Talk about not woke!

He cleared his throat. "I'm going to get some coffee. What do you want?"

Her expression was regretful. "Sorry, I've got to get back to work." She stood and picked up her tray. "Thanks for telling me about the Seiler case."

He could ask her out to dinner; then he'd find out if she had a boyfriend. But did he really want to start something with a work colleague? *Again?* "Good talking to you," he said instead. "I hope you find a place you can afford. I've just moved practically next door to the station, and I'm happy there. But the search was hell, so good luck."

She was standing next to him now, tray in hand. "Yeah, I heard about your separation. That must be difficult, especially for your kids. I'm sorry."

He watched her walk briskly away. She was wearing loose trousers and a long-tailed shirt, so there shouldn't have been anything exciting about her back view, but still, there was something about the way she moved . . .

As he took his espresso to his desk, his mind worked through how to organize the Münster investigation. He should by now have brought Goran into the police station and interviewed him with his parents present, but he'd promised Denis Kellenberger they'd talk again first. He chided himself for such an unprofessional decision, but now he'd stick to it, at least for the next twenty-four hours. The fact that Nathan Winter had said the broken glass wasn't such a big deal removed some of the urgency of the situation since it meant the parish council wouldn't be after Goran's blood. Renzo was eager to confront the teenager, but first, he wanted more background on Katica Horvat's death to help him understand what had triggered the boy's attack. It wasn't the anniversary of his mother's suicide—that had happened in November. Her birthday, maybe? Otherwise, why now?

Now that he had his appointment with Denis's grandparents, he'd see who else he could talk to about Frau Horvat. The priest who'd served the Croatian population back then? He or his successor might be able to put Renzo in touch with the dead woman's friends.

There was Samuel Grossenbacher, too, the homicide cop who'd investigated Katica's death. But if he'd handled the case just before his retirement, he'd be around eighty now. Would he remember it? Would he still care?

Renzo pulled his laptop toward him and typed in "Croatian Catholics in Bern."

10

D enis opened his eyes. Where was the anesthesiologist he'd just been
talking to? Wasn't his operation any minute now? Then he realized
that the strange weight he could feel on his stomach was his lower arm,
now in a cast. Several hours must have passed since his last memory. It
was a jarring feeling, being knocked out—nothing at all like falling
asleep. Instead, you dropped off the face of the earth in the middle of a
sentence and surfaced to find you'd lost a chunk of your life.

And it was possible he'd lost his future, too, unless the surgeon had
been able to give him back normal movement in his arm and hand.
He wanted to ask about that, but glancing around, he could see that
he wasn't back in yesterday's ward but instead parked in a private
cubicle. It was still and quiet, and he didn't feel woozy at all, just gently
stoned. Soon, he guessed, he'd start to feel pain—maybe a lot—but
right now, he felt warm and cozy and well looked after. It reminded him
of spending the night in the tower, snug in bed in his tiny room high
above Bern, knowing that his grandparents were only a few feet away.
At the thought of his grandparents, a pang of remorse shot through
him. Why hadn't he called Nathan earlier with news of his fall and
asked his boss to tell his family? He tried to come up with a reason he

could give everyone for not letting them know—a better reason than simply not wanting the fuss. Now he'd have to watch them try to hide their hurt feelings. *Why did everyone have to make such a big deal out of everything?* he thought for the umpteenth time. *The problem with you, Denis,* he could hear Nathan saying, *is that you don't understand the difference between being independent and being inconsiderate.*

Well, at least there was a silver lining: his mother wouldn't find out he'd shared some important part of his life with his grandparents but not with her. This time, he hadn't told *anyone* anything, so he'd hurt everyone equally.

If he could figure out where his phone was and get his hands on it, he could text Nathan. But sitting up seemed like too much effort. Besides, he was pretty sure the phone was with the rest of his stuff in a locker back on the ward.

Accepting there was nothing he could do for the moment except wait, he tried to recapture his state of dreamy semiconsciousness and found himself thinking about love. When you turned eighteen, he decided, you should be able to send a written statement to everyone you loved that said, "Okay, I love you. This is all the proof you need, and now let me get on with my life without having to worry about demonstrating it to you all the time." You'd have to renew and revise your declarations, though. Not just with girlfriends you broke up with, but . . . would he have told his father he loved him when he was only eighteen? Probably not. Of course, he *had* loved him—he knew that now—but in those days, he was still clinging to remnants of resentment.

There were other problems with his plan, too, he reflected as he snuggled into his cocoon of bedcovers. For example, would each declaration of love have to have a rating on it, expressing how *much* you loved each person? After all, he couldn't really love his father as much as his mother, not when they only saw each other for two or three weeks in Florida every summer. And yet the intensity of that time with his dad was precious. He and his mother had nothing together that compared to it.

Seemingly out of nowhere, it came to him with total clarity that he had loved Zora Horvat, loved her with all the force his ten-year-old self had been capable of.

Had she known it? Had she loved him back?

Had she told her brother Goran to try to kill him?

The cop who'd come to talk to him had promised not to confront Goran—yet. Right. So, he and this guy Donatelli could find Goran, and after that, he needed to find Zora. It had suddenly become important to know if she remembered their year of shared childhood as he did, full of happiness and close friendship, or if she still only thought of him as her mother's killer. Maybe she'd had nothing at all to do with Goran's attack. Maybe by now, she'd forgiven him. After all, he was only a child who'd failed to check a few doors.

But that was the thing. Denis *hadn't* forgotten to lock the door at the foot of the tower nor to make sure the doors into the nave were locked; he was sure of that. The problem—the *real* problem—was that he'd done something much worse, something she couldn't possibly know about. And now, even after all these years, he felt desperate to confess it to her.

11

Renzo stood up from his desk chair, rolled his shoulders, turned his head slowly right and left, raised his arms, and bent to touch his toes, easing back up inch by inch. Rolf had approved Renzo's presence on this case, but that didn't mean he could request a couple of uniforms and a fellow Fahnder to help him gather information on the Horvats. So, he'd been at his desk for four hours, doing the work himself, and he didn't have much to show for it.

Take the priest, for example. Finding an address for the Croatian Catholic Mission in Bern hadn't been difficult, but it had taken ages to locate the priest who'd worked with the immigrant community fifteen years earlier. Unearthing the man's name at last, Renzo learned that he'd returned to Croatia, but no one knew where he was living. Renzo had phoned Zagreb and spoken a slow mixture of English and Italian with a harassed-sounding woman at the central administrative office of the Croatian Roman Catholic Church, who'd promised to look into the priest's whereabouts and get back to him. Despite channeling all his charm into the request, Renzo doubted it had gone anywhere near the top of her to-do list.

He'd also read the 2015 press coverage of Katica's death, which was astonishingly little, and some background stuff on the breakup of Yugoslavia that had started in 1991, caused a war that lasted until 2001, and brought hundreds of thousands of refugees to Switzerland. Thanks to the Secretariat for Migration, he now had a record of Katica Horvat's arrival with her husband Lovro in March 2000, but tracking that down had taken ages as well.

And he still hadn't been able to find an address or phone number for the cop who'd handled the suicide, Samuel Grossenbacher. Renzo thought homicide detective Erwin Sägesser might know, but Erwin was out on a case of his own; Renzo had left him a message.

He stretched his back again and sat back down at the computer, wondering what his next step should be. Just then, Erwin poked his big, crew-cut head around the door. "Beer time. Let's go downstairs."

Showing up at the Kellenbergers that evening smelling of beer was a bad idea, but Renzo figured one glass wouldn't hurt, so he followed Erwin to the cafeteria, where he ordered them glasses of lager. Erwin paid, despite Renzo's protests, and they spread out at a table for four. After a gulp of beer and an *ahh* of pleasure, Erwin said, "Samuel Grossenbacher, huh? Why do you need him?"

Large, tough, and blunt, Erwin had initially intimidated Renzo, but they'd worked together a lot during the past year, and now Renzo considered him if not a friend then certainly a kind of mentor.

Renzo told him a condensed version of the story: the attack on Denis, its possible link to the suicide, and his desire to find out more about the old case. While he was speaking, he realized how hard it was to justify his interest in Katica's death as anything more than curiosity and a chance to show off to Rolf, the top homicide detective.

But Erwin didn't challenge him. Instead, like Giuliana, he said, "I remember that woman's death." He cocked an eyebrow at Renzo. "And I also remember how annoyed Sämu Grossenbacher was at having his investigation shut down by the Münster's top dogs."

"What?" Renzo sat up sharply.

"Well, not quite shut down, but certainly cut short. Not surprising, really, when you think how bad it is for the church and for Bern's image to have people jumping off the tower. Might become a fad."

"Now I *really* want to talk to Grossenbacher."

"Well, he's living in a retirement home in Köniz—wife died five or six years ago, and I guess he couldn't manage without her." There was a hint of scorn in his tone. Erwin's most recent wife had left him when he was in his fifties, and no doubt he expected other men to learn to cope on their own, as he had. "The place is one of a Swiss-wide chain of homes for oldies. Name starts with a 'T.' You should be able to find it; otherwise, let me know. I can see what rings a bell on Google."

Renzo raised his glass to Erwin. "Thanks. Anything I should know about him?"

Erwin frowned. "I've been debating with myself about that. But I guess giving you useful background on him wins out over protecting his privacy." Erwin took a deep breath. "Couple of years before he retired, he started drinking heavily—he was functional but . . . you know what I mean. Not at the top of his game. I saw him about six months after he retired—still drinking. When he turned eighty, I phoned him—that's how I know he's in a home. He sounded completely sober at that point. But who knows?"

"Okay, thanks. Anything else?"

"I've known him since my first week as a uniformed cop. Until he became a drunk, I thought he was a good detective. But I don't think he was too comfortable with women on the job. Giuliana worked with him, didn't she?"

"Yeah. She found him distant and formal, she said."

"Probably kept his distance to hide the drinking. Maybe also because he didn't know how to treat her." Erwin finished his beer and set his glass down, then pointedly looked at his watch. "It's after six. I'm heading home to have a bite before I head out to a club on Aarbergergasse."

"Dancing?" Renzo raised his eyebrows.

"Kid stabbed there," Erwin answered. He stood up and gave a lopsided grin. "So, nobody's going to see me do the Funky Chicken tonight. Their loss."

"What the hell's a funky chicken?" Renzo called as Erwin walked away. Erwin glanced over his shoulder, flapping his elbows, and Renzo laughed.

As he jogged back upstairs, he thought about what Erwin had told him. If Grossenbacher had been prevented from doing a thorough investigation—and struggled with alcohol on top of that—then Renzo wasn't just chasing some daydream of a big success to lay at Rolf's feet along with his application for homicide detective. The supposed suicide really did need to be re-examined. God, he wanted so badly for it to have been a murder.

He only hoped it would also turn out to be one that he could solve.

12

Kirchenfeld, Wednesday evening, June 26

Renzo hadn't climbed the Münster tower since he was a teenager. But he knew that Hans-Peter and Ursula Kellenberger's apartment there, two hundred and fifty-four steps above the ground, must have been crowded. He pictured them squashed in there with their grandson Denis like hermit crabs. Although he knew they now lived in the most expensive section of a fancy neighborhood, he was still jolted by surprise to find them occupying an entire house with a generous front garden. It was as if those tiny crabs had taken up residence in a conch shell.

The Kellenbergers themselves were anything but tiny. The white-haired, well-padded professor was over six feet tall in spite of a slight stoop. He led Renzo to the back of the house and into a comfortable room with an enormous, elaborately patterned sofa. Large open windows let in the light of a warm June evening. In one of the burgundy leather armchairs beside the sofa sat a slim woman who set her book on the carved wood table in front of her and stood to greet Renzo. She, too, was tall, and it was clear from whom Denis had gotten his striking blue eyes.

As Renzo sat down in the second armchair, Herr Kellenberger—Renzo had started with Herr Professor, but the older man had waved that away—began to talk. "Denis has called to say that he's doing well, and the doctors are confident his wrist will be as good as new. He's agreed to stay with us for a few days while he recovers."

The professor shared a wry look with his wife after this last sentence, giving Renzo the impression they'd had to persuade Denis to accept their help. He wondered why. But right now, he had more important questions to ask.

"I'm glad to hear Denis is recovering. Now let me tell you why I'm here. There's a strong possibility that his fall was caused deliberately by a boy named Goran, who's the son of Katica and Lovro Horvat. As you know, Frau Horvat died falling from the Münster tower fifteen years ago. I understand that Denis was made responsible, and there were consequences for all of you. And somehow, the Horvats—or at least Zora and Goran—have ended up blaming Denis, too."

Frau Kellenberger groaned. "Oh, no, not this horrible business again."

Her husband leaned toward Renzo, lips tight with anger. "Are you telling us that Goran tried to kill Denis because of this ridiculous idea that Denis didn't lock the tower door?"

"That's part of what I'm trying to find out," Renzo said. "I'll ask Goran himself, but first, I'm gathering some background."

The couple stared at each other for a long moment, their faces bleak. Frau Kellenberger closed her eyes and shook her head. Her husband sighed. "Denis should never have been involved in any of this," he said. "I'd already decided to tell the police that *I'd* done the doors because I didn't want the boy caught up in it. But the sexton, Klaus Friedli, bumped into Denis that morning on his way to school before we'd had a chance to tell him anything. Apparently, he asked about the tower door, and Denis, who was proud of his responsibilities, said that, yes, checking the doors was one of his chores."

"That man," Frau Kellenberger burst out. "He never liked Denis spending time in the church, although it didn't bother the minister at all. *He* was a lovely man, gentle and caring, and he was delighted with how well Denis got to know the church and how much he enjoyed being there. But the minister was too gentle, really—he got pushed around by that officious sexton with his connections on the parish council."

"So, you were asked to leave?" Renzo knew the answer, but he wanted to hear what they had to say.

"Yes," said the professor. "It wasn't as bad as it sounds because we were due to go in less than a year anyway, and we owned this house, so we just had to give our tenants here notice. The worst thing was that Denis was banned from the Münster, although he was still living with us. He could only go in and out of the apartment, up and down the tower stairs, and in and out of the church through the shop, nowhere else. It was horrible."

"That *wasn't* the worst thing," his wife said, her voice raised. She sat on the edge of her chair, head thrust forward. "It was the gossip. For weeks, people talked about Denis having played some part in Katica's death. Even a few kids at school. Oh, it was so malicious." She slumped back in her chair, a hand over her eyes.

Renzo took a spiral notebook and pen out of his shoulder bag. "That must have been a bad time. Couldn't Denis have gone to live in another school district, with his mother, perhaps? I don't want to be insensitive, but I'm wondering why he was raised by you instead of his mother or father."

"I don't see why that's relevant," Denis's grandfather said stiffly, then relented, adding, "Our daughter Anja was a teenager when she had Denis, and his father was an American who moved back to the US when Denis was under one. They never married, and Anja wanted to get on with her life, so we offered to raise the boy. He visits his father in Florida once or twice a year and sees his mother regularly, but we are—we *were*—his legal guardians."

Nothing especially out of the ordinary, Renzo thought, although "get on with her life" seemed like a rather calculated way of viewing Anja Kellenberger's rejection of motherhood. He wondered how Denis felt about her decision. "Thanks for explaining," he said. "Now, can you tell me whatever you remember from the day Frau Horvat died?" The professor made a sudden, restless movement. "Did you have a question, Herr Kellenberger?"

The white-haired man's eyes narrowed. "Well, yes. The death was declared a suicide. Is there some reason why you doubt that verdict?"

"Did *you* have reason to doubt it at the time?" Renzo countered.

Kellenberger glanced over at his wife. "I think we always wondered whether Katica might have fallen rather than jumped. From what we knew of her." He shook his head doubtfully. "But if she had, I'm sure we would have heard her scream." He steepled his fingers under his chin, and Renzo pictured him at a podium in a lecture hall. "It was very windy that night. But even so, how could Katica have been on the balcony right outside our windows without us hearing? I'm a heavy sleeper, but Ursula isn't."

Renzo wished he'd climbed up to the big balcony around the tower to get a sense of the layout for himself. "It *is* odd that neither of you heard anything," he agreed. "Now, what about the day itself? Frau Kellenberger, I think you went to fetch Herr Horvat? What about before that? I've been told someone from the Münstergasse food market found the body early in the morning, so . . ."

The woman's expression became reflective, and she picked up the story in a slow, husky voice, quite different from her husband's lecturer's tone. "It was one of the butchers. Poor man. He used to fill a bucket from the Moses fountain on the Münsterplatz so he could sluice down the section of street where he set up his stand. He saw Katica." She used the dead woman's first name quite naturally, as if she'd been fond of her. "A pile of clothes, he thought at first. When he realized, he ran straight for the church because he knew the sexton got in early on market days. The butcher told Herr Friedli about the body, and Friedli woke us up."

Kellenberger couldn't resist taking up the tale at this point; Renzo had the feeling he was used to doing the talking. "I suppose when he looked at the body, he recognized Katica. And since she'd obviously fallen from the tower, the first thing he asked us was if she'd been staying in our apartment. Which she hadn't."

"That's right," Frau Kellenberger said. "Zora had spent the night with us a couple of times, but never her mother."

"You said the sexton came to wake you. What time was it, and what did you do?"

The professor answered. "It was a little after six. We were up but not dressed, so we threw on our clothes and ran down the stairs." Renzo winced at the thought of those ancient, winding stone steps and how slick they'd have been on a dark winter morning. "As soon as we saw Katica lying there, I agreed that we had to call the minister."

"Wait a minute. What about the police?"

Kellenberger's face took on a distant look. "You know, it never occurred to me at that point. I mean, it was so obviously a suicide. Or, as I kept hoping, an accident."

Renzo had to stop himself from rolling his eyes. *And whose job do you think it was to figure that out?* "Right. So, the sexton called the minister—what's his name?"

"Emil Graf. But I'm sorry to say he died three years ago," said Kellenberger. Renzo wrote the name down anyway.

Kellenberger's wife continued. "Meanwhile, I went down to the shop in the Matte. The store opened at seven, so I knew Lovro would be up, getting ready. I . . . broke the news, and he went right out the door. I stayed so the kids wouldn't be alone. I wanted to let them sleep as long as possible, to put off having to tell them, I suppose. I heard Zora's alarm clock go off at six thirty. God, the dread I felt when I heard that alarm."

Renzo'd had to break the news of a death several times over the years. The apprehension beforehand was almost as awful as the telling itself. Yet within minutes of seeing Katica's bloody corpse, Ursula Kellenberger had informed the dead woman's husband and accepted the task of staying with her bereaved children. She was an impressive woman.

"Was Lovro awake when you arrived? Did he . . . Look, I'm just going to ask this straight out: Was there anything about his reaction to your bursting in and telling him his wife was dead that made you think he could've had anything to do with it?"

"Really," began Herr Kellenberger, "it's out of the question that..."

"No, it's *not*," said his wife, and there was a message in her glance at him that gave Renzo, once again, the sense of missing a point that he needed to come back to. "I understand you're reexamining the death in light of what happened to Denis, and I wish I could tell you more, but the truth is I... I just don't know. We'd chatted with Lovro a number of times when we brought Zora home, and we made a point of shopping in his store now and then. But I didn't really know him."

"What was he doing when you arrived? How was he dressed?" Renzo didn't expect much from the woman's answer—after all, these were fifteen-year-old memories.

But Frau Kellenberger surprised him again. "Lovro always wore a knee-length white coat, like a doctor's, to work in his shop. He had that on when I knocked on the door. He'd had his daily bakery delivery and was putting pastries and sandwiches into the glass case. I remember the store smelled wonderful, like coffee and fresh bread—and I had to tell him Katica was lying dead at the foot of the Münster tower. He put a loaf down and covered his face with both hands. Then he bent over until his forehead touched the glass counter."

"Did he ask any questions?"

She stared out the window for a moment. "Not that I remember," she said. "He straightened up and took off his white coat. I can't describe his expression, but I know it seemed... real to me. I mean, I never got the sense he was acting or faking. 'I'm going to her now,' he said. And then he left. Walking fast, but not running."

Renzo nodded. It was an excellent eyewitness account. "Meanwhile, were you still at the Münsterplatz, Herr Kellenberger?"

Turning to the professor, Renzo caught him gazing tenderly at his wife, which made Renzo reconsider his first impression of the man. Kellenberger's manner changed as he addressed Renzo's question. "Yes. I remember being aware that I was doing nothing useful there, yet I didn't want to leave Katica alone with strangers staring into her dead face.

Eventually, the minister brought out a blanket and covered her, which helped. Then he dealt with the rubberneckers by calling for a group prayer. *That* made most of them melt away."

The idea of a potential crime scene being so mistreated was giving Renzo a fit, but he tried not to let it show. "Do you remember Herr Horvat arriving?" he asked.

"No, but he got there before the minister. I remember him sitting on the ground by the body, with blood soaking into his trousers. Then *his* priest arrived. There was a cold wind, and it wasn't light yet. The yellow of the streetlamps made everything look . . ."

He didn't finish his sentence, but Renzo could imagine the strangeness of the scene. He remembered Giuliana telling him at breakfast, "Everything was chaos." She hadn't been exaggerating.

He already knew when the police had been called. There might not be notes on the investigation, but the emergency telephone operators kept good records. Someone had noted a call at seven forty-eight a.m. from Olivier Feller, whom Renzo had already looked up. A retired federal bureaucrat, Feller had also been a member of the parish's executive council. Thank goodness someone had finally done the right thing.

"This is all helpful," Renzo said. *Now*, he thought, *let's see if I can figure out what Ursula Kellenberger's been skating around telling me.* "When I talked to Denis, he gave me the impression that Katica was in the cathedral a lot, although she was a Catholic. He told me about her leaving Zora in a pew, sometimes for hours. Do you have any idea what she was doing? Just going shopping, or . . ."

"We don't know," said Herr Kellenberger.

His wife shot him an exasperated look. "No, we don't *know*, but . . ." She gave Renzo a helpless shrug. "I don't want to sound like a gossip. But at the time, we . . . we thought she might have been having an affair."

"An affair." Why on earth hadn't that occurred to him? If Katica had just been going shopping, why wouldn't she have taken Zora with her? "Did the police identify who she was meeting?" Renzo gritted his teeth—what an absurd question. It was *his* job to know what the police had discovered. He felt his face grow red, but neither of the Kellen-bergers seemed to have noticed his idiocy.

Instead, the professor seemed almost grateful that his wife had let the secret slip. "We always thought it might have been one of the workmen," he said heavily. "It went on for over a year. At least, that's how long Katica was dropping Zora off in the church."

Katica had been only twenty-nine when she'd died, Renzo reminded himself, even if she'd had a ten-year-old daughter. He envisioned this young woman meeting a lover regularly. Then something occurred to him. "Didn't Frau Horvat have a baby during that time?"

"That's right," said Frau Kellenberger. "Goran was around six weeks old when his mother died, and Lovro remarried less than a year later. The boy got to grow up with a new mother. But Zora—for Zora, the loss was terrible."

Remarriage within a year seemed like pretty fast work on Lovro's part, thought Renzo. Or had the man been cheating on Katica before she died, just as she'd been cheating on him? That thought was fol-lowed quickly by another: if Katica had been having an affair that whole time, was Goran Lovro's son? Renzo tried to imagine a man meeting a woman for sex throughout her pregnancy when she was carrying another man's child. Surely the lover had known—or at least believed—that the baby was his. And suppose he found out after the birth that it wasn't?

The idea that Katica had been having an affair created a whole set of reasons why someone might have wanted to kill her. There was her husband, her lover, her lover's wife if he'd had one. And if Lovro had had someone on the side, too . . .

The professor broke into Renzo's speculations by getting up to turn on a table lamp at one end of the sofa. The evening light had been steadily fading, and Renzo realized he had been silent, lost in thought, for over a minute. "Forgive me for sitting here taking up your time," he said. "What you've told me has started . . . a new train of thought. I'll need to call the detective who handled Frau Horvat's death and ask him about this lover."

The Kellenbergers were frowning at him. The professor said, "It sounds like you are re-opening this case, and we would hate that. We don't want Denis—"

His wife interrupted, her voice sharp. "We don't want one negative word about our grandson to appear online or anywhere else."

What could Renzo tell them? This was his case, and no one was pushing him to pursue it, so he couldn't take refuge in any kind of "just following orders" defense. "I can't see why any journalist or blogger would want to write about a fifteen-year-old suicide, and I have no desire to call attention to this investigation. But I will need to talk to some of the other people who were involved. I can ask everyone to keep quiet, but I don't have the power to *make* them do it, nor to keep information out of the news."

"So drop the case," said Herr Kellenberger.

"And if someone murdered Katica Horvat and got away with it, you don't care?"

"We *do* care," said Frau Kellenberger, "but I'm not sure I care enough to face all the nasty publicity again."

"I'll be very sorry if you get harassed, and I'll do my best to keep that from happening. But I'm going to keep working on the case."

For a moment, neither husband nor wife said a word. Then Kellenberger surprised Renzo. "Well, if I can't persuade you to give it up, maybe I can speed you along. I think the person most likely to know whether Katica had a workman for a boyfriend would be the manager of the Münster building site, Artur Pereira. He's been supervising renovations for the last twenty-five years. I'll give you his phone number."

Kellenberger got up and left the room. His wife stared after him in silence, then she turned back to Renzo, her face resigned. "I suppose we both know in our hearts that you're doing the right thing," she told him. "Besides, Denis is a man now; we can't protect him forever. Not that we managed to protect him fifteen years ago, either. I guess that's why we still feel so upset."

Kellenberger returned and handed him a neatly written name and phone number. Renzo had one more question. "What was Katica like?"

The older couple looked at each other, and it was the wife who spoke. "She was . . . well, she was lovely. Beautiful and warm and charming and just a little fey, somehow. People felt drawn to her. Denis used to hang on her words. And so did you," she said, smiling at her husband, who spread his hands and made a caught-in-the-cookie-jar face.

"She was beautiful," he agreed, "and she was very loving to Zora and delighted with her little son. I couldn't imagine why she'd kill herself, and I still can't."

"Interesting to know. So that's all I need from you tonight. Except . . . do you know when Denis will be home?"

"We're picking him up tomorrow at ten," his grandfather said.

"Is he okay to move around?"

"He's allowed to do as much as he has the energy for, as long as it doesn't involve his left arm," answered Kellenberger.

"I'll want to talk to him," Renzo warned them as he stood. "Thanks for seeing me." He shook hands with Frau Kellenberger in her armchair and with her husband at the front door before stepping outside into the warm dusk.

As he strolled through the neat front garden, he admired the extravagant peonies blooming on either side of the flagstone path. He'd taken the bus here so as not to lose the parking space in front of his apartment. Now, he decided to walk home. If he went through the Old City, it would take only half an hour. Instead, he turned toward the Aare, the river that looped around the medieval part of the city, cutting it off on three sides from the more modern buildings beyond.

The Kellenbergers' road sloped a few hundred yards downhill to end at a narrow cross street that ran parallel to the river and gave access to the riverbank paths. He could follow these all the way to the Lorraine Bridge, where a long set of stairs would bring him up to his own neighborhood.

It wasn't yet ten, and dim light still filtered through the leaves as he walked along the river, passing the *Englische Anlagen*, the steep forest on the hillside below Giuliana's neighborhood. The slope was thick with trees, and Giuliana's apartment building was out of sight, but still, he glanced up to where he thought it must be and imagined her with Ueli, a dark head and a red one side by side on the sofa as they read or talked—or kissed. The thought of them didn't make him feel as bad as it would have done six months earlier; the pang now was more of loneliness than jealousy.

It made him reflect on his lunch with Madeleine. Now that he'd heard about Katica Horvat's supposed affair, he wanted to interview the retired detective Grossenbacher more than ever. Maybe he'd ask Mädi to come with him.

13

Bern's Elfenau neighborhood, Wednesday evening, June 26

As Renzo was picturing Ueli and Giuliana together, her head was indeed on a sofa cushion next to a man's, but the sofa was at her parents' house, and the head belonged to her brother, Paolo. Every couple of weeks, the siblings met to have an after-dinner coffee with their parents, and Paolo was showing Giuliana a photograph of his thirteen-year-old sons in their ice hockey uniforms, sticks at the ready. The twins' grandparents had already seen the picture, but Aurelia Linder, squeezed into one corner of the sofa next to her children, asked to see it again. Paolo passed his phone over, and Giuliana smiled at her nephews' excited faces. "They're obviously having a great time, but all I can think about is how happy I am that we've managed to avoid hockey. We get up early enough without having to fit in predawn runs to the ice rink."

Paolo gave her a sheepish look. "Mmm. I have to confess that Silvie does most of the carpooling."

"No need to look guilty with *me*. Ueli would probably be organizing the transportation if either of ours was a hockey nut, but so far, neither one seems to have a special sport. What about Theresa?" Paolo's daughter, a second-grader, seemed more content reading than racing around outside. *Good for her*, Giuliana thought; she'd been the same growing up.

Their father, Max, chimed in. "Theresa was here yesterday afternoon, and, thanks to your mother, she discovered a brand-new sport. Aurelia was telling her what *she* liked to do as a little girl, and it turned out the child had never seen a jump rope. So, your mother went down to the basement to fetch a piece of clothesline, and I was roped in"—the retired defense lawyer wriggled his eyebrows at Giuliana and Paolo, who groaned—"to help spin. You'd have been amazed how quickly she picked it up." He beamed as he talked about Theresa's success. He'd always championed Giuliana's small triumphs when she was a child, too.

An unexpected blaze of love made her go to her father and bend to kiss the top of his head. Leaving a hand on his shoulder, she said, "I'm glad you're a fan of us girls, Papa." He placed his hand over hers where it lay on his shoulder.

Her mother glanced at the two of them. "He was proud of me, too, whenever I accomplished something, even if it was learning a new massage technique." Aurelia had practiced midwifery, sometimes full-time, sometimes part-time, throughout Giuliana's life until ten years earlier.

"I profited every time you took one of those courses," her father interrupted, giving his wife a lascivious grin that made Paolo and Giuliana roll their eyes at each other.

"Not *every* time," said her mother. "I didn't practice turning breech babies on you, did I?"

"Hmm. I wonder if I missed something," said Max, which made them all laugh.

In Giuliana's memories of her childhood, her parents always spoke to each other with admiration and affection. It had seemed normal to her, but now she considered what a gift it had been to her and her brother.

"Your mother's done something else I'm proud of, too," said her father, breaking into her thoughts. "She's signed us both up for lifetime memberships in Exit. I suppose, at our age, they should call them 'deathtime' memberships." He was smiling as he said this. Then he looked at his son, and the smile vanished. Giuliana turned and registered Paulo's horrified expression just as he jumped to his feet, his voice loud and shrill.

"Don't you dare tell me you've been hiding something. Are you ill? I can't..."

"No, no, it's not that..." her father began.

Aurelia reached up to put a hand on Paolo's arm. "Sit down, dear. Paps and I are fine!"

Giuliana was sure that her mother would never keep a serious health problem from her—especially not after Ueli's mother had done exactly that with her colon cancer earlier in the year—but Paolo was still upset. She left her father's side and drew her brother back down onto the sofa next to her, putting an arm around his shoulders.

Their mother's voice was light. "This has nothing to do with bad news. Your father and I have been talking off and on for years about living wills, but we hadn't gotten around to getting them done. So, we just—"

Paolo interrupted. "What a classic—the lawyer who puts off making a will!" It was meant to be a joke, but it came out like a jeer, and Giuliana squeezed his shoulder.

Max answered sharply, "You know perfectly well we have regular wills, so..."

"Let me finish, please, you two," Aurelia said. "I didn't just want a health directive; I wanted to sign up with Exit for assisted suicide. Part of their service is all the documentation you need for a living will, as well. I told Max, and we decided to do it together. It's not a secret— I planned to email you copies of the forms as soon as we were registered."

"But why would you do that?" Paolo was shaking his head, gnawing at his thumbnail.

Giuliana, who assumed she and her brother felt the same way about almost everything, was surprised. She shied away from thinking about her parents' deaths, but since the worst thing she could imagine for them was a slow, painful end, their choice of Exit as a just-in-case solution made complete sense to her. But not, apparently, to Paolo.

"Don't you trust me to look after you?" he asked his parents. His voice was shaking.

Whatever annoyance her father had felt with her brother vanished from his face; he looked stricken. "Of course we trust you. This is only about us and what *we* want. About how we want to live—and die."

"Paolo," their mother said, "this is only a kind of... oh, I don't know. An insurance policy. Thousands of people belong to Exit, but most of them never kill themselves. They just know they can if they need to. That's the way it is for us. We want to give ourselves the option, that's all."

Paolo stopped chewing his nails and lowered his hand to his lap. Their mother gently took hold of it.

"All right," he said. "But one reason people join Exit is so as not to burden their kids. I just ... if you decided to kill yourselves because you were afraid we'd get fed up with you—"

Aurelia squeezed his hand. "We're sure you'd take care of us—both of you! Silvie and Ueli and our grandchildren would, too, if it came to it. We *know* that." She put her arm around her son and kissed his cheek, and Giuliana patted his thigh, feeling strangely helpless in the face of her brother's raw emotion.

Their father said, "I'm grateful, son, but maybe I don't want anyone wiping my ass and mopping food off my face. Especially not you and your sister."

Giuliana half expected her mother to say something sharp at this, but she didn't. Perhaps she felt the same way.

The four of them were silent for a long moment, and then Paolo said, "All right. It's your decision, but I hope you won't have to use it. How's that? Now, let's talk about something else. Paps, there's a case I want to tell you about."

To Giuliana's relief, Paolo began to talk about a young couple he was defending at rock-bottom rates. They'd just opened a restaurant on Rathausgasse in the Old City, and one of their neighbors was taking them to court over the noise. "How can someone choose to live in one of the liveliest parts of the city and then have the gall to complain about all the commotion around them?" Paolo rolled his eyes.

Since Paolo had taken over his law practice, Max had stayed out of the office, but he loved hearing about his son's cases. "You're right. But as long as the law doesn't change, it's going to keep happening. The city council needs to get off the fence and decide if it wants Bern to be a modern city with an attractive nightlife or not. Now, if I were you, I'd ..."

Giuliana, who'd worked in both defense and prosecution before joining the police, listened with interest. With all the talk of assisted suicide, it was a relief that no one had brought up the Seiler case. She'd share what *she* was working on another time.

Later, she walked Paolo to his car, telling him about Isabelle's tough breakup with Quentin.

Paolo bit his lip, his face full of sympathy. "For what it's worth, give her my love. Silvie and I are staying in her family's cottage on Lake Neuchâtel for a few weeks later this summer. Tell Isabelle we'd love to have her join us for as long as she likes. I'll email her, too." When they reached his car, he turned to her. "This Exit business. It's just that ... well, parents look after us, and then, when they're too old or sick to cope, we look after them. It's ... I think it's what we do."

And Paolo and his wife *had* done it four years earlier, Giuliana knew, when Silvie's sixty-eight-year-old mother, long divorced, had been diagnosed with pancreatic cancer. She'd lasted less than a year, but they'd been able to hire enough at-home nursing care that she'd never had to stay in the hospital for more than a few days. For the final six months of her life, she'd lived in Silvie and Paolo's guestroom, surrounded by family. *If you were going to have to spend ten months dying,* Giuliana thought, *that was probably the best way to go.* But still, there were so many scenarios where it just wouldn't work.

She chose her next words carefully. "I understand. Still, they may truly not want us looking after them until the very end. Not so we don't have to clean them up. But to spare us seeing them suffer—and suffering ourselves."

"Okay, Gili—I hear you." She smiled; he hadn't called her that for years. "I also hear that you've been assigned to that Seiler case, so you've been thinking about assisted suicide a lot lately, right?"

"Yeah. And that reminds me. When it comes to decisions about putting family members into homes, the law says the spouse decides. Can you think of any exceptions?"

They were standing under a large plane tree, one of a row that stretched along their parents' street, and it was almost dark. "Not offhand," Paolo said, "but I'll check my files."

"Thanks, Lolo." She used his childhood nickname, too. Putting her arms around him, she squeezed him tightly. Then she said, "Give Silvie my love. And let me know when you're on the lake. Whether Isabelle comes to stay or not, I'd like all four of us to come and spend an evening with you. We'll bring the food."

"I like the way you volunteer Ueli to cook for everybody."

She gave his arm a light punch. "Hey, I cook sometimes. In fact, I'll make dessert. Got that? One dessert for nine people, coming up."

"It's a deal." He got in the car and drove off, waving.

Giuliana walked slowly back to the front yard of her parents' building, where all the condo owners had chipped in to have a deluxe bike shelter built. As she pulled her bicycle out of the row, she thought about Werner Allemann's daughter insisting that he go into a home. But, according to the law, what Ruth's stepchildren wanted didn't matter. It was a wife's right to decide how and where her husband was cared for. If Ruth really hadn't wanted him to go into the home, why hadn't she just said no?

14

Renzo was in his tiny kitchen downing a second cup of espresso, waiting for seven thirty so he could call the Münster's construction foreman Artur Pereira. He set his cup in the sink, ran water into it, and then punched in the number Hans-Peter Kellenberger had given him the night before. After two rings, he heard a brisk "Pereira."

Renzo kept it short, adding no word about Katica's possible boyfriend.

Pereira asked, "Do you need to talk today?" When Renzo said yes, he was silent for a moment, apparently checking his schedule. "How about nine this morning at the café on the Pläfe? Grab a table, and wait for me if I'm not there. I'll be the guy in blue overalls with a gray buzz cut."

"Thanks," he said, but Pereira was already gone.

Renzo was at his desk in the Seiler case room by quarter to eight, typing up notes on his meeting with the Kellenbergers. When Giuliana walked in, he swiveled his chair to face her. "The Kellenbergers think Katica Horvat was sleeping with one of the workmen restoring the Münster. That was why she kept leaving her daughter alone on a pew in the church. I'm off in forty minutes to meet with the foreman and ask him about it."

"Interesting." Giuliana opened her desk drawer and set her handbag inside. "I wasn't on the case with Grossenbacher long enough to hear anything about that. But why bring the daughter out with her at all? I mean, I can see her bringing the baby if she was nursing, but..." As she spoke, Giuliana hung her lightweight jacket on the coat rack in the corner, and then opened another drawer to lift out her pistol and hip holster. Once she'd put them on, she spun her chair to face Renzo and sat.

"I'm planning to ask Zora, the daughter, about that as soon as I can. My guess is that she was probably Katica's excuse for going out in the first place."

He'd have to handle that conversation carefully, though. At only ten, Zora probably wouldn't have had much insight into her mother's reasoning. He turned back to his laptop, saying over his shoulder, "I'll send you a write-up of what I've done on this so far."

"No need to report to me; it's your investigation."

"But I want to, in case I need advice," he said.

After typing up his summary and emailing it to Giuliana, Renzo headed for the Münster, walking briskly across the Lorraine Bridge and then turning left to follow the curve of the Aare far below the street. When he reached the Church of Saints Peter and Paul, he turned away from the river toward the medieval town hall and soon arrived at the gate to the Münster platform, passing the place where Goran had crashed into him.

There were still three outdoor tables free at the café, and Renzo, not seeing anyone in blue overalls, took a seat. While he waited, he surveyed the Pläfe. It was too early for many toddlers and mothers to be in the playground, but there were a couple of attractive women at nearby tables. One, her dark hair in a ponytail, looked up from her paperwork and caught him examining her. He smiled apologetically and was relieved when she smiled back before returning to her work.

When he arrived, Artur Pereira, despite his last name, turned out to look more Swiss than Portuguese. He was light-haired and fair-skinned, medium height, strong-looking but spare, and probably about fifty, his face lined by what Renzo thought was the weather, not worry. Despite their taciturn phone call, Pereira had an ingrained cheerfulness that was infectious. As Renzo stood, planning to buy him a coffee, Pereira lifted a hand and strode on toward the café, calling over his shoulder, "Espresso okay?" He was back almost immediately with two tiny cups of coffee, two spoons, and a handful of sugar packets that he set down on the bistro table. He proceeded to add six sugars to his coffee, stir it into a syrup, and drink it in one gulp. Then he set the cup in its saucer. "So, what can I tell you?"

It was a pleasantly cool morning with puffy clouds against a hazy blue sky. An elderly couple sat on a nearby bench, their fuzzy terrier sniffing around their feet. Renzo had already placed his notebook and pen on the table. "How long have you been working on the Münster restoration?" he asked, taking a sip of his own espresso. "I know it's been going on for a long time."

"Yeah—about seventy years, but I only joined thirty-three years ago when I was an apprentice of fifteen. In those days, I carved huge stone blocks to prop up the tower, and now I repair tiny cracks in the nave's vaulted ceiling, but it's all part of the same job."

Renzo heard the satisfaction in Pereira's words. "And how long have you been in charge of it?"

The man raised his hands, palms out, shaking his head. "I'm not in charge. For the last twelve years, I've been responsible for the masons and stoneworkers. Turns out that means a lot of running back and forth, explaining to the workmen—and sometimes the architects—what the specialists have recommended."

"Specialists?" Renzo echoed. He sipped his espresso again and enjoyed the warmth of the sun growing stronger on his face.

"Yes, experts on glass and stone and tile and fifteenth-century painting—all of that and lots more. They come to advise us. Some stay for a day or two; others end up working here for several years. Part of my job is acting as a go-between for everyone. And always having to be careful about their feelings!" Pereira clapped his hands to his head as though holding the lid on his skull, grinning at Renzo. "During the past ten years, things have become more . . . egalitarian. These days, the stonemasons are more likely to tell the specialists to their faces what can and can't be done. But I still do a certain amount of . . . soothing, I guess you could say. And I'm a stoneworker myself, so I'd be sad to give up working on the building—I love that."

"I met one of your specialists recently, a master glassmaker named Nathan Winter. I liked him."

"I've known Nathan as long as I've been at the cathedral. He's great—a great guy and a great craftsman, too."

It was time to get to Katica's suicide before the foreman was forced to return to work. "On the phone, I mentioned Katica Horvat, the woman who died." Renzo paused. "I've been told she was sleeping with one of the men who worked on the restoration. Is that true?" Renzo looked into Pereira's eyes.

The man's lips pressed together for a moment, but he didn't look away. Then he said, "Yeah, it's true."

"Did the police find out about it back then?"

"Yes." This time, the answer came more quickly. "Not that Ben himself told them—he wasn't the type to help the cops. But someone must have blabbed about it because the detective spent a couple of hours grilling him. Ben told us about it. They asked the rest of us when we'd last seen Katica and if any of us were having sex with her as well." Pereira shook his head in disgust. "As if Katica were a slut. I mean, she and Ben were a couple to us, even if both were married to other people."

So, there had definitely been an affair, and the police had known about it. That meant the original investigation hadn't been a farce, not if Grossenbacher had interviewed the lover at length. He still wanted to talk to the retired detective himself, though. "Did all the Münster workmen know about Katica and this Ben guy?" he asked.

"Yes. We saw them together sometimes. I think they tried to meet discreetly, but they weren't very good at it. They acted like teenagers who couldn't keep their hands off each other. We gave him a hard time about it, but we still tried to cover for him. Thank God I wasn't in charge then, or I would have thrown a fit over all his absences. He eventually got fired for missing work so often. All because of his womanizing." Pereira had been playing with his coffee spoon while he spoke, but now he looked at Renzo. "He would have been axed a lot sooner, but he was a brilliant stonemason. A sculptor, really. And also, well . . . he was a pleasant guy. He got on well with everyone, and when he wasn't disappearing to meet women, he worked hard. Sociable, funny, good-looking. I can see why she fell for him. Why they all did."

So Katica hadn't been his only girlfriend. Renzo wondered whether she'd known that. "I'll need to talk to him," he said. "What's his last name?"

Pereira tapped his fingers on the table and frowned. "I can picture him, but I haven't thought of his name in a while. Hmm. A very Swiss-German name—unlike yours and mine," he said, giving Renzo a quick smile. "Oh, of course; it's Schweizer—can't get more Swiss than that. Benjamin Schweizer. He sculpts gravestones now; has a place in Ostermundigen near the Schosshalde cemetery."

Renzo wrote the name down, and Pereira said, "I don't have his number—deleted it when he left the group."

That was odd. If Schweizer was really so talented, mightn't Pereira have wanted to use him again? "Why's that? Did you end up having a serious problem with him?"

For the first time, Renzo read something stiff in Pereira's body language. "After Katica killed herself, Ben's catting around didn't seem so amusing anymore. I often bought lunch at the Horvats' store and chatted with her husband. Seemed like a decent man. He didn't deserve what happened. So, yeah, Ben's number is not in my phone anymore."

Hmm. Pereira had stronger feelings about Ben and Katica's affair than he'd at first let on: contempt for a man who'd apparently walked away scot-free from his involvement in a tragedy. For a moment, Renzo wondered if Pereira, too, had been in love with Katica, but he thought it was more likely to be the stoneworker's innate decency fueling his anger.

Pereira put his palms on the table and leaned forward. "I need to get back to work—is there anything else?"

Renzo fished in his back pocket for his wallet. "Let me pay—I meant to treat you, and you got ahead of me. You're the one doing me a favor, so . . ."

"No, no. Coffee's on me."

As he began to stand, Renzo thought of another question. "One more thing. Where the hell were Katica and Schweizer having sex? Somewhere in the Münster itself? Or in that big storage building you guys have down on the Aare?"

"No, no." The foreman's mouth twisted. "Ben rented a room on Postgasse for taking women to. He had that place pre- and post-Katica, and for all I know, he still uses it now."

Pereira looked anxious to get away, but Renzo went on. "Sorry . . . but is there any way Schweizer could have gotten his hands on a key to the Münster?"

The man laughed. "Oh, sure. Workmen get keys—have for years—then when they finish a project, the keys are returned and checked off the list. Supposedly. We try to keep track, but there are keys that have gone missing—and someone could easily have a copy made. Not just workmen: the organist and his students have keys, for example. Also, the cleaning ladies—and there seems to be a new cleaner every six months. Even the fire department has keys, and the police, too. I'd say Ben Schweizer could probably have gotten in and out pretty easily."

"Into the tower at night?"

"In those days, yes; his work key would have opened the tower door, too," Pereira said. "Now, things are more secure—no more all-purpose keys. But fifteen years ago, it was another story. Friedli, the sexton, will tell you how things have changed."

Renzo wasn't sure he'd get the truth out of the sexton. After all, Friedli was the one who'd blamed Denis for leaving the tower door open. A ten-year-old kid gets called a murderer and feels guilty about it to this day, yet it turns out plenty of people could have gotten into both the main part of the church and the tower. The sexton must have known that fifteen years ago. Why had he insisted on blaming the boy? Was it just to get the Kellenbergers out of the tower apartment? Maybe it had been the sexton himself who'd left the door open, and he was looking for someone to blame.

Renzo imagined Katica climbing the tower stairs alone in the dark. Had she had her own key? Or maybe she hadn't been alone after all. Perhaps the boyfriend, Ben, had unlocked the door with his key and gone up the stairs with her. And if her husband, Lovro, had known about her affair, might he have made a copy of his wife's key in secret, hoping to follow and catch them?

It all sounded like the plot of a Puccini opera. Still, he couldn't dismiss it just because it was melodramatic. He had to find out if Katica's death was truly a suicide. At the very least, if he could find out how Katica had gotten into the tower that night, he might be able to relieve Denis of his guilt.

Renzo rose, saying, "I'll walk with you."

Pereira muttered, "You've made me think again about Ben having that key. Could he have . . . ?" He fell into silence.

"Yeah," Renzo said. "It all needs reexamining. I just hope everyone else has as clear a memory as you do. You've really helped me."

"Good," said Pereira.

They walked across the park, up the stairs to the cobblestoned square west of the Münster's main entrance, and stopped in front of the middle doors. Above them was one of the church's masterpieces, an elaborate and beautifully restored bas-relief sculpture of the Last Judgment.

Pereira shook hands with Renzo. "Guessing from your last name, you were brought up Catholic like me, right?"

"Of course. Although my parents were good Italian communists in their younger days. Don't ask me to explain *that*."

"I know. As for me, I officially withdrew from the church five years ago. It was one revelation too many about pedophile priests. I have three sons." He pointed up to the sculpted scene at Jesus's left hand, which was filled with screaming sinners and devils wielding pincers and spears. "Whenever I pass Hell here, I hope those bastards are in it!"

"Yeah," agreed Renzo. "The Horvats are Catholics, too. I hope Katica didn't believe suicide was a mortal sin when she jumped. *If* she jumped..."

Pereira's eyes were shadowed as he shook his head and walked away, holding up one hand in farewell. "Phone me if you find out anything new," he called. "Or if you have more questions."

Renzo watched the foreman for a few moments, then turned again to the brightly painted group sculpture over the Münster's double doors. He'd already picked out his own saint among the crowd of holy folk at Jesus's right hand. Lorenzo—Lorenz in German—was shown holding a gridiron because he'd been roasted to death by the Romans. That was why he'd been appointed the patron saint of cooks. Not for the first time, Renzo wondered at the Church's bizarre sense of humor.

He remembered wishing the evening before that he'd examined the place Katica had fallen from before starting this investigation. And now, here he was, even if the church was still closed to visitors. So, he apologetically phoned Pereira, who said, "Walk along the north side of the church on Münstergasse until you get to the midwife's door, and I'll let you in. It's the second of the three sets of double doors on that side."

He found Pereira waiting for him. Entering the dimly lit Münster, he heard the whine and buzz of equipment, although he couldn't see the restorers. He followed Pereira across the church and down the south aisle toward the front lobby. A tall, slim woman with dark skin— Eritrean or Somali, Renzo guessed from her features—was methodically dusting the backs of pews. Pereira greeted her by name as they passed; she murmured something but didn't look up at either man.

At the end of the aisle, Pereira gestured to a narrow, closed door that looked like it would open onto the west wall. "That's the staircase going up," he told Renzo. "You'll come down using another set of stairs and end up in the shop. Normally, no one's allowed to climb the tower alone, but I don't think you need me to babysit you. By the time you're ready to leave, the church should be open to the public, but if it's not, give me a call."

Renzo thanked Pereira yet again and opened the door to reveal a steep spiral staircase. The steps weren't worn down in the middle as he'd expected them to be. Nevertheless, he had no intention of running up *these* stairs. Proceeding cautiously, he found the staircase lit by narrow openings every few feet—they were barred by thin stone balusters and open to the outdoors. Now, in late June, the breeze coming through them was pleasant, but he imagined with a shiver what it must be like to climb these steps during winter, in the dark, with an icy wind blasting in. Or even snowflakes.

He climbed steadily, enjoying how the view through the slits changed with every turn: now he could see a section of the Pläfe criss-crossed by trees, walkways, and little patches of lawn; now he looked down on the Moses fountain in the cobblestoned Münsterplatz with a checkerboard of red-and-black tiled roofs beyond it. Another turn brought into view the ethereally elegant copper spire of the Nydegg church, which marked the eastern end of the Old City. When he pulled his gaze back from the distance to study the walls of the staircase itself, the windows showed him bits of carving on the Münster's façade, some-times just a sandstone curlicue, sometimes a serene face on the stone supports, and once or twice an elaborately sculpted bust.

It didn't take him as long as he'd expected to reach the first balcony. During opening hours, someone would have been here to take his ticket and supervise him. But right now, he was alone a hundred and fifty feet above the streets of Bern. Only a few sounds drifted up from the streets below. Despite the blue sky, the line of Alps that should have been on the horizon was mostly hidden by haze. Bern's own little mountain, the Gurten, stood to the south with the alternating greens of meadow and forest on its flanks.

Renzo moved around the rectangular gallery to the section that faced west. Directly below him was the Münsterplatz where Katica had died. Renzo didn't mind heights, but still, his muscles clenched, and his eyes closed involuntarily as he looked down onto the cobblestones. The stone railing reached only to his hip, and the decorative balustrade provided footholds that would make it as easy to climb as a kitchen stepladder. Katica could have jumped—easily. For that matter, a strong person could have lifted her and dropped her over. It wouldn't have been hard.

Then he turned and looked behind him at the enclosed space that fifteen years before had been the tower apartment. The distance between the top of the balustrade and the nearest windowsill was less than three feet. Even if the window had been closed, the bedroom was very small. How could the person sleeping in that room not have heard the slightest sound as Katica climbed up and threw herself over? She must have cried out in terror as she fell. Unless she'd been knocked unconscious. Then there'd have been no scream . . . But if that had been the case, then the killer would have been squeezed into this narrow space under the windows. Could they really have knocked Katica out and tipped her over the railing in complete silence, without any bumps or scrapes, without the slightest moan or grunt? Any way he looked at it, he couldn't imagine how she could have died without someone in the apartment waking up.

He thought of the second balcony, sixty feet above him.

Renzo found a second spiral staircase just outside one of the doors to the apartment. Up he went again, seeing the same views as he wound around the stairs, but with everything on the ground growing tinier as he left it even farther behind. When he walked out onto the second gallery, he gazed up at the intricately carved spire, which looked as delicate as lace from the ground but appeared massive now that he stood with its 120 feet of stone towering over his head.

He paced slowly around the octagonal space, unfastening the security chain so he could circle the tower completely. Once again, he gazed down at the cobblestoned square, which now appeared immensely far away. Here, the railing was higher than his waist, which made him want to know how tall Katica had been so he could visualize where it had come up to on her body. The carved stone balustrade was covered with something like chicken wire, except with larger openings. Large enough for someone with smallish feet to shove the toe of a shoe in and get a foothold. In fact, here, the passage around the tower was so narrow that someone strong and determined could have scrambled up the sloping tower wall using the decorations as handholds, stepped across to the top of the balustrade, and . . . He shivered. No, he wasn't going to picture it all yet again.

Still, he'd found out what he needed to know. Someone could jump off the tower from this higher platform, too. It would have been harder for Katica to climb the balustrade and more difficult for a second person to hoist her up and over, but it could be done. And it had no sleeping people a few feet away.

Renzo stood on the gallery, staring unseeingly at Bern's roofs, spreading out in geometric patterns on three sides of the tower. Then he walked to the staircase on the other side of the balcony and wound his way down to the larger platform below. He glanced at the Alps, still cloaked in cloud, and set off down a second staircase, which ended at another narrow door. He opened this to find himself across from the ticket counter, and there stood the taller of the two women he'd seen on Tuesday, the one who'd rolled her eyes at him while the other had babbled about Denis and drugs. "Oh!" she said. "How . . . ?"

Renzo held out his hand. "Hello. I was here on Tuesday, but I didn't have a chance to introduce myself. I'm Renzo Donatelli."

Smiling, the woman shook hands and came around the counter. "Yes, I remember. I'm Helen Jenzer. Are you still investigating Denis's fall?"

"In a way," he said cautiously. "I met with Artur Pereira earlier this morning, and he said I could climb the tower, something I haven't done in years. That reminds me—he let me in by what he called the midwife's door. Do you know why it's named that?"

The woman cocked an eyebrow at him. "It's part of my job to know. There used to be a font of holy water just inside that set of doors. Day or night, a midwife—or anyone who'd helped a woman through childbirth—could bring a sickly newborn through the midwife's door and baptize it at the font so that if it died, it would go to heaven. We imagine a fair number of those babies were already dead, but apparently, no one questioned the midwives' decisions. It's a rare example of the church giving power to women. Heaven got an extra soul, and the grieving parents got a bit of comfort."

Renzo nodded, feeling moved. He supposed it was the father in him responding to all those babies and mothers dying in childbirth, leaving husbands alone to care for the broken bits of family that remained to them.

He thanked the woman and left the Münster. As he walked across the Old City, he thought of Lovro Horvat, a man left bereft with an infant boy and a ten-year-old girl to care for. According to the Kellenbergers, Lovro had coped by marrying again—and fast. Renzo wished he'd asked them who the new Frau Horvat was. Still, he planned to talk to Lovro Horvat and find out for himself.

He contemplated the morning ahead and decided he'd see if he could locate Zora. *She* might have something to say about her stepmother—and perhaps she could provide insight into her parents' marriage, not to mention their adulteries. She may have been too young to understand what was happening between her mother and father at the time, but a ten-year-old's memories combined with a grown woman's understanding could reveal a lot. It was possible, Renzo thought, that Zora knew more than she thought she did.

15

Renzo was passing the art museum on his way back to the police station when his phone rang: an unknown number.

"This is Denis Kellenberger. I'm at my grandparents' place, and I'm fine. I want to talk to Goran with you. You didn't see him without me, did you? You said you wouldn't. And I can join you. Now, if you like."

The young man took a deep breath, and before he could start speaking again, Renzo took over. "Hello, Herr Kellenberger," he said. "I'm glad your operation went well. I plan to meet with Goran and his parents today, but first, I thought I'd see what his sister has to say. I haven't looked up her address; do you have it, by any chance? Is she still living above the shop in the Matte with her family?"

"Zora?" Denis said. He sounded shocked, and Renzo wondered why. "Well, I . . . A girl we both knew in primary school told me she had an apartment near Ostermundigen, and I have a phone number for her, but . . . well, that was two years ago."

"I'll get someone at the station to look her up," Renzo said. "Listen, there's no way I can take you with me on a police interview." He heard Denis say, "But—" and spoke right over him. "I won't change my mind, so don't waste your breath. Tell you what, though. I'll call you after I've talked to all the Horvats, parents and kids, and let you know what's going on. How's that?"

"But I need to talk to you *before* you see them," Denis insisted.

"Why?" Renzo asked, surprised by the urgency in the younger man's voice.

"Because I'm not going to press charges against Goran. So, there's nothing for you to talk to them about."

"Whoa," said Renzo. "First, we need to make sure it really was Goran who shook the scaffold, and if it was, his parents need to know about it. I'm talking to the three of them no matter what. But more importantly, it doesn't matter if you press charges or not. From a police point of view, this appears to be attempted murder, and—" Again, Renzo had to talk over loud protests from Denis. "I understand you'd like to protect the boy, and I'll try to take that into account, but this isn't something you have control over. As I said, I'll call you as soon as I finish talking to the family. Right now, I have to go."

"Can't we . . . ?" the boy began, but after a firm "Goodbye, Herr Kellenberger," Renzo hung up.

During the call, Renzo had been walking high above the Aare across the Lorraine Bridge. Now he called the station and asked to be connected to anyone junior who was at a computer doing data checks. A young female voice asked what he wanted, and he told her he needed information about Zora Horvat, age twenty-five, probably living on the Bern/Ostermundigen border. She said she'd text him whatever she found, adding, with a giggle, "Is it true you're getting divorced?"

He hadn't registered the woman's name when she'd answered the phone. Did he know her? Was she a friend of Fränzi's? "Yes, my wife and I have separated," he said stiffly. "Why do you ask?"

"Oh, I just wanted to get in line," she said, and while he was still wondering if she meant what he thought she meant, she added, "I'll send the contact info from my *private* phone—then you'll have my number."

She was gone before he could say a word, which was just as well since he was speechless. Then he laughed. Women had been giving him their phone numbers for over half his life, but he couldn't remember ever getting a proposition quite like that before—from a girl he didn't know and had never seen. Although he'd probably glimpsed her around the station if she'd seen him. God, he was getting old—he wasn't even wondering if she was going to send him a picture of herself. Okay, he'd admit to a little curiosity, but . . .

By the time his phone pinged, he was at his desk in the big office he shared with the other Fahnder. Giuliana would probably be wondering why he hadn't stopped by the case room, so he sent her a text explaining what he was up to. Only then did he open his message from the woman who wanted to get in line. Along with Zora's contact information, she'd indeed sent a revealing photo. Smiling and shaking his head, he called Goran's sister's cell.

"Horvat." The woman who answered had a deep voice, and her tone was distant—naturally, since she wouldn't recognize his number.

"Hello. This is Renzo Donatelli, Kantonspolizei. I'm calling about your brother, Goran. He may be in some trouble, and I need to talk to him. I'd like to—"

As soon as he said "*Polizei*," Zora Horvat had sucked in her breath. Now she interrupted. "In trouble? Why?"

"I'll talk to him about that when I see him," Renzo responded.

There was a long silence before she said, "He's coming to my place for lunch around noon. You can talk to both of us; you're not to question him when he's alone. Have you got my address in Galgenfeld?"

"Yes," said Renzo. "I can be there at noon." He looked at his watch. It was ten forty, which meant he'd need to leave in about an hour.

"Good," said Zora and she hung up without saying goodbye.

Renzo settled into his desk chair and hooked up his laptop to the big screen on his desk, glad he had time to record what Pereira had told him and his impressions of the tower's two levels. After that, he'd see what he could find on Katica's boyfriend, Ben Schweizer, before driving to Zora's. Briefly, he wondered what Goran would think when he turned up at Zora's place. This was going to be interesting.

Zora lived a ten-minute drive from Denis's grandparents' large house but in a very different neighborhood, where apartment blocks alternated with small businesses and warehouses. Her apartment was on the eastern edge of Bern, where the city began sliding into the working-class neighborhoods of Ostermundigen. The Kellenbergers lived in Kirchenfeld—church field—and Zora in Galgenfeld—gallows field—which Renzo thought summed up the contrast.

Her building was old, he saw, but the front garden looked tidy, and the balconies facing the street displayed window boxes of geraniums. Renzo realized he was relieved to discover that she could afford a decent place. Why had he expected otherwise? He supposed it was her mother's suicide. As a cop, he knew how often youngsters with traumatic childhoods ended up living in squalor. It looked like maybe Zora had managed to keep a grip on normal life.

Renzo parked his Fiat. At the apartment block's main entrance, he pushed a buzzer marked "Z. Horvat."

"Yes?"

"Donatelli from the Cantonal Police. We spoke on the phone, Frau Horvat."

"I'm on the second floor, 2H." There was a whirr as Zora let him in, and Renzo started up the stairs.

On the second floor, he found a tall young woman in baggy knee-length shorts and a tank top standing outside an open door. She was large, not just tall, with broad shoulders, well-muscled arms and legs, and a full figure that was anything but flabby. A great quantity of dark hair casually piled up on her head made her look even taller. Her mouth was wide, and she had a broad-at-the-cheekbones face that made her blue eyes slant slightly.

She put her hands on her hips and frowned as Renzo approached. Still, she held out a hand for him to shake. "Zora Horvat. You aren't wearing a uniform—how do I know you're a cop?"

Renzo already had his ID in his left hand. Zora studied it carefully, then said, "Let's go inside, Herr...Donatelli. I've been worrying nonstop since you called me. What did Goran do? You know he's fifteen, right?"

He followed her inside. The apartment door opened directly into a room containing both a round dining table and a sitting area with armchairs. Across from the front door, sliding glass panels led out onto a narrow balcony overlooking the back lawn. Zora sat at the round table and pointed Renzo toward another chair. Instead, he stood for a moment, looking around.

His gaze was drawn to the small open kitchen, where something that smelled deliciously of meat and garlic was cooking in a cast-iron pot on the stove. At the other end of the living-dining area were two side-by-side doors in one wall, both closed, presumably a bathroom and a bedroom. There was also a ladder leading up to a narrow platform on one side of the French doors, a loft space containing a single bed, a straight-backed chair, and a small desk piled with papers. A couple of simple shelves fastened to the wall over the desk held books.

Zora followed Renzo's gaze. "I have the bedroom." She pointed at one of the closed doors. "The loft's Goran's. *Please* tell me what's going on."

Renzo chose a chair facing the apartment door. "On Tuesday afternoon," he began, "a young man, a glassmaker, was on a scaffold in the Münster repairing one of the stained-glass windows." He went on to tell what had happened to Denis without using his name, emphasizing how dangerous the fall had been and quoting the words Denis's attacker had said. He watched Zora as he spoke.

She bit her lower lip, and her knuckles turned white as she clasped her hands tight on the tabletop. Her thick brows drew down. "The glassmaker didn't see who did it?" she asked.

Renzo shook his head. "The man told the police that the voice of the person who attacked him was high-pitched. He thought it might have been a girl or a young woman. Later, in the hospital, he told me he thought it was a girl he'd known as a child. He was doped up on pain-killers, you see. Confused."

Zora shook her head, looking puzzled. Renzo continued, "Now I come into the story." He told Zora about the boy who'd crashed into him at the gate, how he'd followed the boy and lost him near her father's shop.

She stared at him for a long time in silence; he imagined her thoughts twisting this way and that as she tried to decide what to do. "I don't have anything to say about this," she said, finally. Her voice shook. "I think you should leave. You'll have to talk to Goran at . . . at the police station, with our father and a lawyer and . . ."

"Isn't Goran due home any minute, Frau Horvat?" Renzo asked.

"It doesn't matter." She stood and crossed her arms. "You can't wait for him here. Get out of my apartment. Please."

Renzo was annoyed and impressed at the same time. He couldn't think of many twenty-five-year-olds who would be able to tell a policeman to get the hell out so calmly and then add a please. In general, most Swiss, even seemingly rebellious youngsters who cursed at cops during demonstrations, tended to cooperate with them one-on-one, especially if they were middle class. And Zora's apartment certainly looked middle class. But, he supposed, even though she'd been born and raised in Bern, her culture wasn't Swiss. Her parents and grandparents had grown up under a dictator in Soviet-influenced Yugoslavia, and maybe he should have known better than to try to sweet-talk her into . . .

The apartment door opened, and a boy walked in. "You won't believe what Frau Zumwald wrote on my German essay, Zora. She thinks I've . . ."

Renzo was fast. Before Goran had registered that his sister wasn't alone, Renzo was behind him, closing the door and standing in front of it.

The small, slight figure—a boy, only just beginning to look like a man—glanced at him with apprehension but without recognition. First, he turned to his sister. "Zora, who's this?" Then he whipped around and stared at Renzo's face. He gave a shriek of rage and flew at Renzo, fists flailing. "Fucking cop!"

He didn't manage to land a single blow; Renzo easily immobilized him in a kind of professional bear hug from behind, careful not to hurt him. Even so, Zora, who was taller than Renzo, was moving toward him like a wolf defending her cub. Now he was going to have to deal with two furious people—without doing either any damage.

Then Goran yelled, "Didn't you know this guy's a cop? What's he doing here? You're crazy to let him in."

All Zora's self-control abandoned her, and instead of attacking Renzo, she began to yell, gesturing wildly with her arms. "You're the one who's gone crazy. He says you—" She broke off as abruptly as she'd begun, and she hurried forward to put a hand over her brother's open mouth. "No," she hissed, sounding panicky, "Don't say *anything*. You mustn't talk."

But Goran was fifteen. No way was he about to listen to his big sister. Even with his arms pinned by Renzo, he managed to shake off Zora's hand. "All my life, I've heard that story about you at Majka's funeral, screaming at Denis"—his voice was venomous—"and saying that he was the reason our mother was dead. I finally did something about it. Then you let this cop into our apartment. What the fuck's wrong with you?"

Renzo had deliberately waited, saying nothing, to see what Goran would reveal on his own—and the tactic had paid off. Zora stepped back from her brother, her face stricken. Renzo could almost see her crumble. How could she protect her brother while he was so busy incriminating himself?

Now it was time to start asking questions. "We need to talk about what happened, Goran," Renzo said, not letting go of the boy, "and why you attacked Denis Kellenberger." He looked up at Zora as he spoke Denis's name; she closed her eyes and put her hand over her mouth. As he'd been convinced since her initial reaction to his story, she'd known nothing about Goran's plan.

"We are going to sit around that table," Renzo pointed with his chin, "the three of us, and no one is going to yell at anyone. Do you hear me?" Still holding Goran, Renzo turned and saw that the key to the apartment door was lying on the floor where the boy had dropped it. "I'm going to let you go, and you're going to walk over to one of those chairs and sit down. Frau Horvat, you sit, too. Right now."

He let go of Goran, who hovered for a second as if still considering flight. Renzo watched him, muscles tense. Then the boy walked to the table and sat, sliding his backpack onto the floor. Renzo scooped up the boy's set of keys and locked the door. As he did, he noticed that the key ring was attached to a disk. On one side of it was the red-and-white checkerboard pattern used by the Croatian soccer team; on the other side, the white-cross-on-red of the Swiss flag. Renzo, both Swiss and Italian, understood Goran's dual loyalties only too well. The key ring made him smile despite the tenseness of the situation.

Pocketing the keys, he joined the kids at the table. No, Goran was a kid. Zora was only ten years younger than Renzo, but it felt like more.

Goran met Renzo's eyes. "Am I going to go to jail?" he asked, a tiny quaver in his voice.

"I don't think juvenile detention is likely," said Renzo, "but I honestly don't know for sure. If you stay calm and explain yourself clearly, first with me and later at the police station, it will help." He got out a pen and his notebook. "So, tell me, what happened on Tuesday afternoon?"

Goran gave his sister a quick look and took a deep breath. "I never expected the guy to fall. When he kind of . . . bounced off the pews and hit the floor, I thought I'd killed him. I was . . . scared." He squeezed his hand into a fist on the table in front of him. "I ran out of the church, and then I crashed into you." He scraped his chair around until he faced Renzo. His face was pale. "You had a gun. I thought . . ." He fell silent.

The boy had dark hair like his sister's but brown eyes, not blue, and an oval face. His hair was cut short and spiked; above one ear, the Croatian checkerboard pattern had been shaved into it. His

Swiss-German dialect was pure Bernese. Renzo wondered if he also spoke Croatian. If the pattern Renzo had grown up with was anything to go by, Goran probably spoke Bernese when he was alone with his sister and Croatian with his father and stepmother.

Zora buried her face in her hands, letting the silence grow. Renzo was just about to ask another question when the apartment buzzer sounded.

Zora looked at Renzo. "Is that someone else from the police?" she asked.

"No," Renzo told her, and with a look of relief, she went to speak into the intercom. But when Renzo heard the voice that answered, he ground his teeth. It was Denis Kellenberger. "*Porca miseria,*" Renzo swore under his breath. "Don't let him in," he said sharply, but Zora, frowning, had already pressed the button.

Damn him, Renzo thought. He should never have told Denis anything about the investigation. He supposed he could throw him out, but he didn't actually have that authority in someone else's house. Also, Zora wouldn't appreciate him coming on like a heavy, and he needed her cooperation. He'd have to make the best of it.

Denis and Zora spent some time in the hall before they came into the apartment, one after the other. Although Renzo had seen Denis already, he was shocked anew by his appearance. The bruises around his left eye and cheek had darkened almost to black; the stitches stood out on his forehead, and his arms, quite apart from his cast, were a mess. He looked terrible. But he was grinning.

Zora put her hand on Denis's good arm and guided him to the table as if he were an invalid. Her eyes were a little red, but Renzo decided that was because of Denis's injuries, not his presence. Goran was staring at Denis, eyes wide, mouth hanging open. *Finally, the little bastard realizes what he did*, Renzo told himself with satisfaction.

As if he'd read Renzo's thoughts, Denis smiled at the kid sitting across from him. "*Tschou!* You must be Goran, and I guess you know I'm Denis. That was quite some shaking you did. As you can see."

Goran continued to gaze at him in silence.

"Hello, Renzo," Denis said. *So, they were using first names now, were they?* Renzo thought grimly. "I'm sorry I'm messing up your interview, but I just . . . I just couldn't stay away."

Tight-lipped, Renzo shook his head. "You shouldn't be here, Denis. You—"

Goran broke in, finally able to speak. "I'm glad you aren't dead. Is your arm going to be okay?"

"It's my wrist—it had to be operated on. But the doctors think it will heal fine. That's important because I work with my hands. I was very worried about it." Denis's voice was even, his face serious, and Renzo was glad. He didn't approve of letting Goran off the hook; being fifteen wasn't an excuse for such violence.

"So do I," Zora said brightly. "I'm a gardener for the city."

This interview is turning into a fucking reunion. Controlling his frustration, Renzo said tightly, "I am here to speak to Goran. If you don't let me do that, I'll take him to the police station." In the silence that followed, Renzo addressed Goran directly. "It's clear that you made an attempt to murder Denis Kellenberger." Zora gasped, but Renzo looked at her sharply. "Now you say you're glad he isn't dead. But after you made him fall, you didn't get help or phone for an ambulance. Instead, you ran home to hide. That means it's hard for me to believe that you weren't trying to kill him, especially when you told him that you hoped he'd bust his head open."

For a second, Goran looked terrified; then he narrowed his eyes. Did he feel any remorse for what he'd done? Renzo still didn't know. "Did anyone tell you to hurt Denis," he went on, "or suggest the idea to you?"

Goran's mouth fell open. "Of course not."

"So, why did you do it?" Renzo leaned back and folded his arms.

"Because . . ." Goran was frowning, his gaze unfocused. Somehow, he looked too puzzled to be searching for a good lie. It was almost as if he was trying to explain his actions to himself. "I've always known about the boy named Denis who lived in the Münster and left the tower door open. It's something my mother talked about."

His mother? Then Renzo remembered that Lovro's second wife was the only mother the boy had known. Had *she* blamed Denis, too?

Goran continued. "About a week ago, one of the Münster builders was in our shop. I asked him if he knew a Denis who lived in the church, and he told me if I ever saw a tall young guy with blue eyes and long, light-brown hair in a ponytail or a bun working on the windows, that would be Denis—but he didn't live *in* the Münster, just near it. So, afterward, for about a week, during my lunch break and after school, I looked for him, and on Tuesday, I saw him. I hadn't planned anything. Well, maybe to talk to him about my mother—my real mother, I mean. But he was working up on the scaffold. I . . . I didn't know I was going to shake it until I just . . . did."

"But why now?" asked Zora, which was exactly what Renzo had been about to ask. "Something must have made you want to track down Denis after all these years."

Silence again. Goran chewed on his lower lip and picked at a nail. "It was because . . . I heard you and Mama talking about Majka."

This time Renzo understood that "Mama" was the second wife and "Majka" meant Katica. "When you were visiting the store last time. About two weeks ago." Zora gasped.

Apparently, she knew what was coming, but Renzo still had no clue.

"You thought I was out playing soccer, but I'd come in the back way. You said something like, 'Do you think I didn't figure that out years ago?' and Mama said, 'Don't say a word to your father. It's bad enough that he lost her without his learning she had been with another man.'" Goran slammed his fist down on the round table. *"Another man!"*

Zora reached for her brother's hand. "Oh, God," she said. "I . . . Ivana and I, we never wanted you to know."

"Ivana is your father's wife now?" Renzo asked, making a mental note of the name.

But Goran was still in full flow. "You weren't going to tell me?" he said, his loud voice cracking. "You didn't think I deserved to know that my real mother was a whore, and Tata isn't my father? That I'm a bastard? It's a good thing I figured it out myself, then, isn't it?" He glowered at Zora, who stared back at him in silent misery.

"That's enough," Renzo said, and the boy stopped ranting, although he was breathing hard.

It was interesting, Renzo thought, that Ivana and Zora knew about the affair and had probably speculated that Katica's lover might be Goran's father. Or perhaps they both knew the truth, one way or the other. But all this still left his question unanswered. "That doesn't explain why you attacked Denis," he said. "What did Denis have to do with your mother's affair? He was only ten when she died."

Goran sat at the table with his shoulders hunched, staring down at his hands. Then he shrugged and spoke without looking up. "Denis is at the Münster, and he knew Majka. Mama always said he was to blame for her death. He . . . he . . ." The boy shook his head, glancing sideways at his sister. "Before you said I'd gone crazy. That's how it feels to *me* now, too, but then, when I was standing at the foot of the scaffold . . ." Finally, he looked up at Renzo. "I don't *know* why I did it. Okay? I don't know. I'm sorry." He started to cry.

The room had grown hot from the noon sun streaming in through the balcony's glass doors, and the rich smell of whatever was cooking filled the apartment. Renzo realized he was sweating. The boy was sobbing softly. Outside, the traffic noises were muted. A nearby church bell rang twice for the half hour. It was only twelve thirty; it felt a lot longer than half an hour since he'd arrived.

As if the bell were a signal, Goran jumped up, and his chair crashed over backward. He stood a moment with his face twisted, then he yelled, "Fuck!" and ran into his sister's bedroom, slamming the door. Renzo heard the key turn in the lock.

For a while, no one broke the silence. Then Denis said conversationally, "What a mess! Well, I'm a bastard, too. Maybe if I tell Goran, he'll feel better about it."

Zora gave a cackle of shocked laughter, and she looked at Denis, her face intrigued. Then she said to Renzo, "I don't know if Goran is

Father's son or not. Maybe our mother didn't know either. In fact, I don't *know* anything. But . . . well, I did finally figure out for myself what had been going on, what with her saying I had appointments that didn't exist and then leaving me in the Münster, sometimes as much as one or two afternoons a week. And disappearing in the middle of the night, too. I remember once waking up because I'd heard the front door close, then looking out my window and seeing her in the lamp-light going along the road."

How could Lovro not have known? Renzo thought. It didn't seem possible, and yet Ivana, his wife of fifteen years, seemed convinced he had no idea.

Zora was speaking again. "Thinking back, I'm pretty sure I know who the man was, although I can't picture him. He used to come into the shop to talk to her, and she'd look at me and then shake her head at him. Or she'd assign me some little job upstairs in the apartment, and I knew it was to get me out of the way."

Renzo found this picture of Katica playing around right under her family's nose disturbing. It seemed so callous, somehow, so calcu-lating. "What was your mother like?" he asked on impulse.

Zora cocked her head. "Why do you want to know?"

"I'd like to understand why she killed herself."

"You think I don't want that, too?" Zora's voice shook. "I've torn myself up wondering why. It made me worry that all the things I thought I knew about her were wrong. She loved me so much. At least, that's what I remember. And she loved my father, too. She kissed him and teased him and chatted to him all day long. I know we were important to her. People remember being angry with their mothers, but . . . not me. And that has made it . . . impossible to bear sometimes. How *could* she have killed herself?"

Denis gave a sudden movement; his expression was bitter. "Do you have a different memory of Zora's mother?" Renzo asked.

"No . . . not at all. She always spoke to me when we were together, and her warmth was like something glowing . . . like embers. When she put her hand on my shoulder, I felt—well, I didn't feel loved, like Zora, naturally, but I felt I was special to her. She was my idea of what a fairy queen must be like."

Zora's smile lit up her face. "A fairy queen," she repeated. "She'd have loved that. She told me lots of fairy tales when I was growing up."

"A fairy?" Renzo mused. "Was she tiny, then?"

"Not really," said Zora. "Maybe five-four or -five. But slim and . . . graceful?" The questioning tone at the end of Zora's sentence made Renzo sad. It was as though she couldn't be sure of her own memories.

"Floaty," Denis said. "Soft clouds of dark hair around her face." He closed his eyes. "Bright clothes that flowed when she moved, hands that darted when she talked. And a voice like a bell."

"Oh, Denis, yes," said Zora, her face a poignant mix of regret and delight. "That sounds so right." She turned back to Renzo, saying, "Looking back now, I see things about my mother I didn't see then. Sometimes she was . . . flirtatious? But more often serious. Fierce, too. I don't think I mean angry, but intensely emotional. And that emotion wasn't always . . . happiness. I suppose there must have been something else inside her. Otherwise, why . . . ?"

Finally, Renzo thought, he was getting a sense of the woman at the center of this case. She was like nothing he'd had in mind. Despite what Denis's grandparents had told him about Katica, he'd formed an idea of her as frivolous—carefree but also careless. This was a woman who'd cheated on her husband and probably given him a child who wasn't his, but maybe she hadn't done it thoughtlessly.

He found himself very much wanting to see Katica's face. "Do you have any photos of your mother?"

"A whole envelope." She looked toward the bedroom door, still firmly closed. "I have some framed, too. They're in the bedroom. Goran has to come out soon—he needs to go back for afternoon school. And I need to get going, too. I don't want to be late for work."

"Okay," said Renzo. "Then stay a minute and let me ask you . . . um, *three* more things. After I have a look at the photos, I'll leave you to eat your lunch."

Zora got up and stood across from Renzo, her hands on the back of her chair.

"Okay, first," he said. "Did your mother have a close woman friend?"

She wrinkled her nose. "Her best friend was Ivana, the woman my father married."

Renzo kept his face blank with some difficulty. What the *hell* . . . ? He was itching to ask more questions, but he felt a need to tread carefully.

Zora was still speaking. "Ivana's ten years older than my mother was—almost my father's age—and my mother used to ask her advice about a lot of things. The two of them could be quite . . . sharp with each other, but that didn't seem to matter. They came from the same village in Istria; they'd known each other for years."

So, not only had the first wife been having an affair, but the husband had married her best friend. Had *they* been having an affair, too? And if they had, did that make Katica's death more likely to be suicide? Or did it point to murder? This story was becoming more convoluted by the minute.

Cautiously, Renzo went on. "Your stepmother believes your father didn't know your mother was having an affair. Do you really think he never figured it out? After all, *you* did."

"I never heard my parents fight about anything like that. In fact, they barely fought at all. He still talks about her in a very affectionate way, and"—she lowered her voice—"he loves Goran and is very proud of him. Would they really be so close if he thought Goran wasn't his?"

Renzo could see Zora was restless, glancing toward the bedroom door, probably worrying about the time. Denis, on the other hand, seemed in no hurry to leave. He was watching Zora, Renzo thought, as though she was the only person in the room.

"Last question," Renzo said. "Have you ever had any doubt that your mother committed suicide?"

Zora's face clouded. "Never. Knowing she killed herself has shaped my life. Not just missing her, but imagining the things she'd never told me, things so bad that she . . ." Then she must have caught something in Renzo's expression because she frowned at him and put her hands on her hips. "What? You don't think that's what happened? So, what did? You think someone *killed* her?" She stared at him, the color rising in her cheeks. "My *father*?"

Had he made a mistake talking to her about this? She'd been coming to terms with her mother's death for fifteen years. He didn't want to say anything that would upset the balance she'd achieved, and possibly for no good reason. After all, he had no proof as yet that the official verdict had been wrong.

He kept his voice light. "I have no new evidence to suggest that your mother's death was anything but a suicide. I just wondered if you'd had any second thoughts over the years."

Zora shook her head without speaking, her face pale.

Renzo got to his feet, and Denis shifted in his chair but made no move to get up. "I'm sorry I've delayed you. If you're late back to work and your boss gives you trouble, tell him to call me." He fished his card out of his shirt pocket, along with Goran's keys, and set them on the table. "May I get in touch again if I have more questions?"

"Yes, but . . . what's going to happen to Goran?" Not waiting for an answer, Zora marched to the bedroom door and knocked. "The men are leaving, Gori. Open up. I need to show the cop . . . show Herr Donatelli my photos of Majka. We're going to have to eat fast, or we'll be late."

The door opened almost immediately, and Goran let her in. Renzo half expected the boy to stay hiding in the bedroom, but he came out and stood with his back to the wall, watching the men at the table until Zora returned with two framed photos, one large and the other a snapshot.

Renzo took the snapshot first. It showed a man of about forty, wearing a navy blazer and holding a baby in a christening dress. Goran's little head leaned sideways on Lovro's shoulder, and his face was screwed up in a fierce yawn. Lovro looked about as happy as it was possible for a person to be. So did the child standing next to him, a leggy Zora with a braid over one shoulder, wearing a blue dress with a full skirt and a sash, light blue tights, and black patent leather shoes. As her father beamed at the camera, she grinned up at the baby, reaching out to hold his tiny foot in her hand.

On the father's other side was Katica.

She wore a pink-and-white dress with a swirly pattern, her hair not floating this time but pulled back neatly, her expression hard to read. She seemed too young to have a ten-year-old daughter, and she certainly didn't look carefree. Along with the slight smile on her lips, there was a crease in her forehead. Renzo glanced away from her face, and when he looked back, the eyes were what drew him: they appeared proud. The little family stood in front of their shop, and Renzo imagined the woman in the photo thinking: *My husband, our shop, our family. Life may not be full of fun, but it's a good life, and I'm grateful for it.* These were the thoughts and feelings of many immigrant parents, including his own.

He turned now to the other picture, a formal head-and-shoulders portrait of the woman. It told him less, except that, yes, Katica had been lovely. He could see a gleam in the warm eyes, slightly slanted like Zora's but brown instead of blue. But there was nothing of the woman's charisma and emotional power, the magnetism Denis and Zora—and the Kellenbergers—had described. Perhaps it couldn't be sensed from paper.

He'd lost himself in the photos, and when he finally set them on the table, he saw that the others were in the kitchen. Goran was talking animatedly to Denis while Zora stood at the sink filling glasses. Renzo felt a flick of loneliness as he looked at the three together. Time to leave. Still, he couldn't go quite yet.

He came closer, careful to stop outside the kitchen area. "Zora," he said, and she finished filling the second water glass and turned. "Goran," he added. The boy broke off the story he was telling Denis. "Here's what happens next. I will speak with your parents and make an appointment for you to come with them to the Nordring police station, where we'll do an official interview for you to sign. Your parents will be there the whole time, and they'll sign, too. You'll probably go before a judge specializing in young offenders, who'll decide what will happen next. You may be required to pay a fine, do community service work, or see a social worker—or all three. I can't control that decision."

Goran was shaking his head. "But what will I say? If my parents are there for the interview, I can't say what I overheard about . . . about the other man. Not in front of my father. Besides, I don't *understand* what made me want to track down Denis or . . . or hurt him. I guess I was just . . . furious with everyone. But I can't say that in the interview—I'd sound like an idiot." Goran turned to Denis and, close to tears again, said, "I'm really sorry I hurt you."

At least the kid was finally using his brain. "I will interview you at the police station," Renzo said, "and I won't ask you *why* you did anything. I'll just ask you to talk about *what* you did. Of course, I can't keep your parents from asking you why. You'll have to work that out for yourself. I won't say anything to your father about the secret you found out unless . . . unless I think it's absolutely necessary. Which it isn't right now." He paused. "Okay. I think that's everything. I'll leave you to eat. Denis, I can give you a ride home if you like."

While he and Goran talked, Zora spooned large helpings of some kind of meat-and-vegetable dish onto two plates. It was obvious Denis was hoping to be asked to stay and share the meal, but with no invitation forthcoming, he reluctantly joined Renzo by the door. Zora shook Renzo's hand; a bit sheepishly, Goran did the same.

"Thanks for meeting with me," Renzo said. "Goran, I'll be seeing you soon."

The smell of the food followed them out the door and most of the way down the stairs. God, he was hungry. As they left the building, Renzo rested his hand on Denis's shoulder. "You could have wrecked my interview by showing up like that. I should have thrown you out."

Denis gave him a sidelong glance. "I know. I just couldn't stay away. I'm sorry."

Renzo rolled his eyes. "You and Goran seem to have a lot in common, giving in to your destructive impulses." Noticing Denis's shamefaced expression, he relented. "Look, I'm starving. Shall we get something to eat? How about a *döner* kebab?"

Denis's worried face cracked into a grin. "Yeah, that sounds great. Maybe you can tell me if there's anything I can do to make sure Goran doesn't get punished. And also, what you know about Katica's death. You think someone killed her, don't you? Yes, I know you said you don't have evidence, but it's what you think, right?"

It was what Renzo had been turning over in his mind since the Kellenbergers had told him about Katica's lover. But until he had evidence—and he wasn't sure if he'd be able to find any fifteen years after the fact—he had to keep a lid on the whole thing.

"This is how rumors get started, Denis," he said sternly as they headed for his Fiat. "I asked Zora if she ever had doubts about the suicide. I didn't say I believed it was murder because I don't. The investigation at the time found that it was a suicide. I'm just asking the questions that policemen always ask. Okay?"

Denis dipped his head, said, "Yep," and got into the car without another word. Renzo studied him. Denis looked like he'd been beaten to a pulp. It didn't matter how sorry Goran was now—it was a miracle the boy hadn't killed Denis. Renzo just hoped Goran realized how lucky he was.

"I'm glad we've got that straight," Renzo said, still using his tough voice. Then he softened it. "Now, let's go get our kebabs!"

16

Nordring police station and the Casino terrace,
Thursday morning, June 27

After Renzo left for his morning interview with the Münster restoration foreman, Giuliana read the notes he'd sent her summarizing his work on the Horvat/Kellenberger case and what he planned to do next. It looked solid—did she have any advice for him?

Then she caught herself. She'd been the one to push Rolf to give him his own investigation—not that it had required much pressure. All Renzo was doing at this stage was keeping her in the loop; she wasn't supervising him. And he hadn't asked for advice—at least, not directly.

She tried to turn her attention to the Seiler case, but she couldn't concentrate. A lurking emotion was still distracting her. She picked away at it. Was she . . . was she feeling *sad* about Renzo's progress? Surely not—and yet . . . Her critical inner voice spoke up: *Not only do you like Renzo wanting to sleep with you, you also like the way he looks up to you as a mentor. But did you really think things could go on like that forever?*

Renzo's separation from Fränzi, along with his need to move up professionally, was going to change their relationship. She knew that—had known it for a while. But she wasn't sure she'd really accepted it yet.

She got up from her desk and crossed the room to its one window, which looked out over Nordring, the main street running through the Lorraine neighborhood. She noticed an old man coming out of the residence for seniors across the street. He was dressed in a pale, lightweight summer suit, and he wore an elegant straw hat with a blue band. There was something confident and cheerful in the way he strolled down the street toward downtown Bern that made her happy and sad at the same time. How did a person manage to age so well? She watched the man in the hat until he was out of sight.

She had to face the fact that Renzo was leaving her behind as a boss *and* an object of desire. If she didn't want to lose his friendship as well, she'd better be ready for what was happening and deal with it gracefully. She closed her eyes and leaned her forehead against the window frame, willing herself to put these thoughts aside and get back to work.

And then, thank God, her phone rang. It was a friendly check-in from Rosmarie Bolliger, the Bern prosecutor responsible for the case against Ruth Seiler. It gave Giuliana a chance to ask about the older couple's money and just how many years in a care home it could have paid for.

Rosmarie assured Giuliana that she and her team were well prepared for challenges on the subject of the couple's finances. "The defense will try to show that Seiler had no mercenary motives when she gave him the overdose. But he was still relatively healthy, physically. He might have died of pneumonia after a year, or he might have lasted into his late eighties. Since there's no way to know, we can definitely argue that there was a risk of his wife being left poor."

She didn't need to add what both of them already knew: that in Switzerland, "poor" rarely meant hungry and homeless. Ruth had worked full-time most of her adult life, which would guarantee her a decent social security payment and an employee's pension. Upon Werner's death, she'd received a twenty percent widow's increase in her social security and sixty percent of *his* pension. Even if the couple's savings had been used up on Werner's care, she wouldn't have starved. But she wouldn't have had much for extras, either.

"Any money of her own that Allemann's kids don't stand to inherit?" Giuliana asked.

She heard computer keys clicking at Rosmarie's end of the phone. "She has her own bank account with just under ten thousand francs, but most of her work income went into their joint account, and I don't know yet if she brought any money into the marriage. Someone's looking into it."

"Thanks, Rosmarie," Giuliana said. "Any idea yet when I can interview her? If she's not well enough for it to be official, could I just talk to her briefly? I've never met her, and it's hard to judge what witnesses tell me without any kind of baseline opinion of my own for comparison."

Rosmarie didn't answer right away. Then she sighed. "Look, I don't want to owe Seiler's defense team any favors, but you may know her lawyer anyway, or at least your brother will. Valérie Imboden. Why don't you give her a call? She might be willing to get you some time with Seiler. As for the deposition, I don't know when we'll be able to schedule it."

Although Giuliana had indeed met Valérie Imboden through her father, it surprised her that the prosecutor was giving her permission to call the defense lawyer. Naturally, the police and the prosecutors had to share all their evidence with the defense. But that wasn't the same as letting her chat with Valérie. "You're okay with that?"

"Why not?" Rosmarie answered. "Just make sure you're the one asking the questions, and she's the one answering!"

Giuliana laughed. "I promise." With a warm goodbye, she hung up.

Returning from her place at the window, she sat again, leaning back in her desk chair. What else was keeping her from evaluating the testimony in the case? It occurred to her that while she knew the bare-bones law about assisted suicide, she had no idea how such a thing was correctly carried out. It was called "assisted" suicide because there was always an assistant: someone who worked for Exit or Dignitas or whichever organization was involved. It was their job to make sure all the legal procedures were followed. Did a complete stranger ring the doorbell half an hour before the set time carrying a vial of poison? Maybe that was all the assistant did. But it seemed unlikely. For the sake of the case, but also in part to satisfy her curiosity, she decided to find out what Werner Allemann and Ruth Seiler *should* have done if he'd wanted to end his life without her being accused of murder.

She googled Exit. A click on "Facts" revealed that it had over 200,000 members in Switzerland. Their contact page gave her an address and phone number in Bern, although their main office was in Zürich.

She called the number, and a man answered. "Exit. Gafner."

"*Guete Tag*, Herr Gafner," she began. "This is Giuliana Linder, Kantonspolizei Bern. I'd like to speak with someone involved in *Freitodbegleitung*." According to Exit's website, that was the job description: literally, free death companionship. You accompanied people as they traveled the path toward a freely chosen death. "Could you give me a list of names to call?"

"Are you a member?" the man asked. "Is this for yourself or a loved one?"

Did he think she identified herself as a cop when she made personal calls? She rolled her eyes but kept her voice pleasant. "No, my questions relate to a police investigation."

The man was silent. What was making him hesitate? She supposed she could imagine why the organization was suspicious of the police. Assisted suicide had been legal in Switzerland since 1942, but there were still crusaders who harassed the people involved in it. Now and then, a public prosecutor filed an accusation of homicide against an Exit employee carrying out a perfectly legal and legitimate assisted suicide because of an alleged procedural flaw. These people were usually acquitted, but still . . . She hoped she wasn't going to have to back up her request with legal documentation—it would waste so much time.

She decided to address his concerns head-on. "Look, I'm not planning to cause trouble; I'm just after some background information. I've read a lot of what you have online, but I'd like to talk to someone who has supervised an assisted suicide. Believe me, I'm no enemy of your organization. My parents belong to Exit," she added spontaneously.

With that, Herr Gafner relented. "Well, if your parents are members," he said, his voice warmer, "I imagine you have a personal as well as a professional interest. Let me email you contact information for some of our local people."

Five minutes later, she had a list of eight names with birthdates, addresses, phone numbers, and a sentence about professions and activities, which she studied on her screen. One name jumped out, and her breath caught in her throat: Ursula Kellenberger. Talk about coincidences! She pulled up Renzo's notes—yes, he'd interviewed the glassworker's grandparents, Ursula and Hans-Peter Kellenberger, at their home in Kirchenfeld, which was where the woman on her list lived.

Perhaps it wasn't *so* surprising that a woman in her sixties who'd retired from an academic profession like art restoration would involve herself with Exit. But now Giuliana was facing a moral dilemma. She'd spent half the morning reminding herself not to interfere in Renzo's case, and here she was, thinking about calling one of his interviewees. There were eight names on the list. All she had to do was contact one of the others.

Instead, she picked up her phone from the desktop and dialed Kellenberger's number.

"Ursula Kellenberger with Exit," a woman's voice said. Presumably, she had a special mobile just for these calls.

"Frau Kellenberger, my name is Giuliana Linder; I'm a detective with the Kantonspolizei Bern. I'm on a case that requires me to understand how assisted suicide works, and I was wondering if you'd be able to answer a few questions. It's not a formal interview. I'm just getting some background."

The woman breathed slowly for a moment. "I suppose this has to do with that woman in the paper and her husband. I've read every word the *Bund* has printed about the case. Frankly, I would enjoy a chance to give the police a piece of my mind about the whole business."

Taken aback, Giuliana almost laughed. "Well, I guess now's your chance. Since this is just information gathering, we could meet in town for a coffee instead of at the station. The sooner, the better, as far as I'm concerned, but . . ."

"I was leaving in ten minutes anyway to do some errands downtown, so I could meet you for coffee at . . . well, to be safe, let's say ten thirty. The weather's good, so how about the terrace at the Casino? I'll get us a table under the trees."

"Thank you. See you there."

Now that was a forceful woman, Giuliana thought with amusement as she hung up. Not everyone contacted by the police was cautious or intimidated, but this was the first time someone had taken an interview request right out of her hands and reserved a table for it.

The Casino, a large and imposing building fronted by Doric columns, was not for gambling. Instead, it housed a restaurant and a concert hall that was home to Bern's symphony orchestra. There *was* gambling in the city, but it took place at "the Spa." Like the Casino that was no casino, the Spa was not a spa. Tourists found this confusing—locals didn't give it a second thought.

A waiter escorted Giuliana to a table in a far corner of the Casino garden. The woman seated there didn't let the young man escape until she and Giuliana had ordered coffee. Then she extended a hand to Giuliana. "Ursula Kellenberger. I'm so glad we're going to talk."

As they shook hands, Giuliana admired the woman's clothes. "What a magnificent jacket," she said, drinking in the unlikely but perfect mix of colors and flowing patterns in the fabric. "If I tried to describe it, it would sound over-the-top, but it's beautiful."

Kellenberger smiled and patted Giuliana's hand. "Thanks. Occasionally something I weave does come out a bit much, but this one worked. Now, let me ask you a question before we talk about Exit. Do you know a policeman called Donatelli?"

Oh, no, thought Giuliana. She cleared her throat. "Yes, he's a colleague of mine."

"It's an odd coincidence, that's all. He called my husband yesterday, wanting to talk about a suicide from years ago, and today you call me about one of *your* cases."

"He's a good man," Giuliana said. "I hope you'll be able to help him." There! She hadn't said anything that could spring back and smack her in the face. She moved the conversation quickly on. "Let me start with my questions, and then you can tell me what we're getting wrong in the Seiler case. Essentially, I'd like to know how assisted suicide is correctly carried out. But first, can you explain how you get assigned to an Exit member and what your work with that person involves?"

Their coffees arrived, accompanied by a small silver pitcher of thick cream and two homemade almond macaroons resting on their own tiny plate. There was a pause as both women added cream to their cups, stirred, sipped, and gave small, satisfied sighs.

Then Kellenberger leaned forward. "An Exit member contacts the main office in Zürich in writing to say they think the time has come for an assisted suicide: a *Freitod*. The request has to be accompanied by all the proper medical paperwork, attesting to a terminal illness, terrible pain or other unendurable symptoms, or a disability that has become too difficult to live with anymore. The person has to be able to take the drug themselves, except in very special circumstances, like paralysis, and they have to understand exactly what's going on."

Giuliana knew how important this part was. It was what made a Freitod so difficult in a case of mental deterioration like Werner Allemann's. How could someone suffering from dementia demonstrate that they knew what they were doing?

Ursula Kellenberger gazed at Giuliana, eyebrows raised as if checking that she was following. "The administrators in the Zürich main office make sure the client's file is complete, and then they circulate the information among several assistants. If I'm the first to say yes to the case, I get the assignment. I call the person, make an appointment for us to talk, and the process begins."

Giuliana's coffee cooled as she took notes. She'd read much of this online, but hearing the steps described was so much better. "How long does your part usually take?"

Kellenberger bit into one of the macaroons, took a swallow of coffee, and said, "That varies a lot. Usually, I visit the person, often with the spouse and children there, so we can talk about what's going to happen; we may meet more than once. When the time comes, I bring the sodium pentobarbital to the person's home, usually in a form to be taken by mouth. Then I witness the suicide, which takes a few minutes—though it's less if the person injects themselves with the drug instead—and deal with the aftermath. Sometimes, the client's doctor calls in the prescription for the drug, and someone with power of attorney picks it up. But that's less common."

"And after the death?"

"That's a vital part. Once the people around the deathbed can handle outsiders, I phone the police and report a Freitod. Then I wait with the body until the police, the district attorney's representative, and the medical examiner are satisfied with the paperwork and the situation as a whole. That can take several hours. Sometimes the family asks me to stay until the undertaker arrives. Once I have the approval of the public prosecutor and it looks like the family doesn't need me anymore, I go home."

"A difficult job," Giuliana said. She was trying to imagine if she herself could cope with it.

Kellenberger shrugged. "Each case is different, but they're all emotional. It's nowhere near as hard as what you have to do, telling family members about accidents or murders."

"Yes, that's tough, but it doesn't happen more than once or twice a year," Giuliana said. "So, what are the criteria for using Exit?"

"Aha," said Kellenberger, "now you're getting to the heart of our problem. The law says that assisted suicide is permitted for people who are not acting on impulse but have shown a persistent desire to die and have not been influenced by someone else. Most cases seem quite obvious, but how can you really know whether someone has been nudged by a husband or wife or an adult child?"

Giuliana pounced on this. "Do you often have your doubts?"

Kellenberger leaned forward. "Almost never," she said vehemently. "I started helping Exit over ten years ago, and I take on one or two clients a month, and in all that time, I've never had the feeling that I should halt a death. But I'm trying to be honest with you. I mean, if a person has been ill for a long time, how can anyone know what kind of 'undue influence' may have been going on? Families are complicated. There can be turmoil seething under the surface, and sometimes it's well hidden."

Giuliana leaned back in her chair. She was thinking about her parents' decision to sign up for Exit and her brother's shocked response. "What about people with dementia?"

Kellenberger met Giuliana's eyes over the rim of her cup. "Did you know that dementia is now the third most common cause of death in Switzerland, after heart failure and cancer?"

"What a horrible thought!"

"Exactly." The older woman frowned and shook her head. "And you say that from the viewpoint of your forties. My husband and I are in our late sixties, so just imagine how the idea haunts *us*. It's a big problem for Exit, too. How can someone who's signed up for assisted suicide make sure they take action before it's too late?"

This was exactly what Giuliana wanted to hear. "But can someone with dementia still use Exit?"

"Yes. Or I guess I have to say, 'Yes, but.' The best possible scenario is that the person contacts us as soon as they're diagnosed and makes their wishes clear. Then we have time to plan what to do when the right moment arrives. It's often too much responsibility for the spouse alone, so we help the client pick friends and family members who will work together to keep an eye on the progress of the disease. Sometimes we assist with that, too."

Giuliana absently finished her cold coffee. She'd had no idea that Exit got so involved. It would have made all the difference to Ruth. "Please go on."

"Determining when the client is still in their right mind but losing enough ground every day that there's only a short time before it's too late—that's very hard. Family doctors can play a role if they're willing, but it's hugely problematic. I think during the next ten years, there will have to be new laws to deal with this situation in a more satisfactory way."

"Which brings us to the matter of Ruth Seiler, doesn't it?" Giuliana said. "Who didn't deal with *anything* the right way."

She was expecting the other woman to launch into a diatribe at this point. But Ursula Kellenberger merely sat back in her chair, her arms folded. Giuliana felt the breeze on the back of her neck; she listened to the Aare rushing under the Kirchenfeld Bridge. The sun filtering through the trees fell in patches on the table. One of the Münster bells rang the hour, and she felt the peace of the moment settle around her.

Perhaps Ursula Kellenberger felt it, too, because when she spoke, she was calm and deliberate. "I don't like the way the news has sensationalized this case, trying to create controversy and force people to take sides. However, I don't have much sympathy for this woman, either. Dementia is a relatively slow disease, and Werner Allemann had plenty of time to sign up for one of the Freitod services or, at the very least, to write down what kind of care he wanted. He was a successful businessman, not some farmhand living in a mountain village; he knew how the system worked. If he didn't take any action, I think it's safe to assume he wanted to die a natural death, no matter what his wife says now."

Giuliana stayed silent. She wanted to hear what else Kellenberger had to say.

"I believe very strongly in assisted suicide," the older woman continued, "otherwise I wouldn't do what I do, but I'm not blind to its dangers. Switzerland has had a more liberal policy than other countries for years, but slowly, the rest of Europe and some parts of the US are catching up with us. Cases like this business with Seiler give what we do a bad name; they could undo all that progress."

Giuliana ate her macaroon as she listened. It was a perfect blend of crunchy and chewy. Swallowing, she said, "But isn't it also possible that the publicity will get people thinking about the problem and persuade them to push for better solutions?"

"Controversy tends to bring out the crazies," the other woman answered, "and they scare the sensible people away. At least, that's what I've observed. But maybe you're right. I hope so because the law definitely needs to change. Maybe for people who don't want to live out their lives with dementia, a written statement could become enough to request a Freitod, with the time of death to be decided by some independent person who is not the patient's heir. But my point is there have to be *laws*, not chaos. Otherwise, we end up in a dystopia where people feel justified in knocking off inconvenient invalids and difficult old folks."

Giuliana found Kellenberger's words so compelling that she thought she'd ask Rosmarie about calling her to testify for the prosecution. She said to Kellenberger, "As a homicide detective, I'm not in favor of a society that treats death lightly, either."

"That makes sense. Thanks for listening to me rant. I hope I've been helpful."

"You didn't come close to ranting," Giuliana told her. "Thank *you* for talking to me. I think we're done as far as the Seiler case is concerned, but if you have time, I'd love to ask you one more question, just out of pure curiosity."

"Of course," said the older woman, although she looked like she was steeling herself for something unpleasant.

Giuliana was about to take a step into what should have been Renzo's territory. She wasn't quite sure why she was asking, except that she was intrigued. "I read that you and your husband used to live in the Münster's tower apartment. What was that like?"

"Oh, thank God," Kellenberger said with a relieved laugh. "I thought you were going to ask me something gruesome. You wouldn't believe how many people are eager to hear details about death. I guess you've seen too many corpses to ask questions like that."

"Unpleasant, isn't it?" said Giuliana. "After a few drinks, people at parties ask me stuff like that, too. It's hard not to be rude."

The older woman grinned and held out her hand for a second handshake. "Call me Ursula, why don't you?" Then she went on. "Well,

I'll tell you about living in the tower. The view was spectacular, and I got used to the smallness of the apartment. Even going up and down all those stairs became normal. But dealing with the tower visitors—now *that* got boring. Answering the same questions over and over and making sure they didn't do anything dangerous. We never anticipated what it would be like to live there with the restoration going on, either. Scaffolding all around the tower—and the workers' break room was above our heads."

Giuliana pulled a face; she would have hated the lack of privacy. "What made you apply for the job?"

Ursula rolled her eyes, but her smile was tolerant. "Hans-Peter, my husband, writes books about the Protestant Reformation in Switzerland. When he heard that the church council was looking for new tenants, he thought it would be an adventure. In many ways, it was, but I'm glad we only stayed two-and-a-half years. Once we left, the apartment was taken over by the builders. And after that, the rooms were turned into event spaces. They can be rented for dinners and parties— by healthy people with very fit guests!"

Giuliana laughed. Thanks to Renzo, she knew why the Kellenbergers had left the apartment after two-and-a-half years, but she wouldn't get into that. She'd already come too close to stepping on Renzo's toes.

She waved over a nearby waiter, paid the bill, and was about to get up when Ursula leaned across the table. "Could you pass something on to your colleague, please?"

Giuliana's heart sank. Was she going to have to mention this discussion to Renzo after all? She could hardly refuse to pass on a message.

"I'm sure you know we were discussing the death of a woman who jumped off the Münster tower fifteen years ago. I believe he's planning to investigate her suicide again. My husband told Herr Donatelli how astonished he was that Katica would kill herself. Because of her children—we were both shocked by that. After she died, I thought a lot about why she might have done it, and your colleague's visit brought that back. In retrospect, I don't think her killing herself is quite so surprising. Not that I experienced her as depressed, but sometimes she seemed . . . overwrought. I used the word 'fey' when I described her to your colleague, but . . . there was something almost *feverish* about her, too. Unstable. I only got to know her after she started leaving Zora while she . . . went off, and a lot of that time, she was pregnant, so perhaps I got a distorted impression of her. Anyway, I should have said all this to Herr Donatelli."

Giuliana typed a few notes into her phone: "overwrought," "fey," "feverish," and "unstable." Now she said, hopefully, "This seems important. I think it would be better for you to tell him yourself."

"Oh, it's no big deal. You can let him know next time you see him, can't you?" She took a deep breath as if relieved to have it off her chest. "Not that I'd mind having Herr Donatelli visit again." She raised her eyebrows. "He's really something, isn't he? If I were forty years younger . . . And I didn't get any gay vibes, either."

Giuliana couldn't help smiling. "No, he's definitely straight!"

The older woman gathered up her handbag and the beautiful woven jacket draped over the back of the chair. "Ah well, those were the days." She held out her hand to Giuliana again. "I enjoyed talking to you. Let me know if I can be of any more help."

"I will," Giuliana told her, shaking her hand warmly. "And thanks again."

She watched Ursula Kellenberger walk away toward Casino-platz. Now she was going to have to tell Renzo about interviewing one of his witnesses, and he was bound to resent her sticking her nose in. Why the hell had she called Ursula Kellenberger instead of one of the other seven Exit people? She could hardly explain it to herself, so how on earth was she going to explain it to Renzo? It wasn't like her to do something so irrational.

But, then, she thought wryly, *is there* anything *rational about my relationship with Renzo?*

17

Renzo's döner kebab was perfect. Thin, juicy slices of lamb; lettuce, tomato, and shredded cabbage; yogurt sauce that was not too spicy; and all of it wrapped in yeasty, chewy flatbread. He leaned forward over the tiny stand-up table on the terrace in front of the kebab stand and took another bite. Grated lettuce fell onto the paper napkin he'd spread on the table, and sauce ran down his wrist. He set the kebab onto his makeshift plate and reached for another napkin from the stack on the table to wipe his hand. He chewed, swallowed, and took a swig of alcohol-free beer. Even that tasted good to him today.

Denis was standing across from him, battling one-handed with his own kebab. "Tell me, is there any possibility Zora's mother might have been murdered?"

Renzo still wasn't ready to talk to anyone about that. He thought he'd put Denis off earlier, but apparently not. He needed to shut this down.

"Well?"

Renzo shook his head. "I understand this is personal for you because you care about Zora, but I'm not going to talk to you about it. You shouldn't have been there today. I already told you that. Zora let you in, so I didn't throw you out. You've heard information that you shouldn't have. It would be completely unprofessional to discuss it with you any further." Denis opened his mouth to argue, but Renzo went on. "I would never insult you by telling you how to make glass, so don't tell me how to do my job, either."

Denis took another bite of kebab and avoided Renzo's eye. The two of them ate in silence until they'd finished their meal. When Denis looked at Renzo, his expression was resigned. "I'm sorry, I won't ask again. But is there anything I can do to help Zora?"

"Zora's not in any trouble, although I'm sure she's worried about Goran. I think all you can do is be her friend."

"What about Goran?" Denis asked. "I really don't think he meant to kill me. He was just . . . being fifteen, you know? There's no way I'm going to accuse him of anything. I've already caused that family enough trouble."

All these years later, Denis was still thinking about the unlocked door. Renzo longed to reassure him, but he'd decided not to mention the tower door until he knew more about who'd had keys that night. "That's your right," Renzo told him. "But, as I told you, the boy committed a crime no matter what you do. Still, I'll make your feelings about that clear when Goran has his official police interview." Renzo wiped his hands. "Now, I need to talk to Lovro and Ivana at their shop— what's it called again?"

"The Golden Goat," Denis told him. "Named after the symbol of Istria, where they're from."

"Right," said Renzo. He took in Denis's cut and bruised face, the stitches on his forehead, one arm in a cast, and the other scraped to bits. And didn't he have a cracked rib or two as well? "Let me take you home now so you can get some rest."

"It was nice of you to buy me lunch, especially when I've been such a pain in the ass. Thank you." Denis held out his hand, and Renzo shook it. The youngster was cocky, but Renzo liked him. "As for dropping me off," Denis went on, "could you leave me at the rose garden? You'll go right past it on the way to the Matte."

"Sure," said Renzo, "although I still think you should go lie on a sofa at your grandparents' place and let them wait on you."

Renzo watched Denis walk away from the car and disappear through an opening in the stone wall around the Rosengarten, a beautiful park with a superb view of the city. Denis raised his hand in farewell, and Renzo stuck an arm out of the car window to wave back. He'd pulled up on a quiet side street to let Denis out, and it was as good a place as any for a phone call to the Horvats' shop in the Matte.

"Golden Goat," said a man's voice.

"Is this Lovro Horvat?"

"Yes. How can I help you?" The man's German was accented, but he sounded comfortable with the language. Renzo was sorry for what was coming next.

"Herr Horvat, I'm with the police. I'd like to talk to you about your son, Goran."

Lovro made a gulping noise. "My God, what's wrong?"

"Don't worry; Goran isn't hurt. I saw him having lunch at his sister's apartment about an hour ago, and both of them were fine. This is about something that happened on Tuesday afternoon when your son deliberately shook a scaffold and made the man working on it fall to the floor. It was a long way down: the man could have been killed."

"You're saying the boy . . . attacked someone?" His voice shook. "The workman . . . is he all right?"

"He's out of the hospital," Renzo said. "He has a great deal of bruising, some cuts, and a broken wrist."

"Thank God for that. I guess he wants to . . . to take legal action. We'll have to—"

Renzo interrupted. "I'd like to speak with you and your wife as soon as possible. May I come by this afternoon?"

"Yes. It's a good time now, after lunch. You know where we are?"

"Yes. I'll be there at about two."

During the five minutes it took Renzo to drive to the Horvats' shop, he considered what he wanted out of the interview. Goran's parents had to be told what the boy had done, but any uniformed officer could have handled that. What Renzo really wanted was to find out more about Katica and the months leading to her death. He thought about the snapshot Zora had shown him of the happy family. Within weeks of that picture being taken, Katica had either killed herself or someone had gotten rid of her. Both her cuckolded husband and the so-called best friend who'd married him made good suspects. But the investigating detective at the time, Grossenbacher, had known about Katica's affair and still decided it was a suicide.

Renzo had to admit that he still didn't know what he thought, and he needed to be careful not to let his desire to solve a fifteen-year-old murder trample on his common sense. *Just treat this like any new investigation,* he told himself. *Ask questions and analyze the answers; don't jump to conclusions.*

When he got to the Matte, he had to park illegally, so he stuck a small sign on the Fiat's dashboard that read "Police Business" and wrote his badge and cell phone numbers on it. Then he walked a block to the Golden Goat.

The sidewalk in front of the shop was swept. Inside, along a shelf spanning the length of the front window, was a row of flowering plants, and among the plants stood a noble-looking, life-size goat carved from wood and painted gold. Renzo grinned to see that the goat was endowed with a long beard, massive horns, a dignified expression—and a large pair of testicles. The guardian spirit of the shop, he assumed.

Looking up from the goat, he realized that a middle-aged man and woman, both gray-haired and solidly built, were watching him from behind the shop counter. The woman's expression was as aloof as the goat's. The man looked worried, and he was already heading for the door. The bell jingled, and Renzo was ushered inside.

Once Horvat closed the door, Renzo held out his hand. "Herr Horvat," he said politely. "Renzo Donatelli. Thanks for seeing me." He turned to shake hands with the man's wife, who touched her palm to his and let him give it a single squeeze before folding her hands tightly at her waist. "Frau Horvat," Renzo said.

"Please come out to the garden with me. Ivana will stay here to mind the shop." Renzo followed Horvat out through an office behind the store that led into a crammed but neatly organized storage room. It opened onto a small back porch. Horvat quietly closed the door they'd come through, and Renzo saw that a few steps led down from the porch to a stone terrace with chairs pulled up to a table holding two glasses and a pitcher of what looked like milky iced coffee. Beyond the terrace was a pocket-sized garden of grass and shrubs made private by a fence on the street side and the walls of adjacent buildings; a single bed of bright summer flowers had been planted in the middle of the lawn.

Horvat led Renzo down the porch steps to one of the chairs, and both men sat. Renzo was delighted to be able to talk to Goran's father and stepmother separately without having to force them apart. It seemed as though Horvat, too, wanted privacy.

"Would you like some cold coffee?" he asked Renzo. Renzo nodded, so Horvat filled both glasses. "Can you first tell me again what Goran did? I can't understand it. We've never had any trouble with him. Maybe skipping school now and then or staying out later than he should, but nothing... nothing violent." He slumped in his chair, shaking his head.

"I'll start by telling you that the young man Goran attacked is Denis Kellenberger, who used to be a friend of your daughter Zora's. You probably remember him." Renzo watched as Horvat's face turned pale and his mouth opened. "Denis is now a glassmaker who works in the Münster. Goran told me he never meant for Denis to fall, but it was definitely an attack, not a prank. Goran yelled at Denis that he was a murderer. He was talking about the role he believed Denis played in the death of your first wife."

Lovro Horvat put his hands over his eyes and leaned forward with his elbows on the table. There was a long pause, which Renzo was in no hurry to fill.

"Goran was a baby when his mother died." Horvat shook his head. "He never talks about her. Where did this craziness come from? From his sister? My God, did *Zora* make him do this?"

Renzo found himself wanting to defend Zora but didn't. "I know Zora got very angry with Denis when he was at her mother's funeral meal," was all he said.

"Yes, because Denis left the tower door unlocked. But it wasn't fair to blame a ten-year-old boy for something like that. I probably said some things that I shouldn't have, but that was long ago." His voice rose. "I had no idea that Zora... Is she obsessed with this Kellenberger? How could she tell her brother to attack someone?"

Renzo left these rhetorical questions untouched. "If Goran was only a baby, how does he know so much about what happened at the funeral and the meal afterwards?"

"The Kellenbergers were with all the friends who came back here with us after the church service for some food, and everyone saw Zora hurl herself at Denis. And they talked about it afterward. My God, how they all talked. For years, they replayed Zora's attack on the boy." Lovro shook his head. "People love stories, and the more often they're told, the more dramatic they become. I suppose, growing up, Goran must have heard the whole tale quite a few times." Lovro's gaze wandered around the garden, coming to rest on the colorful flowers in the center. "And it's possible that Ivana... his stepmother may have talked to him about it. She's his mother in all but blood, you know. She raised him, and she adores him."

Lovro seemed to come out of a reverie. He looked at Renzo, his body tense. "So, what's going to happen? Will we have to get a lawyer?" The shopkeeper said this as he might have said, "Will I have to cut off an arm?"

This was yet another difference between the rich and the rest of society, Renzo reflected. For the rich, a lawyer was someone you hired, like a plumber, to fix something; for normal people, a lawyer was distant and intimidating, not to mention ludicrously expensive.

"Denis Kellenberger told me today that he won't press charges, and I don't think he'll change his mind. Some valuable glass was broken when Denis fell, but I've been assured by the glass master that it can be easily fixed, so that shouldn't be a problem either. As for us, the police, I mean—this is a crime, but it's also a first offense committed by a minor, so I will downplay it as much as I can. Because of his age, nothing will appear on his public record. Still, Goran will have to appear before a judge. You and Frau Horvat will be there, and so will I, and—we'll have to see what happens."

"But . . . his punishment?" Lovro's eyes were pleading. "Will it be a large fine? Prison?"

"Herr Horvat," Renzo told him, "your son attacked someone, and he's old enough and smart enough to understand that actions have consequences. Whatever he *meant* to do, he endangered a life in a deliberate assault, which is a serious offense, and a judge will decide his punishment." Lovro swallowed. "However, I doubt he'll be sentenced to juvenile detention. We'll have to wait and see."

Horvat was hunched forward, his hands intertwined on the table. He looked utterly miserable.

Renzo leaned back in his chair and drained his iced coffee. Now it was time to move on to his real questions. "It would help me to present Goran's case if I understood his mother's death. Could you tell me about it? And can you think of any reason why her suicide would be on your son's mind at the moment?" He knew the answer to the second question already but was curious to hear Lovro Horvat's opinion.

Horvat absently rolled his empty glass back and forth between his palms. He was silent for so long that Renzo, usually patient, began to wonder if he needed to repeat his question.

But then Horvat met his eyes. "I have asked myself so many times—why did she do it? Even now, fifteen years later, that question appears from nowhere in my brain, and I'm driven to think through it all again. At the time, I must have telephoned thirty, maybe fifty people in Bern's Croatian community to tell them about her death and ask if they had any idea why she'd done it."

"And did you get any answers?" The man could not have chosen a better way of demonstrating his role as a lost and grief-stricken husband, Renzo thought. Anyone the police interviewed who'd received one of these broken phone calls—which sounded like half the Croatians in Bern—would want to spring to Lovro's defense.

"No one had any idea. There was only one thing... but really, it was nothing."

"Go on," said Renzo.

"About a week before Katica died, she had a party to show off Goran to some friends, maybe eight women. Zora and Ivana helped her with the food. Goran was about six weeks old. I wasn't there; some of the husbands took me out to eat so we could leave the women to themselves. Afterward, there was... something about her. I don't know—I thought maybe there had been an argument. Perhaps one of the women said something to offend her. She insisted all was well, so I forgot about it, but when she died, I called those women first. Then... well, once I started asking people for reasons, I couldn't stop. I guess I went a bit crazy, but I was..." He paused. "The police talked about her having postpartum depression."

"Did you agree?"

He shook his head. "I think they were just offering me some sort of explanation. And they had to write *something* down, didn't they? Katica had some fits of crying after Goran was born, but the midwife said that was completely normal, that it happened to almost all new mothers."

Renzo thought about Fränzi's state of mind after Angelo had been born. She'd been very anxious, not so much about caring for her son as having lost her freedom. It had probably lasted three weeks or so, he thought, not six.

"We laughed about it, actually. Zora was born five months after we'd moved to Switzerland, and we were so stressed about our new lives here that we decided we wouldn't have noticed any... what words did the midwife use? Baby blues, that's it. We decided they must have disappeared in our general... franticness." He gave a tiny smile. "Is that a word?"

"I'd use it." Renzo smiled back, thinking of his own parents, who had come alone from Italy and met in Bern. Difficult, for sure, but not like leaving a country that had been at war, knowing it might be years before you could get back. And Italian was, after all, one of Switzerland's four national languages, unlike Croatian. "You said the crying didn't last."

"Not that I could see. Katica started getting more sleep as Goran settled, and then it was just . . . well, the normal pressures of work and family. At least, that's what I thought. But there must have been something. God. I'll never stop wondering."

"What about this party, then?" Renzo was intrigued, particularly by the fact that Ivana had been there. "What did the women say?"

"They insisted there was nothing. All of them. Even Ivana, whom I've known since before I knew Katica." That was interesting, thought Renzo. "She said it was a lovely party, and everyone was very kind to each other and to Katica." He shrugged. "I had to accept that my impression was wrong."

If the man knew more about his wife's death—or if he had caused it himself—he was a good liar, Renzo thought. And privately, he was sure that if something *had* happened at the party, the women would have been perfectly capable of closing ranks to lie to Lovro about it. And lie to the police, too, if they'd asked about the party, which Renzo doubted.

Renzo had seen many times how skilled people could be at lying, especially if they were also lying to themselves. And if there was something a man would lie to himself about, it was his wife's fidelity. Horvat spoke now as if he'd known nothing about it. Did Renzo want to be the person who revealed it to him? Suppose, in the end, it turned out there *was* no lover. He needed to talk to this Ben Schweizer and make absolutely sure the story was true. Still, he could ask a general question about infidelity and see how Lovro answered that.

He was on the verge of bringing it up when Lovro poured them more iced coffee. "You also asked me whether anything happened recently to upset Goran. I'd say no, but—well, the boy is fifteen. Six months ago, all he wanted to do was help me in the store, and now he acts like everything is too much effort, even saying goodbye in the mornings." Lovro sighed heavily, and Renzo decided the man was older than he'd first thought, probably over fifty: the backs of his hands had a few age spots, and his shoulders were rounded. "I don't know what's going on in Goran's head, and I don't think Ivana does either. That's why I thought maybe Zora was somehow behind this . . . craziness."

This time, Renzo wasn't going to let it go. "Does your daughter have a history of inciting her younger brother to do violent things?"

"No, of course not," Horvat answered angrily. Then he must have realized how odd that sounded, given what he'd just said. "No, she doesn't. But she's—" He paused, shaking his head. "It's not something I want to go into."

Renzo pushed harder. "When did Zora move to her own place?"

Horvat pressed his lips together. Instead of answering the question directly, he said, "I guess you know that I married Ivana not long after Katica's death. Before Katica died, Ivana was like an aunt to Zora. She worked hospital shifts as a nurse, but she was often here, too. After Katica died, I honestly don't know when she slept. She kept her nursing job, but she was also here helping in the shop. She did most of the cooking for our family and, above all, took care of Goran. Zora didn't like it. They had . . . never warmed to each other."

Renzo could understand that. First, the poor child loses her mother, and then she starts losing her father to a woman she's never liked. He remembered the adoration on Zora's face as she gazed up at her baby brother in the photo and wondered if she'd felt like she was losing him, too.

"Ivana tried to win her over," Horvat went on, "but sometimes she lost her temper with the girl, especially when Zora claimed to know better than she did what was good for Goran. Zora . . . she didn't throw teenage tantrums. But at fifteen, during her first year of *Gymnasium*, she left our shop and started working at a grocery store near her school. Whenever she wasn't in class or studying, she was working, and by sixteen, she'd found a way to move into a hostel for teenage girls who . . . needed to leave home. That hurt. But . . . well, it made things much easier for Ivana. And Zora did come home regularly to eat meals with us and spend time with Goran. She still does."

Renzo thought about how often he still sought refuge with his family, turning especially to his mother. She and his siblings had helped him unstintingly since the separation from his wife. At fifteen, he would never have contemplated leaving home, except for about three minutes, maybe, if his mother yelled at him. His heart ached for Zora.

"So, Zora moved out of your apartment when she was sixteen and Goran was six. Yet you still think she's been a bad influence on her brother?"

"Ivana . . ." Horvat said. Then he looked away, a combination of irritation and shame on his face. Renzo could read it loud and clear: it was Zora's stepmother who blamed Goran's failings on his sister, and Lovro had followed, maybe against his better judgment.

Renzo decided to push back; he would push Ivana, too, if necessary. He wanted to understand the dynamics of this family. Katica's death might be fifteen years behind them, but police work—and his own life—had shown him that when it came to the burdens of guilt, hurt, and rage that families carried with them, fifteen years was no time at all.

"As I told you," Renzo said, his tone conversational, "I was in Zora's apartment this morning. I saw the bedroom she has set up for Goran, and she was making lunch for him as if she did it often. It must hurt your wife's feelings that he enjoys spending time with his sister, especially if she doesn't approve of Zora." Renzo paused. "Speaking of approval, was Zora the only one who was upset when you married Ivana? I'd have thought a lot of the Croatian community might have had a problem with that."

Horvat scraped his chair back quickly, stood, and stalked away from the table. In the enclosed garden, he couldn't go far, but he went to the high gate that led into the alley running along the side of the building and held onto it with both hands. His back, turned to Renzo, was rigid with his effort to control himself. Watching him, Renzo added, "It has occurred to me that maybe your first wife killed herself because she found out you were having an affair with her best friend. If Zora knew *that*, it might explain—"

"What?" Horvat wheeled around to face him. Renzo expected fury on his face, but instead, he only saw puzzlement. Zora's father walked back to the table and stood over Renzo, who kept his face impassive. "You think I was having an affair with Ivana before Katica died? That's..." He shook his head as though baffled by the possibility. Then he sat back down and clasped his chin in his hands. His eyes were red-rimmed; he looked exhausted.

"Katica was eleven years younger than me. I knew her when she was a child, then met her again when I got back from the war and fell in love with her. I married her when she was nineteen and lost her when she was twenty-nine. I was in love with her all that time, even when she exasperated me. I'm a . . . well, I guess you could say I have a dark side. But Katica was full of light. Not all the time—she could be moody—but her joyful side is what I remember. Laughing, singing, teasing me, planning for the future, claiming happiness as . . . as her right, and enjoying every moment of it. I felt lucky to have as much of her as I did, and I would never have jeopardized that by sleeping with another woman. Never."

Was this the truth? Renzo thought perhaps it was, although he'd continue to investigate the possibility of the affair. It must've been exhausting, living with a woman as intense as Katica. Lovro might have sought comfort and relief in the arms of a woman who didn't expect so much. And Lovro's declaration of love didn't make him innocent. In fact, if he'd known about Katica's affair, it made it more likely that he'd reacted violently.

His next question was going to hurt. "Okay, you weren't having an affair; I'll take your word for it. But what about your beautiful young wife? Was she seeing another man?"

Horvat's face grew red, and Renzo could see his jaw working. Finally, he spoke, his voice low and broken. "How can you *suggest* such a thing? It's an insult to her memory." Tears were welling in his eyes. "She was a loving wife and a moral person. A good Catholic, too. I refuse to—" He broke off, stood, and walked away again, pulling a handkerchief from his pocket.

It was time to end the interview. Horvat looked bone weary and probably had hours more work to do before the shop closed that evening. Renzo was sure that some of what the man had said was lies, but he needed to think it all through before deciding what information to question. This was enough for now.

"I'd like to speak to Frau Horvat before I leave," Renzo said. "Let me give you my contact information." He got one of his cards out of his shirt pocket. "Send me an email so I have your address, and I'll let you know when to bring Goran in."

Horvat looked blankly at Renzo's business card. "You spoke to my son today. Do *you* understand why he did this thing?"

"No, I don't," Renzo said, which was mostly true. Could he explain why Goran's fear that he might not be Lovro's son had triggered him to attack Denis? No, he didn't get it either. If anything, it seemed like a cry for help. But what did Renzo know about parenting a fifteen-year-old? Angelo was only six.

Horvat said quietly, "Ivana and I . . . we don't talk about Katica with each other or the children. We never have. Maybe we should."

Imagine growing up without hearing a word about your real mother. It must have been worse for Zora—her family pretending that her mother had never existed. No wonder she'd left. Presumably, *she* talked to her brother about Katica. Perhaps, in that limited sense, she was responsible for Goran's turmoil. But surely sharing memories of their mother was ultimately healthy—for both of them.

Renzo said none of this. Instead, he stood and shook Horvat's hand. "Thank you for your time. Please send Frau Horvat out."

He thought of the dumpy woman with the lined face whom he'd met in the shop and then pictured her predecessor: Lovro Horvat's joyful teenage bride, Denis Kellenberger's floaty queen, Zora's beautiful, loving mother. Poor Ivana, he thought. Imagine trying to fill Katica Horvat's fairy slippers.

18

As a gardener for the city, Zora weeded, watered, and cultivated plants in all of Bern's green spaces, from its playgrounds to the massive concrete tubs of flowers that adorned its sidewalks and squares until the first frost. But the cemeteries were her favorite places to work. Planting English daisies in the spring, ageratum in the early summer, and heather in the late fall on each grave and around each urn and then tending these miniature gardens all year round: this made her happy.

Today, she was working in Schosshalde, which was only a ten-minute walk from her apartment, and she'd been assigned to tidy a wooded walk lined with urns. Ivy covered the ground beside the curving path, narrow silver markers by each urn showed the names of the dead, and cube-shaped stone stands displayed gifts from visitors. As Zora weeded and clipped, she admired the offerings, mostly small flowering plants in terracotta pots, but also the occasional silk flower arrangement or cherub statuette.

Straightening up from a cluster of small shrubs whose leaves she'd been checking for discoloration, she noticed a grave adorned with a collection of Lego knights. That was new! She read the name on the marker—Erna Bühler—and saw that she'd died in her eighties. A gift from a great-grandchild, maybe?

She imagined telling Denis about the Lego figures, and that brought her up short. She hadn't seen or thought about Denis in fifteen years, and now she was talking to him in her head? But it was true; she couldn't get this new, grown-up version of Denis out of her mind. He looked so different. She supposed she no longer looked like the ten-year-old he'd known either, but still. The Denis who'd been her friend had been as skinny as a piece of paper and talked in a squeaky voice. Now, he had broad shoulders and thick hair halfway down his back, and he looked . . . well, hot. Who'd have expected him to turn out hand-some? And taller than her own five feet eleven and a half inches?

Her mind abandoned Denis to worry about Goran again. If only he'd talked to her about what he'd heard instead of attacking Denis. It made no sense on the face of it. Except—he'd wanted to lash out at someone, to hurt the person who'd messed up their family, and the true culprit, their mother, was gone while Denis was right there, a symbol of the Münster that had killed his mother. The more she thought about it, the more it made a twisted kind of sense.

Zora moved her knee pad further along the row of urns, coming to Franz Gnägi, 1925 to 2017. He never had any candles or plants on the stone square in front of his plaque; it was always empty. Perhaps there was a reason for that. Maybe he'd been a terrible husband and father. Or maybe he'd never had a family, and all his friends were dead. She'd given him an extra ageratum plant when she'd done the summer planting, and now the small cluster of soft purple stars stood out against the shiny-leaved box bushes that surrounded Herr Gnägi's space. She did a bit of trimming, her mind still on Goran and his anguished words that morning—that his mother was a whore and Tata wasn't his real father.

Would he insist on a paternity test? She could understand him wanting to know the truth. But if their father didn't know about the affair, he'd be shattered to learn of it now, especially from a son who might not be his—a son he adored. A jumble of painful possibilities churned in her head, although she moved automatically along the path, checking the ground for debris while the pruning shears in her gloved hands snipped and shaped.

A possible solution was taking shape. If a genetic test could identify Goran's father, it could also identify his sister. What if she could find a way to have her DNA and Goran's compared and prove they were full siblings? Wouldn't that set his mind at ease? And if they weren't—well, if they weren't, she'd have to tell Goran, and they'd decide together whether to talk to their father about it.

She wondered if their mother had known whose son Goran was. Zora remembered her parents being affectionate to one another, and they'd slept in a double bed, but what could she really know about their true feelings? She supposed her mother must have talked to Ivana about the affair. Personally, Zora had never been able to understand why the two women, one so cheerful and the other so glum, were such good friends, but she assumed it had something to do with their past in Croatia, as so many things in her parents' lives did.

She finished her work on the path for the day and stood up slowly before lifting her arms to stretch her back. Then she placed her shears on top of the pile of plant debris in her wheelbarrow and pushed it back down the path. After emptying it onto a compost pile, she'd go by the toolshed for a rake and a long pole with a net: the pond needed cleaning. In spite of everything seething away in her mind, she breathed in her surroundings—deep blue sky, sunlight falling through the canopy of trees, swaths of green dotted with gravestones and flowers, the drone of a lawnmower, and the smell of freshly cut grass.

As she tipped out the wheelbarrow, her thoughts moved on to the cop's question about her mother's suicide. And the possibility that it hadn't been a suicide at all.

It should have been horrible, the idea of her mother being murdered. But it wasn't. The more she allowed herself to dwell on the image of someone heaving her mother off the Münster tower, the stranger she felt: lighter, looser, unbound. Her eyes filled with tears, and she gave a sob.

She headed for the pond, which wasn't far from the toolshed, and sat down on one of the benches at its edge. She found tissues in the pocket of her blue overalls, blew her nose, and leaned her head over the back of the slatted wooden bench to stare up at the sky. A mother who'd been killed was a mother who hadn't abandoned her newborn son and ten-year-old daughter, a mother who'd loved them both with all the ferocity Zora knew she'd possessed and who would never have left them to grow up without her. Zora had gotten used to spending time almost every day trying to forgive her mother, even, sometimes, trying not to hate her. The possibility that she hadn't killed herself was ... it was glorious.

But could it be true? Had Majka ever said or done anything that hinted at her being in danger or having an enemy? Nothing came to mind. She couldn't even remember her mother being upset.

At that moment, staring at the sky, a scene from her childhood rose from the depths of her subconscious and presented itself fully formed in her brain. The intensity of it made her breathless.

She was coming down the stairs from the apartment above the shop, and she noticed her mother, very fat because of the baby in her stomach, holding a feather duster. She wasn't dusting anymore, though; she was leaning against the doorframe between the shop and the office and staring at Auntie Ivana, who was sitting at Father's big desk with the chair swiveled to face Majka.

"No, you can't," Ivana was saying. Something in her voice scared Zora. "It's something that can never be fixed. Or forgiven."

She wondered if Majka had broken something valuable with the feather duster that couldn't be glued together again. Not the beautiful golden goat in the window! Or the big round clock over the door between the shop and the office.

"I'd give anything to be able to—" her mother answered, her face pleading. But Ivana was shaking her head, her face as bleak as ever.

Zora clattered down the stairs and rushed into the office, interrupting what her mother had been about to say. "Mamica," she exclaimed, "did something happen to our goat?"

In her mind's eye, both women turned to look at her. Her mother's eyes filled with warmth, as they always did. Ivana's eyes weren't warm at all, but Zora never expected them to be. Auntie Ivana wasn't really her aunt, just a friend of her parents' from before the war, so she didn't feel *too* bad about not liking her. She just wished Ivana wasn't in their shop so often, making Majka sad, like she was doing now.

"The goat is fine, *srce*. Why shouldn't he be?" answered her mother, putting an arm around her. Then she jerked and made a funny noise. "Oof. The baby kicked. My little soccer player is practicing again. Want to touch him, my heart?"

The little film that had played in her memory broke off, and Zora swallowed, her chest tight. Had she touched Goran's tiny foot or knee or elbow as it moved under her mother's taut skin? She couldn't remember now. If only she could still feel her mother's arm around her.

Now she looked back on that snippet of conversation and knew without a doubt that the two women had not been talking about an object. Had Majka said or done something that she regretted and hoped could be put right again? Obviously, the affair couldn't be "fixed," nor could the baby's paternity if it was known to her mother. But it might not have been about an affair. They could have been talking about something to do with her father. Or—she was surprised that this hadn't occurred to her before—was it something to do with Ivana herself? Had her mother done something *to Ivana* that couldn't be fixed or forgiven?

And, if she had, why had they been such good friends?

Zora shook her head as if that would throw off her thoughts and fetched the tools she needed from the shed. After cleaning the pond, she still had to weed the row of English daisies and begonias that grew along the largest set of wall urns. She put her earbuds in and clicked on her beloved collection of Slavic Soul Party songs, turned it up loud, and grabbed the rake and net.

When the pond was as clean as she was going to get it and the wheelbarrow was full again, it was time for a cup of tea. She pulled wet leaves from between the tines of her rake, added them to the pile in the wheelbarrow, and set off back to the compost heap. As soon as she turned her music off, her mother's death flooded back into her mind.

Would it be silly to tell that good-looking cop about the conversation she'd remembered between her mother and Ivana? Denis seemed to know him pretty well—maybe she could ask his opinion. Maybe Denis could ask for the cop's advice about comparing her DNA with Goran's at the same time. She brightened at the idea of taking some action, then remembered that in all the upset, she hadn't asked Denis for his number.

She dumped the second load of compost and headed toward the break room, her mind returning yet again to the idea that her mother might have been murdered. She'd insisted to the cop that her father would never have hurt Majka. But Majka had been cheating on him. Was that what couldn't be "fixed or forgiven"? Or could it only be fixed by death?

No! She stopped on the path, clenching her fists. No, she was not going to think that way. Her father had not killed her mother—she might not be certain of much, but she knew that. And the possibility that her mother hadn't killed herself—the sense of relief and lightness it brought her—even that did not justify entertaining the horrific idea that her father had been the killer. That would unleash more pain than she could bear.

19

After waving goodbye to Renzo, Denis pulled out his phone. Because of his injuries, he was *krankgeschrieben* for at least a week, excused from his job by the hospital doctor. But for Denis, working with Nathan Winter on glassmaking projects was a joy, not a job, so he'd planned to ask Nathan for something special he could do while he was healing. His boss was bound to have a few one-handed tasks for him. At the very least, Denis could watch Nathan work, which was always an education and a pleasure.

But meeting Zora again had changed that plan. Now his only goal was to figure out the best way to see her again. After his check-up with the surgeon the following Wednesday, he'd think about going back to the glass studio, the Münster, or wherever Nathan needed him. But for now ...

For now, he reminded himself, he needed to call his mother. He still hadn't told her about his broken wrist. If he phoned while she was at work, the conversation would be short, which was good. Still, he stared at his cell for ages before dialing.

As usual, she didn't answer, and he didn't leave a message. Instead, she rang back five minutes later as he was walking toward the nearest bus stop. "Hello, Denis," she said. "Do you have any time this afternoon?"

"Hi, Mam," he answered, already cautious. "Some, yeah. Why?"

"There's renovation work going on in Läuferplatz, and the builders called us this morning. Looks like they've found some pieces of armor in what could be a grave. I'm here having a look; why don't you join me, and we'll take a walk."

Denis frowned. *You mean, why don't I come and stand around for half an hour until you can get away?* But he needed to see her—wanted to, as well, if he were honest with himself.

"Be there in about ten minutes," he said. The Rosengarten, where Renzo had dropped him off, was just across the Aare from Läuferplatz, the small cobblestone square where his mother was working. It was an easy walk through the rose garden, down a steep hill to the river, and across the medieval Untertor Bridge.

Anja Kellenberger worked for the city of Bern's *Denkmalpflege*, the Monument Preservation Office. Monuments, in this case, didn't just mean statues of men on horseback but all kinds of structures, particularly historic buildings. Her responsibilities occasionally intersected with the canton of Bern's archeological service, and Denis wondered if this particular find was one of his mother's little triumphs. A chance for her and her colleagues from the city to beat the canton to a significant find.

On his way to meet her, he thought about Zora and her family. Now that he was twenty-five, the knowledge that Zora's mother had had a daughter at nineteen and died at twenty-nine took on new meaning. His own mother had given birth to him out of wedlock at eighteen, and he understood why she'd passed him over to his grandparents to raise; he certainly couldn't imagine fathering a son at that age. Still, hearing Zora describe how her mother had made her feel so loved—that had hurt. At best, his mother made him feel—well, it was slightly better than tolerated, he supposed, but nothing like loved.

He walked slowly across the medieval bridge with its three large arches, glancing down into the swift-flowing Aare as he went. There were sometimes wakeboards fastened with elastic ropes to the lampposts on the bridge so people could bungee surf the river. He'd tried it a few times himself and not done too badly, but he'd never minded handing the board over to the next hopeful challenger. It wasn't really his thing. Today, swimmers' heads bobbed in the river further downstream, but no one was surfing.

In the distance, he could see the cluster of construction equipment half filling the Läuferplatz. Its well-loved statue of a medieval messenger, a *Läufer* in his doublet, hose, codpiece, and feathered cap, had been hidden in a protective cage. Right now, the backhoe wasn't running. Six men and one woman—his mother—were standing around a large hole in the ground, talking.

Denis knew better than to interrupt; instead, he circled the group and took a seat on a squat pillar where his mother would see him. Sure enough, she waved, then did a double take and put a hand over her mouth. It took him a second to realize she'd spotted how awful he looked, with his cast and beat-up face. He raised his right hand back to her with a weary smile. He'd explain it all soon enough.

This time it only took twelve minutes for her to finish what she was doing and head over. He tried to observe her in a new way as she approached, to see her as a forty-three-year-old woman. It was hard to do. All he could see was his Mam—a younger, darker-haired version of his grandmother. Still, she wasn't bad looking. He supposed a man her own age would *not* think of a middle-aged mom when he looked at her. *Of course not,* he told himself. A mother had always been the last thing she wanted to look like. Or be. He knew that better than anyone.

She reached him and gingerly touched the arm that wasn't in a cast. "My God," she said, "what happened to you? A bike accident?"

He leaned in and kissed her cheek. "I'm okay. I'll tell you about it. Let's go for that walk."

Although she still looked worried, she gave him one of her half smiles, affectionate and ironic at the same time. "We're all waiting for one of the canton's archeologists to arrive, so I've got twenty minutes."

They set off along the path by the Aare. They talked better when they were moving; it was easier than sitting across a table, meeting each other's eyes.

"It looks serious," she said. "Explain what happened." He recounted his fall off the scaffold and the operation, and she frowned. "Why would the Horvat boy do that?"

"I don't know," he said, "but I talked to him this morning, and he told me he was sorry." He went on to explain about Renzo coming to see him in the hospital and the way he'd gate-crashed Renzo's interview at Zora's apartment.

His mother shook her head. "It doesn't make sense, but I guess you can say that about lots of things fifteen-year-olds do." She shot him a smile.

They were passing the Längmuur playground now, where he'd spent hours as a boy. "Do you remember Zora from when I was younger?"

"I do. I came to see you once at the Münster when she was having dinner in the tower apartment, and we walked her home, so I remember her *and* her parents. You liked her a lot."

"She's a gardener for the city now," he told her, "and lives near Schosshalde cemetery. She does a lot of work there. She still has that amazing mass of hair, and she's almost as tall as I am."

His mother's smile turned warmer. "You still like her," she stated matter-of-factly. "You're going to see her again?"

"As soon as I can get up the courage to call her." The honesty of his answer surprised him as he said it, and it made his mother laugh—in a nice way.

"Good for you," she said. "I'm seeing someone, too."

Denis knew it was perfectly reasonable for his mother to have boyfriends, but his gut twisted anyway. *No details, Mam, please!* But he forced himself to ask, "Who is he?"

"He's French. A visiting scholar at the University of Fribourg working in medieval European history. Charles the Bold of Burgundy, mainly. We met at a conference." There was a pause in which Denis asked no further questions, so his mother changed the subject. "I haven't seen Ursula and Hans-Peter for a few weeks—they okay?"

Denis was convinced his mother called her parents by their first names in hopes that he'd call her Anja. She'd suggested it when he turned eighteen, but he continued to call her Mam. "They're fine as far as I can tell. I'm staying with them until I can use my arm better."

His mother glanced at her watch. "Time to head back."

They turned and retraced their steps along the Aare. Now that personal topics were out of the way, her voice became animated. "Let me tell you about this find of ours at Läuferplatz. It's a puzzle because men weren't usually buried in their armor—it was too wasteful of good materials that could be melted down. I'm going to have fun trying to figure out what the pieces are doing there."

Denis was intrigued. "Why just melt it down? Why not sell it to be reused?"

His mother seemed to relax. She liked him best when he showed an interest in her work. "A suit of armor was fitted to the wearer, piece by piece. Even then, it was horribly uncomfortable. There was almost no chance that it would fit another man well enough to protect him."

They were passing the long, low building on the Aare that housed the Münster workshop and storage space where the foreman had his office. Years earlier, masons had spent weeks and months there shaping great blocks of sandstone, but now they spent most of their time working inside the Münster. The place must have reminded Denis's mother of his fall because she asked, "What's the policeman going to do about Zora's brother?"

"He's talking to Goran's parents this afternoon. He's interested in the mother's suicide," he added. "He asked *Grosmami* and *Grospaps* a lot of questions about the night she jumped out of the tower."

They were almost back to Läuferplatz, but his mother stopped and turned toward him. "I could never understand why that woman—Katica, right?—killed herself. I'd have said she loved Zora too much to abandon her. And she had a new baby, too."

Again, Denis remembered Zora describing her mother—so full of love for her daughter that apparently even *his* mother, who didn't have a maternal bone in her body, had felt it. Something bitter rose up in him, and he growled, "Right. She cared so much about Zora that she left her alone in the Münster over and over while she went off to fuck some guy."

A wounded look crossed his mother's face, and she strode away from him up the hill and back to her pieces of armor. He was too upset and surprised by his own outburst to say anything as he caught up with her, but he rested a hand on her arm.

She glanced at him, an unreadable expression on her face. "There's the archeologist. Thanks for coming by," she said over her shoulder as she walked back to the dig.

"See you," he called after her, though he wasn't sure when.

His angry comment about Katica echoed around his head as he walked toward his apartment on Herrengasse. He thought about the hurt on his mother's face. Had she realized that the rage was directed as much at her as at Katica? *He'd* certainly realized it as soon as the words left his mouth, and it was too late to take them back. He owed her an apology and maybe a conversation acknowledging that he still had problems with her abandoning him. The idea of having that talk gave him a stomachache, though.

That wasn't the only thing aching. During the past half hour, his whole body had begun to hurt, and he was glad he'd remembered to stick the foil pack of painkillers in his backpack before leaving his grandparents' house that morning. His route home took him up Junkergasse toward the Münster, and he decided to detour into the Münster park—the Pläfe—and sit on a bench to rest.

The view from the Pläfe was beautiful, over the Aare to the woods and houses and hills beyond, but today Denis sat on a bench facing the long south side of the Münster instead. He'd rather admire his church than the woods. From here, he could see the building's two sections, divided by a stretch of red-tiled roof. At ground level, vast arched windows were spaced between monumental columns that stretched up into ever finer and more delicate towers. The upper story had its own row of smaller arched windows, set high in the nave, and at the top soared the enormous peaked roof.

Denis tilted his head back until he could see the tower and stared at the larger of the two viewing balconies that encircled the apartment he'd once lived in. For fifteen years, he'd done his best to forget the night Zora's mother had died, and now Goran had brought it back to him with a bang.

He should have told Renzo right away of his own suspicions about Katica's death. But he hadn't done it because first, he had to tell Zora. He had to explain that she'd been right to attack him at the funeral. Once he'd confessed to her, he could tell the policeman and his grandparents and his boss and anyone else he felt like sharing it with. But Zora deserved to know first.

He got his cell out of his pocket. He couldn't stop thinking about being with Zora; he wanted them to go out and have a great time and end up in bed together. Just the thought of holding her hand excited him—how silly was that? And yet here he was, already planning to sabotage any possible fun by telling her something upsetting about her mother's death, something he'd been ashamed of for fifteen years. He'd kept his secret all this time; couldn't he wait a while longer to tell her?

He sat with his phone in his hand and stared at the Münster, feeling torn. Finally, he called the number he had for her—which was two years old and might not work.

"Hello." Her voice made him smile, although it sounded wary.

"Zora, it's Denis. Can we talk for a minute?"

"Denis, I'm so glad you called. I was upset that I didn't get your number. Sure, we can talk. I'm weeding a long, long row of flowers."

"I've had this number for ages, wanting to call you and not doing it. I came by today while the cop was there because I was worried. I know you didn't need me, but . . . I wanted to be there. And then I couldn't say what I wanted to say with Renzo there. Or Goran. I'm hoping we can have dinner tonight. Is there somewhere you'd like to go? Otherwise, how about eating on the river at the Dampfzentrale?"

Zora laughed, but it sounded affectionate. "Wow. I think you got all that out in one breath."

"I planned it," he answered. "I had to get it said before I got cold feet."

"Well, no need for cold feet. I'd like to have dinner, and Dampfzentrale is fine. Let's meet at seven after I've cleaned up. I'm covered in mud."

Denis couldn't stop grinning into the phone. "Seven. Okay. You'll take the number 10 bus to town, right? So, let's meet at the ice cream shop at the corner of Monbijoustrasse and Eigerstrasse and walk to the restaurant together?"

"Okay, seven o'clock in front of La Golosa. Hey, I'm really happy about this—it will be fun." There was a pause. He listened to her breathing in and out, and for a second, there was so much he wanted to tell her that he couldn't think of a single thing to say. He simply waited, smiling to himself like a loony.

"Got to get back to work. Tschou, Denis."

"Tschou, Zora. See you at seven—and thanks!"

Denis sat on his bench, still grinning. He knew he ought to be worried, but he was too pleased to be meeting with her to feel apprehensive about what he had to say. Yes, he'd decided to tell her. He had to.

He looked at his watch. It was almost three, so he had four hours, and the last thing he felt like doing was going back to his grandparents' house and being an invalid on the sofa.

Nathan had told him he was ready to take on a commission of his own—a small colored-glass window in a front door or on a staircase landing, perhaps. But he needed more sketches of flowers and plants in his portfolio to show potential customers. There was a basement flower shop across the street from his flat whose owner grew her own supply of flowers on the hill sloping down from her backdoor toward the Aare. The florist let him sit behind the shop among her rows of plants and draw. He was close enough to his apartment to fetch his sketchpad, pencils, pens, and watercolors.

But first, he had to call his grandparents and tell them he wouldn't be home until late. They'd be hurt that he wasn't eating dinner with them, and once again, he wished that loving and being loved didn't involve inflicting pain on people so often. And feeling pain? That was true, too, but he didn't want to think about it before his date with Zora, so he pushed the thought away.

20

The Golden Goat, Matte, Thursday afternoon, June 27

Hearing the shop's back door open and close, Renzo turned away from the flower bed in the center of the Horvats' little garden and walked toward Ivana as she came down the porch stairs. Her smile looked forced; no surprise there.

Smiling back as genuinely as he could manage, he approached her but didn't offer his hand a second time. Instead, he waved her to one of the chairs at the outdoor table where he'd just spoken with her husband, waited for her to sit down, and took the seat across from her. He examined her again: gray-brown hair pulled tightly back from her face; brown eyes behind brown-framed spectacles; makeup that seemed to make red cheeks redder; a buttoned-up overshirt in a flowery, old-lady fabric; brown trousers that did nothing to disguise a pear-shaped figure. Like her husband, she had to be over fifty, and he wondered about the woman she'd been in her twenties. Right now, she looked and dressed like someone who wanted to be invisible. Did she do that deliberately, or did it reflect the way she felt about herself?

Once they were seated, she met his eyes and said, "You questioned our son when we weren't there." Her Bernese dialect was less correct than her husband's but more fluent, the Croatian accent milder. Despite the reproach in her words, her voice was flat, and her face was blank.

He wasn't going to apologize, but he could reassure her. "All official questioning of Goran will take place with you and your husband present. The interview will be transcribed, and you'll have a chance to read it and check its accuracy. You'll be able to have a lawyer there, too, if you want one."

She sat impassively, her eyes on his face.

Renzo went on. "Do you know about the serious injury Goran caused Denis Kellenberger, how it happened, and what your son said to Denis?"

"Yes," she said.

"Do you know what made him do it?"

"No," she answered.

Renzo waited for elaboration of some kind, but none came. He was impressed with her restraint.

"Goran told us that you've brought up Denis's role in Katica Horvat's death more than once," he said. "Yet apparently, you believe Zora must have put Goran up to this."

Ivana's brows knotted, and her lips pursed for a moment. Then her face was blank again, and she shrugged. "Zora talks to Goran about my husband's first wife." An interesting way to refer to Goran's biological mother, Renzo thought, especially since they'd once been friends. "It isn't healthy. It . . . makes things like this happen."

It was such a preposterous statement that he had to bite back his first angry response. He took a deep breath. "I understand you knew Katica throughout her childhood and adolescence and that you were her best friend here in Switzerland. I can't imagine why you don't want to share your memories of this woman you cared about with her biological son. Is that because you feel guilty about marrying her husband after she killed herself?"

He was sure this would break through her self-control. Instead, she gave him a small, cool smile. "I don't feel guilty at all. Lovro needed me—to work in the shop, to take care of the baby, and to comfort him. I talked to the priest about it, and he believed it was the right thing to do. I didn't care what other people thought."

Aha, thought Renzo. *So, there had been talk.* There was always talk, especially in small, insular immigrant communities. As a first-generation Italian Swiss, he should know. Had people kept an eye on Ivana's belly after the wedding? That thought made him wonder why she and Lovro hadn't had children of their own; she'd been young enough back then. But there was nothing to justify asking her such an intrusive question except his own curiosity.

Instead, he asked another difficult question. "Do you know why Goran's biological mother killed herself?"

A lightning-fast look of panic crossed her face that was gone before he could read it. But her voice remained soft. "I knew before the boy's birth that she was . . . not herself. But I never imagined she'd do such a terrible thing."

It was an opening, at least. "When you say that she was not herself, are you referring to her affair with Ben Schweizer?"

And then her anger was out in the open, blazing. She leaned toward him, her eyes narrowed, and hissed, "Zora. That—"

"No, Frau Horvat," Renzo interrupted her and then cursed his own stupidity. What might she have said about her stepdaughter in that flash of temper? He should have waited to hear it. Too late now. "Zora said nothing to me about her mother's infidelity. It was Goran."

Ivana covered her mouth with both hands and shook her head, her eyes fixed on him.

"Goran overheard you and Zora talking about Katica's affair. According to him, you told Zora"—he flipped through the pages of his notebook—"'Don't say a word to your father. It's bad enough that he lost her without his learning she'd been with another man.' So now Goran believes he isn't his father's son. And he says it was this that made him attack Denis."

Ivana, hands still pressed to her mouth, hunched over the table like an old woman.

Renzo continued relentlessly. "Goran heard you say that Lovro doesn't know. Are you sure? It seems impossible that a man's wife could go off day and night to have sex with someone else for over a year, and he wouldn't figure it out."

Ivana was shaking her head violently; her hands were squeezed into fists. "I am sure," she said, glancing quickly at the closed door behind her. Then she lowered her voice and glowered at him. "You mustn't tell him. God only knows what he'd do. You don't want *him* killing himself, do you?"

How theatrical, Renzo thought. But maybe she had a point. Was his investigation worth burdening Lovro with more misery? He decided to move on. "Herr Horvat told me he thinks something happened to upset his first wife at a party she gave to celebrate Goran's birth. Were you there?"

"Yes," Ivana answered. "I helped her set it up."

"Did anyone at that party say or do anything that could have pushed Frau Horvat toward her death?"

"No." They both let the monosyllable sit there until Ivana said, "Why are you asking these questions?"

He'd known Ivana would ask this sooner or later, but he thought for a moment before answering. "You and your husband, along with several people who still work at the Münster, have always seemed astonishingly eager to shove blame onto Denis—and only Denis. Zora attacked him at her mother's funeral, but someone else made her believe in his guilt. Children don't come up with these ideas by themselves, especially not about their friends. There were other people in Katica's life at that time who were much more likely to be responsible for her death than a child who might not have locked a door or two. Her lover and her husband, for starters, not to mention you and maybe some of her women friends. And I don't just mean 'responsible' in the sense of driving her over the edge. I am looking into whether someone killed her."

Now Ivana's face filled with horror. "You . . . you can't do that. Another policeman already handled it. It's over now. You can't come back to it after all these years. You can't!" Her voice rose to a wail that made the hair on his arms prickle.

"Do *you* think someone killed her?"

"No," she said loudly. "No, no, no." Her hands gripped the edge of the table. Whether she was saying no to the idea of murder or to the investigation itself wasn't clear. "I am going inside now. I can't answer any more of your questions." She stood, climbed the steps to the porch, and disappeared through the back door.

He gave her a few moments and then went in himself, through the storage room and the back office and into the shop. There, Lovro was ringing up groceries for a customer and helping him pack them into paper bags. The two men were chatting in what Renzo assumed was Croatian. Ivana was nowhere to be seen.

When the customer left, Lovro turned to Renzo. "Are you finished for now?" Renzo nodded. "When do you think you'll be talking to our son again?"

Renzo spread his hands. "Probably not until our official interview at the police station. I'll try to give you some warning about the date and time so you can find someone to work at the shop then if you both want to be with him."

"Good," said Lovro. "And if you talk to him before that, I need to be there."

"I'll let you know."

Outside, the day had grown overcast, and what had been a pleasant breeze now felt like wind. He walked past his car and a little further along Gerberngasse in the direction of the Matte schoolhouse before turning down an alley that he knew from teenage adventures. It ended in a flight of stone stairs leading right into the Aare, which was broad and lazy here beyond the weir. There were a few small figures on the path on the other side of the river, but otherwise, no one was in sight. Renzo sat down on the steps near the bottom, leaned back against the stairwell wall, and watched the gray-green expanse of water glide by. Eventually, he lifted his eyes from the water to stare at the steep forest on the other bank, the Englische Anlagen. The path at its foot was the one he'd taken Wednesday night, walking home from the Kellenbergers' house. Above the forest, almost directly across from where he sat, was Giuliana's apartment building. For once, he didn't think of her; instead, he was considering Lovro and Ivana Horvat.

Ivana was easier to analyze. In spite of her attempt at iciness, her conflicting emotions weren't far from the surface. He thought of Lovro describing how much Ivana had helped his family after Katica's death and what Ivana had said about how much Lovro needed her. Ivana and Lovro had known each other when Katica was only a child, and then he'd married Katica. Ivana might have had some good reasons for wanting her "best friend" dead.

As for Lovro, he seemed calm, forgiving, and reasonable, especially compared to Ivana. But his declaration of love for his first wife was striking. Zora and Ivana thought he hadn't known about Katica's affair. But suppose they were wrong? In that case, he, too, had had a good reason to kill Katica, at least by old-fashioned Balkan standards. Hell, look how he, Renzo, felt about Fränzi having affairs after *he'd* broken up their marriage. Sometimes he understood why women thought men were crazy.

There were definitely grounds to think this could have been a murder. But he kept coming back to the fact that the homicide detective fifteen years ago, Samuel Grossenbacher, had known about the affair and still decided on suicide. He needed to talk to Grossenbacher—and to the stonemason lover, Ben Schweizer—as well as confront Lovro for a second time.

Soothed by the steady murmur of the Aare flowing past his feet where they rested on the second to last step above the water, Renzo decided he'd do those three interviews. If none of them threw up anything suspicious, he'd focus on conducting Goran through the legal system and give up on Katica's death. He'd go back to what he was supposed to be doing on the Seiler case with Giuliana.

He took out his phone to call Giuliana and tell her what he'd decided. Then, with his finger hovering above the number pad, he stopped. He was his own boss for this investigation; Rolf and

Giuliana had made that clear. He could contact Giuliana as a friend, but he didn't need to ask for her approval. He could just get on with his next steps. It was only three forty-five—Grossenbacher might still see him today.

Before he could follow up on that thought, his phone rang. Giuliana.

21

When her meeting with Ursula Kellenberger on the Casino terrace was over, Giuliana called Ruth Seiler's lawyer, as the prosecutor had suggested. The receptionist informed her that Valérie Imboden was out for the morning, so Giuliana left a message saying how eager she was to meet with Seiler. Maybe it wouldn't contribute a lot to her understanding of the case, but she'd read, heard, and thought so much about Seiler that she was impatient to set eyes on the woman.

She checked her watch; it was ten to twelve. She decided to walk back to the station using the Kornhaus Bridge for a change and cut through the Breitenrain neighborhood. It would be good exercise. She knew she should give Renzo Ursula's message; she needed to get it off her conscience. But she was not looking forward to it. What if he thought she didn't trust his investigation skills? Instead of phoning him, she went back to thinking about her own case.

Giuliana found it useful to imagine a mock trial to help her identify holes in whatever information package she was putting together for the district attorney's office. She'd spent several years in her father's defense practice, followed by six months as a prosecutor before joining the police. There was no jury at a Swiss trial to be swayed one way or the other. Instead, a panel of five judges would read casebooks before the trial containing the sworn statements of the doctor and pharmacist who'd prescribed and sold Seiler the insulin. There'd be written testimony from both sides of the case: witnesses to Seiler's movements, friends who'd heard her talk about her husband's condition, medics who'd treated him, and the community nurse who'd shown Seiler years earlier how to administer insulin. There'd be lots of paperwork about the couple's finances, too.

Giuliana crossed the Kornhaus Bridge and turned left, passing the Beau-Site clinic. As she walked along Wyttenbachstrasse with its old-fashioned three- and four-story buildings, she made a mental note to advise Rosmarie to have Sebastian Allemann, and *not* his sister, speak during the trial. Tamara Hofstetter disliked her stepmother so much that she'd be a gift to the defense. The judges would find her vindictiveness distasteful, and it would make the case against Seiler look like a witch hunt—which Giuliana thought Tamara had indeed turned it into. She was just wondering if the defense was planning to call in a moral heavyweight of some kind to justify Seiler's actions—maybe a psychiatric specialist or a philosophy professor with expertise in ethics—when her cell phone rang.

It was Valérie Imboden calling her back. "Hello, Giuliana," she said. Giuliana smiled. Thank goodness Seiler's lawyer wasn't going to insist on the formality of last names just because they were on opposite sides. "You left a message about talking to Frau Seiler."

"Thanks for calling back, Valérie," said Giuliana. "Rosmarie told me it would be okay to request a chat to give me a chance to meet her before I depose her."

Giuliana heard Ruth's lawyer inhale deeply on a cigarette. "You've never met her? How can that be? I know Adam Neuhaus was originally the detective on the case, but I assumed you—"

"Nope. I took over from Adam unexpectedly two weeks ago. I guess you heard that his wife has been in the hospital with complications since the birth of their second kid. He needed to take time off to help out, and it's turned into a six-month leave of absence."

Giuliana reached the intersection at the end of Wyttenbach-strasse, where there was a paved picnic area, and sat down on a bench under a tree. It was hot. Since taking off her cotton blazer would reveal her gun, she was glad to be in the shade.

"So, you're having to put together a case against a woman you've never met." Valérie sounded sympathetic. "Well, as long as I'm in the room, I think we can risk a conversation. Ruth is still not completely recovered, though."

Giuliana had half wondered if Ruth Seiler's pneumonia was real or if it had been cooked up by her defense team to postpone the deposition. Now she said, "I understand. You and she can decide on the rules, and I'll stick to them."

"How about meeting at Ruth's house tomorrow morning at ten? But come by yourself, will you? You can take notes, but they won't be transcribed, and I don't want to submit her to a crowd."

Giuliana had been hoping to have Madeleine Trachsel come with her as a substitute for Renzo, whose job it should have been. Two cops were certainly not a crowd, and she'd have liked to discuss her impressions of Seiler with someone else. But it was worth cooperating with Valérie's requirements for the sake of goodwill.

"Thanks very much. I'll come alone and ask questions, but you can cut things off if you decide Frau Seiler is getting too tired. You'll give me at least twenty minutes, though, won't you?"

"Sure," said the defense lawyer. "And more—unless Ruth becomes exhausted. We'll play it by ear."

"Good. See you tomorrow at ten."

She made her way into the police station by the back door and headed upstairs to the detectives' shared office, where she found that her colleague Sabine Jost hadn't gone to lunch yet and was happy to join her. Over cold cucumber soup in the cafeteria, they exchanged news.

"I'm close to having enough evidence to charge a man who killed his wife," Sabine told her.

"I heard about that," Giuliana said through a bite of whole wheat roll. "The guy who beat his wife to death?"

"That's the one," Sabine said grimly. "And this time, nobody can look away from the problem by blaming it on macho foreigners or poverty or alcohol. It's a classic femicide. The family is Swiss, white, and middle-class; the man's an accountant, and everyone involved was sober. And still, the bastard punched and kicked his wife until she died while their three-year-old son sat in his highchair watching and screaming."

Despite all Giuliana's years in homicide, there were still things that shocked her into silence. Sabine also seemed to feel she'd said enough, and both women ate quietly for a few minutes, hunched over their food. Finally, Giuliana asked, "Is Madeleine working with you?"

"Yes." Sabine smiled broadly. "She's doing a great job. Top organizational skills and good self-control. And on top of that, she can make me laugh."

"I'm impressed with her, too, *and* I like her." Guiliana had finished her soup and was buttering the last piece of her roll. "I was going to have her accompany me to talk with Ruth Seiler tomorrow, but now the defense has asked me to come alone."

Sabine pushed her tray away and leaned back. "You're finally getting to meet Seiler, huh? Well, at least she didn't kill her spouse in front of their grandchild."

"Actually, the poor man never got to see his grandchildren. His daughter never forgave him for finding a new wife. She—the daughter, I mean—kept herself and the kids away from him. Now she's convinced Ruth Seiler killed him for his money. I don't think the daughter wants any money for herself, by the way; she's very rich. She just doesn't want Ruth to get it."

Sabine shook her head. "Families!" she said as she stood and picked up her tray.

After lunch, Giuliana tried to concentrate on the case, but in the back of her mind, she continued to worry about Ursula Kellenberger's message to Renzo. Finally, midafternoon, she fetched a coffee from the Nespresso machine down the hall and dialed Renzo's number.

"Ciao," he said. "How's it going?"

She could hear the rush of water behind his voice and was suddenly desperate to get this over with. "I . . . I need to tell you something. I saw Ursula Kellenberger this morning at the Casino for a coffee and a chat about her work for Exit because of the Seiler business. I didn't mention your case, but she asked if I knew you, and when I said yes, she wanted me to give you a message. Since you talked to her, she's been thinking about Katica's death and feels more convinced that it was suicide. She said that Katica always struck her as somewhat unstable; she described her as 'feverish' and 'overwrought.' Anyway, I'm just . . . passing on the information."

For a long time, all Giuliana could hear was water flowing and Renzo breathing. Then he said flatly, "It sounds like you couldn't resist getting involved."

"I know. And I'm sorry. When I saw her name on the list of Exit volunteers in Bern and realized how close she lives to me, I . . . well, I guess you're right. I couldn't resist."

"When she said she had information for me, why didn't you give her my phone number and tell her to call me?" His voice was still hard.

I tried, Giuliana wanted to say, which was true: she'd suggested that Ursula contact Renzo herself. But she could have refused to carry the message altogether; that would have been the right thing to do, given that the woman was Renzo's witness. She hadn't insisted on Ursula calling Renzo because she was so used to working with him—and she enjoyed it too much.

"That's what I should have done," she said to him now and repeated, "I'm sorry. I'm having trouble . . ." She trailed off. How could she say *I'm going to have trouble separating my work life from yours*? Then she thought, *Work life? Or life as a whole?* Had she really become this dependent on their relationship?

"Giuliana." His tone had changed. Now he sounded tentative, shaky, even. "Mädi," he said softly, "Madeleine Trachsel. I'm going to see if she has time to talk to Grossenbacher with me this afternoon. And . . ." Giuliana waited, her heart thumping. "I'm going to ask her out. I have no idea if . . . I mean, she may not be interested, but . . . I wanted to tell you before I say something to her because . . ." He stopped. There was no need for him to explain further. "I'm sorry," he mumbled after a long pause.

Giuliana was furious with herself. As if *he* should be feeling guilty about anything. Of course Renzo should ask someone out! And Mädi—well, at least Giuliana knew and liked her. "You have *nothing* to apologize for," she told him. "In everything that has happened between us, you've never done a single wrong thing. Remember that."

"Then why do we both feel so bad?" He spoke so quietly that she almost didn't hear him over the sound of the water.

She did feel bad, and she didn't mind his knowing it—but now, in a hurried phone call, wasn't the time to talk about it.

"I'm glad you told me about Mädi," she said with a catch in her voice. "I hope you have a nice dinner with her. And I'll try not to interfere with your case again."

"Right. Thanks. And I'll keep in mind what Frau Kellenberger said about Katica," Renzo responded. "What's going on with *our* case?"

"Tomorrow, I'm talking to Ruth Seiler. At last." Before Renzo could have an attack of conscience about putting his case first, she added, "Even if you were free, I couldn't take you with me. Seiler's lawyer is insisting on only one person. But I'd like to talk about my impressions, either tomorrow afternoon or over the weekend if you have time."

"Naturally I have time, Giule. I'm still on the Seiler case with you." He sounded more exasperated than apologetic, but then his voice softened. "We're never going to stop being colleagues and discussing cases with each other. That's invaluable to me. And . . . and it's fun. More than fun. It's—"

She knew he was trying to comfort her, but it was too painful. "Well, maybe we'll talk tomorrow then," she said quickly.

After they'd hung up, she sat at her desk and tried not to think about Renzo and Mädi. Drawing her laptop closer, she opened a Word file and named it *Questions for Ruth Seiler*. She contemplated the screen for a moment, took a deep breath, and typed: *Why does her husband's daughter hate her so much?*

22

R enzo stayed for a while on the steps leading down into the river. His chest felt tight. If he kept on throwing the women he loved out of his life, he was going to be very lonely.

Finally, he pulled himself together and phoned Mädi. When she didn't answer, he refused to take it as a cosmic message about his love life. Instead, he sent her a text: *"Time this afternoon or evening to interview a retired detective w/me who handled part of my case 15 years ago?"* Then he called the residence where Grossenbacher lived. He'd found the place online the night before with the information Erwin had given him.

The woman who answered connected him to someone else, who said, "Herr Grossenbacher is reading in the garden right now. Why don't you ring his cell in five minutes, and I'll send someone out to tell him he's about to get a call. Does he know you, Herr Donatelli?"

"No, but I think he'll want to talk to me. I'm with the Kantonspolizei like he used to be, and I need to talk to him about a case he investigated before he retired. Can I ask, is his memory sharp enough for questions?"

"Hmm." The woman went quiet for a moment. "He's certainly not suffering from dementia, if that's what you mean. He's smart, and he likes talking about the past. If he's willing to see you, I think it could be worth your while. Just don't expect too much detail. He *is* eighty years old." She paused. "Shall I give you his mobile number?"

"Yes, please." Renzo wrote it down. "Thanks. I'll phone him in five minutes."

Time to leave the Aare behind. Thinking about what Grossenbacher might have to tell him, Renzo jogged back to his illegally parked car, feeling recharged. There was a parking ticket under the windshield wiper, and he snatched it up, only to find that whoever had left it had written him a note on the back saying, "Good luck with your case." He grinned and, as he was crumpling it, heard his phone buzz. *"Can meet you at four thirty,"* said Mädi's text. *"Station parking lot?"*

Renzo's grin widened. If he couldn't see Grossenbacher today, he'd use the time to fill Mädi in on the case and ask her to come with him to see Katica's lover, Ben Schweizer, tomorrow. But first, he had to call Grossenbacher.

The old man answered on the first ring and agreed to a five o'clock meeting. "I'll be waiting in the lobby," the former detective told him, sounding eager.

Renzo got back to the station in time for a trip to the bathroom that included a quick check in the mirror. He thought he looked tired—or was it just looking thirty-five? In any case, he needed a haircut—his hair was probably longer than Mädi's. The thought of her bristly hedgehog hair made him smile. He just hoped she wouldn't bristle for real if he asked her to have dinner with him. He'd see how things went with Grossenbacher and then decide.

She was waiting for him in the parking lot, wearing loose gray chinos, a white T-shirt, and a long vest-like thing in a stripy red pattern. Her platinum hair was in its usual spikes, and she had on red earrings and a tiny red nose stud.

They got into his Fiat, and as they pulled out of the lot, she said, "Thanks for asking me to come with you. What do I need to know?"

He concentrated on squeezing into a gap in the traffic on Nordring before saying, "First, I'll tell you what I know about the retired cop we're going to see. Giuliana worked with him when she was a brand-new detective, and Erwin told me he had an alcohol problem. I'm hoping now that he's in a retirement community—or whatever it is—he's sober. Still, he's eighty, and it all happened fifteen years ago, so who knows how much he'll be able to remember? Erwin said Grossenbacher complained that he was pressured to get the investigation over with as quickly as possible. We'll need to ask him who was behind that."

He glanced over at Mädi briefly—she was nodding. "You think maybe he missed something because he was rushed or because he was drunk? But what's this fifteen-year-old case anyway, and why are you looking into it now?"

Renzo took a deep breath. He was looking forward to hearing what she made of the whole thing.

Instead of starting with the attack on Denis, he began with Lovro Horvat and his pregnant wife Katica coming to Switzerland during the Balkan wars, followed by Katica Horvat's body being found in the Münsterplatz ten years later and, fifteen years after that, Denis Kellenberger being shaken off his scaffold by Goran. He listed everyone he'd talked to so far and tried to give her a sentence or two about each person. Mädi listened and wrote something on her phone now and then; she was much faster typing with her thumbs than he was.

He'd just finished telling her about the rest of the interviews he had planned when they pulled into a parking space behind a high-rise apartment building with plenty of windows. It was surrounded by a large, well-landscaped garden with benches, paved paths, and a sunny terrace where umbrellas provided shade for chairs and tables.

The clock on the Fiat dashboard told Renzo they were a few minutes early, so he didn't get out. "I know that was all very rushed, but do you think you have enough background? And have you got any questions?"

Mädi had unfastened her seatbelt, but she wasn't in any hurry, either. "I have lots of questions," she said, "but nothing urgent. I can see why you decided to have another look at this suicide, which does sound suspicious—or at least . . . odd. I'll take notes on the interview. Do you want me to keep my mouth shut?"

"Absolutely not," said Renzo. "Ask anything you think needs asking. That's why you're here. I've gotten to the point where I need someone to discuss this with."

They got out and walked side by side to the automatic doors opening into the lobby. "I thought you always discussed everything with Giuliana." Renzo felt his face flush, but then Mädi added, "Of course, she's busy on the Seiler case. You're lucky to have her support as much as you do. I look up to both her and Sabine, but Giuliana's the one I feel like sending fan mail to."

That remark made Renzo want to laugh and hug Mädi at the same time. But they were in the lobby now, so he said, "I know. I *am* lucky."

Together they headed for the one white-haired man sitting by himself. In the photo Renzo had found of the detective from just before he retired, he'd been florid and overweight; now, he was neither of those things. His face was deeply lined, and he was neatly dressed in a short-sleeved blue shirt.

"Herr Grossenbacher?" Renzo called.

The man was already getting to his feet, slowly but steadily. He held out a hand. "Herr Donatelli?" He eyed Renzo with an expression that Renzo was used to in older policemen and quite a few members of the public. It said, "This pretty boy's a cop?" This time, though, the man also stared at Mädi, with her spiky dyed hair and nose stud.

Renzo had worked hard to come to the point where these reactions no longer annoyed him. He put on a polite face and waited for a joking remark about police standards slipping, but it never came. Instead, Grossenbacher spoke with unexpected warmth. "Good to meet you," he said and turned to Mädi. "I'm sorry, I don't think I got your name. Trachsel? A pleasure, Frau Trachsel. I've reserved one of the private dining rooms for us. Let's go."

They signed in at the front desk, and Grossenbacher led them out of the lobby and into the main dining room, leaning on the cane in his left hand. Opening a door in one wall, he ushered them into a wall-papered room with a round table and chairs seating eight, two large windows looking out on the garden, and, to Renzo's delight, a pitcher of water and a coffee thermos with glasses, cups, sugar, and cream.

As soon as they were all seated, and Renzo and Mädi were filling cups for themselves and their host, Grossenbacher said, "Tell me how I can help."

This time, Renzo did start with Goran and Denis and how the fifteen-year-old's irrational attack had made him curious about Katica's suicide. "I certainly don't want to offend you by questioning your conclusion at the time," he said, "but when I heard about the woman's affair and the possibility that the son might not be her husband's, it sounded . . ."

Before he could find the right words, the old detective interrupted. "I agree with you. There was a lot of potential there for someone, either the husband or the boyfriend, to have thrown that young woman off the tower. From a practical point of view, it could have been one of those two academics living right there at the top, but I couldn't find any motive for either of them. And it's hard to believe they would have done something like that with their ten-year-old grandson sleeping a few feet away."

Renzo grinned at the old man. "I see you've got the case at your fingertips."

"I kept a few notebooks on old cases that bothered me, and that was one of them. So, after you called me, I went straight to my notes. It's not every day I get fellow homicide detectives coming to pick my brain."

"Mädi and I are both Fahnder, actually, but we do a lot of work for homicide, and the current head of the division, Rolf Straub,"— Grossenbacher nodded in recognition—"has asked me to handle this investigation independently. Erwin Sägesser sends his greetings, by the way. He helped me track you down. When I reminded him of the Horvat suicide, he told me that you were under pressure to deal with it quickly."

Grossenbacher's cheerful face darkened, and his lips tightened. "Yes, there was hellish pressure—the worst of my career, I think. The

Münster's executive board was full of bigwigs who didn't want the church's reputation sullied, especially not by a suicide. They got the federal tourist board and the mayor's office involved. Then there was the fact that the dead woman was Catholic—the Croatian priest seemed to hover around the investigation almost as much as the Münster's minister."

Mädi looked up from her note-taking, eyebrows raised. "The Catholic priest wanted a finding of suicide?"

Grossenbacher snorted. "No one *wanted* a suicide, exactly, especially not the Catholics. And the Münster Protestants were afraid of copycat jumpers. But I think a sordid murder worried everyone even more. They all wanted it to disappear. And meanwhile, I was concerned for the husband and daughter, wanting to keep them out of the public eye. Still, I managed to soldier on for a few days, trying to get answers out of the boyfriend."

"I've focused so far on the Horvat family and the Kellenbergers," Renzo said. "I haven't gotten to Schweizer yet. I'd be very interested in hearing what you thought of him."

"Above all, he's one of those men who simply can't keep his prick in his pants." The retired detective shook his head, then glanced over at Mädi. "Sorry, Frau Trachsel."

"Don't mind me," said Mädi. "I believe in calling things what they are. Are you saying that sleeping with Frau Horvat wasn't a big deal for him?"

"To be fair, he seemed upset by her death. He insisted he'd been in love with her and got very emotional when he talked about her. But I don't think he was seeing her exclusively. His best buddy at work and his neighbors in the Postgasse apartment were convinced he was meeting at least two other women off and on during his affair with Frau Horvat. When I asked him about them, he said they weren't important—Frau Horvat was."

Renzo considered this—it matched what the Münster foreman, Pereira, had said, too. "Did you ask him if they talked about Frau Horvat getting a divorce?"

"Yes," said Grossenbacher. "He said he asked her once, and she got angry and told him never to ask her again. When I pushed, he said it had been a stupid question since he couldn't afford to get divorced anyway. I checked, and he had two kids then, with a third on the way."

"Did you talk to his wife?"

"She was his alibi for the time of the death," answered Grossenbacher. "They lived outside Bern in Münchenbuchsee, and she said he was at home in bed with her all night."

Mädi looked up from making notes on her phone. "You thought Schweizer might have something to do with Katica Horvat's death, then, if you got his alibi."

"I suspected the hell out of him, just on principle, but he didn't seem to have a motive, and his wife stuck to her story."

"Could he have killed Katica to keep his wife from finding out about her?" Renzo asked.

Grossenbacher shrugged. "I'm almost sure the wife knew he played around, and I don't think Schweizer cared that she knew. I got the impression she was weary of his cheating and of him, but she still confirmed his whereabouts for the night Katica died."

"And no sign that he was in the Old City?"

"Not so many surveillance cameras around fifteen years ago, don't forget. We tried to find a witness who'd seen Schweizer after midnight, but no luck. Same with the Horvat woman's husband. Not one jot of evidence that he or Schweizer was at the Münster then."

"What about texts on Katica's phone about meeting Schweizer?" Renzo asked.

"She had two one-hundred-franc bills in her back pocket. That was all there was on the body. No wallet, no keys, no phone. We searched for the phone in and around the Münster, in the Horvats' shop and apartment, in Schweizer's Postgasse room, and everywhere else we could think of. We never found it." Grossenbacher leaned back in his chair and let out an exasperated sigh.

The former detective was turning out to be tremendously useful. Renzo vowed he'd bring the man a couple of bottles of really good

Italian wine as soon as—no, bad plan if he'd been an alcoholic. Maybe chocolates? "Both the current Frau Horvat and Zora, the daughter, are convinced that Lovro, Katica's husband, never knew about the affair and still doesn't. What do you think?"

The ex-cop rolled his eyes. "It was a dilemma. The woman's family and friends were overcome, and her husband's grief seemed genuine. If he was ignorant about what had been going on, God knows I didn't want to add to his suffering. I didn't want to have to tell *anyone* who cared about her what she'd been up to. But at the same time, I was trying to find out if someone had killed her because of it."

"I'm struggling with this, too," admitted Renzo. "If her husband *did* know about the affair, he had a huge motive, especially if the boy wasn't his. But you'd think if he wanted to kill his wife, he'd find a better way than throwing her off that tower with three people sleeping inside it."

"Unless he followed her, and it was a spur-of-the-moment thing," Grossenbacher said, frowning as though he was beginning his investigation all over again. Then he sighed and thumped both palms onto the table. "Anyway, in the end, I'm ashamed to say that I did what everyone wanted me to. The death was ruled a suicide."

"What else could you do?" Renzo said, reaching out to touch the age-spotted hand on the table. "You can't fight for more time when you don't have the ammunition. And the evidence just wasn't there, was it?"

"Maybe if I'd kept pushing, something would have emerged. Who knows? But imagine how pleased I am to have *you* looking into it, although whatever evidence I might have found is probably long gone or forgotten by now. Like the phone texts I never asked for."

Mädi shifted in her seat. "What about the boy, Goran? Did Schweizer show any interest in finding out if he was the father?"

Grossenbacher reached for the water pitcher. Renzo had been wondering whether he ought to pour another glass for the old man, but Grossenbacher picked up the pitcher with a steady hand and managed it himself without spilling a drop. His voice was hard as he answered. "As far as I know, he doesn't care who fathered the boy as long no one asks him for money."

"Another question," Mädi continued. "When you think back, is there anyone or anything you wish you'd followed up on or taken a deeper look at?"

The old man leaned forward, elbows on the table, fingers steepled under his chin. "I wanted more time with the boyfriend and the husband, but I got a fair bit out of them in the time I had. There was one person whose testimony made me uncomfortable, though, and I didn't have time to follow up. It was the dead woman's friend. I wrote her name down." He pulled a tiny yellow Post-it out of his shirt pocket. "Ivana Pavić."

"Ivana," echoed Renzo. "I don't need to find her—she's Ivana Horvat now. She married Lovro less than a year after Katica's death."

Grossenbacher's chin sank into his palms, and he smiled. "Now, why am I not surprised? She was constantly at the shop. I got the impression she'd been hanging around for years. At one point, the little girl said to me, 'Oh, she never invites us to her house. She only comes here.' The more I dealt with Ivana Pavić, the more I thought, 'If anyone knows what really happened to Katica Horvat, it's this supposed friend of hers.'"

"Supposed?" Renzo was frowning.

"I'm probably not being fair. She just . . . Something about her disturbed me. And it wasn't that she didn't like cops. I'm used to that with Eastern Europeans."

"She doesn't like me, either," Renzo said, "and I also thought she was holding back." The two men exchanged wry smiles.

There was a brief silence. Renzo could hear footsteps moving slowly into the main dining room and the murmur of voices. The evening meal was about to begin, but the old man didn't seem in any hurry.

"Is there anything else you think we should follow up on?" Mädi said.

He looked thoughtful. "Well, it sounds like a small thing, but some of the business with the family living in the tower, the grandparents and grandson, bothered me. There was a sexton then"—the old man checked his note—"named Klaus Friedli—"

"He's still there," Renzo put in.

"Right. Friedli was part of that whole gang who were keen for the case to disappear. Yet he kept trying to make trouble for the tower family, the Kellenbergers. I think he enjoyed having power over them. That doesn't make him guilty of anything except being an officious son of a bitch, though." The old man gave a shrug. "I can't give you a reason to follow up with him—I guess I just didn't like him."

"The Kellenbergers told me about the sexton and how he was against them and their grandson living in the apartment," said Renzo. "Perhaps he couldn't stand them sharing his kingdom." Nevertheless, Renzo made a mental note to talk to the sexton properly before he wrapped things up. He pictured Friedli's prim, holier-than-thou face and thought that, at the very least, the man would have plenty to say about the Kellenbergers. How much of it would be true, Renzo would have to figure out for himself.

It was time to leave before he and Mädi outstayed their welcome. "This has been very helpful, Herr Grossenbacher. Thanks for your time." Before they got up, Renzo added, "I don't know if you remember Giuliana Linder, who was a newly promoted homicide cop when you were dealing with this case. We both work with her often. She suggested I talk to you as soon as she heard I was interested in the Horvat suicide."

The old man slowly got to his feet, leaning on his cane. "During the three years before I retired, I was an alcoholic, including when I handled this case. I've been sober for twelve years now, and maybe I'd have found Katica's murderer if I'd been sober then. I remember Giuliana—she was young and sharp. I don't like to imagine what she remembers about me." He met Renzo's eyes. "Tell her I say hello. And Erwin, too. Is he still scaring all the rookies?"

"Oh, yes, he's still going strong. It took me years not to quiver like a rabbit whenever Erwin growled at me."

"I have trouble imagining Giuliana at my age," Mädi put in.

"She was . . . forceful." Grossenbacher opened his eyes wide and raised his hands palms outward in a warding-off gesture. "But I could see how good she was at the job already and how much better she was going to become with experience."

Renzo was also trying to picture a thirty-one-year-old Giuliana, four years younger than himself. Would he have fallen in love with that young Giuliana, or would he also have found her too "forceful?"

Grossenbacher led them through the crowded main dining room and out the front doors of the building. "I'd love to hear what happens," he said as they shook hands in the garden.

On their way to the car, Mädi said, "The Giuliana we know would have tried to get Grossenbacher into a drying-out program. But it wouldn't have been easy back then, with an officer over thirty years her senior."

"I wonder if she even knew about the alcohol," Renzo mused as they got into the car. "It was Erwin who told me about it, not Giule."

"She knew. She was just being discreet. Believe me, if someone you deal with regularly is an alcoholic, you know it." She said this so emphatically that Renzo glanced at her, eyebrows raised. She caught his look. "My father," she said dryly.

"Still?" he asked.

"Yep." She pulled on her seatbelt. "All my life, basically."

"Then you know what you're talking about," he said softly and shut up in case she wanted to say more. When she remained silent, he looked at his watch. It was five forty-five.

"Our next step is Schweizer. Since we're in the car already, why don't we swing by his business in Ostermundigen?" If this had been his week with the kids, he wouldn't have been able to meet with Grossenbacher at five, let alone go afterward to see Schweizer. "I can always drop you off and see Schweizer by myself. Or we can wait until tomorrow."

"I don't have plans. Let's do this."

Renzo searched for the address of Schweizer's gravestone business and programmed it into his car's navigation system.

"What's the main thing you hope to get out of him?" Mädi asked after they'd pulled out of the parking lot.

"I keep wondering why Katica went to the Münster that night." Renzo had chosen a route that avoided the highway, but the rush hour traffic on Schwarzenburgstrasse was bad. He wasn't looking forward to the snarl of cars, buses, trams, bikes, and pedestrians at Eigerplatz, either. "Did she sneak out knowing she was going to the tower to jump? If so, she must have had a Münster key—although there was none on her body. Or was she simply planning to see Schweizer, and something happened that made her jump? Did they meet, and he killed her? Or did Lovro follow them and kill her?"

As he spoke, Renzo felt a growing sense of dissatisfaction. He'd insisted on turning Goran's attack on Denis into a full-blown reinvestigation, and after forty-eight hours of reviewing the case, he wasn't any closer to deciding whether he was looking for a murderer or not. If he didn't get it together, he was going to end up looking like a fool.

But Mädi only nodded, her brows drawn. "If Schweizer *was* out with Katica, how did he get his wife to agree that he was at home in bed with her? And I wonder if she's still willing to alibi him." She cocked an eyebrow at Renzo. "What do you reckon? Because I bet if we ask her again now, she'll tell a different story."

Renzo had been wondering how they were going to pressure Benjamin Schweizer to talk to them, much less tell them the truth. Now he gave a short laugh. "Great! Let's do exactly that. Call the station and get someone to track down the wife's full name and cellphone number—and her landline if she has one. We've got his name, we can estimate her age, and we know the couple used to live in Münchenbuchsee. I think they'll be able to find her."

"Ha!" said Mädi, taking her phone out of her pocket. "Now that's what I call leverage."

23

Ostermundigen, Thursday evening, June 27

It was ten after six when Mädi and Renzo arrived at the stonemason's shop. The border between Bern and Ostermundigen ran right through the Schosshalde cemetery, and Ben Schweizer's gravestone business was on the cheaper Ostermundigen side of the graveyard, just off Güterstrasse.

Renzo parked on the street a few doors down from the single-story building, which looked like it had once been a family house. The front garden displayed sample gravestones carved and decorated in various styles, plus statues of angels, crosses, and some abstract sculptures. As they got closer, they saw the house was only part of the operation. A long driveway led behind it to a low gray building from which they could hear the whine of a power tool.

"He's good," Mädi commented softly as they climbed some steps to a small porch. "Not that I'd want a four-foot angel on my grave, but this stuff isn't kitsch. Look at that curved bluish stone with the flowering vine carved up the side. It's realistic *and* subtle."

They hadn't been sure the place would still be open, but a sign on the door told them to ring the bell and walk in. They found themselves in a front room with several comfortable chairs and two small sofas, bookshelves full of binders in muted colors, and a desk where a very attractive blonde woman of about thirty sat behind a computer. She stood when she saw them, displaying a navy suit, a white blouse with navy pinstripes, and pale pink lipstick. As she stepped out from behind her desk, Renzo saw her red stiletto heels. *Interesting. The suit was for the bereaved clients, but the heels were for herself—or perhaps for Schweizer?*

Renzo gave his name and asked if they could speak with the boss. They'd decided they wouldn't out themselves as cops until they had to.

"He's with clients right now, but there are no appointments after that. He might be able to see you when these people leave. I'll text him that you're here. Have a seat."

Renzo and Mädi sat next to each other on the sofa facing the desk. Almost immediately, the receptionist's phone pinged a reply. "He should be finished any time now. If you can wait, he'll be glad to see you. You're lucky he's in. He usually only sees people for a few hours in the morning and spends the rest of his time in the workshop." She gestured with her thumb over her shoulder to indicate the gray building behind the house.

Renzo doubted that Schweizer would be at all glad to see them, but he assured the woman in the red heels that they'd wait. She was clearly waiting, too, with her computer turned off and her red handbag sitting on the desk. She disappeared briefly, and they heard a toilet flushing; when she returned, her lipstick had changed from pink to the red of her shoes.

Renzo skimmed general emails from the police department, a task he saved for quiet moments like this, and Mädi flicked through one of the loose-leaf binders, which displayed photos of gravestones. A door opened out of sight, and they heard a voice say, "Take those photographs with you. I'm sure the rose-colored granite would be an excellent choice. Call me by next Monday with your decision."

A well-dressed man walked in. He was in his forties with a slim body, a boyishly attractive face, and golden-yellow hair, escorting a couple who looked to be in their sixties. The man and woman had features so similar that they could only be brother and sister. Strolling between the pair, the blond man gave Renzo and Mädi just the right kind of smile: grave enough to satisfy the recently bereaved, genial enough to charm them if they were merely looking for a statue. Then his attention returned completely to the couple he was ushering out. Closing the door behind them, he turned to the secretary. "You don't need to stay, Aline. I'll finish up here." Then he drew close to Renzo and Mädi, who'd stood, and spread his arms in welcome. "Please, come with me," he said in a warm, deep voice and led them down the hall.

Schweizer's office was big enough to contain not just a desk but a comfortable sitting area, to which he motioned them. Mädi walked toward a loveseat but didn't sit. Renzo waited until Schweizer was in the room before moving behind him and closing the office door.

Halfway to two armchairs facing the loveseat across a coffee table, Schweizer stopped and looked first at Renzo, then at Mädi. He clasped his hands at his belt buckle in a gesture that should have looked relaxed but instead made him seem immediately nervous. "What's this about?"

"Benjamin Schweizer?" asked Renzo. "I'm Renzo Donatelli of the Kantonspolizei, and this is my colleague, Madeleine Trachsel." Schweizer said nothing. "Let's sit down," added Renzo.

Without a word, Schweizer continued to one of the chairs while Renzo took the other, and Mädi sank onto the loveseat. The man's silence wasn't the response Renzo would expect from an innocent person. Where were the anxious inquiries about relatives' safety, the nervous jokes about unpaid speeding tickets? Instead, the man seemed watchful.

"We're reinvestigating the death of Katica Horvat, who jumped or was pushed from the Münster tower fifteen years ago." A look of pure astonishment flitted across Schweizer's face before he assumed a bland half smile. "I know what you said to the police then," Renzo continued, "and I'd like to go over it."

"Certainly," Schweizer said pleasantly. "But I told that older cop everything I knew. I'd been sleeping with Katica for a little over a year when she killed herself; we mostly met at a tiny place I had on Postgasse. I saw her every two weeks on average. Sometimes I wouldn't see her for three weeks—over Christmas, it was a month—and other times, we'd manage it twice a week."

"What about at the Münster?" Mädi asked. "Did you have sex there? In the tower, maybe?"

"The tower? Of course not." He shook his head. "The couple and their grandson slept up there."

Renzo picked up the theme. "There are lots of other places in that church you could have met for sex. After all, you had the keys, didn't you? Did you let her into the Münster the night she died?"

"I wasn't there, remember? Besides, why would I? She could let herself in just about anywhere."

And there it *is*, Renzo thought. Katica had her own key to the Münster and the tower. *No one* had left any doors unlocked. He would tell Denis. And Ivana, too, so that she'd never again be able to blame the boy Denis had been.

"So, you met in the church to screw," Renzo pursued, sneering deliberately. "Was she into kink? Maybe you tried the altar." He waited to see how Schweizer would respond to his provocation.

The man's lover had been dead for fifteen years, but still, he leaned toward Renzo, fists clenched at his sides. "There wasn't anything strange about us being in the Münster together. I worked there for years; it was my place. And Kati, she loved it. She didn't care that the Münster was Protestant, and she was Catholic. For her, it was holy."

Renzo glanced at Mädi, who gave him a tiny nod as if to say, *Well, you've gotten a rise out of him now.* She joined in, her voice gentle. "And the tower? Was that especially important to her?"

Schweizer leaned back in his chair and combed his golden hair with his fingers. "Um . . . maybe. One evening, she got away from the shop and her family, and she wanted to watch the sun go down from the highest point in the Old City. It was a June night, still light, so we went up to the second gallery and . . ." His eyes went distant for a moment before he caught Renzo staring. "The view was spectacular," he finished with a smooth smile.

"That means you *were* with her in the tower," Renzo said evenly.

"Yes. But not on the night when she died. When that happened, I was at home in Münchenbuchsee, in bed with my wife." Schweizer sat back, arms folded across his chest. The way he trotted out his alibi, unsolicited, made Renzo doubt its truth even more. He looked across the coffee table at Mädi and raised his eyebrows.

"Are you and your wife still together, Herr Schweizer?" she asked.

He unfolded his arms and shifted his body. "No, we've been divorced for over ten years."

Mädi raised her eyebrows. "And she'll still alibi you for the night Katica died? Given how much you slept around, I mean. You think your wife's forgiven you for all that cheating?"

Schweizer didn't answer, but there was nothing relaxed about his posture now.

Mädi got out her phone. "What do you think, Renzo? Shall we see what Frau Schweizer has to say *now*?"

"Wait," said Schweizer. "Don't—" He stood up so abruptly that he banged his shin against the coffee table. "You aren't really going to phone her." As Mädi started pressing buttons on her phone, Schweizer moved behind his chair and grabbed the back as if for support. "She'll tell you I wasn't there out of spite—you can't believe anything she says about me. The divorce was . . ."

Renzo saw that the man's hands were fists again, his jaw tight. The phone rang and rang. Would his ex-wife pick up if she didn't recognize the number?

Finally, the call was answered. Mädi switched it to speaker, and the three of them heard a woman's voice say, "Schweizer."

Mädi succinctly explained her reason for calling, and Schweizer dropped back into his chair, hands cupping his nose and mouth. If Renzo'd had to put money on it, he would have wagered he was looking at a guilty man. But guilty of what?

There was a long pause, and for a moment, Renzo wondered if Schweizer's ex had heard the question. Then she said quietly, "That's right. He was with me that night, and I'm a very light sleeper, so I'm sure he was there."

Renzo's breath caught, and he almost turned wide eyes on Mädi to share his surprise. Instead, he forced himself to continue observing Schweizer and was glad he did. The man's mouth opened, and his eyebrows shot up in unconcealed amazement.

Meanwhile, Mädi thanked the woman and ended the call, her voice staying steady and her face impassive. Renzo was glad he and Mädi were better at controlling their surprise than Schweizer was, but he was worried. Their ace had turned out to be a deuce. What would they use to pump the man for information now?

He told himself to stay calm. Yes, things hadn't worked the way they'd expected, but maybe their idea hadn't been a complete dud after all. Schweizer had been stunned by his ex-wife's answer. But what did that mean? Were they left with a smug bastard who would now turn smugger? Or could they use these first unsettled moments of his to their advantage?

Schweizer certainly wasn't looking smug. He was staring down at his hands, clasped in his lap, and shaking his head. Renzo turned to Mädi with a finger at his lips, and she nodded. Together they waited in silence.

Schweizer mumbled something that sounded like, "Why did she . . . ?"

Was he talking about his wife? Renzo wondered. Or was he talking about . . . ?

"Katica?" Renzo asked gently.

Schweizer raised his head. "There's no point telling you the truth. You won't believe me."

"You mean your alibi—what your wife said—that's *not* the truth?"

Schweizer's head jerked. "She knew about Katica, or at least, she knew some of it. But she still . . ." His voice cracked. "She's good to me. Better than I deserve."

Renzo kept pushing. "Are you saying the alibi was a lie? You *were* there when Katica died? Were you up the tower with her?"

Schweizer looked at him and shook his head vehemently. "No. *No.* I had nothing to do with what happened. I loved her. I couldn't bear it . . ."

Renzo saw a question on Mädi's face; he nodded very slightly. "Did you want her to leave her husband?" she asked sympathetically. "And she refused? Then you argued . . ."

But Schweizer kept shaking his head, his hands over his eyes. "Don't you get it? I watched her die! I saw her fall from the same place where I'd watched the sunset with her, and there was nothing I could do to save her. She hit the Münsterplatz fifteen feet away. It was . . ." His indrawn breath sounded like a sob.

Renzo glanced again at Mädi, and she leaned across the coffee table toward Schweizer, reaching out to give his knee a brief, gentle touch. "I'm so sorry. That must have been terrible. The police assumed she jumped from the lower gallery, but you say it was the higher one?"

Schweizer took his hands away from his face, which didn't look so boyish anymore. "I was standing in the Münsterplatz, waiting for a delivery van to show up, and I didn't see the moment when she . . . when she actually . . . came away from the tower. She didn't scream, but . . . I must have heard something because I looked up, and it was . . . I can still hear the noise when she landed on the cobblestones. I ran to her. Her eyes were open—I don't know if she could see me. God!" He covered his face with his hands again as if he could block out the image in his mind.

"Had you just broken up with her?" Mädi said in the same soothing voice she'd used before. But, this time, her tone didn't work.

Schweizer leaped from his chair, which made Renzo get up as well. The man looked back and forth between them wildly. "No. She came up the stairs from the Matte and met me on the Pläfe in the middle of the night. I thought we'd grab some time for sex, but no, she'd come to break up with *me*. Said we had to stop."

Renzo raised his eyebrows at Mädi. So, Katica broke up with Schweizer and then jumped to her death. *That* was certainly news. If it was true.

Before either of them could ask a question, Schweizer went on. "It wasn't my fault—truly! When I left the church to wait for the van, she was sitting in a pew. She'd come to tell me goodbye, and I thought she was about to go home. She was calm; *I* was the one who was upset because I didn't want things to end. Next thing I knew, she was falling through the air in front of me. The horror of it. I—" He broke off and walked away from them to stand behind his desk with his back to them, looking out the window and drawing shaky breaths.

Renzo wanted to keep him talking about the past. "You didn't want to end the affair; you must have been angry with her."

Schweizer spun to face them. "Katica was the most exciting woman I've ever slept with. She was... on fire. Not demanding... I don't mean that. Just... totally there, pouring herself out, like there was no 'off' switch. All the time, not just in bed—being with her was amazing. I was *always* afraid she'd end it—first with the pregnancy and then after the boy was born. But she kept wanting to meet, even with that tiny baby screaming his head off beside us in the bed. Then, all of a sudden, it was over. And before I could even... deal with that, she was dead. Angry? I didn't have time to get angry. I was crushed."

Schweizer's voice caught at these last words, but after that, he seemed to pull himself back into the present. He returned to the chair he'd abandoned and sat back down, running his fingers through his hair again—it was a gesture that reminded Renzo of Giuliana, but in Schweizer, it was preening.

Mädi was nodding at Schweizer understandingly. "Do you think she broke up with you because she was planning to kill herself, or did she break up with you for other reasons and then... something happened to make her jump?"

"I've already told you nothing happened. I know what you're getting at—you want to know if I did something to her. But I didn't. Yes, I begged her to reconsider, but I didn't yell at her or hit her. I was too sad. I had to leave her to meet the van. She was sitting in the nave of the Münster then, but I assumed she'd go home to the baby—and to be there when her husband and daughter got up. The truth is, I was upset but still hoping she'd get over her attack of conscience and we'd be back together in a couple of weeks. We were... so good together. I didn't think she could give that up for long."

You mean you didn't think she could give you *up for long,* Renzo thought. Something self-satisfied about the man rubbed him the wrong way, but he reined it in.

"Herr Schweizer." Mädi leaned forward. "I want to know if, looking back, you think she was already determined to commit suicide when she met you in the park that night."

"Absolutely not!" he said violently. Then, in a softer voice, he added, "I don't know. The idea never occurred to me. Nothing she said made me think she had that in mind. Otherwise, I'd never have left her side. I swear it."

Something turned over in Renzo's mind. "You said you didn't look up until Katica Horvat was already falling. Would you have been able to see someone else up there as she fell? *Did* you see anyone?"

Schweizer frowned. "I guess you really do think someone killed Katica." His reaction seemed genuinely puzzled, as though he was considering this possibility for the first time. Renzo didn't think he was faking it. But maybe the man was a good actor. Someone who cheated on his wife so persistently would have to be, wouldn't he?

"Did you see anyone?" Renzo asked again. "Or . . . was there something about the way she fell that makes you think an attacker could have knocked her out and thrown her over? Especially since you say she didn't make a noise as she fell."

Schweizer bit his lip. He was shaking his head again. "Who would have killed her? Who could have had a reason to?" Then he realized Renzo was still waiting for an answer. "It was too dark for me to see if anyone else was up there in the tower. All I saw was Katica falling. No . . . flashlight beams from the gallery or lights in the apartment."

"But you're sure she came off the upper gallery, not the lower one?"

"I must have looked up only a second after she jumped. She was just at the level of the apartment. I watched her fall past it. There was no way she could have come off that lower balcony." Schweizer closed his eyes, pressed both hands to his chest, and took a shaky breath. Again, it *seemed* genuine—a man picturing a woman he loved hurtling to the ground.

Renzo changed tack. "Do you think her husband knew about your affair?"

"Katica told me he had no idea." Schweizer considered their question. "Lovro?" He shook his head. "You think Lovro killed her? I doubt it. I often saw them together in the shop, and he never acted like he wanted to keep her away from me. I asked her, early on, if he was ever violent with her, and she became furious. Told me never to say or even think anything bad about him because he was a good and honorable man who loved her, and she loved him, too." His mouth turned down. "Maybe if he'd been a worse husband, she might not have felt so guilty about cheating on him, and she wouldn't have broken up with me."

Renzo sighed and heard Mädi make a similar sound of frustration at Schweizer's focus. It appeared he was too self-involved to give them useful insights into Lovro as a husband or Lovro and Katica's interaction with each other. He could only talk about Lovro's reaction to himself.

"In any case," Schweizer continued. "I'm sure Katica would have told me right away if he'd confronted her about our affair."

Mädi was ready with the next question. "Do you believe Goran is your son, Herr Schweizer?"

"I . . ." He paused, and a stubborn look came over his face. "We used condoms. I couldn't afford another kid back then, and now that I'm paying child support and alimony to my ex-wife, I can afford it even less. Do *you* know something about Goran that I don't?" Without waiting for an answer, he hurried on. "Honestly, I don't think Katica knew herself, and she didn't want to. We never talked about it."

"A few more questions," said Renzo. "First: What time was it when you left Frau Horvat sitting in the Münster and went out to meet the van in the Münsterplatz, and how much later was it when she died?"

"It was Tuesday morning, Münstergasse market day, and the van was due at four thirty, so I must have gone out to wait for it at four twenty, maybe a bit later, because I didn't want to leave Katica. The van was late, and I was really pissed off, but I stayed out there. It must have been just before five when . . . she jumped." He shivered.

"Why didn't you call the police or an ambulance?"

"The police?" Schweizer sounded as if the idea had never occurred to him. "I just . . . couldn't. The van . . ."

Renzo was struck by something that should have been obvious. "Does the reason you couldn't call the police have something to do with what was inside the delivery van you were meeting at four thirty in the morning?"

Schweizer opened his mouth, then closed it again. A cagey, mulish look came over his face. Perhaps he was remembering the alibi his wife had given him and the reason he'd needed it in the first place. Maybe he was regretting his sudden attack of honesty.

The man said nothing more; the three of them sat in silence for a few moments.

Finally, Renzo spoke. "Do you know what a statute of limitations is?"

Schweizer stared at the table in front of him.

"In Switzerland, there is a statute of limitations on most crimes, except for terrible ones like having sex with children. After a certain number of years have passed, you can no longer be prosecuted for breaking the law. I assume there was something—or someone—stolen or illegal in that van. Were you helping to bring children into Switzerland to be sold for prostitution?"

"God, no." Schweizer looked horrified. "It was nothing like that, *nothing*. Not people, not drugs. Just . . . it was just . . ." Renzo watched him wrestle with himself for a couple more seconds. Then he shrugged. "It was cigarettes. Smuggled cigarettes."

Renzo and Mädi's eyes met again as Schweizer went back to staring at the table. Mädi looked amazed, and Renzo could see why. It was such a . . . well, old-fashioned crime. Even fifteen years ago, there couldn't have been too many people making money from selling illegal cigarettes in Bern; the big bucks would have been made by the middlemen shepherding them *through* Switzerland from one destination to another.

"You're telling us that, in addition to working as a stonemason, you were receiving and selling smuggled goods?"

"No," began Schweizer yet again. "Not me. I was a customer. That meant I knew about the business, and when I stayed over at my Postgasse place, I sometimes got up early and came over to help unload the van in exchange for a few free smokes."

Renzo was willing to bet there'd been more to it than that. More like cartons of cigarettes that Schweizer could sell to his fellow workmen at the Münster and at his local bar in Münchenbuchsee. But still, hardly the crime of the century. For a moment, it seemed to Renzo inconceivable that something so trivial had made Schweizer keep silent about Katica's death for fifteen years. If he'd called the police back then and told them the whole story, Grossenbacher's investigation would have gone so differently. No one would have been able to shut it down.

Even now, he couldn't be sure Schweizer was telling the truth. But at least no one was trying to end *his* inquiry, as they had Grossenbacher's. He'd simply keep going until he had the whole story.

He turned his attention back to the others. Mädi was smiling at Schweizer. "We don't care about illegal cigarettes, do we, Renzo? We're just grateful for what you've told us. Talking to the last person who saw Katica alive is—"

"Not me," he said quickly, shrinking back. "*I'm* not the last person to see her alive—except for when she was falling."

Renzo reached out and grabbed Schweizer's wrist before he could stop himself. "What do you mean?"

Schweizer glanced down at the hand gripping his wrist, then looked back at Renzo with mild surprise. "When I went out to meet the van, I left her in the church with the sexton," he said simply. "With Klaus Friedli."

"Friedli!" Renzo thought of his encounter on Tuesday afternoon with that pompous man. "I don't understand. Was he standing with you in the Münsterplatz when Katica jumped?"

"No. That's what I'm telling you. He always waited for deliveries inside the church—in his comfy office. I was the one outside in the cold," he added with a whine.

"You're telling us," Renzo said incredulously, "that the Münster's sexton takes deliveries of smuggled cigarettes and sells them . . . from the church?"

Schweizer looked at him for a long moment, apparently trying to work out how much to say, even after he'd revealed so much. At last, he spoke. "Well, yeah. I wasn't going to tell you now that I've kept it quiet for so long. Honor among thieves and all that." Renzo thought it more likely that the man had been protecting himself, not the sexton. He let Schweizer continue. "But I don't owe Friedli anything. And besides, I doubt he's still doing it. The profits were already drying up before he took over the business from his father, and when I knew him, he often talked about packing the whole thing in."

"But where did he hide the cigarettes? Among the bells?"

Schweizer laughed this time. "The workmen would have stolen them if he'd put them anywhere in the tower. No, there's a wine cellar that can only be accessed from his office. He kept them there, underground, where it's nice and cool."

Mädi was shaking her head. Renzo reminded himself not to let this revelation—however unlikely—distract them from Katica's death.

He cleared his throat. "So, Katica knew about Friedli's business, and she came up the stairs from the Matte at three thirty in the morning to talk to you because she knew you'd be there helping Friedli unload the cigarettes?"

"More or less. Since it was a market day, she assumed I'd be at the Münster with Friedli, but she texted me to meet her on the Pläfe half an hour earlier. She said she needed to talk." Schweizer shifted restlessly in his chair. "Can we stop now? I'm tired, and I need the bathroom, a drink, and some dinner. I've told you everything I know. Maybe I'll remember something new later in the week. But right now, I'm done."

Renzo felt exhausted, too. He'd started the morning having coffee with Artur Pereira, the works foreman; it seemed long ago. Then he'd spoken to Zora and Goran; Lovro and Ivana; Grossenbacher; and, now, Schweizer. He didn't think his brain could absorb any new information. He needed to sift through what he'd already taken in, and he wasn't sure he'd find the energy for that this evening.

Renzo turned to Mädi, who was frowning in concentration. "Do you have any more questions for Herr Schweizer?"

"Not tonight." She extracted two Kantonspolizei Bern cards and a pen from her handbag. "One card has all my information in case you want to tell us anything. Please write your private address and cell number on the other."

Renzo watched as Schweizer wrote his name down, reflecting on how much they'd learned in a short space of time. It was enough to take things in a completely different direction, he thought, certainly enough to give them some new leads. That was, assuming Schweizer was now being honest. Because, Renzo reminded himself wryly, the man had been lying about this for fifteen years. Why should they trust him to be telling them the truth now?

24

Lorraine, Thursday evening, June 27

Five minutes later, Renzo and Mädi were sitting in the Fiat. It had been a mostly sunny day with a brisk breeze, and now it was turning into a warm, golden evening—an evening for sitting outside, hopefully not alone.

"I know we're both exhausted," Renzo said, "but I want to talk about all this while it's fresh in my mind. Do you want to come back to my apartment and discuss what we've gotten from Grossenbacher and Schweizer over some takeout? Do you like Indian food? Okra's right around the corner from my place."

Mädi paused for a moment. "Sure, but only if we eat first and then talk. I'm starving."

"See if you can find the menu on your phone, and we'll call it in. I already know I'm having the spinach and lamb curry with a side of naan. And a Kingfisher beer."

"Make that two naans and two beers." Mädi was scrolling through Okra's dishes. "I'm looking for something with eggplant and ginger."

By the time they got to the restaurant in the Lorraine, their order was ready, and Renzo found a parking place a few blocks from his apartment. He led Mädi up the stairs and into the main room. She looked at the three stools at the kitchen island, the dark blue sofa, and the glass coffee table and laughed. "Shall I assume the bedroom contains a mattress on the floor and an orange crate with a lamp on it?"

"Ha! Not quite. I went to IKEA and got a nice big bed with two night tables and two lamps. The tables even have drawers." Renzo grinned as he defended himself.

"Hmm," said Mädi. "Why am I not surprised that you'd spend money on a big bed before getting any kind of table to eat at?"

I'm not the one bringing up the bed here, thought Renzo, but he knew better than to treat her comment as a come-on. Not tonight. Instead, he said, with pretend indignation, "What do you mean? There's a lovely bistro table with two matching chairs out on the balcony." He got plates and cutlery. "Do you mind if I take a quick shower?"

"Go ahead," said Mädi. "I'll put the food out."

When he returned, showered, barefoot, and dressed in a white T-shirt and baggy black cargo shorts, he noticed that Mädi was also barefoot. She was over at the kitchen's back wall looking at a corkboard filled with photos of the children, drawings they'd made for him, and a piece of printer paper containing his son's name: Angelo. The capital letters meandered up the page; the "G" was a "C," the "N" was backward, and one of the arms of the "E" was very long and slanted downward, but it was readable. Renzo walked up behind Mädi, careful not to get too close. She half turned toward him, smiling, and tapped a finger on the name. "I bet he wishes you'd named him something shorter. How old is he?"

"He's six. One year of kindergarten to go. His sister is four. Wait until she has to write her name: it's Antonietta."

Mädi moved her finger to a snapshot of Renzo sitting in a garden chair with a child on each knee. Angelo was laughing, Antonietta was snuggling into her father's shoulder, and Renzo . . . well, he thought of it as his happiness picture. "My brother took that."

"It's lovely." There was a pause in which he was sure Mädi was about to say more. Instead, she moved past him to the food on the countertop. "Come on, it's getting cold."

The balcony table was a little small for all the cartons, but they managed to fill their plates with dal, rice, curry, and torn pieces of naan. As they ate, Renzo told her a few funny stories about the kids and asked her about her new nephew with the unfortunate name of Elvis. Then Mädi told him more about her father.

"I'm not sure I ever saw him sober. He treated hangovers with more alcohol, but most of the time, he was a loving drunk—or a sleepy one. As a small child, I thought he was lots of fun and couldn't understand why my mother and older sister were usually upset with him. But then I started to see how irresponsible he could be. Always late, always forgetting to do or buy things. But never violent, thank God."

Renzo thought about his fireman father who, because of shift-work, was sometimes home for several days at a stretch. During that time, he was his children's primary caretaker while their mother worked in a factory. Loving and fun, yes, but also utterly dependable, a tower of strength in his family's lives. "It must have been especially hard on your mother."

"They divorced when I was twelve. We still saw him regularly, at least one weekend a month, but he wasn't allowed to drive us anywhere. The judge made sure of that after she saw all those drunk driving charges."

Renzo explained the system he and Fränzi were trying, with the kids staying in the family apartment and the two adults moving back and forth between the same small apartment. "It's working so far," he told her.

"How long have you been doing it?" Mädi asked.

"Less than a month," he admitted.

Mädi drank the last of her Kingfisher. "Well, it may be complicated, but it's a lot cheaper and easier than finding two three-bedroom apartments near the kids' school, one for each of you. I've been apartment hunting for months now, so I should know."

Renzo watched Mädi while she talked. He imagined stroking her close-cropped hair the way he would an animal's fur. *That's right*, he told himself, *keep your fantasies focused above the neck*. He glanced away from her and at the balcony across the street, where his retirement-aged neighbors both waved enthusiastically. He waved back, imagining them speculating about him sitting here with a woman.

Mädi waved back, too. "I bet they wonder why sometimes they see only you out here and sometimes only your wife."

And probably my wife with one man after the other. Renzo wanted to growl out the words, although he knew how idiotic that would be, especially with Mädi sitting beside him. "I'll clear this up." He pointed at the cartons and dirty plates. "Then let's go over our notes from the afternoon."

She got up to help, and with both of them barefoot next to each other, he could see that she was about half an inch taller. It didn't bother him. Like her skinny frame, it was part of what made her different. She was unlike either Fränzi and Giuliana, and that was good.

They sat on the balcony and talked over what they'd learned from Grossenbacher and Schweizer.

"Everything Grossenbacher told us confirmed what I'd heard so far," Renzo told Mädi. "Which was good. It reassured me that I haven't missed anything crucial. Even his distrust of Ivana Horvat—it convinced me that my own reaction to her was legitimate."

"And what he said about the sexton, Friedli," Mädi added immediately, "combined with what Schweizer told us afterward. Now we know why Friedli didn't call the police straight away, and also why he wanted the investigation to be over as quickly as possible—because he was afraid of the police finding his cigarettes." She was smiling triumphantly at Renzo. Then she caught something on his face and gave him a worried look. "Or . . . do you think I've got it wrong?"

"I think you've got it absolutely right," he assured her. "I just keep wondering how the sexton got away with running an illegal business out of the church for so long. I think he must have an accomplice on the parish council. Frau Kellenberger said something about that yesterday evening, and I haven't followed up. It sounds like I need to talk to the minister again—Frau Zehnder. Although, honestly, those cigarettes aren't my priority right now."

They sat for a moment in silence before Mädi said, "And then there was Schweizer. That trick with his wife: he was stunned when she confirmed his alibi. Yet, in spite of that, he told us a whole new story." She faltered again. "You didn't expect that, did you? Should I have seen—?"

She broke off, and Renzo wondered why she sounded unsure of herself. Was he doing something to knock her confidence? He couldn't imagine what it could be. He'd felt like they worked together smoothly. But had he told her that? Maybe not. He was being so careful not to come on to her that he'd forgotten to praise her in case she took it the wrong way.

"I *did* hope threatening to call his wife might make him nervous," he told Mädi, "and it certainly rattled him, but everything else was as much of a surprise to me as it was to you. All of that talk about watching her fall—God, how awful. If it's true! This could be a new ploy. He's been lying for years. Maybe now he's trying to make us believe he was outside watching her fall rather than up in the tower, throwing her off."

Mädi clasped her hands in front of her on the metal table. "You're right. I was taking it for granted that he was finally telling the truth. Stupid, huh?"

"Mädi," he said, reaching out and covering her hands with his own. "Don't say that. You're great at this and an excellent interview partner. Why do you think I asked you to come with me? I remembered how smart you were when we worked on that bicycle murder together. This is my first case alone, and I wanted your help. And your opinion, so, tell me: Do *you* feel Ben Schweizer is telling the truth at last?" He realized he was still touching her hands, so he sat back and crossed his arms.

She bit her lip. "Well . . . he thought his wife was going to rat him out. When she didn't, he was off the hook! All he had to say was, 'See, I told you. I *was* at home.' Instead, he spilled everything. Why would he do that unless he had a real attack of conscience?"

"That's just how I see it. But—"

Mädi interrupted. "But he could have been manipulating us, letting something slip at just the right moment. And 'confessing' about the cigarettes would be a good way of deflecting us from the bigger crime of murder."

"Yeah," Renzo agreed. "We'll have to get him to tell us all about it *again* to see if we can catch him in any inconsistencies. To me, his story—and his emotions—seemed real, but I've been fooled before. At least we have Friedli to interview for confirmation. If only Schweizer doesn't get to the sexton before we do and tell him what to say. But I don't think Friedli's going to feel like doing Schweizer any favors, not now that he's told us about the cigarette business."

"So, the next step is Friedli," Mädi said. "But I can't join you tomorrow. Sabine and I are spending all morning with the prosecutor discussing our wife murder, and I think there will be a lot to deal with that afternoon, too. I'm disappointed to let you down. I hope you understand."

"Of course I do," Renzo said. "I respect you for not running out on your case. Or on Sabine. I hope *you* understand that I'm planning on talking to Friedli first thing tomorrow anyway. I'm supposed to be on Seiler with Giuliana, you know, and I need to get back to that next week."

Renzo felt like offering her more to eat and drink. No, what he actually wanted was to grab her hand and take her to bed. But all he did was stand up.

"Thanks for dinner," she said.

"Thanks for letting me pay for it this time," he answered. "And for brainstorming with me. I'll let you know what I get out of Friedli and whether I have to go back to Schweizer right away and . . . what comes out of all this."

She picked up the two empty bottles and walked back indoors to set them down on the kitchen island. Then she turned and faced him. Their eyes met, and she took a small step toward him. For a moment, he was sure she was going to put her arms around him; his breath caught in his throat. Then, before anything could happen, she shifted backward and held out her hand. He took it, and she gave him a smile so full of regret and promise that his disappointment vanished.

"You can tell me the whole Horvat story once you figure it out," she told him. "We'll do it over takeout at my place, okay? I might have my own apartment by then. It's just possible I've found something in Breitenrain. *Daumen drücken!*"

He wished her good luck by squeezing the thumb of his right hand in his fist. She bent to slip on her shoes, and when she straightened, he opened the door for her.

Their eyes held again; Renzo knew he was beaming at her, and he didn't care. In the hall, she raised a hand. "See you," she said. "Good luck with Friedli."

"Same with your wife murderer."

He watched her start down the stairs and listened to her footsteps as she ran all the way to the ground floor, just like he always did. *A woman after my own heart,* he told himself, and then felt a pang.

Giuliana. He hadn't thought of her since their phone call about Ursula Kellenberger. Not with his usual lust and longing, nor as someone whose support he needed. It came to him that what he wanted to do instead was present her with his finished case like a tomcat proudly depositing a disemboweled rat at the feet of his mistress.

Snorting at the image and what it implied about him, he went to clean up the kitchen.

25

Sitting on a canvas stool in the florist's steep garden, Denis spent three hours drawing dark-blue delphinium stalks, balls of pink hydrangea, and salmon-colored gerbera daisies, breaking only to chat briefly with the shop owner and her assistant and drink a glass of water.

Then he went back to his apartment to change. Before he could take a shower, he used masking tape to fasten plastic shopping bags around his cast, a slow process with only one useable hand. It was a beautiful, warm evening, so he decided against jeans and put on loose, brightly patterned shorts that he could easily pull up and down with one hand and a T-shirt with the sleeves cut off so he could get his cast through the armhole.

When he finally looked at himself in the mirror, he saw that it didn't matter what he wore—he still looked like the living dead. One side of his face, the inside of his good arm, and the whole front of one leg were black. The stitches on his forehead were swollen and red, and there were smaller cuts and bruises scattered over the rest of him. Should he cover it all up again? No—he really couldn't be bothered to wriggle in and out of more clothes. It would have to do.

Normally, he'd have ridden his bicycle to meet Zora, but with a broken wrist, that was out of the question, so he decided to go on foot. As soon as he left his building, he became aware of people doing double takes or wincing as he passed. He walked as fast as he could, which was slower than usual, first to the Kirchenfeld Bridge, which he crossed before heading down Aegertenstrasse to tackle the Monbijou Bridge. Approaching the ice cream shop on the far side, he saw Zora immediately. She was wearing dark-purple pants that came to just above the knee, as tight as jeans but made of thinner material, and a long, pale-purple T-shirt that unfortunately covered her ass. She had on comfortable sandals, not the thin, strappy ones that so many women wore. Good. It drove him crazy to be with girls who couldn't walk normally.

She turned and saw him, and instead of waiting, she moved toward him, looking so glad to see him that it made his chest hurt. He stopped a foot away from her, not sure what to do. She looked horrified at his injuries, but without a word, she put one hand gently on his shoulder and leaned forward to give him the traditional three kisses, her lips barely touching the side of his face with the worst bruises. As she moved from cheek to cheek, he smelled the woodsy, musky scent of her dark hair, loose in a dense cloud around her face and shoulders. He put his good hand on her arm as she greeted him.

"I'm really happy to see you, Denis," she said, looking into his eyes.

"I'm happy to see you, too," he answered, smiling back.

They turned and crossed the street without any discussion about the route to the restaurant, two people who knew the city inside out. Denis let Zora lead—although they walked side by side—to the long stairway that led down from the bridge to the river and the Dampfzentrale restaurant, where Denis had reserved a table outside.

When they were seated so both faced the river, Zora leaned toward him. "I promise I'm only going to say this once, Denis. I'm sorry Goran hurt you so badly. Thank God you didn't die."

Denis took her hand in his good one. "I'm okay. And I honestly don't think Goran wanted to kill me. Let's not talk about it."

They ordered food and beer, and the splash of the river was in their ears as they ate and drank and talked. They mostly told stories about their apprenticeships and their jobs, one with plants and the other with glass, but both with color. Zora told him how her father had wanted her to go to university and study botany instead of becoming a gardener and how they'd compromised on her attending Gymnasium so that she'd have the credentials to switch to university someday. Denis explained how the same thing had happened to him, but worse. Instead of getting to start working with Nathan Winter at fifteen, as he'd wanted to, his mother and her parents, waving their doctorates in his face, had insisted that he not only attend Gymnasium but get a university degree.

"They were sure that once I had a bachelor's in art history, I'd want to go on studying, just as they had. But the day after my sixth semester of Uni was over, and I had all the credits I needed for a BA, I showed up in Nathan's studio, and he hired me as an apprentice on the spot. Actually, it wasn't a standard apprenticeship because I'd been working for him off and on since I was a kid, plus full-time during summers, so I already knew a lot. But we wanted to make it official, so we filled out all the paperwork, and I jumped through the hoops. I've been a full-fledged glassmaker for over two years now."

After they finished eating, they ordered more beer and watched as the Aare darkened except where streetlights sparkled on its ripples and eddies. Their chairs were touching, and Denis put his right arm around Zora's shoulders, which felt broad and strong and somehow just right, and she leaned her head against him. When she straightened up, he took his arm back, and she asked him an unexpected question. "Why did you live with your grandparents? Instead of with your mother and father, I mean? I know they're separated, but that's all I remember."

He'd rather have talked about almost anything else. But if anyone had the right to ask about mothers, it was Zora.

He kept his voice as light as he could. "Do you want a two-sentence explanation or the whole story?"

"Story, please," she said.

He took a sip from his glass and began. "My mother's name is Anja, and my father is Robert Tracey, called Robby. When my parents met, they both wanted to be artists—my father a painter, my mother a sculptor. She was eighteen and still in Gymnasium, and my father was twenty; he'd already been to art college in the US. He was an American from a small town near Boston, and he'd come to Bern because a Swiss artist visiting his college had offered to work with him. They met at a party, my parents, and that was it. As in, two days later, my mother moved out of my grandparents' place and into an apartment that my father was sharing with a bunch of other people." He rolled his eyes at Zora as if he were the parent and they the foolish kids—which, in comparison to the person Denis was now, they had been.

Zora chuckled. "I moved away from my father and Ivana's at sixteen, so I'm not going to disapprove of your mother for that."

"Fair enough," Denis agreed. "I guess I'm cynical mainly because I know what happened next. For a while, they worked on creating art. My father really can paint, and my mother can carve wood and stone and weld metal. But the whole thing was more about rebelling against what their parents wanted them to do—and having sex, naturally! Both of them admit that now. Anyway, after five months of living with Robby, Anja got pregnant with me. As far as she was concerned, this was a huge mistake that would fuck up her life. But my grandparents and, surprisingly, Robby..."

Zora interrupted. "Do you call them by their first names all the time?"

Denis shrugged. "It's what they both want me to do and mostly I think of them that way. But I make a point of calling my mother 'Mam' to her face to remind her who she is."

"I see," said Zora, in a voice that suggested she wasn't sure she did. "Sorry I interrupted. Back to the pregnancy."

"Anja wanted an abortion, but the idea made her parents and Robby hysterical. At least, that's how she tells it. Apparently, my grandparents barely spoke to my father, but on this subject, they were allies. It didn't have anything to do with religion; I guess they were just obsessed with their genes or something."

"You say that like it isn't *you* you're talking about. *Your* genes. I don't think you're being fair. You must feel at least a little bit grateful to them. *I* certainly do."

"Thank you," he said mockingly and received such a fond, quirky smile from her that his chest tightened again, and he had to take a deep breath. "Sure, I feel glad to be here," he told Zora, "but I'm on Anja's side. Nobody should be able to tell the *mother* of a baby how to handle being pregnant. And Anja, who was supposed to be such a rebel, couldn't stand up to all the pressure they put on her. She told them she'd have me, but only if my grandparents would take care of me. Once I was born, she handed me over, finished Gymnasium, and went off to Uni Bern."

"If your father made her keep you," Zora asked fiercely, "why isn't he around?"

"He wised up. He went back to the US, got a business degree, and took a job selling real estate with his uncle in Florida. Eventually, he married a lawyer named Vicky, and they have two daughters, my half sisters. Painting is just a hobby for him now."

"But why aren't you *with* him?" Zora's face was full of indignation.

"Don't be mad at him. He's a good guy, Robby. He stayed in Bern six months after Anja left him, and that whole time, he kept me with him. He painted during the day and worked in a bar at night, and when he couldn't get one of the people sharing the flat to babysit me, he'd take me to the bar and either wear me on his chest as he served drinks or set up a little folding crib for me in a backroom. I was under a year old, so I don't remember any of it, but he really tried. When he decided to go back to the US, he wanted to take me to live with his parents while he figured things out, but my grandparents were desperate to keep me in Bern, so eventually, he agreed. After that, I didn't see him for a while, but since I turned five, I've gone to Florida for a month every summer and for Christmas, as well, a couple of times. I love him."

He stared out at the Aare, thinking about how uncomplicated and happy his relationship with his father was and wondering, not for the first time, why he resented his mother's neglect of him but not his father's. Probably because his father texted him often, sent him emails, remembered his birthday, and spent lots of time with him when he was in Florida—time that Denis knew his father enjoyed. But that wasn't the only reason he forgave his father. Like most people, he expected more of mothers.

After a brief silence, he gave Zora a sidelong glance.

Her eyes were fixed on the river. "I was born five months after my parents got married, so I guess I was a mistake, too. My father was thirty, my mother nineteen. They got married a few weeks before they left Croatia, and I was born here in Bern."

She sounded sad, so he said, "Hey, this morning you talked about how much your mother loved you, so you can be sure you weren't a mistake. Besides, you must know lots of couples, like I do, who live together until a baby's on the way and then get married. Maybe that's how it was with your parents."

Zora shook her head and grinned at him as if he were a lovable idiot. "I don't know much about the small town in Istria that my parents come from. But I know enough to be sure that in those days it wasn't a place where a teenage girl wanted anyone to think she'd *had* to get married."

Denis figured he might as well reveal the true depth of his ignorance about Croatia. "What about the war?" he asked. "Is that why your parents came here?"

"Now it's my turn to ask if you want the long version or the short one."

"Whatever you want to tell me."

It was almost nine thirty now, and the sky had turned pink and orange. Zora's beer glass was still half full, and she held it without drinking. "Croatia's war started in 1991," she told him, "when it declared independence from Yugoslavia, and it ended in 1995 when we'd won back all the territory the Serbians occupied. Everything was chaotic by then. Whole cities and towns had been destroyed, and hundreds of thousands of Croatians had been made homeless. We also took in Bosnian refugees. Things were worse for them, without a doubt."

"When was that terrible killing? Serbrenica?"

"*Sre*brenica," she corrected, changing the first syllable, accenting the "i," and making the "c" sound like "ts." "That was 1995. Eight thousand men and boys, Bosnian Muslims, were massacred by Bosnian Serbs, while the UN did nothing. The UN troops were caught in a bind, I know that, but I still . . . Hmm. By that year, Croatia wasn't losing many people. But we had our massacre, too, in Vukovar in 1991."

"I'm sorry," Denis said. "I don't know anything about it."

"You're not the only one who hasn't heard of it. Vukovar is a town in Slavonia that was besieged by the Yugoslav People's Army. Our fighters had defended the city for eighty-seven days. When it fell, Serbian paramilitaries dragged off prisoners of war and civilians, shot them, and buried them in a mass grave."

Denis listened numbly. He almost wished he hadn't asked; he should have realized how difficult it would be for her. The fall of a city under siege—for him, that was *Game of Thrones* stuff, not real life. Not real death. But these things had happened to her fellow Croatians less than a decade before he was born.

"What about *your* family? Did anyone—?"

"It affected them and all their friends. My father went to fight in 1993 and served for about two years, winning back land the Serbs had taken. He doesn't talk about it, but he has a big scar on his back from when he was a soldier. Even afterwards . . . So many people were left with no homes or jobs." She trailed off, looking at Denis almost apologetically. "I wouldn't want you to think I'm obsessed with all this. It's just . . . it's my history. I've read a lot about it. But my father won't tell me which battles he was in. He isn't angry that I'm curious; he just doesn't want to remember it."

Zora's father might be the only person Denis knew who'd fought in a war. Like most Swiss his age, he had great-grandfathers who'd guarded the border against invasion during the Second World War—an invasion that, thank God, never came. But you couldn't call that fighting. There were people all over the world killing each other in wars small and large, but as a Swiss, his chances of ever having to face something like that were almost nonexistent. How little the Swiss, with their precious neutrality, had suffered over the years. It made him feel incredibly lucky but also somehow . . . ashamed.

Before he could try to articulate this, Zora said something that surprised him. "The person who really suffered was Ivana, my stepmother. She was supposed to marry her older brother's best friend. He and her brother were policemen. Since Croatia had no army when it declared itself a country, the police ended up fighting at the beginning. First her brother was killed, then her boyfriend. They were twenty-five. *Our* age, Denis. I might not like Ivana, but whenever she starts criticizing me, I try to remember what happened to those men she loved." She gave him a rueful grin. "Of course, sometimes I lose my temper at her anyway, or at least I used to."

Imagine becoming a village policeman with your best friend, figuring the most you'd have to do would be get drunks home safely and stop teenagers vandalizing the school, and then finding out that you were expected to fight a war against ridiculous odds with no training.

"God, that's so sad," he said, knowing even as he spoke how inadequate it was. "I'm going to tell Renzo. What those Croatian policemen had to do."

"You like him?" she asked curiously.

"I do, yeah."

Zora touched his arm. "In that case, can you see if Renzo will do me a favor?"

"I can ask," he said, surprised. "What is it?"

"Goran's desperate to find out whether he's really our father's son. I'm afraid he's going to confront Tata about it. I thought if we could get tests done showing that we're brother and sister, it might satisfy him. But he can't request a DNA test until he's eighteen. Except I bet Renzo knows a way Goran and I can check. So could you find out?"

He could see why Zora had come up with this idea. But still . . . "What will you do if you're only halves?"

She frowned. "We'll deal with that if it happens. If it doesn't, then the problem is solved, and Tata never has to know."

"I'll call Renzo tomorrow. Will you both have to go to a lab to collect the DNA?"

"I don't think so. I think we just have to scrape our mouths with something. I googled it." Zora looked as if he'd lifted a burden off her shoulders. He just hoped he could deliver. Perhaps he was imagining it, but her smiles had started to give him a lot of promise.

He didn't want to break the moment, but there was one more conversation they needed to have, and he hadn't managed to get to it yet. He decided he'd ask for the check, and then, during the walk home, he'd do it.

They strolled back along the bank of the Aare in the June twilight. A couple of blocks before the Golden Goat, they turned away from the Aare and down the short road toward the staircase and, beside it, the elevator leading up to the Münster platform. His apartment was only a few minutes' walk from there. It wasn't yet ten o'clock, so Denis decided to ask her to come to his place. Maybe there, within his own safe walls, he'd manage to get his story told. And then . . . they'd see.

Denis turned toward the stairs, but Zora caught his arm and pulled him to her side. "Where are you taking me?" he asked her.

"You'll see." Her face was full of mischief.

Beyond the staircase and the elevator was the high stone wall that supported the Pläfe. She led him along it to some unobtrusive steps that climbed up to a small door in the wall. She took a ring of keys from her daypack, unlocked the door, pushed it open, and turned to him with wide eyes and raised eyebrows, holding a finger to her lips.

Not daring to whisper, he followed her through the door, which she closed and locked behind them.

The sun had just set, but the sky was still light, and Denis could see that he was on the threshold of a tiny one-room cottage made of wood—a shack, really—that housed a cluttered office of sorts: a desk with a chair facing the entrance and shelves holding books and brochures. There were also food products for sale: jams, bottles of wine and fruit syrups, and jars of tomato sauce for pasta.

Looking around, he realized that the shack was actually a lean-to built against the Pläfe wall. An open door led into a garden, and Zora took him out onto a strip of flat land from which terraced rows of plants and trees flowed upward toward the outer walls of the Old City. High above them soared the tower of the Münster with its stone fili-gree tip; closer, but still far above his head, were the white walls and tall windows of a great patrician townhouse that now housed govern-ment offices.

Zora smiled at his astonished expression.

"Where are we?" he asked in a soft voice.

"It's called the *Stiftsgarten*," Zora told him, waving at the expanse of flowers, vines, and trees. "The land belongs to the canton. It used to be a wilderness, but a woman named Angela Losert has been fixing it up with the help of volunteers."

"You're one of them?"

"I've been helping here since I was fifteen. There are grapevines for wine, fruit trees, heirloom vegetables, and rare plants, all of them organic. Lots of little creatures live here, too, right in the middle of the city. I want to give you a tour."

"I'd love that. But first . . ." Denis took a deep breath and exhaled shakily. "First, I need to tell you something."

She stared at him, her delight in sharing her treasured place draining from her face. "Okay," she said, motioning toward four mismatched metal chairs and a little table that sat facing the garden not far from the ramshackle cottage. "What's wrong?"

Denis sat down in the third chair in the row and waited for Zora to take the seat next to him. Instead, she perched on the first chair, leaving an empty place between them, and he realized that everything won-derful about the evening was about to end. But he had to do this, and he was going to go through with it.

"It's about the night your mother died."

Her eyes widened, and she raised one hand to her cheek. "Oh, no," she whispered. Then, in a louder voice, "Tell me, Denis. Now. You're scaring me." Her fingers were pressing into her cheek. "Please. Just get it over with."

He'd thought he might feel relief, but instead, he was overwhelmed with dread. "That time after the funeral, when you said I'd killed your mother—"

"I never said that. Or, at least I . . ."

He held up a hand to stop her. "You . . . you were right," he said. "I've never stopped feeling responsible."

She clenched her hand into a fist and banged it on the thin metal table; the noise seemed to shake the garden. "Tell me what you're talking about."

Denis began speaking fast. "The night your mother died, I was awake because of the wind, and I heard someone on the balcony. I never saw them, but I could hear that it was a woman. She was panting in high-pitched moans, almost like little screams. Then the noise stopped. I figured she'd gone upstairs to the higher balcony. I got out of bed to wake my grandparents, and . . . I heard heavy footsteps."

Zora tipped her head back and stared at the cathedral tower that dominated the evening sky in front of her. Behind the tower, the setting sun had left streaks of pink. "You heard someone following the woman."

"I was terrified. The man stopped right outside my window, catching his breath. I was still standing in that tiny bedroom, and he was just on the other side of the window. We were less than six feet apart, and I could see his outline against the lights shining up from the city. Now I realize he couldn't see me in the dark room, but then I thought he'd spot me if he turned his head. I forgot all about the woman because I was so afraid of the man, afraid he was going to do something to me and my grandparents. In those days, they seemed frail to me because they were so much older than my classmates' parents. I used to worry they'd die."

"You're saying that you didn't go and tell them about the woman who was moaning." Zora spoke in a flat voice, and Denis felt tears come into his eyes.

He got a grip. "Oh, God, Zora, I wish I had. Instead, I got down on the floor and crawled back to my bed, sliding into it like a snake. I put the pillow over my head and pulled the covers up over me, and I lay there for a long time, waiting and listening to the wind, which was very loud. Suddenly, it was morning, and my grandmother was waking me up and telling me that your mother had died—a terrible accident, she said." Denis reached for Zora's hand. "I'm so sorry I didn't do anything to save your mother. I only thought about saving myself."

Zora was staring at him in a way that made him let go of her hand. "But when you heard that Majka was dead," she said, "didn't you tell your grandparents? Didn't you think the police should know that someone had chased her up there? The man you saw might have thrown her off!"

He had known these questions were coming, and now he cringed at Zora's incredulous tone. He'd never been able to justify his behavior to himself, so how could he explain it to Zora? "I . . . what can I say? It seems unbelievable now, horrible, but . . . everyone just wanted to get me out of the way and off to school so they could deal with the crisis. No one wanted to listen to me. No one asked me if I'd heard anything in the night. My grandparents kept saying Katica had fallen—they didn't mention suicide—and everyone seemed convinced that she hadn't gone up to the higher balcony, that she'd 'fallen' from just outside our apartment. I started to doubt my own memory, everything I thought I'd witnessed in the night. And then Friedli, the sexton—remember him?—he got hold of me to find out whether I'd checked the doors and made sure they were all locked. He made me feel so terrible that I couldn't bear to get into even more trouble by talking about the man I'd seen. I didn't want to be the reason that your mother was dead."

"You were ten years old," Zora said thoughtfully, which sounded forgiving, but she didn't look at him, just kept gazing at the dark garden.

Thank God he was almost finished. "But being afraid of being blamed—that wasn't the biggest reason I was silent, not really. I was *ashamed*. I hated what a coward I'd been, and the older I got, the more

I saw that if I'd fetched my grandparents as soon as I heard your mother—or when I saw the man outside my window—she'd still be alive."

Zora kept staring out into the darkness. "Did you figure out who the man was? Have you seen or heard him again since that night?"

"I never heard him speak, just wheeze, and all I saw was an outline. I still have no idea who he was."

Zora shook her head and finally looked at him. "God, Denis, you don't know if the woman *was* my mother. Maybe my mother was quiet and *crept* up the stairs, and it was a second woman you heard. It could have been Ivana or . . . or any of my mother's women friends. Maybe the man you saw was Majka's boyfriend, or my father, or someone else. All these years, I've been worrying about why my mother killed herself. Maybe now I don't have to anymore. Instead, I have to worry about whether my father killed her!"

Denis didn't know what to say. He breathed in the scents of the garden, wanting only to disappear into its darkness.

"Have you told Renzo about this?" she asked.

"No. But I will," he said. "I had to tell you first. I should have told you as soon as I was old enough to realize how much it mattered. I know I could have found you at the store, at least before you moved out. But I felt so guilty, and you were already angry with me." He gave a bitter laugh. "First, I was a coward for hiding from that man, and then I was a coward for not telling you the story. Until now."

He needed to see her expression in the faint light to know what she was thinking, so he slid over into the middle chair between them and took her hand.

She looked at him levelly. "You were only ten, Denis. Your fear of the man in your window was normal. Afterward, you didn't tell me what you'd seen because I was so cruel to you after the funeral. That was an awful thing for me to do to my best friend." She reached out and touched his cheek. "I need to tell you that *I'm* sorry." Her fingers were only on his face for a few seconds, and then she stood and started to make her way back to the little office.

Denis stood, too, maneuvering himself from behind the table. He was not going to get a tour of her hidden garden. All he could do was hope he'd get another chance. "Was I wrong to tell you, Zora?" The question burst out of him. "Should I have kept it to myself?"

She walked through the office and onto the top step, where she pointed toward the alley and locked the door. Coming slowly down the crooked stairs, she joined him, and they walked back to the long staircase leading from the Matte to the upper town. Finally, she said, "I don't know."

They climbed the one hundred eighty-three steps to the platform in silence. On their right, the staircase was open to the steep ground that had for centuries separated the poor along the river from the rich high above it. It was almost dark, the sky a deep twilight. Denis noticed all this dully; he was grappling with the idea that his brave act of telling Zora the truth might have been a mistake, something he'd done for himself, not for her.

They reached the top of the stairs, where the eastern end of the Münster, rounded by the shape of the chancel, loomed over them. They turned to go through the gate into the park and walked along the cathedral's south wall, past its flying buttresses. On that warm night, the benches and chairs scattered throughout the park were still occupied; other people were stretched out on the squares of grass between the trees, talking softly. But Denis didn't consider asking Zora to sit with him again.

At the end of the path, they passed through another set of gates and into the cobblestoned Münsterplatz at the church's western end. Denis suddenly feared that Zora would want to walk to the place under the tower where her mother had fallen, but she continued across the square to Denis's street, Herrengasse.

He stopped in front of his building. "This is where I live."

Zora stood close to him on the sidewalk, looking into his face, and Denis felt overwhelmed by affection and longing for this girl whom he'd loved as a child. "Zora," he said, trying to put everything he was feeling into her name, including his regret.

She stepped toward him, put her arms around his waist, and rested her head on his shoulder. His right arm encircling her, he pulled her in and rested his chin against her hair. They didn't move for a long time. Then Zora lifted her head and said into his ear, "I'll call you tomorrow. I need to think."

He let go, and she said, "Will you ask Renzo about the DNA test?"

God, he'd forgotten. "I will," he promised. "I'll tell you as soon as I know."

She set off at a jog toward the clock tower and the number 10 bus. He watched her go and then headed into his building, comforted by the long hug but still not sure that anything had been resolved.

This DNA test, he thought, shaking his head as he went up the stairs. He would do what Zora wanted, but it was a bad plan. Why take a step that could cause so much disruption? *After everything that has happened*, he thought, *the Horvat family has had enough pain.* Did Zora truly want to risk inflicting even more?

26

Ruth Seiler and Werner Allemann had lived together in Felsenau, a small patch of buildings on the Bern side of the Aare River, famous only, as far as Giuliana knew, for its large brewery. Giuliana usually drank wine, but now and then, during the summer, she enjoyed a Berner Müntschi, one of Felsenau's most popular beers. The brewery was a nineteenth-century building complex that had spread itself out along the bank of the river; around it, a collection of houses, shops, and small businesses had sprung up. It was like a village nestled on the riverbank below the "real" city. A charming place to live—unless the Aare flooded.

As Giuliana drove her Volvo downhill along Felsenaustrasse to the address on Tunnelweg where she was due in five minutes, she tried to remember if she'd been here before. She and Ueli had passed the brewery a few times, walking along the river path, but this little neighborhood was new to her. The houses were small but individual-looking, with attractive gardens.

She parked in Ruth Seiler's driveway behind an Audi and walked up the flagstone path. Valérie Imboden, Ruth's lawyer, answered the door. In her mid-forties, Valérie had carefully maintained dark-blonde hair worn loose to her shoulders. She'd probably left the house in a suit jacket, but at nine in the morning, it was already warm, so she'd pared down to a sleeveless silk blouse and dark linen trousers.

Waving her inside, Valérie gave Giuliana a genuine smile—evidence that she wasn't going to be adversarial at this stage—and told her, "This neighborhood was a surprise for me, and I've lived in Bern for twenty years." As they chatted about Felsenau, she led Giuliana into the living room, where a slight woman sat in an armchair.

Ruth Seiler, at last.

Despite the June heat, Ruth was wearing a navy cardigan over a white blouse patterned with small dark blue flowers; her trousers were also navy. Her pale face was oval, her features small and regular, her eyes light blue under naturally thin brows. Parted in the middle and pushed behind her ears, her mousy gray hair was chin length. The smile she gave Giuliana was a courtesy, no more, as she stood carefully and shook hands, moving like someone unsure of her balance, probably due to the pneumonia. She looked older and frailer than she should have at seventy-eight, but Giuliana wasn't going to underestimate her because of that.

Valérie gestured to the end of the sofa near Ruth's armchair and then sat down across from Giuliana and leaned back, seeming to offer her the first word. Fine, then. She was ready.

Giuliana took a spiral notebook and pen out of her handbag. "Frau Seiler, I'm here to ask about your husband's death. I'm going to take notes, but I won't transcribe what you say verbatim and hand it over to the prosecuting attorney. Still, that doesn't mean I can't use what you say to help me build a case against you—I'm here as a policewoman." She paused. "To start with, I'd like to know more about your husband and your relationship with him in the years before he developed dementia."

"That's exactly where *I* want to begin, Frau Linder," said Ruth, "with Werner and what was important to him. I want you to understand *why* I did what I did. That's what matters most to me now."

Giuliana assumed this was no surprise to Ruth's lawyer, but she resisted the temptation to look at Valérie. Instead, she kept her eyes on the woman she'd spent the last two weeks trying to understand. "Please go ahead."

Ruth looked off into the distance. It was obvious she'd thought about what she wanted to say, and she began smoothly. Although she paused now and then as if to shape her thoughts, she carried on without stammering or losing her thread.

"When I started a relationship with Werner, which was soon after we met, he'd been separated from his wife for four years. He was fifty-eight, and I was fifty-three. There was physical attraction and affection, which eventually grew into love, but the main thing that brought us together was that we both wanted to live with someone. I lost my first husband when I was thirty-six, so I'd been alone for a long time."

Giuliana already knew that Ruth, with a full-time job at the cantonal tax department, had lived comfortably after her first husband died of cancer. She must have lived carefully, too, considering how much she'd managed to save in her special tax-free "old-age" bank account. Giuliana murmured, "I see," and gave Ruth an encouraging smile.

Ruth nodded back. "Werner could never get over the way his son and daughter abandoned him after their mother left. He didn't understand why they were punishing *him* when she'd been the one who'd had an affair." She pressed her lips together as if she couldn't bear to mention Werner's children. Giuliana also didn't know why Sebastian and Tamara—especially Tamara—seemed to have chosen their mother over their father. Was it possible that he'd done something to them as children?

As if she could hear Giuliana's thoughts, Ruth said, "Werner sometimes talked to me about how he and his wife had raised the children. He wanted to know what he'd done wrong. I asked him outright if he'd hit them or yelled at them or mistreated them in any way, but he said no. The mistake he dwelled on was that he hadn't played with them— or just hung out with them. He always focused on teaching them: how to ski or ride a bike or kick a ball. Looking back, he thought he'd expected too much of them instead of just enjoying them. But that doesn't seem like enough to have driven them away from him." Her eyes narrowed slightly. "It sounded to me as if their mother alternately indulged them and lost her temper with them. Maybe she was the real problem. Or maybe he was hiding something from me, but I don't think so. To this day, I still don't understand that family."

Ruth glanced at her lawyer. Then she leaned back in her chair and closed her eyes for a moment, which gave Giuliana a chance to look around the living room. It was crowded with furniture, the surfaces covered with ornaments, vases of flowers, framed photographs, and plants. It should have felt cluttered, but Giuliana found it cozy.

"Are you all right, Ruth?" the lawyer asked when she'd been quiet for almost a minute. "Do you need to stop the interview now?"

"I *am* tired," Seiler answered, "but I'd like to go on." She looked at Giuliana. "Do you mind that I'm just talking like this? You can ask me specific questions if you'd prefer."

"As long as you're telling me what I want to know, I'm content. I'll interrupt if I need to."

Ruth sat up a bit straighter. "I'm sorry I haven't offered you anything to eat or drink, but Valérie and I decided not to waste time with all that."

"It's fine," Giuliana told her. "This information is what's important."

"Right," said Ruth. "Well, I'm talking to you about Werner and his relationship with the children because I think that's key to understanding what happened, and I doubt *they've* told you what I'm telling you now. For example, I don't imagine Tamara described what an effort Werner made to improve his relationship with her and especially with his grandchildren. During the first ten years that he and I were together, we visited them three or four times a year, and we'd have gone more often if she'd allowed it. Werner visited her alone, too. I made him do that because I hoped that if I wasn't around, she'd warm up. But it was no use. As for her visiting us, she brought the grandchildren once a year for a few hours around Christmastime."

Giuliana shook her head. The drive between Zug, the city where Tamara lived, and Bern was under two hours, and the train trip was even faster, so it wasn't the distance that had been the problem. "And Sebastian?"

"We visited Sebastian in Hamburg three times during those first ten years, and once Werner went alone. I don't think Sebastian was intentionally cruel; the first evening we arrived, each time we came, he always took us out to dinner at a nice restaurant and made an effort to be pleasant. But for the rest of each visit, he just couldn't be bothered." Ruth paused again, and, looking up, Giuliana saw she was quietly crying. "I'm sorry. I wanted to tell you about Werner, and now I'm complaining about his kids. But he was so hurt and . . . and *bewildered* by the way they treated him, and there was nothing I could do about it. It made me hate them, for his sake."

Valérie Imboden cleared her throat noisily. It wouldn't do Ruth any good at her trial to confess to hating her stepchildren, even if it wasn't one of *them* she'd poisoned. But Giuliana understood Ruth's feelings. Her mother-in-law blatantly preferred her older son, Mike, to Ueli. Ueli loved his mother anyway, but Giuliana was less forgiving.

"Don't worry about it," said Giuliana, which made little sense since the trial and its consequences gave them a lot to worry about. "Let's just say this. I've interviewed Herr Allemann's children, and . . . well, nothing you've said about their behavior comes as a surprise to me."

Swiping at her tears, Ruth gave Giuliana a grateful look. "I need to talk about Werner's attitude to money because that's important, too. You see, his father had an accident with a factory machine in his midthirties and couldn't work after that, so Werner grew up poor. He was very proud of having earned enough to help his kids. He longed to give Tamara and Sebastian gifts of cash and interest-free loans, but once they finished their studies, they never asked him for anything. For that, at least, I respect them, but he saw it as part of their rejection of him, and it hurt him all the more."

Interesting, Giuliana thought. This fit with the children being willing to put their father in a home, although it would probably have cost them their inheritance.

Ruth paused as if to check that Giuliana understood, so Giuliana nodded and Ruth continued. "The kids rejecting his money made Werner want to leave them as much as possible in his will. He never actually said it, but I think he liked imagining how terrible they'd feel when they got their inheritance and remembered the way they'd ignored him."

This made sense to Giuliana. As a small child, she'd once been so furious with her parents for something—she couldn't remember what, now—that she'd "run away" to a nearby park, where she'd sat on a bench for an hour gloating about how sorry they'd be when they realized she was gone. Werner's plans for his kids' inheritance had been his way of gloating.

"Do you think he was right?" Giuliana asked. "*Would* they have felt sad and guilty?"

Ruth snorted. "Of course not." She leaned forward. "Well, to be fair, I suppose Sebastian might have felt a twinge of remorse, but it would have disappeared quickly. Tamara wouldn't have wasted a second's thought on whether she deserved to profit from her father's death or not: as his daughter, she was his heir, and that was that. In fact, I already know that she's sorry she ever agreed to let me stay in this house."

Giuliana remembered: the house belonged to the stepchildren. It was common in Switzerland to make property over to heirs under the condition that the original owners were granted usufruct, which meant the right to continue using it until their deaths.

"He turned the house over to them twenty years ago. Apparently, they signed the usufruct agreement then without a second thought. Now Tamara wishes she hadn't done it—she's made that clear to me—but it's too late."

Ruth raised her eyebrows with a wry smile; it gave her face a charm Giuliana hadn't noticed before. As Giuliana smiled back, Ruth said, "That's just one example of Werner starting to plan for his death much earlier than most people do. Long before he was experiencing any of the effects of the dementia, he was talking to me about how he wanted his affairs handled. He wanted me to know I would be taken care of so I wouldn't worry about how much money was going to his children."

"Did he discuss all this with a lawyer?" Giuliana asked.

"Yes, he wrote up what he wanted and took it to a lawyer he knew in Bremgarten, and they redrafted it together. Eventually, it was notarized in front of two witnesses."

Giuliana couldn't remember having Werner's lawyer on her list; she'd need to check with the prosecutor. She'd certainly want to talk to the man and read through the will. "How did you feel about all these plans?"

Ruth shrugged. "Oh, I was fine with everything. If they'd been *my* kids, those two monsters, I'd have wanted them to get nothing; I'd rather have given everything to Doctors Without Borders. I'd probably have left a nasty letter to be read out to them after my death, too. But Werner was a better person than I am."

Giuliana was interested in Ruth's opinion of her stepchildren. But it was time to focus on Werner's death. "While Werner was talking about all this, did he ever bring up the subject of a living will?" Ruth shrank back into the armchair, and Giuliana added, "That's written instructions about his end-of-life medical care."

"I know what a living will is," snapped Ruth. Then she gave Giuliana an apologetic look. "I know. And I tried. If I could have seen into the future, I'd have recorded our conversations on my phone, but it never occurred to me that I'd need evidence of my husband's state of mind." She rubbed her forehead with a hand. "He was stubborn; you have to understand that. No matter what I suggested, all he'd say was, 'I want you to handle everything, Ruthie. You're younger than I am, and women live longer than men, so you'll be here to make decisions.' I begged him to write something down, but he wasn't having it."

"What about a care facility?" Giuliana persisted.

"He didn't want to go into a nursing home. But even after telling me that, he also said that if I decided a home was best, he'd be okay with it." She sighed helplessly. "He kept insisting that he trusted me, no matter what."

Suppose in thirty years Ueli said something like that to her. Would she want to make these kinds of decisions on his behalf?

Without any guidance? "Did you ask him what he'd want if he was, say, in a coma?"

"I certainly did." Ruth raised her arms in the air and let her hands flop down to her thighs in exasperation. "I thought he'd understand what a burden he was putting on me. But he said, 'How can I know now if I'll be in a coma where my brain is dead or one that I have a good chance of waking up from? You'll have the facts, and you'll make the decisions. Whatever you tell the docs will be what I want.' From then on, all I got out of him was variations of the same thing: that he trusted me to choose for him. When I reminded him that Tamara might fight me, he'd always say, 'But the law says it's your right, so she won't be able to interfere.'"

Giuliana opened her mouth and then closed it. Being permitted to decide if life support should be turned off or if it was time to put a spouse in a home—yes, the law supported a husband or wife's right to do that. Being permitted to decide if it was time to kill your spouse, no. Assisted suicide in Switzerland was just that—suicide. The person took an overdose of sedatives with full knowledge of what they were doing, as Ursula Kellenberger had explained.

But there was no need to say this. Ruth knew it. Her hands were gripped in her lap, her face drawn.

Before Giuliana could ask if she was all right, Valérie said, "We've tried to reproduce as many of their conversations on this topic as Ruth can remember, although after Herr Allemann told her what he wanted, he avoided the subject. He said it was morbid. This was before he showed any signs of dementia, so it was all in the abstract."

"He *hated* talking about it," Ruth added fervently.

"And after he had dementia?" Giuliana asked, not sure which of the two women would answer.

Valérie said, "You know it's not easy to draw lines like that, right? Before and after the dementia, I mean. It's never clear when the illness starts."

"I understand," Giuliana said. "Still, I need to know what was discussed when."

With a deep sigh, Ruth leaned forward. "Around the time Werner turned seventy-six, I started to notice him losing his keys more often and doing and saying odd things occasionally, like . . . well, you know what the signs are. But many people have memory lapses as they get older, and they aren't necessarily serious. Werner still read, watched TV, went out alone for walks, socialized easily, and when we went out in the car, even on long vacations, he drove. I thought I would know if it was something serious."

Giuliana thought of her parents. Her father was seventy-six, her mother seventy-seven. She'd never noticed them forgetting anything, but still, an icy hand squeezed her heart.

"Life seemed normal," Ruth went on. "Now . . . now I know I was stupid—I should have tried harder to make him talk to me about what was going on in his brain. Although knowing Werner, he probably would have lied. Who . . . who has the courage to face something like that honestly? It's—" Ruth broke off.

It's unbearable, Giuliana finished for her. Giuliana had friends whose parents had Alzheimer's. After it was diagnosed, you couldn't imagine why you hadn't seen it from the beginning, but beforehand, you honestly weren't sure. Or, maybe you tried not to notice what was right in front of your eyes because it was too horrible. "You weren't stupid," Giuliana said. "You were frightened."

"Thanks, but . . . it's still hard to forgive myself." She folded her hands in her lap. "That's how life went along until Werner was seventy-nine, and then—I started noticing details. Like, he didn't turn the pages in his book often enough, or he wasn't really following what we watched on TV. I began paying more attention, and I figured out . . . a lot of things. For example, that his walks alone were essentially round and round the same few blocks, so he wouldn't get lost. I was devastated. I tried to get him to go to a specialist, but he kept denying that anything was wrong. That was . . . very hard for me, and I got angry with him, but at the same time, I understood. It's not like getting cancer diagnosed so you can start treatment. With this, there *is* no treatment." Ruth took in a shaky breath as if she was fighting tears. Giuliana waited.

"That's why I didn't tell anyone what was going on, because Werner himself was completely in denial. He kept pretending all was well, lost his temper with me when I pushed him to go to a doctor, never talked to me about problems. So, there was no chance for us to decide together what to tell friends and family. No chance to talk about the next steps."

Giuliana wondered if she and Paolo would someday have to go through this with their parents, whose Exit membership would be no help if they denied what was happening until it was too late to act.

She fought to push these private worries out of her head. "When did you decide that you had to acknowledge his dementia, even when *he* wouldn't?"

"I'd read quite a lot about Alzheimer's by then, and I studied the stages. They're described online. Sometime between seventy-nine and eighty, he'd moved into what's called the middle stage. He . . . well, he wet himself a few times, and there were some personality changes. I'd already talked to our family doctor about what was going on, so I called him after one of Werner's accidents, and he made Werner an appointment with a neurologist. Then I tricked Werner into going by lying; I told him he had a checkup for glaucoma with the eye doctor. And somehow, it worked. The neurologist asked him a lot of questions he couldn't answer and told him the truth, and hearing it from the doctor made him accept it. Thank God."

"Did you ever discuss assisted suicide?" Giuliana asked. Valérie shifted in her chair, and Ruth glanced at her lawyer. Giuliana couldn't decipher what message passed between them.

"I brought up Exit. First, long before any signs of dementia, when we were talking about his will, I mentioned the idea of us both joining Exit as part of the process of planning for the future. That's when he told me he wanted me to make his health decisions, but he didn't say . . . he didn't say those words specifically in the context of Exit. Just about his health in general. After that, I tried . . . well, several more times, including once before we went to the neurologist and once afterward.

But he wouldn't listen. So, I guess the answer to your question is no because, although I brought it up, there was never any discussion."

Giuliana was surprised. What was Valérie's defense strategy going to be? Giuliana would have expected her to advise Ruth to show more hesitation, to leave the question of Allemann's attitude toward assisted suicide more ambiguous. Instead, Ruth was making it clear that when the subject came up, Werner closed it down.

"You're telling me that, although he didn't actively reject assisted suicide, he *did* actively refuse to talk about it."

Valérie intervened. "I'd put it this way. He didn't refuse to talk about assisted suicide as much as reject the idea of planning *anything* to do with his health."

Hmm. Giuliana thought this was splitting hairs, but she wanted to keep the conversation going. "You mentioned the problem of telling friends and family." She was remembering Sebastian's story of arriving to see his father and not being recognized. "Sebastian Allemann told us that he visited last fall and learned only then about his father's mental state. He said he was . . . I think his words were 'very sharp' with you."

"Yes, he was," Ruth agreed, "and I was sharp right back at him. I told him maybe his father would know who he was if he'd ever come to see him. Or if he phoned Werner more often than just on his birthday and Christmas or sent him an email or a text now and then."

Giuliana saw her point. But she still had hard questions to ask. She glanced down at her notebook. "This was when Werner was eighty-two. But the neurologist diagnosed Alzheimer's when Werner was seventy-nine. You had three years to tell the children about their father's illness, yet . . ."

"I should have, and I wanted to," Ruth said, and for the first time, Giuliana didn't believe her, given how much she disliked Sebastian and Tamara. Some of her doubt must have shown on her face because Ruth added bleakly, "Oh, not out of kindness. I've told you what I think of them. It was because I wanted to avoid exactly the kind of situation that

I experienced with Sebastian. But right after the diagnosis, Werner could still make decisions, and he insisted he didn't want me to tell them. He didn't want his kids to see him as a witless old man; they had enough contempt for him already. That was . . . it really tore me apart. I hated how bad they'd made him feel about himself. So, I went along with it."

Giuliana was about to speak when Ruth added, "Besides, I told Werner that Sebastian was coming, and Werner recognized him and spoke to him more or less normally for at least the first half hour. He only forgot who Basti was after that, when he got distracted."

Valérie joined in. "Tamara never saw her father a last time because she made no effort to visit him, although Sebastian says he informed her that Werner had Alzheimer's. And now she has the gall to play the loving daughter with an evil stepmother."

The lawyer had let the questioning continue for an extraordinary amount of time; Giuliana could only be grateful for the information she'd gathered and the impressions she'd been able to form. She'd run out of background questions, though, so she had to decide if she was now going to ask Ruth directly about poisoning her husband and risk the defense lawyer ending their discussion.

Choosing to move things along no matter what happened, she took a folded page of dates from her handbag. "Sebastian's visit was in the middle of October, and by the end of October, you'd received a registered letter from Tamara Hofstetter informing you that she was looking for a place in a care home. She told you she expected her father to be moved there as soon as possible. You wrote back that you would continue to look after Herr Allemann yourself because it was what he'd wanted and the law gave you the right to make that decision. You told her, if necessary, you'd hire a lawyer to see that his wishes were respected. Then *she* got a lawyer, so you had to get your lawyer involved, too, and after that—"

"After that, she had her lawyer threaten that if I didn't get better care for Werner by putting him into a specialized facility, she would file charges of abuse against me with KESB."

"What?" Giuliana drew in a sharp breath and heard Valérie do the same; Ruth's lawyer had apparently not been expecting her to reveal this.

Giuliana was shocked. KESB meant the Child and Adult Protection Services for the canton of Bern, and despite all the good work they did, most people were afraid of the power they had to interfere. If Tamara had made an official complaint to KESB, it could have made Ruth's life hell, even if, in the end, the authorities decided there were no grounds for the charge.

Giuliana turned to Valérie. "Why am I only hearing this now?"

Valérie met her eyes briefly. "The complaint never got filed, so there was nothing to report. The threat wasn't in writing, so . . ."

"But surely you've talked to Tamara's lawyer to verify what was said."

"I've tried to, but I think the only way to get him to tell the truth is in front of the judges, with a threat of perjury facing him. And even then, he may still lie or refuse to answer."

We'll just have to see if the police can get him to tell the truth. She needed to discuss this with Rosmarie. Why hadn't Adam, the detective on the case before her, left any notes about this KESB business?

"Written or not, that threat scared me," Ruth said. "All this was happening over the weeks leading to Christmas. I thought Sebastian would show up again to see his father, but he didn't even phone. In mid-January, Tamara's lawyer let me know that a private room at a care center in Bern would be available sometime in February, and I'd need to take up the place by the end of March or suffer consequences. Our lawyer tried to calm me down, but I was very worried. I decided to visit the center."

She paused to drink from a glass of water that sat on a little table to her right. Giuliana was prepared for her to launch into a rant about the care home, but once again, Ruth surprised her. "I don't have one bad thing to say about the place," she said. "As far as I'm concerned, the staff there are superhuman. Most of the old people have no idea who or where they are or what's going on. They wear bibs and incontinence pads, but the staff get them out of bed, dress them in decent clothes, make them comfortable, and help them feel like guests rather than inmates. It was heartbreaking to see how hard everyone worked to preserve their dignity. It was all so well-meaning and well-done—but that home was still one of the most awful places I've ever been."

Giuliana's great-aunt had been in a nursing home for six months before she died, so she knew what Ruth was talking about. She nodded at the older woman, who gave Giuliana the ghost of a smile before continuing. "I knew from my lawyer that this place was top of the line. We talked about how I could afford it. I couldn't sell the house because it already belonged to the children. Werner's and my pooled worth was over a million francs, but I didn't want to touch the money Werner had meant for the kids. Even investing every penny, *including* what he'd set aside for the children, wouldn't have been enough to cover the costs for as long as Werner might need. And that was with contributions from Werner's health insurance. It was . . . impossible. We talked about my renting out the house and moving to a cheap apartment, assuming the usufruct agreement would permit that."

Giuliana's impression from her talk with Tamara Hofstetter and Sebastian Allemann was that their stepmother had just put her foot down and said, "No home, no way," without considering the options. She should have known better than to believe anything those two said without checking it. Here, she thought, was the truth, although it, too, would have to be verified. Ruth had visited the home, checked the costs, and tried to come up with a plan to pay for it that wouldn't touch the precious capital that Werner so desperately wanted to leave Tamara and Sebastian.

"If you'd rented out this house and used that income and all of your future inheritance from Werner to help pay for his care, what would you have lived on?" asked Giuliana.

Ruth shrugged. "My life might not have turned out to be all peace, joy, and pancakes, but I'd have been fine. I have my social security, my work pension, and some savings of my own. The lawyer thought I should use a share of my inheritance—before investing it to create an income to pay the care home—to buy a one-bedroom condo so I wouldn't be at the mercy of rising rents. God knows I'd rather have this house and my half of the money as Werner had planned. But the alternative wouldn't have been so bad. Not for me, anyway."

It didn't seem to Giuliana as though Ruth was merely trying to sound noble and self-sacrificing. Calculations like these went on all over Switzerland and probably all over the world as people tried to figure out how they could afford the best possible care for a loved one and still support themselves. Ruth was better off than many, and she sounded sensible enough to know it. But the last words of her sentence stood out.

"What you're telling me," Giuliana said, watching her carefully, "is that *you* could have lived with the new situation, but you didn't think it was best for Werner to move him out of your care."

"Not just *my* care," Ruth said. "A male nurse came in six days a week, usually for two hours but sometimes four. Werner enjoyed seeing him, and the carer did a lot of personal stuff for him. He also got Werner out of bed and moving, at least around the house and sometimes outdoors. It gave me time to get out to have coffee, meet a friend for dinner or a concert, or just take a walk. Compared to what the care center cost, I could have increased my home help for only a pittance—and part of that expense was covered by insurance."

Giuliana thought she had the whole story now. Werner was content for Ruth to take care of decisions about his health and well-being. He'd made her promise that she'd ensure his ungrateful, unloving children got half of his money. Ruth was no martyr, but she was willing to care for him in their home, with help, until his death. That was her decision, the one Werner had trusted her to make and which, by law, she had the right to make.

Then along came Tamara—Giuliana guessed that Sebastian was only going along with the expensive care facility to placate his sister—who hated Ruth for all kinds of irrational reasons. As a result, she was determined to take her father out of Ruth's care and put him in a home where all his money would be used up. She was willing to deprive herself and her brother of their inheritance as long as Ruth didn't get the other half of the cake. Talk about cutting off your nose to spite your face. And yet Ruth was determined to preserve Tamara and Sebastian's half of the money because it had meant so much to their father to be able to leave it to them.

"Did you talk to Werner's GP or his neurologist about whether they thought he should go into the home?" Giuliana asked. It seemed important to get a sense of how advanced the man's dementia was at this point, a medical opinion rather than just Ruth's feelings. "In mid-October, you said he had a reasonable conversation with Sebastian. How were things five months later?"

"He seemed quite a lot worse to me," Ruth said. "I didn't take him back to the neurologist, but I emailed the man in mid-February with a list of Werner's symptoms. Our GP, a gentle soul in his sixties, paid us a house visit as well. He spent half an hour with Werner and then spoke with me in private. Both he and the neurologist felt that Werner was entering the last stage of Alzheimer's. He wasn't really able to carry on a conversation anymore; he was having trouble walking and feeding himself, even swallowing sometimes. Our GP didn't just take my word for the changes: he offered Werner food, asked him to accompany him to the next room, things like that. He—the GP, I mean—was upset."

Winning the GP as her ally had been smart; Giuliana wondered if Ruth was already planning to administer the insulin overdose to her husband when she called the two doctors.

"You've given me a good picture of the weeks leading up to the night Werner received the overdose from you. Now, I'd like to talk about his death."

At Giuliana's mention of the overdose, Valérie sat up straighter and leaned forward; Ruth clasped her hands in her lap and bowed her head.

"Frau Seiler," Giuliana continued, "I know the date you bought the additional insulin you needed and the pharmacist you bought it from. I know that sometime during the evening of the twentieth of March, you said goodbye to your husband and injected him. You messed up a bed in the guestroom, so it looked like you'd spent the night there and hadn't found Herr Allemann dead until morning, but we think it's more likely that you stayed next to him all night. Then, at about eight in the morning, you called the family doctor. Your husband was eighty-two and suffered from other conditions besides dementia—high blood pressure and mild type 2 diabetes, among other things—and your GP had seen him less than a month before. So, he was perfectly willing to provide a death certificate without any fuss, and the body was picked up by the mortuary service."

Valérie was listening with fierce attention. Ruth was slumped in her chair, and tears trickled from her eyes, but she seemed calm. Now and then, she swiped her cheeks with the sleeve of her navy cardigan.

"Then came your big mistake." At this, Valérie stirred, but she didn't stop Giuliana. "You let your GP call Tamara immediately to break the news of her father's death. I can see that you didn't think you should do it yourself, but you should have had someone more forceful call the children. Ideally, a family friend who'd known Werner for years—someone they'd never suspect of being on your side. He could have started by phoning Sebastian, offering sympathy but making it clear that this sudden but not unexpected death was a blessing for everyone. Sebastian would certainly have agreed with him, if only because it meant he'd get his inheritance. Maybe then he'd have stood up to his sister's craziness."

Her unexpectedly honest speech seemed to have frozen Valérie and Ruth in their seats. Maybe it was because she'd just acknowledged that the prosecution's main witness, Tamara Hofstetter, was unreliable.

"Instead, the family doctor called Tamara right after he signed the certificate, and let her scream herself into hysterics about her stepmother killing her father for his money. And because she was questioning the death certificate, he felt he had to agree to label the death suspicious. Even then, you might have been all right because too much insulin is very hard to detect in an autopsy. If the pathologist had been too busy to get to the body until twenty-four hours later, I don't imagine he would have found any evidence of insulin poisoning. But he had time to do the autopsy right away. So, the insulin was discovered in Herr Allemann's system."

No one spoke. Giuliana listened to the clock ticking and the twitter of birds outside the living room window and waited, hoping Ruth would respond.

But it was Valérie who finally said, "I think that's a good place to end this discussion."

Ruth looked up, and Giuliana caught her eye. "Do you have anything you want to add to my reconstruction of your husband's death, Frau Seiler? I've read the confession you signed that describes your actions step by step, but it's just a statement of the facts. Do you want to add information about your state of mind? Your decision-making process?"

Giuliana imagined Ruth's mind racing with all kinds of justifications and self-recriminations. But surely her main regret had to be that she hadn't planned the killing well enough to get away with it. And that was not something she'd want to share with the police.

"No," Ruth said at last. "I have nothing else to say. But thank you for listening. I needed the police to hear the reasons for what I did, and now you've heard them." She paused and tucked her two wings of straight hair behind her ears. "Will you be at the trial?"

Giuliana rarely attended trials that she'd worked on unless she was required to testify; there were too many of them. But she'd already made up her mind to be at this one.

"I won't speak at the trial, but I'll be with the public," she answered.

"Good," said Ruth.

Valérie Imboden rose from her armchair. "I'll see you out."

Ruth Seiler struggled to her feet. "Thanks," she said again and held out her hand.

Giuliana shook it gently. "And thank *you* for taking this time to talk to me, especially when you're not well. You've done an outstanding job of giving me the background I need."

Ruth withdrew her hand quickly. "The background you need to send me to jail?"

Giuliana shook her head. "Background to help the prosecutor build a fair case."

"Fair." Ruth's lips tightened. "Nothing has been fair since Werner got Alzheimer's." She gave Giuliana a last long look, then headed for the kitchen while Valérie herded Giuliana toward the front door. As Valérie opened the door, Ruth turned and said, "Goodbye, Frau Linder. I'm sure we'll be seeing each other again before the trial."

"I appreciate your setting this up," Giuliana told Valérie when they stood outside on the front steps.

The defense lawyer looked for a moment like she wanted to say a lot of things about Ruth's case that she shouldn't say to a cop, but all she did was smile. "You're welcome."

"Good luck," Giuliana called as she got into her Volvo. It was an idiotic statement from a detective working with the prosecution, but it was what she found herself wanting to say.

Driving up the hill away from Felsenau, she thought about the interview. It had given her a wealth of new information without really clarifying her thoughts about the case. If anything, Ruth's story had only increased her confusion.

Giuliana was too experienced a police detective to believe that right and wrong could be distributed into their own neatly labeled shoeboxes. But her job would have been far easier if the interview had convinced her that Ruth was greedy and selfish, or if the older woman had come across as a liar or a wife who'd wanted to free herself of a burdensome husband. But she didn't appear to be any of those things. She'd broken the law, and maybe that should have been enough to make Giuliana want to see her punished. But it wasn't. Giuliana desperately needed someone wise to talk this over with. Ueli, she decided—and not casually, at the dinner table, with the kids around, as they'd done Tuesday night, but seriously, when he could give her his full attention.

It wasn't until a few minutes later, as she was passing the Innere Enge Hotel and thinking she'd like to have dinner in its garden before the summer ended, that she registered her plan to discuss the Seiler/Allemann complications with *Ueli*. Not Renzo. That was interesting—and probably a good thing. But it made her sad.

27

Renzo woke up Friday morning at five forty-five, rolled out of bed on autopilot, stumbled in and out of the bathroom, pulled on his workout clothes, and left the apartment. At the gym, he moved from bench presses to squats to pull- and push-ups, all the while thinking about the sexton, Klaus Friedli, and how soon he could interview him.

Getting ready for bed the night before, he'd decided he needed to interview Friedli at the police station, not in the church where he would be distracted by the demands of his job. The idea of talking to him over coffee, as he had with Pereira, the restoration foreman, made Renzo uncomfortable. If Schweizer had been telling the truth, Klaus Friedli had run an illegal business—albeit a small one—that had been part of a vast criminal network. Even if he was no longer involved in international smuggling, he might still have ties to organized crime. Renzo didn't think that was likely, nor was he interested in talking to Friedli about anything but his memories of the night Katica died. But he wanted the man in an official interview room.

Renzo had the authority to insist that Friedli leave his job and accompany him to the station, but he thought it would be a good idea, as well as a courtesy, to talk to the minister, Selena Zehnder, first. Not only could she give him another perspective on the sexton, she could show him the wine cellar that Ben Schweizer had told Renzo and Mädi about, the place where the sexton had hidden his cigarettes, and they could check if he was still hiding anything there. He wondered how early he could call her.

By seven twenty, he was home from the gym, showered, and dressed for work in black trousers and a short-sleeved white shirt. The morning was overcast, hot, and muggy; according to his phone, there was a seventy percent chance of a thunderstorm later. While waiting for his coffee to bubble up in the old Bialetti espresso pot, he buttered two slices of the loaf he'd bought at the bakery café where he and Giuliana usually had breakfast after their joint workouts.

The end of his week in the apartment was coming up. On Sunday night, he and Fränzi would switch, and he'd go to Wabern to be with the kids. He needed to change the sheets, run a wash, and vacuum. *You can do it on Saturday*, he told himself. Maybe by then, he would no longer be in this state of limbo, his thoughts flipping back and forth over Katica's death with every new piece of information he took in.

Sighing, he took his breakfast out onto the little balcony and spent fifteen minutes reading the news on his phone, soccer first, as usual. Then he finished his bread, drained his espresso, and looked at his watch. Quarter to eight. Hopefully not too early to call Frau Zehnder—after all, given her job, she probably dealt with crises at all hours. He found the card she's given him and dialed her number. When she answered, he asked to meet with her as soon as possible.

"When can you be at the Münster?" she asked him.

He'd be faster walking than driving, but he'd need the car to bring Friedli back, and he still had to walk over and pick it up from the police station garage, too. "Fifteen minutes," he said.

A quarter of an hour later, the minister let him in by an enormous set of double doors close to her office on the south aisle. The office was small but cozy with two armchairs in one corner so that she didn't have to speak to visitors across her desk. She took one of them and waved him into the other. "I can give you half an hour now, and if you need more time, I can find it, but probably not today." She gave him a crooked smile, her expression weary. "It might surprise you to hear how much time ministers spend in meetings. Time that we'd rather spend counseling and—" She caught herself. "Sorry. You didn't come to hear me grumble. How can I help?"

"I have a lot to tell you," Renzo said, "but first, I have a question, and I'd like you to answer it honestly rather than tactfully—in other words, without charitable Christian restraint." Her eyebrows rose, but she said nothing. "How do you feel about your sexton, Klaus Friedli?"

She put a hand on her chin, looking at him thoughtfully, head inclined. "I can't say I'm friends with him." Renzo waited. "But I respect how good he is at his job, and I'm dependent on him."

Renzo tried not to look disappointed. This wasn't the juicy inside information he'd been hoping for.

"I've been the minister here for almost five years," she continued. "But Klaus has been here for over twenty. He's fifty-eight, and he keeps this church running like a brand-new Rolex. Repairs get done. If he can't do them himself, he hires the right people—and he makes sure the cleaning staff comes and goes at the right times. Weddings, funerals, and all our public concerts are set up properly; our volunteers are given their tasks; the shop ladies sell their tickets, books, and trinkets; the tower guardian is kept informed. And, of course, he has years of experience coordinating with the architect's staff and the restoration people. He's very, very good at his job, and he does it as if it were second nature."

"Is there a but?" Renzo asked, still hoping for something useful.

"Not really. Except that . . . well, I suppose he's just . . . not easy to warm to. He's stiff and overly correct, if you know what I mean. Like I said, we're not friends. But none of that means that he's a bad man. I suspect he's finding it hard to adapt to a woman minister. Quite a few parishioners find it a challenge, you know."

Renzo was almost sorry to break Zehnder's trust in her sexton, but she needed to know about the illegal cigarettes, if only so she could keep an eye on him in the future.

"Thank you for that," Renzo said. "Look, I have something to tell you that might surprise you. The police have been told that fifteen years ago, and probably for a while before and after that, your sexton was selling smuggled cigarettes from the Münster, taking deliveries on Münstergasse market days and storing his wares in the wine cellar."

Frau Zehnder's mouth opened, and she gave an incredulous little laugh. "That's . . . hard to believe."

"It is," Renzo agreed, "and we're still verifying the story. But right now, I'm assuming it's true. I think Friedli may have sought out the job as sexton because it gave him a legitimate reason to work in the center of the city and have contact with anyone who walked in the door. I'm glad he has been such an efficient sexton, though. Perhaps the job started as a cover, but he ended up enjoying it."

The minister was gripping the arms of her chair, but her voice was still controlled. "If he really did that, then . . ." She broke off and took a deep breath. "Using this magnificent, holy place for an illegal business—and selling *cigarettes*, of all things. Poisoning parishioners and making money from it!"

Better tobacco than crystal meth or fentanyl, Renzo wanted to say, but he didn't think Frau Zehnder was in the mood for that comment. "I'm going to take Herr Friedli into the police station to talk to him about all this," he said instead. "Not actually about this business but about a suicide that happened fifteen years ago on a morning he was taking a delivery of cigarettes. The attack on Denis Kellenberger may have something to do with that death. Is Friedli here right now?"

Selina Zehnder looked at her watch. "He normally begins at seven thirty, but tonight he's staying late because of an organ concert, so we agreed he wouldn't come in until nine."

"That's ideal," Renzo said, "because I need to check the wine cellar below his office and see if he's still storing anything there. I would be very surprised if he's still selling cigarettes. There's no money in that these days. But he could be hiding stolen goods, or . . ."

Frau Zehnder jumped up. "Let's go now, in case he comes in early. My God, if he's still carrying on something criminal from this church,

I'll—" Her lips moved furiously as she banged through the door and out into the aisle.

"He can't be prosecuted for cigarette sales that took place fifteen years ago," Renzo told her.

She slowed down a little. "Oh. You mean that crime has expired. I guess . . . I guess that's fair. Still, if he used his position here to help him commit a crime, I don't think I want him as sexton. I'd miss his efficiency, but knowing about this . . . this *disrespect* for the church and what it stands for, even if it's not going on anymore, I don't feel I could continue working with him. But I'd need the parish council behind me on this, and he has at least one supporter there. Hmm, this could get complicated."

She was still muttering, half to Renzo and half to herself, as she stopped in front of a door at the southwest end of the aisle just to the right of the ramp leading into the choir. She took a bunch of keys from her jacket pocket and fitted one with a bright red label into the keyhole. Opening the door to the sexton's office, she held it for Renzo and then closed and locked it behind them. "Now, let's check out this wine cellar."

Renzo had expected ancient stone steps, but the stairs leading down from the sexton's office were concrete, wide, and well lit. By contrast, the room at the bottom felt as medieval as the rest of the cathedral—it was chilly, with a rough stone floor and a low, barrel-vaulted ceiling. It was also clean and empty, except for half-full racks of wine bottles along three of the walls.

"Do you see anything that shouldn't be here?" Renzo asked.

She frowned. "I don't come down very often, but I would say this is what it looked like, give or take some bottles of wine, when I arrived five years ago."

Renzo checked his watch: his half hour with Zehnder was almost up. "You can go back to your office if you need to," he told her. "If you don't mind lending me the keys, I can take a more thorough look."

The minister glanced around the room, sighed, and handed Renzo the ring of keys. "Thanks. I pray you don't find anything illegal down here. I'll be in my office for another twenty minutes."

"I won't need that long," Renzo said.

True to his word, he had the keys back to her ten minutes later. "I don't have the tools or the skills to search for secret rooms and passageways behind the walls or under the floor, but I had a quick look. I also poked around the wine racks, and I think the bottles are filled with nothing more than wine. But if there's cocaine dissolved in them, I wouldn't be able to tell."

Zehnder was at her desk, peering at her computer; now she stared up at him, her eyes wide. "Cocaine?"

Renzo nodded. "It's a way of smuggling coke that's hard to detect. Still, the police aren't going to pull the cellar apart looking for drugs, not without evidence. I'm hoping that even if Friedli is still a criminal, he's stopped running his business from here."

"I sincerely hope so, too." Her voice was icy.

He held his hand across her desk, and she shook it. "Thanks for your help," he said. "I've relocked everything, so I'll go wait for Herr Friedli to arrive. You get on with your day, but do let me know if he phones to tell you that he'll be later than expected."

"I will." The minister paused, tapping a finger on her chin. "But first, I need you to tell me more about what's going on. Do you suspect him of something—something else, I mean? I promise not to gossip or make false accusations. Imagine if a word of anything against him reached Frau Arnold in the shop; she worships the ground he walks on."

Renzo decided it couldn't hurt to tell her the bare facts. "Fifteen years ago, a woman named Katica Horvat died falling from the tower. You might already know that. We just learned that Frau Horvat's boyfriend sometimes worked with Friedli on his cigarette business. Allegedly, Friedli was the last person to see her alive, so I'd like to hear what he can tell us about her death. That's all I can say right now."

"Thank you. You'll let me know if you verify this story about the cigarettes?" She stared at Renzo until he nodded. Then she turned back to her computer, and Renzo left her to her work.

He went to sit in a pew at the back of the church. From there, he'd see and hear if the sexton came in, and he wouldn't be disturbed by

tourists or worshippers since the doors didn't open until ten. He got
out his phone, saw he had no new messages, and put it away again. He
knew he was jittery, but he didn't understand why, so he gazed slowly
around the nave, taking in the rows of pillars and the vast stained-glass
windows. Then he leaned his head against the back of the pew and
stared up at the intricately vaulted ceiling with its stark black decorations, squinting to make out the coats of arms on the bosses where the
ribs met. He felt calm start to seep into his being.

The church bells were sounding the last strikes of nine when the
doors from the Münster platform opened, and Friedli slipped through
them, unlocked his office, and went in. A moment later, Renzo got up
from his pew, walked across the nave, and knocked.

"Just a minute," came a voice. Renzo did not wait a minute—he
tried the door, which was locked. Interesting.

It was several minutes before the sexton opened up, looking totally
composed. Renzo saw again the tall, bulky figure in neat clothes, with
shirt buttons straining against a paunch, gray, slicked-back hair, and an
unremarkable face with a pleasant, helpful expression. If he hadn't
known about the cigarettes, he would have seen only a man in his late
fifties with a responsible job.

"Yes," Friedli said, planted in the doorway. "May I help you?"

"*Grüessech*, Herr Friedli." Renzo offered his usual automatic
handshake. "I'm from the Kantonspolizei. You may remember that we
met on Tuesday afternoon after Denis Kellenberger was hurt. That
incident has led me to reopen the investigation into the death of Katica
Horvat, and I now know that you were the last person to see her
alive, a fact which you didn't share with the policeman looking into
her death fifteen years ago. I'm here to ask you to accompany me to
the police station so we can have a talk about that."

Friedli did not speak. His mouth opened, then closed again. His
face worked, his brow wrinkled, and his whole expression became
one of intense concern. There was no indignant outburst of "I can't
imagine what you're talking about." Instead, he said quietly, "Of
course! It's no trouble at all. I'm glad to help you get to the bottom of

this. Let me just put a note on my door first." He went back into the office, and Renzo followed, alert to his every move. But all the man did was take a plastic sign from a wooden file box on his desk and hang it on his door; it said, "Away all morning." Then they walked out of the office, and Friedli locked the door.

After that, he said nothing.

Walking close beside him on the way to the car, Renzo hoped he'd be able to pry information out of this man. In spite of Friedli's helpful manner, there was something tight and controlled . . . something exceptionally *watchful* about him. Renzo had a feeling that the interview was not going to be easy.

28

Renzo let Friedli get into the passenger seat of his car instead of putting him in the backseat like a criminal. He wasn't arresting Friedli—he had no cause to—but the tension in the car made him feel that he had. On the short drive between the Münster and the police station, he got a text, which he read when he reached the parking lot. It was from the woman at the reception desk: *"Denis Kellenberger to see you. Says it's important. Waiting at front entrance."*

He cursed under his breath at the timing. Still, Denis might tell him something that he needed to hear before talking to Friedli. He made a quick call to request someone to take the sexton to the interview room he'd reserved, get him mineral water or whatever he asked for, and make sure he stayed there until Renzo got back. When he explained the situation to Friedli, the sexton only nodded—which Renzo found odd.

A few minutes later, a woman in uniform came to relieve him of Friedli, who had remained sitting patiently in the passenger seat when Renzo got out of the car. As she led him away, the sexton threw Renzo a long look over his shoulder that he couldn't read. He walked briskly through the ground floor to the front of the station, waving at the receptionist as he passed, and saw Denis sitting in the waiting area. Sketch pad open in his lap, he was drawing the large fern on a table under the front window.

As Renzo approached, Denis closed the pad and shoved it into the daypack at his feet. He stood and shook hands but didn't smile. "I have something I need to tell you about the night Zora's mother died, something I should have told the police fifteen years ago. But I had to tell Zora first. I did that last night, so now I can tell you."

Oh, shit. Renzo had absolutely no idea what was coming. Had one of the Kellenbergers seen something—*done* something? He looked around the waiting area, then took Denis by his good arm and led him to the farthest corner of the room.

"Now," he said when they were both seated again, "tell me."

He listened with growing unease as Denis described waking inside the tower apartment to hear a woman's moans coming from the balcony and then disappearing, followed by a set of heavy footsteps. He heard about the man outside the window who'd so frightened Denis that instead of fetching his grandparents, he'd hidden in bed, waking the next morning to the news of Katica's death.

Denis stared at his feet as he spoke. When he finished, he raised his eyes. "If I'd called my grandparents, Zora's mother would be alive. I can't tell you how sorry I am. I've felt guilty about this for fifteen years. That's why I barely defended myself when I got accused of leaving the doors unlocked."

Well, that, at least, Renzo could make him feel better about. "Katica had her own key to the Münster," he told Denis. "Her lover gave it to her. She could have gotten into the nave and up to the tower whether you left the doors unlocked or not. And I don't think you did, in any case."

Denis seemed too full of guilt to be comforted. "Listen," Renzo began again, but Denis interrupted.

"I know you're going to tell me I was only ten, so it's okay. But it's not. A ten-year-old may not be old enough to fight a man, but he *is* old enough to wake up two adults or call 117. Or just scream and yell and bang on a window to scare someone away."

Renzo's comforting words died before he could get them out. Denis was right, and yet he wasn't. A child could do those things, yes, but in such mysterious, frightening circumstances, he might not understand why they should be done.

He didn't know how to ease Denis's guilt, but there was one thing he *could* say. "Well, I'm a policeman, and *I* don't blame you for Katica Horvat's death. Perhaps now that we know about this man outside your window, we'll be able to find out who he was. Is there anything you can remember about his appearance?"

Denis closed his eyes. Finally, he said, "No. I was too scared to look at him closely."

"That's okay," Renzo told him, although it wasn't. "It's important that you told me all this, and I can see how hard it was for you. So, thank you." *But why the hell couldn't you have told me while you were lying in your hospital bed that first night?* He swallowed the reproach before it slipped out. Maybe showing Denis a lineup that included Ben Schweizer would shake something loose in his memory. Although a silhouette he saw in the almost dark fifteen years earlier? Renzo wasn't hopeful.

"There's something else," Denis said. "I have a favor to ask. Actually, it's for Zora."

"What does she want?"

Instead of answering right away, Denis unzipped an outer compartment of his pack and pulled out two small, sealed white paper envelopes. He held them out to Renzo. "Goran is desperate to find out who his real father is. Zora understands his wanting to know, but she'd like to find a way of doing it that won't cause too much upset. She's hoping your police lab could . . . if maybe you could order a DNA test to find out if she and Goran are full or half siblings. They both swabbed the insides of their mouths with Q-tips this morning, and she brought the samples to my apartment. She thought you could slip these in as part of your investigation into the Münster mess."

Renzo raised his eyebrows. "Don't you think this test could lead to even more misery?"

"I *do* think that. But, I believe she and Goran are prepared to cope with the results, whatever they show. It's being left in the dark that's tormenting Goran. He says if it turns out his father is this other man, he'll deal with it—but he needs to know."

Renzo didn't think *he'd* want to know if the sperm that had made him hadn't come from his tender, funny, and now deeply missed father. No DNA test could take his beloved *Papà* away from him. But it was hard to imagine how he'd have felt at Goran's age if he'd known that his mother had a lover when he was conceived.

Denis was watching his face anxiously, his fingers gripping the envelopes. Finally, Renzo reached out for them. "I think either way, the Horvat family is headed for a big blowup, but I'll see what our DNA specialist has to say. He'll probably need to send the swabs out somewhere, so I don't know how long it will take, but I'll ask. It would be helpful to my case to know whose son Goran is."

"Thank you. Zora will be relieved." Before Renzo could remind him that this DNA business might not work, Denis went on. "Is there anything I can do to help with your investigation? I mean . . ." He grinned and cocked an eyebrow at Renzo. "Actually, I have no idea what I mean. I'm just eager to help Zora any way I can."

"Thanks for asking, but—" Renzo broke off, adding, "Actually, I might need you to testify in front of a magistrate. Either way, I'll need a signed statement about the attack, which I'll write up from the notes I took at the hospital and ask you to read. But right now, that's it. I'll let you know when the statement's ready."

Denis nodded and stood up. "All right," he said, and with a wave, he was gone.

Renzo checked his watch. Time to grab an espresso, and then he'd tackle Friedli. Thanks to Denis, he now knew a man had chased a woman up the tower staircase in what Denis had thought was the middle of the night, but which could easily have been four forty-five on a cold November morning. Had it been Schweizer? Lovro? Or Friedli, for a reason that he couldn't imagine? Or it could have been someone he'd never heard of. After a moment of self-doubt, he told himself to get a grip and focus on the upcoming interview.

Renzo considered the uneasiness he'd felt bringing Friedli into the station. His original plan for the interview had been to cross-reference Friedli's statement with Schweizer's, maybe get the sexton's take on Schweizer's relationship with Katica, and ask him broadly about seeing Katica in the church that night. But he realized there was now more he needed to ask.

He swallowed his coffee in two gulps and made a snap decision: he would phone his favorite narcotics detective and try to persuade him to get a warrant to search the sexton's office and the wine cellar, plus his home, with drug dogs.

His cop's instinct was clamoring at him. Whether or not the sexton had anything to do with Katica's death, Schweizer's story about the cigarettes meant that the man had been living a double life for years. He knew how to play a role and get away with it. And that . . . that could make him dangerous.

29

Renzo and the sexton were in one of the smaller basement rooms. It had pale green walls, no windows, harsh lighting, a small metal table, and a couple of chairs and lacked two-way mirrors or any fancy equipment. Renzo would have liked to have Mädi there, but she was on Sabine's case, so he was on his own, except for a uniformed woman taking notes on a laptop.

Renzo stared across the table at Klaus Friedli, who gazed levelly back at him. Unlike most innocent people—and many guilty ones as well—he didn't ask why he was there, rant about his rights, or seem particularly worried about anything. He just sat and waited. Renzo recognized this as the behavior of a professional criminal, and he was determined to confirm Schweizer's story about the man.

"Herr Friedli," Renzo began, "I understand that your father sold illegal cigarettes and that you took over the business from him. I think you took the job as sexton so you could run sales from your office in the Münster, take advantage of the street market on Münstergasse twice a week, and store the cigarettes in the wine cellar."

Renzo kept his eyes on the sexton's face as he spoke. The man swallowed, and his folded hands clenched slightly at the mention of cigarettes, but that was all.

Since Friedli said nothing, Renzo went on. "Ben Schweizer used to help you unload and store the cigarettes, which were delivered by a van on market days before the vendors started to set up their stands. Fifteen years ago, on the night Katica Horvat died, she met Schweizer on the Pläfe at three thirty in the morning. Then she came into the Münster and sat in a pew while he went out to wait for the delivery, which was due at four thirty. A little before five, Ben says, he was still in the Münsterplatz when he saw Frau Horvat fall off the tower from the higher balcony. She lay dead on the stones until almost six o'clock when one of the market vendors saw her body and ran into the church to tell you. Although, in fact, I believe Schweizer told you about her death just after it happened."

More silence.

"All of this means that from four twenty until she climbed the tower, Frau Horvat was alone with you in the Münster. I want you to tell me about those forty minutes."

A look almost of relief came over Friedli's face. Perhaps he'd thought Renzo had been going to make trouble over the cigarettes. For whatever reason, he seemed to feel he was on safer ground than he'd expected. That was interesting.

The man leaned forward. "There's really nothing to tell. It wasn't the first time Ben had one of his lady friends with him on a market day morning. Katica was different from most of them only because she often prayed at the Münster, although she was a Roman Catholic. I suppose she needed to ask God to forgive her for breaking the seventh commandment." He snickered. "In any case, I wasn't surprised to have them come into the church that morning."

This Friedli wasn't stiff and oily like Friedli-the-sexton. In fact, he was almost relaxed, though Renzo could feel his watchfulness just beneath the surface. Maybe this was who Friedli was in private. Or was it just another role he was playing?

"That morning," Friedli continued, "I figured they'd just come from Ben's place. He was in a state, so cut up that even I noticed, and she was kind of teary-eyed, too. Something was going on, but I didn't care about their tiffs. I told Ben to go out and wait for the van and text me when it got there. Then I'd come out with the second handcart so we could get the stuff unloaded and out of sight as fast as possible. I was always cautious, but"—he shrugged—"at that hour, there was no one around, and if someone did see us, they'd have thought we had something to do with the street market."

Yes, thought Renzo, *it was a clever place to conduct your business.*

He was finding the sexton's sudden honesty strange. Perhaps he was trying to win Renzo's trust; perhaps he genuinely didn't feel he had anything to hide now that Renzo knew about the cigarettes.

"I was waiting in my office to hear from Ben, and Katica was sitting in a pew near the altar. She did this during the day, too, stopping in on her way back from an errand. I was used to it. But this time, she didn't leave after two or three minutes, so I figured she had more to say to Ben and was waiting for him to come back. Just like I was waiting for a text from him."

"Were you able to see her from where you were sitting in your office?"

"No," Friedli said a touch impatiently.

"Could you have seen or heard someone who came into the Münster at that point?"

Friedli frowned. "The three main double doors in the west front were still locked and bolted, and workmen like Ben only used the smaller doors on the north and south aisles. All of those were locked except the one outside my office. It's hard to be sure, but I don't think anyone could have come into the church without my hearing them. The Münster's as quiet as the grave at that hour."

"All right. Go on."

"Well, as I said, there's nothing much to tell. I wasn't thinking about the girl. Then, all of a sudden, Ben stumbled through the door by my office, screaming, 'She jumped! She jumped!' He was crying, and his hands were bloody; he claimed he'd seen Katica throw herself off the upper gallery."

Renzo noted the word "claimed." Did that mean Friedli thought Ben was lying? Or was that just what he wanted *Renzo* to think? The casual way Friedli spoke about Katica's death and Ben's grief made him angry. "And you didn't want to call the cops," he said, "because you were still waiting for a delivery of cigarettes and probably still had some cartons hidden in the cellar. So, first, you had to cancel the van and then get rid of the boxes in the wine cellar *and* Ben Schweizer. After that, you sat at your desk until a butcher came running in to tell you he'd found a dead woman lying in the Münsterplatz. Even after that, you tried to delay getting the police there for as long as possible, and you made sure every possible person *except* the police was called in to mess up the scene. Am I right?"

"Katica was dead," he said calmly, "and dead women don't get any deader from lying on cold stone for a couple of hours. You can't charge me with failing to render first aid to a corpse." There was almost nothing of the pious, helpful sexton left in his face. Who *was* this man?

"What about murder?" Renzo snapped. "I could arrest you for that." He had no basis for the accusation. Friedli had no motive that he could think of. But he was impatient to provoke some sort of genuine reaction.

Friedli's face went pale. "You can't . . ." Finally, there was a squeak of fear in his voice. He took a deep breath, and when he spoke, he sounded composed again. "The woman jumped. Ben said so. I was in my office. I had no idea she'd left the nave."

"A minute ago, you told me the Münster was dead quiet. Yet now you're saying you didn't hear Frau Horvat get up from her pew, walk down the aisle, open the tower door, and let it close behind her? Certainly you would have heard her."

Friedli said nothing. He looked at Renzo through narrowed eyes.

"But that's beside the point anyway, Herr Friedli. Because the Kellenberger boy was lying awake in bed. He heard Frau Horvat run up the stairs to the apartment, stop to catch her breath, and continue toward the staircase leading to the upper gallery. Then he heard and saw *you* coming up after her." Renzo felt no compunction about this lie, and he pushed on relentlessly. "You stood right outside his window, and he stood inside, staring out at you and listening to you pant."

There was a long pause. "That boy—has it occurred to you that he's lying? He left everything wide open, and he . . ."

"We know that isn't true. Frau Horvat had her own key."

Another pause. Renzo watched thoughts chase themselves over Friedli's face. Perhaps he was wondering what else Renzo had found out. "If that's what the boy says, then it's what he says. But it wasn't me outside his window." His voice was icy.

"Then who? You've confirmed what Schweizer told us: you were in the church alone with Frau Horvat. *You* say you would have heard someone come in. So, who could have been in the tower besides you?"

The man watched him steadily. Finally, he spoke. "Who do you think? Schweizer, of course. Who else?"

Renzo gave an exasperated laugh. "So, now you're telling me Ben Schweizer came back into the Münster? Although you just said you saw and heard no one?"

Friedli put on a smile that didn't quite work. "Come on, you're a cop; you know how it is. He and I worked together. We looked out for each other. The verdict was suicide, and that suited me; a murder investigation would have caused problems. Ben wasn't a professional. Eventually, he'd have told the cops about the cigarettes. But I'm not going to keep lying for him if he's telling you I was the last person to see the Horvat woman, especially not when you accuse *me* of killing her."

Renzo's mind was racing, but he kept quiet, hoping Friedli would keep talking.

Which he did. "The truth is that Ben got tired of waiting outside, came back in, and he and his tart carried on fighting. She ran away from him up the tower stairs, and he went after her. Eventually, he came downstairs alone and went out the door without speaking to me. I assumed he went back into the Münsterplatz to wait for the van. But twenty minutes later, I got a text saying the van wasn't coming that day. And there was no Ben—he was gone. I stayed at my desk until the market guy arrived to tell me about finding Katica's body."

"You are telling me Schweizer killed Frau Horvat and then just walked away? Yet you described him coming into the Münster crying and bloody . . ."

"Well, I didn't actually see him throw her off the tower, but it's obvious he did. Why else would he tell the police that he was at home in Münchenbuchsee all night?"

Oh, God. Renzo felt like banging his head on the table. Not another story he couldn't prove true or false that contradicted what he thought he knew! This case was a nightmare.

Then his investigative experience kicked in. It made sense that Schweizer might have killed Katica if she'd just broken up with him. He'd loved her—the emotion he'd shown in his office had been real. Perhaps Schweizer couldn't bear the thought of her going back to her husband. And yet his description of standing on the ground and seeing her fall toward him had been utterly convincing.

Friedli was still talking. "You can bet his ex-wife won't back up his fake alibi anymore, so the fucker had to make up a new story accusing *me* of killing her."

Renzo's head snapped up, and he stared at Friedli. That was the key, wasn't it? Schweizer had confessed to being at the Münster that night although his ex-wife *had* given him his alibi yet again. He'd never have done that if he'd killed Katica. He'd have grabbed gratefully at the old story and kicked Renzo and Mädi out of his office with a smirk on his face. Which meant that in spite of Friedli's best efforts to shift blame, Schweizer had been telling him the truth about standing on the cobblestones and seeing a woman he loved fall to her death. And *that* story tallied perfectly with what Friedli had told him about Schweizer coming into the church distraught and bloody. Only after Renzo told the sexton that Denis had seen him standing on the tower balcony had he come up with a completely different account of Schweizer's behavior.

Trust your gut, he told himself, knowing that his "gut" was actually the unconscious pattern recognition that years of police work had given him.

"Nice try, Herr Friedli, but it doesn't work. We checked Schweizer's alibi, and his ex-wife is still insisting he was at home in bed with her. Despite that, he told us all about the cigarette scam and being there when Katica died. He had no reason to tell us anything, but he did. And he didn't even *try* to point the finger at you, except for saying that you were inside waiting in your office. You're the only one who seems to think he's accusing you of something. Is that because you have a guilty conscience?"

At these words, Friedli's face twisted, and he smashed his fist down on the table. "Fuck you. I did *not* kill that Yugo cunt, and I'm not going to let you pin it on me. You've got no proof."

The policewoman taking notes started, and Renzo's heart was beating faster as he leaned back in his chair and stared at Friedli. He kept his voice calm. "Hate speech toward women and foreigners is a crime, Friedli. I'd be careful if I were you."

Friedli's face was red. A strand of hair fell forward over his eyes. Nevertheless, he took a deep breath and managed to calm himself. "I didn't kill her, and that's all I'm going to say. I'm finished." Then a thought seemed to occur to him. "Martin Rohner from the parish council will vouch for me. I'm done with you and your bullshit!"

Renzo tucked the name away to think about later. What now? Should he keep pushing Friedli? There were other things he needed to be doing, and he thought Friedli meant what he'd said—he was done talking, at least for now. Perhaps he'd insist on a lawyer. And anyway, what Friedli had said was true: Renzo had no *evidence* that he had killed Katica. Denis couldn't identify the figure outside his window; he didn't know if the man had continued up the second flight of steps or gone back down. Schweizer had seen Katica falling, but not someone on the upper gallery. It was all, still, a mere hunch. But Friedli was lying—about Ben Schweizer coming back into the church and only God knew what else. Renzo felt certain.

How could he find *facts* about what Friedli had been doing during that short time he was in the Münster with Katica? He'd check with Denis's grandparents again, but he knew it would be useless. If they'd heard or seen anything suspicious, they'd have told Grossenbacher fifteen years earlier—or at least Renzo now. And what really troubled him was the question of motive. What reason could Friedli possibly have had for killing Katica? What, if anything, had happened while the sexton was alone with the woman that could have made her run up the staircase? If she'd been running away from him, then why hadn't she pounded on the Kellenbergers' apartment door?

He felt stuck. He'd made progress, yes, but there was more to uncover here. Standing, he went to the door of the interrogation room and called to the uniformed man on guard in the hall. "Let's get this guy put away."

Despite the lack of evidence and motive, after Denis's story about the man in his window and Friedli's obscene outburst about Katica, coming on top of the man's lies about Schweizer, Renzo now considered the sexton a suspect. So at the very least, he was damn well going to keep Friedli locked up while he figured out how to get more information about that night.

30

Renzo made sure there was a free jail cell at the *Amthaus* to hold the sexton for twenty-four hours. Then he went upstairs to his desk in the Fahnder office and called Sven Huber at the Institute of Forensic Medicine. They'd known each other since Gymnasium and still got together a few times a year to kick a soccer ball, play cards, or watch a game on TV. To his surprise, Sven said he could test the siblings' DNA by midday Sunday and promised to send Renzo the results, although an official report would take longer. Renzo walked the swabs over to the police lab so they could go out in that afternoon's delivery to the institute. Then he returned to his desk to call the Münster's Frau Zehnder.

The minister didn't answer her cell, so he left a message. "I'm keeping Klaus Friedli for twenty-four hours. I know it will inconvenience you, but I think it's important."

Within a minute, Frau Zehnder called him back. She sounded out of breath, and he could hear street noise in the background. "Have you found out anything concrete?"

"He confirmed selling smuggled cigarettes. That's all I can say right now. But I'd like to ask you if . . ."

"Sorry, I need to go," she said. "But I'm very grateful you called about Friedli. Please tell me anything else you find out about him. As for your question, could you try me tomorrow?"

Renzo was disappointed that he hadn't been able to ask her about the parish councilor the sexton had given as a reference, Martin Rohner. He'd have to follow up on that himself. But first, he called Oliver Leuthard, the public prosecutor he knew and liked best, and gave him a very brief summary of what he was working on, with an emphasis on the sexton's past and perhaps present crimes. "I'm leading up to letting you know that I'm putting him in the Amthaus jail."

"I figured that was coming. And in theory, I ought to come and question him during the next twenty-four hours, but let's leave it like this: if you find new evidence that might lead to a formal accusation, let me know before tomorrow noon, and I'll make sure a prosecutor talks to him. If you have nothing by then, no need to get back to me. Just let him out, and all's well."

Renzo nodded to himself. This was why he liked Oliver. The man cared deeply about fairness and the law, but he didn't always need to dot every i.

"Great, Oli, and thanks. I wanted to be sure I wasn't messing up the case, assuming we get the evidence to indict him later."

"No sweat, Renzo. Your ass is duly covered."

What else could he do? Jürg Thönen in Narcotics should by now have gotten permission to check Friedli's office and the wine cellar for drugs, although he'd told Renzo when they'd talked earlier that he'd never get a warrant for a home search unless they struck gold at the Münster. It would be a while before Renzo heard more about that. It was time to call Friedli's buddy on the council.

It was easy to find Martin Rohner in the databases the police had access to. He was sixty-nine, originally from the canton of Saint Gallen, a lawyer retired from a large, well-respected Bernese law practice. He had a wife, two children, five grandchildren, a holiday house in an Alpine village between Zürich and Saint Gallen, and an apartment just across the Kirchenfeld Bridge from the Münster. Not, at first glance, a very likely associate of the sexton's. Renzo called his landline.

"Rohner." The man who picked up the phone had a strong voice.

"This is Renzo Donatelli of the Kantonspolizei, Herr Rohner. I'm calling about a matter related to the Münster. I understand that you serve on the *Kirchgemeinderat* in a position of responsibility?"

"I've been on the council in a variety of jobs for over twenty-five years now," he answered, "but it sounds as if you need the council president, not me."

"Perhaps I do," Renzo agreed courteously, "but right now, it's you I want to talk to. May I come by your home on Weststrasse this afternoon at two? Or would you prefer to meet at the police station? I don't want to intrude on your privacy."

There was a long silence, and Renzo pictured the man trying to imagine what this was all about. "It's fine for you to come by our apartment, Herr Donatelli," Rohner said at last. "May I . . . can you let me know what you'd like to discuss with me?"

"I'd prefer to get into that when we meet, Herr Rohner. Thanks for making yourself available. I'll see you this afternoon at two."

Renzo sat back and considered what else he could do to collect information about Friedli. Perhaps there was some sort of connection between him and Katica Horvat that he couldn't imagine. He still had very little background on Katica's life in Bern, her marriage, and her past. The obvious person to ask was Ivana, who had grown up in the same village and had known Katica since childhood. But he didn't trust Ivana to tell him the truth. There had been other women friends; Renzo remembered the party Lovro had mentioned.

Renzo found Zora Horvat's number, picturing her spooning out that delicious-smelling home-cooked lunch for her brother. He looked at his watch and saw it was close to noon. Not the best time, perhaps, but he dialed anyway.

Her phone rang for a long time, and he was about to hang up when she answered. "Sorry," she said. "I was up to my elbows in mud. Did you find something from the swabs already?"

"Not yet. But a guy I know is working on them, and there's a chance we'll have something by Sunday afternoon. Just try to be patient, and tell Goran not to explode."

"That's great! Thank you so much. I don't think I'll see Goran until Sunday at our family lunch. Maybe we'll have the results by then." Her voice rose in excitement.

Renzo tried to dampen her zeal. "I doubt it. Listen, there's something else I'd like to ask. I've been thinking about your mother's state of mind before she died, and I know she gave a party to show off Goran. Apart from Ivana, of course, did you know any of the women who were there?" When Zora didn't answer right away, he added, "I'm interested in talking to the one who's most likely to reveal everyone's secrets, including your mother's."

"Tetka Jelena!" Zora burst out. "I remember my mother joking to my father, 'If you want to pass a piece of news to every Croatian in Bern, just tell it to Jelena!' She's the one. I *think* she was at Majka's party. I mainly remember her from church. I liked her."

"Is Tetka her first name or her surname? Do you spell Jelena with J or Y?"

"Tetka means 'Auntie,' her first name is spelled with a J, and I don't remember her last name, but my father will know it, and I can make up a story about seeing her on the tram and wanting to send her a note." She sounded pleased with herself.

This whole business could turn Zora's life upside down—again. Renzo felt he owed it to her to warn her. "You know," he said slowly, "by the time I'm finished with this investigation, I might have found out things about your mother that will . . . well, that might make you sad. I hope—"

Her voice cut in. It had turned hard. "Sadder than knowing my mother used me to cheat on my father? Sadder than feeling I wasn't worth her staying alive for? How much worse can I feel?"

"Much worse," he said because it was true.

He could hear Zora breathing deeply in and out. "Not knowing *why* she died is the worst burden," she said at last. "Anything that reveals that is a gift. I think it's worth any short-term pain to get to future peace, um, closure—or whatever you want to call it."

"I don't want you to regret having helped me or blame yourself for whatever comes out of all this," Renzo told her.

"You're a strange policeman," Zora said with a smile in her voice, and Renzo knew it was a compliment. "Isn't it your job to squeeze people for information and to hell with the consequences?"

"I only do that when I'm looking for killers, and right now, I'm still not sure there is one."

"Yeah." Neither spoke for a moment. "Okay, I'll get Jelena's last name from my father. Let me know as soon as you have the test results."

"All right. Thank you, Zora."

Jogging down the four flights of stairs to the basement cafeteria, he went over what he knew about the long-ago party for Goran's birth. Lovro thought it had upset his wife; Ivana claimed she'd had a wonderful time. Maybe this "Auntie" of Zora's would know which of them was telling the truth.

31

Bern's Bärenplatz and Weststrasse in Kirchenfeld,
Friday afternoon, June 28

While Renzo was making his series of phone calls, Giuliana was on her bicycle, heading to lunch with the Seiler case's prosecutor, Rosmarie Bolliger. They were meeting at Luce, an Italian restaurant on Bärenplatz with tables outdoors. Although the "outdoors" in question was a wide strip of concrete surrounded by buildings, eating outside in June was always a pleasure.

She locked her bike to a stand near the restaurant, found the table for two labeled "Bolliger," and sat down facing the tall, moss-covered cylinder of the Meret Oppenheim fountain. Then she opened her phone and began a list of follow-up tasks to her morning's interview with Ruth Seiler. Some points in Ruth's story still needed checking, and there was digging to be done on Tamara's lawyer before she confronted him about the bogus complaint over Ruth Seiler's care of her husband. Had the man approached anyone at KESB, the Child and Adult Protection Services? Put anything in writing? Or had it remained a verbal threat, never carried out?

Valérie Imboden should have told the police about that threat long ago. And why hadn't the police known about Ruth's visit to the care facility? Both those pieces of information would make the prosecution's case harder. Valérie could talk about the stress that the threat of being reported to KESB had placed on Ruth. It would make the court sympathetic to her dilemma. Hell, it made *Giuliana* sympathetic, as well, and that made it harder to do her job. She'd started to feel she was on the wrong side of the courtroom.

Elbows on the table, she propped her forehead in her hands and closed her eyes. Not for the first time, she wondered how thoroughly Adam, her homicide colleague, had investigated this case before his leave of absence.

Her phone pinged with a text; it was the prosecutor apologizing for running ten minutes late. Giuliana sent a thumbs-up and then opened the notes on her phone. But instead of reading over what she'd learned from Ruth, she found her mind on Renzo. She needed him back on her case to help her with this new to-do list. Yet having him out of the way these past few days, involved in his own case, had made her life easier. Once he was back on the Seiler case, she'd be sitting in that case room with him again, smelling his clean male scent, listening to him curse in Italian under his breath, and knowing that every ten minutes or so, he'd share a thought about their case that would make her think—or laugh.

When he'd told her about asking Mädi out, she'd known it was his way of pushing the reset button. It was best for both of them. She thought of that quote about putting away childish things. It was never too late to do that, even at forty-seven. Then she wondered how Renzo would feel about being called a childish thing and teared up. Blinking, she got a tissue from her pocket and blew her nose.

The noise caught the attention of a passing waitress, who came over to chat and see if she wanted anything. Giuliana ordered sparkling mineral water, and by the time that was done, she was calm.

Looking out across the expanse of pavement, she saw the prosecutor walking toward her, waving. Rosmarie was small and brisk, in her early fifties, with short brown hair going gray. Giuliana smiled inwardly, as always, at how Rosmarie's wardrobe of pastel-colored suits and matching kitten heels contrasted sharply with her relaxed, no-nonsense manner and dry humor.

Giuliana waved back and stood so they could hug each other. She wasn't sure how this meeting would go. What would Rosmarie make of her ambivalence about their case?

They ordered food. "Tell me about your interview with Seiler," Rosmarie said.

"Yes." Giuliana took a deep breath and began explaining about Ruth's husband's trust in her decision-making, his almost irrational desire to leave money to his children, and his refusal to make plans for his death.

The waitress brought them their water and a basket of the warm, delicious *piadina* Giuliana loved. But instead of taking some of the flat-bread, she kept talking. "Then, right after the interview with Ruth was done, I managed to get both Allemann's lawyer and his doctor to talk to me, although, at first, they said they had no time. I should have interviewed them earlier instead of trusting the previous investigation. The lawyer went over the will with me. After making sure his wife was taken care of financially, Werner focused on the children. He talked to the lawyer at length, not just about what he wanted in his will but about his old age in general. So, the lawyer can testify that Allemann wanted his wife to take care of him at home and did not want to go to a care facility unless his wife felt it was absolutely necessary because she could no longer cope."

She reached for a wedge of folded piadina and bit off one pointy end of the triangle while she waited to see if Rosmarie had a comment.

"But there's no legal document confirming that?" asked the prosecutor.

"Right. The lawyer says he encouraged Allemann to let him create some sort of health-related or end-of-life directive but got a firm no. Allemann said he'd leave all those decisions to his wife, and that was that."

Their food arrived, and they ate for a few minutes. Then Giuliana continued. "In other words, the lawyer backed up what Seiler told me, and it was the same with the doctor."

Rosmarie's mouth was full of pasta, but she nodded.

"Seiler said by the time Allemann died, he was into the severe stage of Alzheimer's, no longer following conversations and having trouble feeding himself. The doctor agreed; he had visited a week or so before Allemann's death. He also told me he was perfectly satisfied with the death. No one could have been more surprised than he was when the forensic pathologist found too much insulin in Allemann's system."

Rosmarie raised an eyebrow. "And you believed him?"

"No, but I understand why he said it. And that's part of my problem. I know Seiler broke the law, but I am also convinced that the doctor approved, although I don't believe he assisted in any way. He would have quietly let the killing go if that vindictive daughter—who I believe is truly unbalanced—hadn't scared him into contacting the prosecutor's office. This *should* have been a fully legal assisted suicide, and if you and I were members of the public instead of a policewoman and prosecutor, we'd want Seiler to get off. And there are other things you don't know. At least, I didn't."

Rosmarie swallowed her bite. "What? Information that Valérie Imboden is planning to use in Seiler's defense? Tell me."

Giuliana summarized what Ruth had said about visiting the specialized care facility and sitting down with her lawyer to see if she could work out how to pay for it while preserving the children's inheritance. "I verified that with the lawyer," she added, "as well as something else. Do you know that Tamara Hofstetter got her lawyer to tell Seiler that if she didn't put her husband into the care facility by the end of March, they would report her to the KESB for abusing her husband?"

Rosmarie paused, a bite of food halfway to her mouth. Then she set down her knife and fork and wiped her lips with a napkin. "You're talking about blackmail."

"Yes." Giuliana paused, hoping Rosmarie would anticipate what she was about to say. "Rosmarie." She took a deep breath. "It's getting hard for me to pursue this case."

"Are you serious?" Rosmarie's voice was sharp. "Come on. This business about KESB is a minor problem at most. Seiler would have been cleared easily. The family doctor would have vouched for her doing a good job, and there was a home healthcare worker who could also have spoken in her defense. Nobody in their right mind would have taken that threat seriously. Assuming it isn't something Ruth made up."

Giuliana didn't answer straight away. She was disappointed that Rosmarie didn't see things the way she did. But the prosecutor hadn't heard Ruth's voice or seen her tears. She didn't grasp the dilemma the woman had faced.

Maybe she needed to try a different approach. "Look at it this way. If I, a member of the police force, don't want to see this woman go to jail for premeditated murder, what are the judges going to think? Valérie is a good lawyer, and Seiler is a convincing and touching witness. If she explains to the judges even half as well as she did to me, I think you're going to lose your case."

"Our case," Rosmarie snapped. Giuliana nodded but didn't let herself get sidetracked.

"I have to make sure that everything Seiler and her lawyer told me is true. But let's assume we can confirm her visit to the care facility, which shows good faith, *and* the KESB threat. Suppose the home really was too expensive for her means, especially if the children inherited what their father wanted them to." Giuliana stopped for a breath. "Assuming all that, I want us to meet with Valérie and see if we can come up with another way to present this case in court. I'd say we need to consider reducing the charge to manslaughter."

Rosmarie was frowning, but she tilted her chin. "Go on."

"If we talk to Sebastian Allemann alone, without his sister putting him under pressure, I think we could persuade him to take his inheritance and be done with it. Perhaps Valérie would agree to our letting Sebastian see the evidence from the doctor and lawyer showing that Ruth was acting in his father's interests *and* according to his wishes. We need to get him to change sides before we go after the sister."

Rosmarie didn't say anything, so Giuliana went on. "Then—I wonder if Valérie has considered insisting on Tamara having a psychiatric evaluation? She was such a terrible daughter to her father, never phoning, barely letting him see his grandchildren, and now she's set herself up as his champion. It makes me sick." Privately, she was wondering what Valérie could legally reveal to the *press* that would expose Tamara, but she didn't breathe a word about that to Rosmarie. "Whatever we do, I'd like the judges to consider a suspended sentence or house arrest instead of sending her to prison."

"She committed a crime," Rosmarie said.

"I'm not suggesting she should get off," Giuliana said, although she was hoping very hard for a suspended sentence. But that wasn't her decision. "Just that we keep all the extenuating circumstances in mind and don't charge her with premeditated murder."

Rosmarie was staring out over the concrete square. Finally, she cocked her head and gave Giuliana a sardonic smile. "Why am I not more surprised? You're your father's daughter, even as a cop."

Giuliana took that as a compliment. She wanted to add *Don't forget that I'm Paolo's sister, too.* Instead, she said, "The biggest strike against Ruth, besides the killing itself, is that she didn't hold her ground although the law was always on her side. The *spouse* decides what happens in cases like this, not the children. So, why didn't she just dig in her heels and tell Werner's kids to go to hell, which was her legal right? I think she lost her courage when the KESB threat showed her just how far Tamara was willing to go to control her. That's what we need to emphasize. The judges will already know that most people are terrified of the protection authorities, but let's highlight that in our reports."

"Hmm," Rosmarie said. That noise gave Giuliana hope. "I'll ... think about it. In the meantime, you work on verifying the KESB business. And play the defense for me: make me a list of all these extenuating circumstances you expect Valérie to bring up, including any you haven't mentioned today. I'd be sorry to lose the case if I could win it by changing the charge and working out a compromise instead. But— there has to be a clear acknowledgment that Seiler broke the law."

"I agree." Giuliana remembered Ursula Kellenberger saying that cases like Ruth's gave legitimate assisted suicide organizations a bad name. Seiler couldn't just get off. Still, Giuliana could go back to the case with a clearer conscience now, gathering evidence to both prosecute and defend Ruth. And she felt she'd managed to keep Rosmarie's trust—that was important, too.

"Do you have time for us to order coffee?" she asked Rosmarie.

Martin Rohner, the parish council member that Klaus Friedli considered his friend, lived on the beautifully renovated ground floor of a large, late-nineteenth-century villa. Renzo turned down coffee and asked Rohner if they could sit outside, so the lawyer led him to a round table in the back garden, shaded by a tree. There was no sign of the afternoon's predicted thunderstorm. As Renzo retrieved his pen and notebook, he decided that straightforwardness was his best approach. Someone like this lawyer was probably better at setting verbal traps than he was.

"Let me first assure you that *you* are not in any trouble with the police, Herr Rohner," Renzo began. "But the Münster's sexton, Klaus Friedli, is; we're holding him in a cell in the courthouse. He told me you would vouch for him, but what I'd like you to do instead is tell me about him, starting with his selling smuggled cigarettes out of the sexton's office." Renzo paused, but Rohner was pressing a fist to his lips, shaking his head, so Renzo added, "I believe he started doing that soon after he got his job at the church twenty years ago, and you told me on the phone that you've been on the council at the Münster for almost twenty-five years. Were you involved in hiring him?"

"Friedli." Rohner breathed out the name and put both palms flat on the table. "For years, I've worried that a journalist or a cop would ask me about that man, and now that it's happened, I find I'm relieved. And . . . ashamed. I'm glad to say that I was *not* responsible for his employment, but soon after that, I found out about the cigarette business and did nothing about it. Which I suppose is why he expects me to vouch for him." He paused. "Look, can I tell you this in my own way instead of answering questions?"

"Of course," Renzo said. "I'd prefer that."

"I'm from the city of Saint Gallen, and my father was a house carpenter, so my parents were surprised when I chose to go to Gymnasium and university. After three years of studying law in Saint Gallen, I transferred to the University of Bern and got my law degree here. I did the whole program, internships, exams, and everything in Bern and joined the bar. I was lucky to get a job with a decent firm, but I didn't have local connections to help me bring in clients. So, on top of all the work a young attorney is expected to do, I started looking for ways I could volunteer in the city of Bern." He raised his eyebrows at Renzo. "Did I work in a soup kitchen or with recovering heroin addicts? No, I did not. I joined organizations that would bring me into contact with the 'right' people."

Renzo could imagine where this story was going, but he was still eager to hear it. "I suppose getting involved with the folks who ran the Münster was a triumph." Unlike Rohner, he didn't speak sarcastically. As a first-generation Italian immigrant, he had sympathy for outsiders who needed to find a way to fit in and make a good living.

"I was already established in Bern by the time I joined the parish council, but, yes, I was very pleased. And although the work for the parish grew out of my campaign to make connections, it has come to mean a lot to me over the years. Except for anything related to the sexton." He sighed. "How could he possibly believe I would put in a good word for him? I'd rather tell you how he got his claws into me."

Aha, thought Renzo. *Friedli has a hold over this man.* That did not surprise him.

As if he were reading Renzo's mind, Rohner said, "Don't feel sorry for me. I cared too much about public opinion. If I hadn't, I wouldn't have kept silent about the way he was abusing the Münster and the parish's trust in him."

Renzo waited, and Rohner went on without faltering, his eyes meeting Renzo's. "You see, Friedli's father ran a little shop only slightly bigger than a kiosk that sold cigarettes, gum, candy, a few grocery items, little toys—all kinds of stuff. It was just off the Länggasse, right in the middle of the university area, and it seemed as if half the student population—including, ironically, quite a few of my law student friends—knew that he sold exceptionally cheap cigarettes to 'special' customers. This was fifty years ago, and we all smoked tobacco then, and a lot of us smoked marijuana, too, which we also bought from him, but not often because we could usually get it cheaper from friends."

Renzo couldn't resist breaking in. "But you can't have known the younger Friedli in those days. He's fifty-eight, so when you were a law student, he'd have been a kid."

"Although I'd stopped smoking weed by the time I took the bar exam, I kept buying those cheap cigarettes until I was around thirty, and by then, Klaus was nineteen and helping his father. He'd done an apprenticeship and had a job in retail somewhere else—I don't know what firm—but most weekends, he was in the shop. I never paid attention to him, except to say hello and goodbye when I noticed him, but he knew all about me. His father had made everyone who bought the extra-cheap cigarettes sign up with him. He talked about his 'club' and left our names on our packages of smokes as if we were special customers. I was studying law when I gave that crook my name! How *could* I have been so stupid?"

"Not stupid, just naïve," Renzo corrected. "Do you still smoke?" He asked to gain some insight into how seriously the man took illegal tobacco sales at this stage of his life.

"God, no." Rohner sounded disgusted. "My wife and I stopped smoking soon after our older daughter was born. She has been fine for years now, but when she was tiny, she had a lot of respiratory problems. Believe me, knowing your secondhand smoke is making it harder for your baby to breathe can scare a craving for tobacco right out of you."

Renzo had smoked as a teenager only because his friends did and used the excuse of soccer to stop in his early twenties. Still, he knew quitting was much harder for some people.

"That was a lot of background," Rohner said apologetically, "but now I'm coming to Friedli after he became sexton. I wasn't on the committee that hired him, which included the minister, Emil Graf. Later, when the full council held a *pro forma* vote to accept his employment, I didn't recognize him, either by name or by face. Friedli is a common surname, and when I last saw him twenty years before, he was a teenager, not a thirty-eight-year-old man."

"Did he tell you who he was?"

"Definitely not, and I don't think he ever would have, but about a year after he'd become sexton, I was helping to prepare for a social event in the Münster, and the organizer needed more wine. Friedli was away on an errand, so I was given a bunch of keys and sent down to the wine cellar. No one told me the bottles I was looking for were on a shelf, so I began searching the floor for cases of wine, and I came across cartons of Ukrainian cigarettes. By the time I found the wine and brought it upstairs, I'd started thinking about the name Klaus Friedli and what it meant in relation to those cigarettes."

Renzo was amazed that no one fetching a bottle from the cellar had discovered Friedli's illegal inventory before that. Maybe the cigarettes weren't normally so blatantly left around. "That must have been eighteen or nineteen years ago." In the three or four years between then and Katica's death, Renzo supposed Friedli must have figured out a better way to make sure no one else searching for wine could uncover his cigarettes. Maybe he bought a big wardrobe and locked them away in it. "What did you do?" This was the point, he knew, when the story would start getting uncomfortable for Rohner.

"That same day, I called him and made an appointment for the following Sunday after the service, and I confronted him. I thought he was using the wine cellar as extra storage for the shop near the university, and I was indignant about that. Once he got over his initial shock, he told me about the location of his new shop, right there in the church. The more upset I got, the more he gloated. He'd done his research and knew all about my job history. I was by then quite senior at my law firm and handling some delicate cases that were of interest to the press. First, Friedli told me he had his father's records of me buying not just illegal cigarettes but marijuana and threatened to share that information with a reporter at the *Blick*. Frankly, that terrified me, but I still tried to hold my ground. Then he said that if I blew the whistle on him and got the police involved, he'd say I'd been in on the whole thing from the beginning and helped him get hired as sexton. A bit of fact-checking would have shown I had nothing to do with his getting his job, but public opinion is rarely swayed by facts." With that, Rohner got up. "I need some water," he said and went inside.

Renzo finished writing notes on what the man had said and looked around him. It was midafternoon, but the garden had grown dark because the sun had been swallowed by a tower of dark clouds. The air under the tree was still hot, but now it was so heavy with moisture that it felt gluey. Renzo, who had not expected to feel sympathy for Rohner, found that he could identify with the man's dilemma all those years ago. It was all very well to expect people threatened with blackmail to yell, "Publish and be damned." But he could imagine what it would mean to face a barrage of whispers and a threatened reputation.

Rohner returned with two glasses of tap water; his was already half empty. Renzo took the other glass gratefully and drank it down before taking up the reins of the interview.

"Did you tell anyone about Friedli's second, illegal job in the Münster?"

Rohner's shoulders slumped. "I didn't. I just walked away and did my best to have nothing to do with Friedli from then on. Until a young mother jumped out of the Münster tower and killed herself. That happened on a market day, so I knew he might have been there when she jumped because how else had she gotten into the church? At the very least, I suspected he might have seen her go up the tower stairs or discovered her body and just waited for someone else to find her so he wouldn't have to explain what he was doing there at that hour. His callousness made me furious, and that gave me courage. I still wasn't brave enough to tell the police, but a week after that poor woman died, I went to him and said I'd give him a month to close down his shop, and after that, I'd find an excuse to check the wine cellar and bell chambers and other hiding places in the church, and if I found anything, I'd go to the detective who'd investigated the woman's death and tell him everything, including about Friedli blackmailing me."

"And you think Friedli stopped his sales from the Münster?" Renzo was skeptical. The sexton would know every hiding place in the church, many more than Rohner could come up with. "I could be wrong, but I feel convinced he did stop. I didn't just search the place for cigarettes; for a year after that, I popped up at the Münster now and then at five in the morning on market days. He was never in his office or anywhere else in the church. Each time, I'd wait for him to arrive at his normal time and make sure he knew I was still checking on him. I think those surprise visits of mine, plus having the police all over the church after the woman's suicide, made him decide it wasn't worth it. Whether he set up shop elsewhere, I don't know. However, I'm sure he didn't need to—he earned good money as a brand-new sexton, and he's had quite a few raises since then. I know because I'm on the personnel committee now," Rohner added, looking around and noticing the darkening sky. He made no comment about ending the interview, though. "I'm deeply sorry. I should have called the police as soon as Friedli told me what he was up to with those cartons of cigarettes I found. When I finally did stand up to him, it was too little, too late." Rohner paused. "I can't imagine why he'd tell you I'd speak in his favor. How could he see me as still under his thumb now that I'm retired from my law practice?"

"I think he was pretty rattled when he mentioned you. I've started reinvestigating the death of the woman who fell from the tower, Katica Horvat, and I've found evidence to suggest it wasn't a suicide. You're right. Friedli *was* in the Münster when she jumped, and he's accusing her lover, who was a stoneworker doing renovations, of pushing her off. But the accusation isn't convincing. I have no evidence that Friedli killed the woman, but his whole demeanor makes me suspect him. Do you know anything that would help me learn the truth?"

At that point, Renzo noticed a couple of raindrops on the garden table. The two men stood simultaneously and moved toward the open glass doors leading back into the apartment. With both of them still on their feet in the living room, Rohner said, "I could believe anything of that man; he's amoral to the core. But I know nothing that could help you arrest him for the woman's death. Still," he paused and seemed to come to a decision, "as the head of the parish personnel committee, I have access to files going back decades. Let me spend some time with the paperwork. Maybe I'll find something you can use to put that *Souhung* in jail."

Renzo was content. Whatever wild hopes he'd had about evidence against Friedli, he'd gotten more out of the man than he'd expected. Before he left, though, he had one more question to ask.

"Herr Rohner, do you like the Münster's current minister?"

There was only a quick frown of surprise before the lawyer smiled. "I like Selena Zehnder very much, and I respect her, too. She manages to be as tough as that job requires without losing her warmth and compassion. I'm sorry I don't know her as well as I'd like to."

"Well," said Renzo, "if I were you, I'd enlist her help in your research on Friedli. You don't have to explain to her why you despise the man, although I think it would be a good idea to trust that compassion of hers and tell her the same story you told me. I can assure you that she is very angry about Friedli abusing his role within the church all those years ago and would be glad of your support in getting him out of the Münster forever. Apparently, thanks to what he's apparently told her, she thinks you're Friedli's buddy. She'd be relieved to know you're on her side, and perhaps, between the two of you, you can fire him and, in the process, find me evidence that would help me arrest him."

Rohner seemed energized. As they shook hands, he said, "You can't imagine what good it has done me to tell you everything and feel like I'm doing the right thing at last. If Selena and I can take steps against Friedli, that will make me feel even better. Thanks for listening without piling on the guilt and for giving me such a good plan of action, Herr Donatelli. Here, let me see you to the door."

Renzo hurried through the rain to his car. Driving back to the station and his long-abandoned desk in Giuliana's case room, he only gave a brief thought to Rohner, accepting that nothing the man had told him would allow him to keep the sexton in jail beyond Saturday at eleven, which was twenty-four hours after he'd been booked. Still, Rohner's involvement had increased Renzo's chances of learning more about Friedli in the future, and for that, he was grateful.

The next day, he'd see what Zora's Auntie Jelena had to say about what had really happened at that party.

32

B ack in the case room, listening to rain fall outside the open window, Renzo was reading Giuliana's notes on her interview with Ruth Seiler and the follow-up talks with Ruth's doctor and lawyer. It was a lot of new information, including this whole business involving the Child and Adult Protection Services. For the first time in several weeks, he was finding the Seiler/Allemann case interesting. He'd almost finished going through the doctor's statement for a second time, trying to read between the lines to determine what the GP had suspected about Werner Allemann's death, when Zora phoned.

"I can't talk long. I've only got a short break, and I used up most of it getting Jelena's number out of my father. Then I called her, and she wouldn't let me go. It was great to hear her voice, though, after so many years. She's a good person. She says you can come and see her tomorrow. I'll text you her phone number and address; her last name's Tomić. The only thing is, she insists I come, too. I explained about your being police and wanting to ask her questions about my mother's death, but it was no good. She wants us both there."

Renzo spoke fast so they could get this sorted out before she had to hang up. "Do you have time to come with me? And are you *willing*?

I'm going to ask her about the last weeks of your mother's life, and it will be hard. She might not be as straightforward with you there as she'd be without you. Or maybe your presence will help her open up. I don't know. In any case, it's terrific she's willing to meet with us—if you can handle it."

"Of course I can handle it. I want to hear what she has to say, too. I *need* to." He could hear the determination in her voice. "Just text me where and when."

"I'll pick you up at home, and we'll drive to her place together," Renzo told her.

"Thanks! I'm texting you Jelena's number now. See you tomorrow."

Renzo forgot about the Seiler case as he waited for Zora's text. As soon as it arrived, he called Jelena Tomić, who knew exactly who he was. "I was so happy to hear from Zora." Her dialect was fluent, but her Balkan accent was still there in the background. "I haven't seen her since she was about fifteen and turning into a woman almost as gorgeous as her mother. So tall, though—whew! Tell me, now, what is it you want? Zora didn't make that too clear—or maybe she did, and I didn't take it in. Anything I can do to help the poor child . . ."

Hastily Renzo stemmed the flood of words. He'd already thought about how to present his interest in Katica's death without lying. "We'd be very grateful for your help, Frau Tomić. The police are taking another look at Katica Horvat's death to be sure it really was a suicide, and it would be ideal if someone like you, someone close to her, could tell us what you know. Her husband thinks something might have happened at the party she gave to celebrate Goran's birth, and Zora decided you'd be the best person to ask. Do you think—?"

Jelena's angry voice cut him off. "Are you telling me that Ivana Pavić—I suppose I have to say Horvat now—never told Zora what went on at that party? I assumed Ivana talked to the police about it right after Katica killed herself." *Why didn't you talk to the police?* Renzo felt like asking, but he held his tongue. "All right," Jelena continued. "It sounds like I need to explain some things to Zora and—well, maybe it's time for me to tell someone in authority, too. Like you!"

"I'd appreciate that, Frau Tomić. It's especially good of you to see us on a Saturday."

"As it happens, Saturday afternoon is perfect since my husband always spends it with his mistress." Renzo's speech of thanks died on his lips, but Jelena continued as though she'd said nothing out of the ordinary. "Why don't you bring Zora to my place at two o'clock, and I'll give you coffee and cake. It will be so nice to see how the child turned out, and I hope I can help. I'm only shocked to have to do Ivana's job for her," she tutted. "I knew she'd be happy to raise the baby and even happier to take Katica's place in Lovro's bed. But there was never any love lost between Ivana and Zora, so I guess I should have known *that* wouldn't work out."

Finally, thought Renzo, *finally* it sounded as though someone would be able to give him the truth about Ivana's role in this whole mess. Ivana had told him to his face that nothing had happened at the party, yet Jelena was suggesting that whatever had gone on was serious enough that the police should have been informed. He gritted his teeth. Why couldn't the Horvat case run in a straight path, with all the evidence pointing in the same direction? He took a breath. "It sounds like I have a lot to learn about the second Frau Horvat as well as the first one. Zora and I will be there at two tomorrow, Frau Tomić. Thanks again."

"I'll expect you," she said. "It will do me good to talk about Katica after all these years. Not that I've ever forgotten her, because . . ."

Renzo cut in quickly. "Until tomorrow," he said and disconnected. He texted Zora that he'd pick her up the next day at one thirty and got a thumbs-up in reply. That done, his next step would be to find out if anyone at KESB had heard the name Ruth Seiler. Then he'd do a background check on the lawyer who'd threatened Ruth.

As he put his phone back to his ear again, his mind ran over his interview with Ivana Horvat. He'd *known* she was keeping something from him—why hadn't he pushed her harder? And Lovro, too. Renzo's sympathy for the man had made him go easy on him. Suppose they'd *both* been lying. What could he do to make them tell him the truth?

33

Cleaning the apartment to prepare it for Fränzi, Renzo was grateful that Saturday morning was cooler than Friday had been. He dusted surfaces and vacuumed everywhere, wiped down the tiny toilet and sink off the foyer and the full bathroom that served both bedrooms. Then he mopped the floors.

Housecleaning always made Renzo think of his older sister, Bianca. Their mother had been busy earning money when he was small, so Bianca had made sure he did his share of the housework—and showed him how. Bianca's bossiness was a joke among her three siblings, but Renzo didn't think any of them had ever truly resented her. With their parents so busy, Bianca had been a huge source of affection and stability in their lives. And look how useful everything she'd taught him about cleaning, ironing, and doing laundry had turned out to be!

He couldn't change the sheets until Sunday morning, but he sorted the rest of his laundry and began a wash. Once the second load was in the machine, he grabbed an empty backpack and set off to the nearby grocery store, enjoying the sunshine on the back of his neck in spite of the heat the afternoon would bring. Fränzi could get her own food, but he wasn't going to leave her without milk, her favorite flavors of yogurt, and some fresh fruit. Plus, he needed something for his dinner that night. He'd get Fränzi a loaf of bread at the bakery just before he made the exchange the next day.

Finally, chores done, he pulled a stool up to the breakfast bar and phoned to authorize Friedli's release from his jail cell. There was no way around it. That done, he opened his laptop and began writing a report for Rolf on how he'd investigated the attack on Denis Kellenberger and, in response to it, reopened Katica Horvat's death. Rolf hadn't said he expected a report, but Renzo thought this was a good way to show the head of homicide how he'd worked the case. He hoped Rolf would give him useful feedback and think a little harder about making him a detective. If this meant he was becoming a suck-up, so be it.

At twelve thirty, Renzo ate a thick slice of braided white bread with butter, some garlicky salami, and a handful of the dark-red cherries he'd bought for Fränzi. Then he left to pick up Zora.

When she got into the Fiat, Renzo saw that she'd taken a polite step or two toward conventionality for the sake of her mother's old friend. Her wild curls were partially contained by a red plastic headband, her jeans were clean and more stylish than the baggy shorts he'd seen her wearing for work two days before, and instead of a T-shirt, she wore a short-sleeved red blouse.

"Thanks for doing this," he said.

"Thank *you* for having the idea," she answered. "I want to hear what Jelena has to say. Every word about my mother will make me happy . . . even if it makes me cry. I suppose you can understand that."

Renzo nodded but kept himself from reaching out and comforting her with a hand on her arm. He would have liked to tell Giuliana that he was working to stop himself from casually touching women—if only they were still discussing things in their old, thoughtful way. He wondered if they'd ever be able to talk like that again. God, how he would miss it if they . . . If they what? Broke up? How could they break up when they'd never been together?

He dragged his mind away from Giuliana. "How old do you think Jelena is? Do you know how your mother knew her?"

"Majka would be forty-four now, and Jelena must be at least five years older, maybe more. She already had two children when Majka was pregnant with me. They met at some kind of church supper in Bern before I was born, and Jelena took my mother under her wing. She's Slavonian, not Istrian, and the war was harder on that province, so she and her husband came to Switzerland earlier. I think she was my mother's best friend until Ivana showed up, which was when I was seven. Ivana sort of... took over my parents after she moved to Bern. At least, that's how it seemed to me. And I didn't like it."

Renzo digested Zora's words. He thought about how Jelena had talked on the phone about Ivana's failings as a stepmother. Now it sounded like Jelena might have reason to be jealous of Katica's old friend, so he'd have to watch out for that.

Before Renzo had finished parking in front of the Tomić house—and it was a house, too, not an apartment—Jelena was hurrying toward the Fiat, her arms open. Despite the eye roll she gave Renzo, Zora jumped out and fell into Jelena's ferocious embrace. They spoke in animated Croatian for a few moments, and then Jelena ushered the two of them through the house and onto a shady back porch overlooking a garden, bringing them cups of coffee and slices of cake tasting of almonds and oranges.

For some time, Jelena Tomić grilled Zora about her life, this time in German for Renzo's benefit. He was wondering whether he ought to rescue her when she saved herself.

"Aunt Jelena," she said, laying a hand on the woman's arm. "It's wonderful to see you again, but I'm not here to talk about myself—I want you to tell me about my mother. Please! In all these years, no one's ever talked to me about why she killed herself. If you have any ideas about what might have been going on, please, you have to tell me."

Renzo quietly got out his notebook and pen and tried to make himself unobtrusive.

Jelena patted Zora's hand. "Of course, dear girl, of course you want to understand why. But *no one* can comprehend something so terrible, can they? At least I can tell you what happened at the party.

That cursed party! Looking back now, I know I should have told the police about it. Talking about women's business to men, let alone to Swiss policemen. I wasn't brought up that way. I thought it was better to keep quiet. But now . . ."

Renzo should have been delighted, but there was a knot of tension in his stomach. He couldn't help remembering Denis finally telling him about the figure he'd seen in his window, the best evidence so far for Katica's death being a homicide. Only the afternoon before, he'd listened to Rohner's confession. Now Jelena had yet another version of the story to share. How many more people were going to come forward and tell him they'd decided to talk at last? The first big case he'd ever handled alone, and after five days of questioning, he was still bogged down in secrets, lies, half-truths, and decades-old, highly selective memories.

Jelena paused and carefully poured herself more coffee from the old-fashioned china pot on the table. She seemed to be reveling in the drama of the moment. Zora looked over at Renzo and raised her eyebrows skyward; he gave her a tight smile. Together, they waited for the woman to begin her story.

34
Before

Fifteen years earlier
In the apartment above the Golden Goat,
almost midnight, mid-November

Jelena took another sip from her shot glass and pursed her lips appreciatively as she held the homemade *biska* in her mouth before swallowing. The flavor was new to her. The plum brandy—*rakija*—that she knew from her hometown of Daruvar wasn't flavored with mistletoe the way this Istrian stuff was. Still, it went down smoothly. There was a pitcher of apple juice in the middle of the table so the women could dilute their drinks, but only the youngest, Branka's daughter Lucija, had bothered.

Two of Katica's nine guests had left soon after dessert, worried about their babysitting arrangements, but seven remained, and all of them were getting steadily tipsier. Jelena had gotten a ride with Dunja, which meant she could drink as much as she wanted, although she hoped Dunja wouldn't overdo it. She grinned as she imagined how surprised their husbands would be to see them downing straight biska. None of them ever drank hard liquor in front of the men, except at weddings, where they all acted like it was much too strong for them. Oh, well. As she'd said many times before, what the men didn't know couldn't hurt them.

Nela was complaining about her husband, as she always did. They all complained about their men now and then, except for Lucija, who was madly in love with yet another Swiss boy. And Ivana, who was still unmarried at thirty-seven and, as far as anyone knew, had never been attached to any man—except Father Marko, the priest in charge of Croatian services. Not that Ivana would dream of flirting with him, nor would Father Marko be interested. Jelena suspected he had different tastes altogether.

"I can smell her cheap perfume on his shirts when I wash them," Nela was saying shrilly, and the women around the table nodded sympathetically, although Jelena was sure they were as bored as she was of hearing about Nela's husband's little sexual adventures. Jelena had asked her own husband if Nela had anything to worry about, and he'd scoffed. "Just the occasional afternoon with a waitress at his regular *Beiz*," he'd told her. "She's married too and, anyway, not a woman that any man would leave his family for." Jelena had felt relief at his words, and not just for Nela's sake. Unlike her friend, though, *she* didn't air her—or should it be her husband's?—dirty laundry in public.

"Maybe you should talk to Father Marko about it," said Ivana, who had been listening gravely.

They all turned to look at Ivana, and Jelena wasn't the only one who rolled her eyes. Trust Ivana to suggest something so silly. Nela was normally patient with Ivana's piety, even when it slid toward self-righteousness, but tonight she'd had too much to drink to keep her mouth shut. "Why in the world would I talk to the priest about my husband cheating? He'd probably say it was my own fault because I wasn't a loving enough wife. As if *he* knows anything about that!"

Ivana's prim face took on a holier-than-thou expression. The atmosphere had shifted. The evening, which had been a lot of fun so far, could be about to end badly. Jelena willed the two of them to let it go; she shook her head at Nela. But Nela was staring at Ivana, her face growing redder than it already was.

Katica clearly sensed danger, too. She stood up and grabbed a plate from the sideboard, saying loudly, "More cookies? What about coffee?"

But Nela wasn't going to be deterred. "The priest isn't the only one who knows nothing about how things work between men and women. Neither do you. So keep your useless advice to yourself."

Even after that, the evening might have been saved if Ivana had backed down. But she'd been drinking biska, too. So she said, "I don't need to be married, Nela, to understand that your nagging would drive any—"

"I've been nagging *my* husband for weeks now to fix one of our shutters," Jelena broke in desperately. Katica, still standing, plate of cookies in hand, also began to speak.

But it was no use. Nela jabbed a finger at Ivana. "How dare you try to tell me how to please my husband, you pathetic old maid?" She was leaning so far forward across the table that she was almost lying on her empty dessert plate. "What's wrong with you? Are you *proud* of being a virgin, or what? Why didn't you become a nun if you're so scared of locking your legs around a man?"

Ivana's mouth shut tight; her face went blank.

"Nela, please!" Katica was truly distressed, tears springing to her eyes, and Jelena remembered that their hostess was the only person at the table who knew anything about Ivana's past. Had Nela crossed some line that none of them knew about?

The women were silent now. Ivana pushed her chair back robotically and stood up. She stared over their heads at nothing, talking almost to herself.

"I'm not a virgin," she said dully. "I slept with my fiancé Anto, my brother's best friend. He died—at Vukovar. After that, I didn't want another man."

Vukovar! Jelena clutched her face with her hands. As the only Slavonian, she probably knew more about the horrors of that massacre than the other women at this table. And Ivana had been carrying this burden all these years. She'd never liked the woman, but still, her heart went out to her.

Nela began speaking, her voice soft now. "Ivana, I—"

But Ivana wasn't finished. "Then, when I was twenty-seven, Katica took me to a café, a place where UN soldiers hung out. She went off with some man she knew, and another man—I don't know what country he was from—bought me a drink. We spoke a little English together, and he was nice to me. He told me he'd take me to Katica, but instead, he led me into a dark room with a stinking mattress, and when I said that I didn't want to be with him that way, he raped me and left me lying there. So, if I'm scared of being alone with any man but a gay priest, I think I've earned that right. Don't you agree, Nela?"

Eyes wide, Nela nodded rapidly, her lips pressed together. The horrible silence seemed to stretch and grow.

Then they all heard a noise, something like a whimper. But it wasn't coming from Ivana; it was Katica. The cookies slid to the floor as she clutched the plate to her chest. "Ivana." It came out as a croak. She began to cry, looking pleadingly at Ivana, tears running down her cheeks. Then she covered her face with her hands and sobbed. She was trying to talk, but the words came out as gasps, and it took a while before Jelena could understand that what she was saying, over and over, was, "I never knew. I never knew."

Jelena stood up to console Katica, but Ivana got there before her.

She put her hands on Katica's shoulders. "I didn't tell you because . . . you were so young then. It seemed too cruel." Jelena wondered why Ivana didn't put her arms around her friend. "You never asked me, though, did you? You never tried to find out what happened after you left me at that bar. You never came to see me while I stayed in bed for over a week, pretending to be sick."

Katica was still crying, but her voice was more under control. "I'm sorry, Ivana. I'm so sorry." But still, Ivana held her at arm's length.

Stop now, Ivana, Jelena prayed silently. *It's enough.*

But Ivana didn't want to stop—or maybe she wasn't able to. "Then you and Lovro disappeared with barely a goodbye. You left the country with *Lovro*, the man I . . ." Her face twisted. ". . . The man I'd fallen in love with. A year later, you were writing me all about your wonderful baby girl, and at the same time, I was finding out that the man at the café had given me gonorrhea, and I hadn't known it. The doctor told me . . ." Ivana drew in a deep breath, and her whole face quivered with emotion. "She told me that the disease had gone untreated for so long that my body was damaged, and I could never have a child."

A sigh like a moan escaped from the women around the table. No babies—that was a tragedy every one of them could relate to. *Stop talking*, Jelena thought again. *You've got our sympathy now.*

"You took Lovro from me, stole him away." Ivana's voice was low, almost a hiss. "How could you be so *selfish*?"

Katica took her hands away from her face, which was red with crying. "You're right; I was selfish, and I'm so sorry for that. But . . ." Her voice became earnest, as though she was trying to reassure Ivana. "But Lovro didn't love you, Ivana. He would never have married you. He told me so."

The women around the table gasped. "I think it's time for us to talk about something else," Jelena said loudly. No good could come of all this honesty. She was sure of it. "Let's leave the past alone now."

Ivana still had hold of Katica's shoulders. Now she shook her violently, several times, and shoved her away. Katica's hip hit the edge of the table, and she fell to her hands and knees. Ivana stood over her, glaring, and for a moment, Jelena thought she was about to step on Katica's fingers, or kick her, or . . .

But all Ivana did was say in a flat voice, "You destroyed my life." With that, she walked out of the dining room and down the staircase to the dark shop.

By then, Nela and Milena were helping Katica to her feet, and the other women were out of their seats, too, beginning to talk again, their voices tinged with hysteria and growing louder. They crowded around Katica with expressions of concern. Only Jelena went to the top of the stairs to watch and listen as Ivana separated her coat from the pile on the counter, unlocked the front door, and went out into the street.

Jelena could tell she'd left the door open because she could hear Ivana's footsteps growing fainter along the sidewalk, so she went downstairs to lock it.

When Jelena got back to the dining room, Katica was on her feet, and everyone was talking at once.

"I'm just going to the bathroom," mumbled Katica, untangling herself from the women gathered around her and moving past Jelena into the upstairs corridor. Jelena started to speak but let it go. Instead, she moved to the head of the table, thinking that they all needed to do something useful to distract themselves. "Let's get all this stuff cleared, shall we?"

They sprang into action, finding a tray, piling dessert plates and glasses on it, carrying everything into the kitchen. The room was really too small for six, but they all managed to cram in. Again, they began to rehash everything that had happened, and Jelena felt desperate to stem the flood of gossip.

Then Branka spoke above all the voices, repeating a single word of Ivana's outburst. "Vukovar," she said. Silence fell; the women were frozen. "That was 1991. Ivana must have been just a teenager, the fiancé who was killed not much older."

It was all that was needed to still the chatter: this reminder of their own and their friends' losses and the devastation that had brought them to Switzerland.

Then Katica was at the kitchen door, her face clean, her hair tidy, and her hostess persona hauled back into place. "I'm so grateful for your help, but you're not allowed to lift another finger at my party," she said. She began pulling and pushing them out of the kitchen. "No, no, don't do another dish, Dunja. Things may have ended badly, but it's still a party. What good friends you are! Do you all have a way to get home?"

It was obvious Katica was eager to have them gone. She was trying hard to be upbeat, but her voice shook, and something in her eyes made Jelena want to stay and check that she was going to be all right. The problem was that Dunja was driving her and Milena home.

In the end, as they were saying goodbye with kisses and compliments about the food, Jelena contrived to leave her handbag behind. Then, once they were in Dunja's car and the other women were fastening their seatbelts, she ran back to the side door and rang the bell.

Katica opened the door immediately, holding the handbag, but Jelena stepped inside and closed the door behind her. "Why don't you let me spend the night? Or stay, just for another half hour. You don't have to tell me anything. I think you need a friend to—"

All of Katica's energy had drained away. She answered hoarsely, "No, Jelena. I know you mean well, but I need to talk to Ivana. That's all that matters now."

"What happened to her was vile. I'm sick at heart for her, but can't you see . . . ?" Katica's face was empty of emotion, and Jelena broke off. She wanted to warn Katica against Ivana, just as she'd tried to do four years earlier when the woman had shown up in Bern and taken over Katica's family and her life. But criticizing Ivana at this point would backfire. "Don't torture yourself about leaving her at that bar. We all make mistakes when we're young."

Katica shook her head. "She never told me. The rape. Her infertility. God forgive me, I was only thinking about myself, just like she said."

Oh, no, Jelena thought. Katica was *already* beating herself up about this. Outside, a car horn beeped—Dunja.

She put both hands on her friend's cheeks and looked into her eyes. "Katica, listen. Don't try to reach Ivana tonight. Don't call her tomorrow, either. Wait until the following day, when she's calmed down. If you call her now, she'll say . . . hateful things."

"Whatever she says, I deserve it." Katica gently pulled her face from Jelena's grasp. "I ruined her life."

Katica always had to be histrionic. Jelena was starting to lose patience with this wallowing in guilt. "Don't be silly," she said sharply. "*You* didn't rape her."

But Katica was looking at her stonily. "I'm selfish, like she said. I'm a bad person, Jelena. I've tried to be a loving wife and a good mother, but I've failed."

Exasperated now, Jelena stepped back. "You are *not* a bad person, my dear. You are a normal person, and normal people can be thoughtless." She tried to figure out what else she could say and heard the car horn again. "Call me if I can help," she said, but she didn't think any call would come.

She left Katica standing framed by the light from the apartment door. "Promise me you won't call Ivana for a couple of days," she said again. Katica's lips were pressed into a thin line.

Jelena whirled around and moved as fast as her good shoes would carry her to the waiting car. By the time she'd settled into the back seat and glanced toward the building, Katica had closed the side door and gone back into the apartment.

For a few moments, there was silence. Zora's face was white. When she spoke, she sounded furious. "Are you trying to say my mother killed herself over *Ivana*? That she left Goran and me and Tata alone forever because she felt guilty about walking away from Ivana in a bar?" She leaned forward, her eyes blazing. "Is that what you're telling us?"

Jelena was looking at Zora sympathetically. "I'm telling you what I directly experienced—what I know for sure. Anything that happened between the party and the night she killed herself...well, I don't know about that."

Good point, thought Renzo. He'd been deep in thought, scribbling in his notebook. What *had* happened during the following week, leading up to the night when Katica had died? Had Katica called Ivana in spite of Jelena's warning? Had Ivana taken revenge on Katica for "destroying her life," perhaps by telling Lovro about the affair? Or had she gone further, following Katica to the Münster and attacking her?

Suspicious as he was of Friedli, Renzo could see Ivana taking shape as a potential killer, even as he reminded himself—with a feeling close to despair—that everything he'd learned also explained why Katica might have killed herself. All this new information and he was still lost in his intolerable limbo of indecision.

Zora took a deep breath. "Surely afterward, you all talked about it?"

"There was talk," Jelena admitted, "but only among the six of us. We agreed that we mustn't tell anyone else because that story would've followed Ivana around forever. I've never heard a whisper about Ivana's rape since, so I think everyone kept their promise. But the six of us, yes, we spoke about it, particularly after your mother's death." For the first time, she seemed to waver. She put a hand over her mouth and shook her head. "You don't have to tell me," she said to Renzo. "I know I should have talked to that policeman, the one who questioned us."

"Did it . . . did you ever wonder if Ivana had killed Majka?" Zora asked in a whisper.

Renzo looked up from his notebook, waiting for Jelena to speak. Her complete lack of surprise at Zora's words was all the answer he needed. "Of course we discussed that! We could all imagine Ivana—I don't know—poisoning Katica and trying to make it look like suicide, or stabbing her in a rage and then calling the police, or more likely Lovro, to turn herself in." She shrugged. "But pushing Katica off a tower? Honestly, I doubt Ivana had ever been in the Münster, let alone the tower. She was never one to do touristy things around Bern. Climbing God knows how many steps in the middle of the night, hauling her childhood friend over the railings? I just can't see it, no matter how angry she was."

Renzo found himself wondering if Jelena had also known about Katica's affair. Ben Schweizer now took a distant second place in his mind to Friedli as a murder suspect. But Jelena was a sharp observer. It would be interesting to hear what she had to say about Katica's adultery. Reluctantly, however, he decided he didn't have a strong enough justification for staining Jelena's dead friend's reputation. Not yet, anyway.

Jelena Tomić looked exhausted—and sad, too, he decided. Even now, fifteen years later, it was clear that Katica's death weighed on her. But she pulled herself together and turned to Zora. "More coffee, *draga?* I'm sure *you'll* have more, Herr Donatelli. And cake, too, I bet."

"No, thank you, Frau Tomić," he said gently. "It's delicious, and I'm grateful for what you've told us. But I need to go away and think about what it means."

"I'm going home, too, Auntie," Zora said, her voice warm again. "I have company coming for dinner, so I have to cook. What you've said about that night—it was hard to hear, but it means a lot to me. And, well—you were very good to Majka. Thank you for that."

Jelena waved a dismissive hand. "We were friends," she said as if that explained everything. Then her face sharpened. "Company for dinner, eh? A young man?" She raised her eyebrows at Zora.

"If all goes well, I'll come by and tell you about it another time, okay? I'm very happy to have you back in my life. I promise not to wait so long before seeing you again."

The two women stood up and embraced, and Renzo got up, too. He headed straight for the front door and out to his car to give the women a chance to speak Croatian with each other.

But Zora didn't keep him waiting long; within a few minutes, they were driving to her apartment. Renzo was still musing over Jelena's story when Zora said, her voice tight, "Ivana has kept all this from me."

Renzo nodded. Monday morning, he'd make another appointment with Ivana and confront her. But until then, he didn't feel he could. This cold case wasn't urgent to anyone but him—and now Zora. He wouldn't bother the Horvat family on a Sunday.

"Enjoy your dinner tonight," he said as he dropped Zora off. He wondered if it was Denis she was cooking for. But he didn't ask. "If the DNA info comes in tomorrow, do you want me to wait until evening to call you? I'd hate to be responsible for destroying your family's Sunday lunch."

Zora had already gotten out of the car, but now she bent down and leaned through the open door, a feral grin on her face. "Are you kidding? After this, *I'm* going to destroy the lunch. Goran's paternity will just add weight to the wrecking ball. Let me know the results the minute they come in. Please," she added, as if realizing how imperious she'd sounded.

He was only a decade older than Zora, but at that moment, he felt like her grandfather. "Zora . . ." She opened her mouth to argue, and he added, "I'm not trying to protect Ivana, although you've said yourself that her life has been sad, and now we know it's even sadder than we thought. But what about Goran? Look at his attack on Denis—he could so easily lose control again. And think of the pain you'll cause your father."

Zora glared at him, her jaw jutting forward. "Goran and I deserve the truth for a change." Then she let out a breath. "But I guess you have a point. I promise to stay calm." She closed the car door and smiled again through the open window; this smile was kinder. "Thanks for the ride and for giving me a reason to get back in touch with Jelena. It reminded me of the time before my mother died. I'm definitely going to see her again."

"I'm glad." Renzo watched as Zora walked down the path to the door of her building. Halfway there, she waved, and as if on cue, he heard a clap of thunder. Dark clouds had piled up in the sky, and rain was on its way again.

He headed toward his Lorraine neighborhood, thinking of Zora's romantic dinner, feeling wistful. He had to get back into the habit of setting up dates for Saturday nights—when he wasn't in the middle of a bad case, on call, or with the kids. He sighed. Why hadn't he asked Mädi if she wanted to do something?

The gym across from the police station was open for two more hours, and he kept clothes and towels there. He could work out until the place closed, go home, eat the ready-made tortellini he'd bought that morning, and add to his report about the Horvat case.

Driving on autopilot, his mind seesawed between Ivana and Friedli. Ivana had bitterly resented Katica—or perhaps it had been a more complicated mixture of love and envy that had grown toxic. But rationally, he couldn't picture Ivana being responsible for Katica's death. He was sure Jelena was right that Ivana would have been very unlikely to follow Katica up the tower. Not only that, but Friedli would have seen or heard her enter the church, and he had no reason to keep quiet about that, especially now that he was under suspicion. Ivana would make as good a scapegoat as Ben Schweizer.

Renzo wanted desperately to know more about what had happened between Katica, Ivana, and Lovro during the week after the party. If Katica's death was truly a suicide, then he felt he was far closer to finding out *why*. But if he was looking for a killer, he had to focus on Friedli. Then he corrected himself. What he needed to be looking for was the truth, and he was certain that Friedli was lying—about Ben, about Katica, and about everything that had happened that night. And if he was lying, that meant he had something to hide. Renzo knew he had glimpsed something dark inside the man, and he was determined to expose it. The question was how to dig it out.

35

On Friday morning, after telling Renzo about hiding from the man in the window and giving him the swabs, Denis called Zora at work. She said little except to thank him for sorting out the DNA test. That made him afraid she was going to shut him out of her life again. Then, before she hung up, she asked him to Saturday dinner. He reminded himself that the evening could easily turn into a politer, more grown-up version of her rejection of him at her mother's funeral fifteen years earlier. But when he remembered the way she'd hugged him in front of his doorway the night before, he couldn't push down the hope that it was something else.

He spent the rest of Friday with his grandparents and truly enjoyed himself. For once, their obvious pleasure in his company, their interest in his daily life, and their tentative questions about his future plans didn't make him feel like a specimen under a microscope. Nor did their gentle hugs and pats on the shoulder burden him with the usual feelings of responsibility and guilt. For the first time in years, their love seemed less like a constraint and more like a favorite set of old clothes. He told them about being out for dinner the next day, and they were fine with it—even pleased for him—and took care to avoid nosy questions.

After helping his grandmother set up a new warp on her treadle loom, he went outside to do some one-handed weeding with his grandfather, who told him all about his latest attempts to make mead. This project had been going on for years, and Denis had been tasting the brew—honey, water, and yeast—since long before he was old enough for alcohol. Now, his grandfather had him doubled over with laughter at tales of his recent failures.

Later, he called his boss, Nathan, to ask if he needed any help. The glassmaker sounded delighted to hear from him. "I've got a whole set of panels due for a student fraternity event next week, and I'm running behind. I'd love as much time as you can spare."

"I've got one hand completely out of commission," he reminded his employer.

Nathan didn't sound concerned. "Well, come along, and we'll see what you can manage."

So, on Saturday afternoon, Denis stood at one of the worktables in Nathan's Altenberg studio across from the Aare, thinking about Zora yet again. His tools were laid out, and he was going to see what he could do with one hand on a set of fifty-three eight-inch-square glass panels, each bearing the elaborate coat of arms of one of the oldest student fraternities in Switzerland, with its name in fancy lettering underneath. The panels had been ordered as gifts for a number of the fraternity's *Altherren*—former students at the University of Bern, many of them now elderly men, who were still active in the *Studentenverbindung*. The glasswork was done, but the frames needed a discreet hook soldered onto the back so they could be hung up. Nathan had decided he could let Denis try that work without too much risk.

Soldering required one hand to grasp the tool and another to secure the hook against the lead frame. Luckily, the cast on Denis's left wrist left his fingers free. He'd be slow, but he could do it.

Denis soldered the first frame in silence. Since it went well, he decided to risk starting a conversation. "I can't believe these boneheads still fight duels," he said to Nathan, who was at a nearby worktable sketching a kingfisher on a piece of glass that would later be etched and colored for a child's bedroom window.

It took Nathan a moment to answer because he was controlling his breathing to keep his hand steady. "This fraternity doesn't allow dueling anymore. Some of the boys fence, that's all. And they aren't trying to give each other cheek scars; that's not considered sexy these days, thank God. I bet a few of the old guys who'll get these panels have a scar or two, but is a dueling scar any more lamebrained than a tattoo?"

Denis lapsed into silence for a while. In spite of his intense concentration, his mind was full of Zora, so full he could hardly keep it in. Suddenly, he blurted out, "I think I'm in love."

"Damn, boy," said Nathan. "You surprised me so much I almost . . . nope, everything's okay." He looked up from his work. "This the first time?"

"I don't know. I guess so. It feels different from all the other times I wanted to be with a girl. With a particular girl, I mean." He kept his eyes on his work so he wouldn't have to risk meeting Nathan's gaze.

"How different?"

"Calmer, maybe. Excited, yeah, but also content. Not so focused on . . ." Denis broke off and looked up.

His boss was grinning at him. "Not so focused on getting laid?"

Denis smiled back sheepishly. "I don't know if I was going to *say* that, but it's probably what I meant. We're not that far yet, but I already feel . . . attached, somehow."

Nathan bent over his drawing again. A minute or two later, he asked, "Am I allowed to ask this person's name?"

Denis didn't want to tell his grandparents about Zora yet, but he didn't see why he couldn't tell Nathan. "You can if you keep it to yourself. It's Zora Horvat. I met up with her for the first time in years on Thursday; we went out to dinner that night, and, well, we're having dinner again tonight at her place. It's like . . . like we never stopped being friends, only now I feel like we're more than friends. I don't know how she feels, though."

"Zora!" exclaimed Nathan. "I remember talking to her in the Münster and also a few times when I stopped by to have a drink with your grandparents, and you and she were playing in the apartment. Was it that Italian policeman who got you two back together?"

"Yeah, Renzo."

"I'm glad," Nathan said, and that was all.

Denis was working faster now that he'd figured out exactly how to position his injured arm at the correct angle. He did ten hooks in silence before saying, "I saw my mother yesterday afternoon; she was gloating over some medieval armor that had been discovered at the Läuferplatz." To his own surprise, he added, "She has a new man, she told me. French. And a historian like Grospaps. Which I find a bit weird."

He glanced up at Nathan and caught his boss giving him a sympathetic glance, which made him realize that he wanted Nathan to tell him more about Anja. All this talk of Zora's mother filled him with questions about his own.

He put his soldering iron down on the stand. "Do you want tea?" he asked Nathan.

"Sure," the glassmaker agreed. "I'll take a break when it's ready."

Denis had been making Nathan pots of black tea with lemon and sugar since the age of ten, and now he put Russian-style tea glasses into metal holders with wooden handles and set them down on the coffee table in front of the battered red sofa. As a child, he'd admired the tea glass Nathan always used. Its surface was subtly patterned (later Denis learned Nathan had created the design with a swan's feather), and the holder for the hot tea glass had been formed from small silver roses soldered together.

"This belonged to a set I made for my parents years ago," Nathan had told him then. "Would you like me to make you one? Tell me what you want it to look like."

At twelve, Denis had wanted his glass to be yellow and black (because those were the colors of Bern's soccer team) and to have a swirly, almost psychedelic surface; he'd asked Nathan to make his metal holder out of small soccer balls instead of roses. As he set this garish masterpiece on the coffee table now, he shook his head at his childhood lack of taste—but he still loved it.

Making tea one-handed slowed Denis down, but at last, he poured the liquid from the brown china pot into the glasses. Once Denis had taken his place on "his" side of the sofa, Nathan left his work and plopped down next to him with a sigh, picking up his tea and taking a noisy slurp.

Denis held his hot glass by the wooden handle that Nathan had made from a piece of walnut dowel he'd polished to a dark gleam and strung onto a thick piece of wire attached to the metal holder. He studied his tea and his thoughts and finally spoke. "Mam said something about how much Zora's mother loved her. She sounded... respectful. She meant it as praise. But, well... it made me wonder why she's never felt that way about me."

Whew! What a question. But at least it was out. Denis gulped his tea, grimacing at how hot it was.

Nathan examined him thoughtfully over his glass. When he spoke, he surprised Denis by evading the question, which wasn't like him. "You probably know that I met your grandfather when I was twenty-two, but I don't think I ever told you it was because my father and I were doing some work on the Three Kings window in the choir. I wanted to read historical records about the window, so I made an appointment with a professor at the university who I thought might be able to help me. That was your grandfather. He was thirty-eight, and I found him intimidating but also impressive. He must have realized how much I looked up to him because he invited me to his home for dinner with your grandmother and your mother, who was eleven then."

Denis couldn't imagine where Nathan was going with this story of his, but he watched him sip tea and waited.

"Your grandmother was researching and restoring early medieval fabrics at the Abegg-Stiftung, and I was captivated by her. By the end of the evening, I probably had a bit of a crush on her. But the most extraordinary thing about that dinner was the way your mother joined our conversation."

"My grandparents talk about what a scholar she was, even then." Denis had always imagined his mother as an insufferable child, one of those competitive kids who sucked up to teachers and showed off in class. Had she had any friends her own age? Maybe she'd been bullied by her classmates. "You've told me before that she was slightly strange."

"It was upsetting, watching such a young child try to win her parents' attention by one-upping them in their professional fields. What was valued most in that household was control: being in control of yourself, your work, your future. Setting goals and achieving them. I'm not saying the three of them didn't love each other, but . . . well, even a teenager needs teasing and hugs and expressions of affection from her parents." Here he stopped to drink more tea.

"So, I guess the 'expressions of affection'"—Denis made air quotes with his fingers—"that she wasn't getting from Grospaps and Grosmami, she started getting from my father."

"Yeah. You know Anja and Robbie started living together in a place that was supposed to be an artist's studio, not a residence. No bathroom in it, only a shared toilet down the hall. She was eighteen and thought she was rebelling—but she still had the same goals I'd been hearing about since she was eleven."

Nathan wasn't one to spell things out—unless it had to do with getting a piece of glass right. Maneuvering awkwardly because of his cast, Denis set his cup down and pulled his legs onto the cushion so he could sit cross-legged with his back against the arm of the sofa and observe Nathan's face. "Okay, I get it, but only up to a point. Having a baby at eighteen would have ruined her plans, and she should have had an abortion. But everyone else said they'd raise the baby, so she handed me over. I can see that, and I forgive her for it." Nathan was nodding slowly. "But then her plans worked out: she built up a successful career, and meanwhile, I got older and wasn't such a nuisance. So why didn't she . . . ?" He stopped, unable to articulate what he was feeling. Tears came into his eyes, and he wiped them away angrily. He wasn't ashamed of Nathan seeing them; he just didn't want to feel this way. "Jesus, why the *hell* can't I let this go?"

Nathan moved along the sofa toward Denis and put his arms around him. Denis rested his head on his friend's shoulder, and tears leaked from his eyes onto Nathan's coveralls. Nathan didn't pull away, and, for just a minute, Denis let himself be held. Then he loosened himself from Nathan's grasp and went to the wardrobe, where Nathan kept ratty old towels for cleaning up messes. He washed his face at the industrial-sized sink in the corner near the door and toweled it dry. Then he sat back on the sofa, finished his tea, and poured himself another glassful. Nathan was smiling at him.

Denis grabbed the shoulder he'd been crying on and gripped it. "I know my grandparents love me, and I love them. But you . . . you're the one . . ." He paused, trying to find the right words. "You're the one who taught me what it's like to feel valued just for being alive."

"I'm glad. You make that easy, Denis. You were a good boy, and now you're a good man." He gave Denis's cheek two quick pats with his fingertips. "Don't forget, I'd had a lot of practice when you showed up in my studio, more than your grandparents and your mother ever did. First, I had four little brothers and sisters to care about, and then my own three kids."

"That's what my mother never had," Denis said. "You don't think of people needing lessons in showing or feeling love, do you? But I can see that's why she doesn't know how to act like a mother with me."

Nathan shook his head. "Poor Anja. At least your grandparents learned from their mistakes and did a better job with you." He stood up, itching to get back to work. As he returned to his table, he said, "As for why you can't let this business with your mother go—well, I'm still dealing with my father's way of loving *me*, and he's been dead for seven years. Dead or alive, however they raised us, our parents haunt us. That's part of being human. Now, any more questions? About love, mothers, or anything else? Otherwise, back to work."

"Just one."

Nathan rolled his eyes so extravagantly in feigned exasperation that Denis laughed. "What did you think of Katica Horvat?"

"I only saw her briefly now and then, but every time I did, I spoke with her, just to be near her. She pulled men in like a magnet without meaning to. And not just men—everyone. But . . . well, I think she consumed herself with all that allure. She was a candle burning at both ends. Like your mother, different as they were, she lacked balance. I wasn't completely surprised when she killed herself."

Renzo's continuing investigation had half convinced Denis that Katica had been murdered, so he was interested to hear Nathan's take on her death.

The master glassmaker got up from the sofa and walked to Denis's worktable. "Now, I'll have a squint at how you're managing to do that soldering one-and-a-half-handed."

"Yes, do." Denis waved at the stack of glass panels. "I'll wash out the teapot." He carried the pot to the sink and came back for Nathan's empty glass, leaving his own full one on the table for later.

"All of the frames look good except this one," Nathan said.

Denis knew exactly which of the panels Nathan was going to point out. He'd already planned to fix it, and he was pretty sure he knew how to do it. But maybe his boss could show him a better way.

Good old Nathan, thought Denis, heading back to the worktable and his friend.

36

Bern's Galgenfeld neighborhood, Saturday night, June 29

When Zora decided to invite Denis to dinner, she wanted to make a traditional Croatian dish. She'd thought about her favorite recipes—most of them Ivana's, because, whatever her faults, her stepmother made delicious food. Pork stew with beans, homemade pasta with meat sauce, fish soup. The problem was that nobody wanted to eat stuff like that on a hot summer evening. Besides, with part of Saturday taken up with meeting Jelena, she didn't have time to make anything complicated. Eventually, she'd decided on chicken salad. She'd put veggies in it—diced cucumber and grated carrots and chunks of red pepper—and maybe slivered almonds and curry, too. Should she put in chopped apples? Or should she make a fruit salad with whipped cream for dessert?

After the thunderstorm Saturday afternoon, it was still raining at ten to seven in the evening, but through her bedroom window, Zora could see patches of blue sky and occasional gleams of sun. She smoothed her hair in the mirror one more time and went onto the balcony to find, as she'd hoped, that it was much cooler and the rain was only a drizzle. The apartment was clean, and the huge bowl of chicken salad was taking up most of a shelf in her small fridge. Given how much food fifteen-year-old Goran put away these days, she figured Denis must eat like a bear. She'd bought four kinds of rolls at the bakery to go with the salad and planned on serving homemade hummus and toasted pita triangles to start. The fruit salad was cut up in a glass bowl, sitting on the kitchen counter. It hadn't fit in the refrigerator, but fruit tasted better at room temperature, anyway.

At five after seven, Denis buzzed at the downstairs door, and she went out into the hall to meet him. When she saw him walking slowly and carefully up the stairs, grinning at her through his bruises over a huge bunch of delphiniums wrapped in newspaper, it seemed natural to move toward him. Only his injuries and the mass of flowers stopped her from throwing her arms around him. She took the flowers and smiled first at them and then at him while he wrapped his good arm around her shoulders and gave her three proper cheek kisses.

"You smell good," she told him.

"I was about to tell you the same thing," he said.

Instead of putting his long brown hair into a ponytail or a bun, he'd brushed it back into a single braid at the nape of his neck. In the apartment, she made him turn around so she could look: the braid was perfectly plaited. "Your grandmother did that for you!" she crowed.

He laughed, not at all embarrassed. "You're right. No way I could do it, not with one hand. The blue flowers are from their garden. I wasn't sure you'd want them since you look at flowers all day long, so what *I* brought you are two pints of ice cream from that great place at the Tramdepot, one chocolate and one blackberry. They're in my backpack, melting."

"These are not just 'blue flowers,' they're perennial delphiniums, and they're gorgeous. I think they're Blue Nile." She moved into the kitchen, and he followed. "Thanks for the ice cream, too; it can go right into the freezer. I'll get the wine out of the fridge, and you can open it while—oh, you can't, can you? Not with one hand. Never mind. I'll get the wine glasses and a vase for the flowers. Actually, they're so tall that I'll put them in a plastic bucket for now and figure out what to do with them later."

They started with their wine and hummus at the table where they'd sat with Renzo and Goran only two days before, and Denis told her about working with Nathan despite his cast. He described the glass panels with their coats of arms that were Nathan's bread and butter, supplying him with the money that let him work on more complicated commissions for reasonable prices and even produce a piece for himself now and then, something he could show at a gallery or sell to the Swiss Museum of Stained Glass in Romont.

"Is that what you plan to do, as well?" she asked him.

"Right now, I want to work on mastering all the different glass-making techniques the way Nathan has, and I'm happy doing that. Really happy. At the same time, I'm creating a portfolio of my own designs to show clients when I'm ready to produce my own stuff—which Nathan says will be soon." He paused. "I talked to Nathan this afternoon about my mother and growing up without her in a way I never have before. I've been thinking so much about *your* mother and what it must have been like for you and Goran not having Katica in your lives. Well, I don't want to ruin this evening the way I wrecked Thursday night in your special garden, but . . . I need to know. Are you mad at me?" He trailed off.

She'd hoped this invitation to dinner would be enough to convince him that she'd put his confession behind her, but she saw he needed more. "I want to spend time with you, okay? This evening for sure, and after that, who knows?" They locked eyes, and she reached out and touched his good cheek for a moment before looking away. "As for you not being able to save my mother's life when you were ten years old . . . She died, and I have to accept that I might never understand why. Whether she killed herself or someone killed her, she's not coming back. Your story shocked me, but it doesn't change a thing. Maybe it does for your cop friend, but not for me. So, let's not talk about mothers tonight. Let's talk about us."

And they did. Through the rest of the hummus, they talked about their work, and then, with the rain truly over and the evening sun giving the world back its gleam, Denis helped Zora dry off the chairs and table on the balcony, and she brought out the rolls, a block of butter, and the chicken salad. While they ate dinner and finished the wine, they recalled memories about each other from childhood and recounted stories of trips they'd taken when they were younger. Denis told her about his two half sisters in Florida, teenagers whose lives seemed straight out of a Hollywood high school movie. "One's a cheerleader, and the other's a junior lifeguard at the local beach. When they aren't on their phones, they're at the mall. They seem so immature and overprotected to me—but they're very sweet."

Zora told him about the few times she'd been to the part of Istria where her parents grew up and described the month-long trip all over Croatia that she'd taken two years earlier, by herself, to get a sense of her roots.

At nine thirty, when the blue of the sky was just starting to darken, she suggested a walk. She led Denis through a corner of the Schosshalde cemetery where the graves were a mass of flowers. "Thanks to you," commented Denis when he admired them.

She laughed and took his hand. "Thanks to me *and* a bunch of other gardeners," she said, and they were still holding hands when their path joined Melchenbühlweg.

Passing elegant family houses and embassies and then green fields, they reached Wittigkoffen Castle, part medieval and part baroque. "It's still in private hands," Zora told Denis, and they shook their heads at the idea of anyone owning and living in a castle, even such a small one.

Standing in the castle's shadow, Denis held her face with his good hand and kissed her cheek. He drew back a little, and she heard him murmur her name, a question in his voice. In answer, she put her arms around his waist, raised her face toward his, and kissed him on the mouth. As she sank into the kiss and his body, she could hear a voice in her head, full of wonder, saying, "This is Denis," and everything felt right.

She wanted to kiss Denis forever, there by the castle with night falling, but a car was heading toward them, catching them in its lights. She let go of Denis and grabbed his hand to pull him back into the shadows. Kissing wasn't enough—it was time to go home. They started to hurry back the way they'd come until one or the other of them would stop to catch their breath, and they'd start kissing again, locking their bodies together until they were breathless before breaking apart with groans and giggles and continuing on their way.

They trotted as fast as Denis could move through the darkening cemetery, which Zora knew as well as the back garden behind her father's shop. She considered all the half-sheltered places she knew of where they could find privacy, but deciding she wanted the comfort of her own bed, she resisted Denis's fumbled attempts to back her up against walls and start taking off her clothes. "Next time," she finally said to him, pushing him gently away once more. "Next time, we'll be outside. I promise."

"You're promising me a next time before the first time. That's . . . reassuring." The look he gave her seemed more intimate than a kiss.

By the time they burst into the twilit apartment, she felt almost out of her mind with longing, and she knew Denis did, too. She led him straight into the bedroom, where her windows were wide open, and the bed with its white duvet glowed in the last of the light from the night sky. Now that they were finally here, standing next to her bed, there seemed no need to hurry anymore.

Denis must have felt the same because he reached down for the hem of her lightweight dress and lifted it slowly over her head, then watched her take off her bra and panties. She helped him undress, too, easing his clothes over his battered body and drawing in a sharp breath at the sight of his hip and one side of his torso, which were still purple black.

When they were naked, they stood a foot apart, drinking each other in, until Denis suddenly frowned and crouched awkwardly to pull his jeans off the floor and fumble around in his pockets. Finally, he produced some condoms and fanned them out with a triumphant flourish, like a magician producing the ace of spades.

Zora giggled. She'd needed that moment of lightness to ease the tension. "*Four*? You're very ambitious. And hopeful." Then she swung around, opened the drawer in her night table, and showed him her own stash. "Brand new," she told him. "I was hopeful, too."

Denis grabbed her then, and they fell onto the bed. He yelped with pain, and Zora started to draw back, but he locked his good arm around her and rolled on top of her. She found herself laughing—at nothing but the delight of being there with Denis. Then he kissed her, and she stopped laughing, although her happiness kept growing.

37

R enzo sat next to his mother, eating the roast pork, buttery polenta, and fennel with parmesan she'd made for Sunday lunch. His younger sister Valentina and her husband Patrizio, who were expecting their first child in two months, were also there. In between bites of delicious food, Valentina was lamenting the number of girls and women with eating disorders who came to her psychotherapy practice for help.

When Renzo's cell phone rang, he left the table for the nearest bedroom, closing the door behind him. It was his geneticist friend. "Hi, Sven," Renzo said.

"Your brother-and-sister result came in. I know I said I'd text you about it, but I had a moment, so I thought I'd call. They're only halves, not full siblings. Does this tell you anything useful about your case?"

Renzo sighed. Poor Zora and Goran, not to mention Lovro. Or did Lovro already know, and had he confronted his wife with that knowledge before she died? Yet again, he found himself musing over Lovro's motive for murder, set against Friedli's insistence that no one except Ben Schweizer had come into the church that night. God, here he was again, drowning in uncertainty.

"It doesn't solve anything," he told Sven, "but it adds interesting dimensions. And it sure is going to shake up the family." Like Goran shaking the scaffolding, he thought grimly. Would this set the boy off on another rampage? Renzo decided he'd better tell Goran the results of the test face-to-face in case the kid lost it and Renzo needed to intervene. "Thanks for doing the test so fast. Let me take you out to dinner, okay? And when I do, I'll tell you the whole story if you're interested."

Renzo put his phone away and went back to the others. "Sorry, Mamma," he said, switching back to Italian. "I was waiting on some lab results for a case."

She smiled up at him. "No damage done. I put your plate in the oven."

They went back to eating and chatting; they'd switched from Valentina's work to joking about their unborn son's name. Patrizio's latest contribution was Genghis.

Renzo was only half paying attention. What should he do with the information he'd just received? The easiest solution would be to call Zora later when her family lunch was over, and she was back home, and tell her the results of the test had only just come in. Or he could go to her apartment that evening. Goran might be there, too.

Zora had assured him she'd stay calm. But she was bound to confront her family with Jelena's revelations, wasn't she? He ought to be there now instead of waiting until Monday. He was tired of pussyfooting around, trying not to hurt everyone's feelings. Ivana and Lovro Horvat clearly knew more than they'd told him. He needed to put pressure on them, and the sooner, the better. Maybe that meant using the news about Goran's paternity to do it.

His mother put an espresso in front of him and laid a hand on his shoulder. "That phone call is bothering you, isn't it? Don't worry. Go do what you need to do so you can get it off your mind."

He put his hand over hers. "I'm sorry," he said to his sister and brother-in-law. "It's great to see you guys. I know I'm being rude."

Patrizio grinned and shrugged, and Valentina made shooing motions with her hands. "Go on, go on," she said. "The last thing we want to do is give you a hard time about your job the way Fränzi always did."

Renzo gulped his coffee, hugged his mother and brother-in-law, kissed the top of his sister's head so she wouldn't have to get up, and drove off. It was a sunny day but blessedly cooler since the previous afternoon's thunderstorm. On the green meadows surrounding one of Bern's big public swimming pools, groups of teenagers, parents with small children, and older sun worshippers were spreading their towels on the grass and stretching themselves out among the trees. He wondered briefly if Fränzi had taken Angelo and Antonietta to the shady baby pool at Marzili.

He reached the Matte neighborhood and the Horvats' shop and parked the Fiat. Heading for the Golden Goat, he tried to plan his next steps and realized that he couldn't. There was simply no way of predicting how everyone would react.

Approaching the side door that led into the apartment rather than the shop, he could hear Zora's voice coming from the back garden, though the high wooden fence around it hid her from view. Renzo walked down the side street to the tall gate, took a deep breath, and knocked. Zora's voice stopped immediately and Goran threw open the gate. The boy grabbed Renzo's arm and dragged him into the yard.

The remains of a meal littered the table on the terrace, but only Lovro was still sitting in his chair. Ivana, separate from the others on the back porch, held a folded paper in her hand. Zora and Goran stood by their father and faced her, scowling.

In a low, choked voice, Goran said, "Show the cop the note my mother wrote you. I want him to know what kind of person you are."

Renzo had been expecting to create a confrontation—now he saw he'd stepped right into one. Apparently, Zora's wrecking ball was in full swing. Ivana's eyes were swollen, her face full of despair. Renzo expected her to run into the house to get away from his intrusion, but she just stood on the small porch, head down. Goran gave a hiss of impatience, darted up the stairs to her side, and snatched the paper out of her hand.

Ivana dropped to sit on the porch steps and rested her forehead on her knees.

Goran handed the note to Zora. "Translate it," he commanded.

She opened the folded note and gave Renzo a questioning look. He nodded, but instead of reading the note, Zora turned to look first at Ivana, hunched on the step, and then at her father, still sitting at the table, his face bleak. Finally, she dropped her eyes to the note and haltingly began to read, translating into German as she went.

"You have been like a big sister to me for most of my life," she read. Renzo watched her face, imagining Katica forming the words, struggling to find the right things to say to Ivana. *"As I got older, I realized you disapproved of me. Now I know that you have given up on me. Since the party, you've called me a terrible wife and mother, a useless friend, a bad Catholic, and a whore."* Renzo's eyes went to Lovro's face. The man's lips were pressed into a tight line. *"You're right. I've betrayed and damaged everyone around me. Especially when it comes to Lovro. I've repaid all his kindness and care with deceit.*

"I'm going to end things with Ben and never see him again. That's one of the few things I can do to put my life right. But still, you plan to tell Lovro about him. Thank God I will be gone before you hurt Lovro in this way. You are cruel—not just to me, but to him, the person you claim to love. I am all the things you say I've been, but you, Ivana, are a hypocrite. How could you pretend for all these years to be my friend while hating me for what happened at the bar? Hating me for stealing Lovro from you, too, when he was never yours to begin with. And all that time, I loved you. I was a fool."

Lovro's hands were bunched into fists. Other than that, he showed little emotion. But of course, everyone here had already heard this letter in Croatian. He, Renzo, was the only one hearing it for the first time.

Was this a suicide note? Not necessarily. "I will be gone" did not mean "I'm going to kill myself." Perhaps she was only talking about getting away from Lovro. She couldn't have been planning to run away with Ben Schweizer, though, if she'd gone on to end things with him right afterward, as Schweizer confessed that she had. But what if

Schweizer had been lying? What if Friedli had told Renzo the truth after all? Could Schweizer have begged Katica to come and live with him in the room on Postgasse? If Katica had refused, what might have happened then? *No,* Renzo told himself. *You've already been through this. Ben had no reason to tell you about being at the Münster, yet he did, and freely. Why would he have done that if he'd killed Katica?* He forced himself to focus.

Zora was wiping away tears. Renzo held out his hand for the note and put it in the breast pocket of his shirt. "I'll get a copy made and have it officially translated for the record. You'll have it back by Tuesday." He turned to Zora's father. "Herr Horvat," Renzo said, and the man finally met his gaze with eyes that looked hollowed out. "When did you first learn about the existence of this note?"

"When my wife produced it fifteen minutes ago, and each of us read it," he answered woodenly. Was he telling the truth? At this point, Renzo didn't trust *any* of them to be completely honest.

"Did you know about Ben Schweizer before you read the note just now? Did your wife—did Ivana tell you about Katica's affair, as she planned to?"

Ivana moaned something almost inaudible in Croatian. Lovro didn't answer.

Suddenly, Zora spoke up so loudly that Renzo winced. "Do you have something to tell us, Renzo?" Her eyes sparkled dangerously. Goran made a noise that sounded like a whimper and moved closer to her.

Renzo took a step toward them and said in a soft voice, "I'm so sorry, but the test shows you're only half siblings."

Goran closed his eyes and clenched his fists. His body tensed until he was trembling. Zora put her arms around him and pulled him to her. For a moment, he let her hold him, then yanked himself away and ran to Lovro, who jumped to his feet, face pale. Goran pounded his fists on the man's chest. "Tata," he sobbed. "Tata." Only Lovro *wasn't* his father.

Zora had fresh tears on her cheeks, too. *Jesus,* Renzo thought, *look what I've done.*

Ivana came down the stairs and began asking something, repeating the same words over and over with increasing hysteria.

Lovro cut her off with a few stern words and glared at Renzo. "What did you do?" he asked Renzo. "Did *you* tell him about Katica's affair with the stonemason?"

"He already knew," Renzo said. "So did Zora." And so, it now seemed, had Lovro.

As Goran began to get control of himself, Lovro helped him into one of the chairs and sat back down next to him. Then he closed his eyes for a moment.

"Yes," he said heavily. "Ivana *did* tell me about the affair. Fifteen years ago. When Katica wrote Ivana that note, she thought Ivana hadn't said anything yet, but I'd already known for several days. I . . . I confronted Katica about it, God forgive me. When you were here on Thursday afternoon, you asked me if my wife could have been having an affair, and I told you not to insult her. It was my pride. I didn't want to tell a stranger about . . . something private. I thought you'd let the thing go."

He was speaking in German, but it seemed to Renzo that he was really addressing Ivana, who stared back at him from where she stood apart from the rest of the family, her hands pressed into her cheeks as if she were trying to keep her head from splitting apart. She looked as though she wanted to rush to Lovro, but something in his expression must have held her back. Goran was sniffling, swiping at his eyes. Zora was glaring at Ivana.

"Yes, Ivana told me about the stonemason," Lovro repeated, "and she wasn't the only one to call Katica a whore. Come and sit down, the rest of you. It looks like we're going to have to share all our secrets with this man"—he jerked his chin at Renzo—"whether we like it or not. Zora, fetch another chair."

By the time Zora had grabbed a folding chair for Renzo, Ivana had joined Goran and Lovro at the table; she was folding and refolding her hands in an agony of tension.

Had Zora already screamed out the story of Ivana's rape to her father and brother? Perhaps Lovro still didn't know the terrible thing that had happened to his second wife. It was possible the Horvats might retain a few of their secrets, and at this point, maybe that wasn't such a bad thing.

Lovro faced Renzo while he told his story, perhaps because it was less painful than watching his family.

"Ivana's brother and her fiancé Anto were best friends, but I was close to both of them, too. Especially Anto. When they were killed, I was twenty-one. I mourned them *and* felt guilty because I hadn't been there with them, although I was relieved about it. I was so ashamed of that relief. In fact, I was a mess, but I tried to act normal."

Only twenty-one, and already facing so much pain. Renzo reminded himself that this man had lied to him more than once. But he didn't think this was a lie.

"So, I ran the smaller of my father's two stores. I spent time with Anto's parents and little brothers, trying to comfort them, and I talked about Anto with the girl he'd planned to marry: Ivana. In late 1993, I became a soldier, and it was when I was leaving for the military that I realized Ivana had fallen in love with me. I'd never offered her any encouragement, and it was partly to avoid that complication that I got a job in Zagreb after I was discharged."

Ivana had a hand pressed to her mouth as she watched Lovro, her eyes dull. Lovro's face was sad but resolute. He seemed determined to tell these truths, hurtful as they might be.

"In 1998, my father wanted me to take over from him at the family store, so I came back from Zagreb. And I fell in love with Katica, who'd been a smart and amusing child when I went away. She was almost eighteen and very beautiful, while I was twenty-eight and average in every way. I tried to get her interested in me, but it was no use. She liked me but didn't love me. In fact, she told me she was in love with someone else, although I had no idea who that could be. Meanwhile, Ivana paid *too* much attention to me, my father bossed me around day and night, and the Serbs were still killing people, this time in Kosovo." He shook his head wearily. "I knew lots of Croatians had emigrated to Switzerland, and I decided to do the same—to make a new life there. That was when Katica came to me and told me she wasn't in love with the other man anymore. She asked me to take her to Bern as my wife."

Lovro glanced at Ivana, his expression sadder than ever. "We both abandoned Ivana—I, the man she was in love with, and Katica, the girl she'd known for years. We said a kind goodbye and then disappeared and forgot about her, except for an occasional postcard. Seven years later, Ivana moved to Bern. She was thirty-four, had learned German, and had trained and worked as a nurse. With those credentials, she got a job quickly. Katica welcomed her like a long-lost sister. I was worried but did my best to resume our friendship."

"A long-lost sister," Ivana muttered, staring at the tabletop. Renzo couldn't read her voice. Was she repeating the phrase in contempt, remembering how her so-called sister had left her to be raped, or was she echoing it with guilt over the way she'd contributed to Katica's death?

Zora was also watching Ivana. Renzo could imagine that, for a girl born in 2000 who'd grown up in the capital of Switzerland, Katica's "crime" of leaving Ivana alone at a café would seem like no offense at all, just an incident. But this had been in a Southern European Catholic village; Ivana would have been naïve and trusting, even at twenty-seven. It wasn't either of their faults. Only the rapist was to blame.

Lovro finished a glass of water, then refilled it from a carafe on the table. "Tata . . ." Zora murmured, leaning toward him, but he held up a hand and said, "Let me finish." She sat back in her chair.

"I think Katica started meeting Ben Schweizer about a year before Goran was born; I'm not sure. It seems incredible to me now that I didn't notice what was going on, but I was busy with the shop, and I thought we were happy. Katica always had a good reason for why she was going to be out for an hour or two, whether it was coffee with a friend, an errand, or Zora's physiotherapy appointments."

Zora broke in again, and this time, her voice was louder. "I'm so sorry I lied to you, Tata. I didn't know what to do. It seemed so important to Majka, and I wanted to make her happy."

Lovro lifted his daughter's hand from the table, pressed the back of it to his lips, and spoke lovingly to her. Though Renzo couldn't understand the words, their meaning was clear. He glanced quickly at Ivana and caught her giving father and daughter a bitter look. So—had she transferred the jealousy she'd felt toward Katica to Zora? Or had she been jealous of both mother and daughter since the day she arrived in Bern?

Ivana spoke for the first time, spitting out something in Croatian.

"Ivana says I was blind to the affair because I wanted to be. But I didn't stay that way. After the party for Goran, Ivana insisted on meeting with me while Katica was minding the store, and she told me all about Ben Schweizer. Months earlier, she'd followed Katica to his apartment and figured things out. When she'd confronted Katica, Katica confirmed it all." He fell silent.

That meant Ivana had kept Katica's secret for quite a while. Why hadn't she revealed it to Lovro sooner? Had she wanted leverage over Katica? Or had some part of her cared about the younger woman, even while she resented her? Renzo was sure he'd never know what had been going on in her mind.

Zora and Goran were both staring at Ivana. Zora's eyes were narrowed, her lips curled. Goran's face was pale, and his eyes red. *Poor kid*, Renzo thought. *He probably doesn't know what he feels right now.*

Lovro went on, his speech halting. "When Ivana told me, I . . . I became desperate. You see, after Zora was born, we'd wanted more children right away, but over the next seven years, Katica had three miscarriages."

Zora gasped, and Renzo saw Ivana's eyes widen. She hadn't known about this.

"So, when this pregnancy worked out, and Goran was born, we were both so happy. Then, when Ivana told me about Schweizer, my first thought was that Goran wasn't mine. I couldn't bear it. I was furious with her for cheating on me but even more upset to think that

Goran wasn't my son. I put off telling her I knew about the affair because . . . I couldn't stand to hear what she might say about Goran."

This made sense to Renzo. Lovro's fury and his fears about Goran's paternity—all this was how Renzo thought he, too, would feel as a betrayed husband. But what was it revealing about Katica's death? It certainly seemed to give Lovro a motive for murder. Could he have come to the church that night? But if he had, surely Ben Schweizer or Klaus Friedli would have known. They had no reason to lie for Lovro.

As if Lovro had read his mind, he looked up. "Yes, I was furious with my wife. But I didn't push her off that tower. What I did was—" His face worked to control his emotions. ". . . It was almost as bad. I woke up at three in the morning when she was creeping out of our bedroom. I watched her get dressed, and I followed her to the door to be sure she was really going out to meet that son of a bitch. And then I went crazy. I grabbed her shoulders and shook her until I thought her neck would break, and I called her . . . terrible things. I'd admitted to myself by then that she'd never really loved me. At least, not in the way a husband wants to be loved by his wife. She listened to everything without speaking, and when I was finished, she just said, 'I know, and I'm sorry. That's why I'm going.' I thought she meant she was leaving me to live with Schweizer, so I said, 'You're abandoning the children?' She didn't answer, just walked away, and I told her she was a monster. The way she looked back at me then—like she was broken. I wished I could take those words back. A few hours later, she was dead."

There was a long silence before Goran asked, in a timid voice, "And what about . . . him?"

"Who?" Lovro asked sharply.

Goran swallowed. "My . . . my blood father. Did you see him after Majka died? Did you say anything to him?"

Lovro burst out in a flood of passionate language that Renzo didn't understand.

Goran shrank back, frowning, and turned a face full of confusion to Zora.

She looked at Renzo. "Tata says he had a paternity test done right after Majka died, and they told him Goran was his. Then he had a second one done by another lab, just in case, and it was the same. Are you sure your friend didn't screw up?"

Lovro snapped, "Why were you doing the test in the first place?"

Goran raised his voice, too. "Because Zora said . . ."

Suddenly, the four of them were talking at once in Croatian, gesturing angrily, interrupting each other, their voices getting louder and louder. Renzo let it go on for a couple of minutes, then he took a glass from the table and hit it with a spoon until the Horvats stopped yelling and stared at him.

"Listen to me, all of you. When Goran overheard Frau Horvat and Zora talking about his mother's affair, he wanted to know if he was your son. He and Zora decided to give me DNA swabs, and I asked our police lab to see if they were full siblings or not. The test showed that they are only half brother and sister, and I have no reason to doubt the finding, but I suppose it could be wrong. In either case, I apologize for . . ." At that point, his voice trailed off.

Lovro got up from the table and walked a few paces away. He stood with his back to them, breathing heavily. No one spoke.

Finally, he turned around, and it was Zora he looked at. His lips twisted into a smile, loving and rueful but tinged with exasperation, too. She looked back at Lovro, bewildered, and he offered her his hand, saying a few soft Croatian words to her.

Zora's mouth dropped open, and she stared at Lovro for a few seconds. Then she spoke to Renzo. "I'm . . . um . . . going for a walk with my father now. I'll see you later."

"Tata?" Goran said shakily.

Ivana got to her feet but made no move to join them. Lovro said something soothing as he opened the garden gate, and then he and Zora were gone. Renzo could hear their footsteps on the side street, heading toward the Aare.

Good God, thought Renzo. *Not another secret!*

Any plans he'd had to confront Ivana with her lies about the party seemed superfluous. He needed to go away and think—right away.

He stood and looked down at Goran, still in his chair at the table, his eyes wide and confused. "Goran, I'll be in touch next week about your case," Renzo said. "Frau Horvat, I apologize for interrupting your Sunday lunch."

Ivana gave a tiny, bitter laugh. She walked him to the garden gate and saw him out with a curt nod. "Goodbye, Herr Donatelli, and please don't come back," she said as she closed the gate behind him.

Renzo hurried away, heading not toward the Aare, as Zora and Lovro had done, but to the main street. There he turned left and walked briskly in the direction of the long staircase leading up to the Münster platform, the place where Goran had crashed into him, and this whole investigation had begun. He climbed the stairs so fast that even *he* got out of breath. At the top, he went through the gate leading to the park and headed straight for the tiny café in the corner. He had to think—and for that, he wanted coffee.

He took a seat at a table with a view of the soaring Kirchenfeld Bridge. If he looked up through the branches of the tree over his head, he could see the Münster's tower looming over him.

He sipped his coffee and started with the dates. When Lovro returned from working in Zagreb in 1998, he fell in love with Katica, but she told him that she was in love with someone else. In 1999, when she was eighteen, she was familiar enough with a café where UN soldiers hung out to bring Ivana with her. There she'd disappeared with a man. Shortly after, she'd come to Lovro and asked him to take her to Switzerland. They married, and in 2000, Zora was born.

Fifteen years ago, Lovro had paid for two paternity tests confirming that Goran was his son, yet Goran and Zora were half siblings.

Renzo shook his head. It was clear to him now what had happened. This damned investigation and the DNA test had forced Lovro Horvat to reveal to his beloved daughter that someone else, probably a UN soldier, was Zora's biological father. No wonder Lovro had felt so betrayed by Katica: he'd protected her secret and taken care of her and her baby, and she'd paid him back with infidelity. Perhaps he had not been too surprised. After all, he must have known that she'd been in love with someone else when they married—the father of her baby, who'd probably deserted her. Perhaps the inevitability of her betrayal had hurt him all the more.

Renzo felt respect for the man and sympathy, too. But despite all he'd learned, he still didn't feel sure that Katica's death was a suicide. She'd said she was leaving. What had she meant? If only he knew for sure what had happened between Schweizer, Friedli, and Katica that night, what had taken place in the last hour of Katica's life.

He finished his espresso, tipping his head back to get the last drops, and as he did so, was confronted with the tower. The hundred-foot Gothic structure, with its tall arched windows and pierced stonework, filled him with sorrow. Katica had fallen in love twice, neither time with her husband and both times with disastrous results. The first time, pregnant and probably abandoned, she'd managed to salvage a good life for herself, but without passion in her marriage, it hadn't been enough for her. So, she'd fallen in love again, and going to the Münster to break up with Ben had led her to die that night. If she had truly decided to kill herself, he knew she would have found another way, another time. But perhaps something else happened that night that made the insults Ivana and Lovro had showered on her literally unendurable and caused her to jump off the tower. Or had she met her killer in the cathedral? He still didn't know.

Renzo was veering into melodrama, but he couldn't seem to help it. What else could you call Katica's story—or, for that matter, Ivana's or Lovro's? It all went back to the war and to Anto being murdered by Serbs at Vukovar. Out of that ghastly death grew Lovro's guilt and his attention to Ivana, which led to her unrequited love. And so, it went on and on, now affecting Goran's and Zora's lives in ways he knew he would never fully understand.

He needed to tell someone about all of this—and he knew exactly who he most wanted to talk to: Giuliana.

38

*Kirchenfeld, Sunday late afternoon and
early evening, June 30*

As they often did when they were reading, Giuliana and her husband
Ueli were at either end of their long sofa, half sitting and half lying,
with their legs intermingled on the middle cushion. Giuliana was
reading Michael Connelly's most recent crime novel. She found it fas-
cinating to compare the workings of the LAPD, with its ten thousand
cops and three thousand civilian employees, to Bern's Kantonspolizei,
with just twenty-five hundred men and women responsible for the
whole canton. Meanwhile, Ueli had finished his sweep of the newspapers in search of story ideas and was now deep into Joël Dicker's latest
novel.

Next to her on the coffee table, Giuliana's phone rang. When she
saw Renzo's number, she wriggled off the couch and took the phone into
the kitchen. Usually, he began with a bit of self-deprecating humor, but
today, there was no preamble.

"Listen," he said, "I'm feeling overwhelmed by what I've learned
about Katica Horvat's death. I need to get it off my chest. Can we . . . ?"

"Just a minute." She put the phone down and walked back into
the living room. "Ueli," she said, and he looked up from his book.
"Renzo wants to talk about a case he's been working on. Can I invite

him to dinner? I'm sure we have enough lamb stew, and we can defrost another loaf of bread if we need to."

"Sure, ask him. I like him." But when Giuliana relayed her invitation, Renzo declined. "I'm switching places with Fränzi at seven tonight. I'll be back in Wabern with the kids until next Sunday. So, I don't have time for dinner at your place—sorry."

"Then come at five for a glass of wine on the balcony. We're on your way. Is Ueli allowed to listen in?"

"Um . . ." She pictured Renzo running through the Horvat case in his head. "Yes, as long as he doesn't write about it."

"That won't happen," Giuliana assured him. She could tell he was taken aback by her suggesting they discuss work with Ueli there, but she was determined to show him that she'd accepted the change in their relationship and was moving on. Maybe next time, she'd ask if she should invite Mädi to dinner as well. She found herself wondering if he and Mädi had already gone out together and what it had led to. Then, chiding herself for these thoughts, she went back to her Michael Connelly.

At ten to five, Giuliana checked that there was a bottle of good white in the fridge. She put three wine glasses and a mug filled with breadsticks on the counter and made sure the awning on the balcony was lowered against the hot sun. Isabelle was doing her homework in a deckchair out there, and Giuliana warned her that she'd have to find somewhere else to sit when Renzo arrived.

"The guy you work with, the one Lukas met? Can I meet him, too?"

"Of course. He's my favorite work colleague." Giuliana flashed for a moment on the idea of Isabelle, still mourning her breakup with Quentin, falling for Renzo. But he was twice her age. *Don't be silly*, she told herself.

Just then the door buzzed, and she ushered Renzo into the kitchen, where Isabelle was grabbing a few breadsticks. She turned and shook the hand Renzo offered her. Her English homework was lying on the kitchen table, and Renzo pointed at the novel she was reading, Nick Hornby's *About a Boy*. "Does that mean you've been spared *Animal Farm*?"

Giuliana laughed. "I had to read that, too."

Isabelle rolled her eyes. "We had it last year. Definitely way past its sell-by date." Then she headed to her room without a backward look. Giuliana breathed a secret sigh of relief as she and Renzo carried the wine, glasses, and snacks to the balcony.

Later, sitting at the table under the awning, sipping from his glass of Petite Arvine, and crunching on a breadstick, Renzo began the story of Goran running into him on the Münster platform and continued from there. Giuliana already knew a lot of it, but it was helpful to hear how Renzo put the information together. At some point, Rolf was bound to ask her what she thought about Renzo being promoted to homicide, and she wanted to be able to provide good examples of why she thought he had the organizational skills to do the job. Besides, she enjoyed listening to him.

He ended with Lovro and Zora leaving the garden together so Zora's father could tell her how she was conceived.

"I got a text from Zora half an hour ago," Renzo added. "She found out her father was a Dutchman, which helped her understand why she's so much taller and bigger-boned than everyone else in the family. Her mother was utterly in love with this man Bram, Lovro said, and apparently, he was good to Katica while he was in the Balkans but refused to take her back to Holland with him. She didn't realize she was pregnant until after he left, and then he never answered her letters."

"So, she had the sense to ask Lovro to take her away with him," Giuliana said. "I just hope she told him about her pregnancy."

"Zora said it was the first thing Katica told Lovro, before she asked about going with him. I'd like to believe that's true." Renzo shook his head at Ueli's offer to refill his wine glass. "When Zora was born, Katica wrote down the man's name for her, along with everything she knew about him, and handed the paper to Lovro so he could be the one to tell her whenever he thought the time was right. If she wants to, Zora can go and find him. She wrote me that she won't because it wouldn't be fair to Lovro. But I bet she will, someday in the not-too-distant future. I'd love to see the man's expression when a striking six-foot-tall young woman who's the image of his former lover shows up at his door." Renzo's grin faded. "Still, if I did it again, I wouldn't get those swabs tested. I don't know why I agreed to do it."

Ueli gave him a wry smile. "Maybe it had something to do with Zora being a striking young woman."

"You're probably right. But it was not a good thing for that family."

"I don't know," Giuliana said. "Lovro would have had to tell Zora the truth about her real father sooner or later, and she's twenty-five, which seems like a good age to find out. What's bad is the ton of guilt the parents—Ivana and Lovro, I mean—have been carrying around. That can't be healthy."

Renzo cocked his head. "I think Lovro feels guilty, but not Ivana. I think she's just...bereft. On the surface, she won. With Katica gone, she could marry the man she'd set her sights on after her fiancé was killed, and she got Lovro's baby to raise in spite of her infertility. The life she'd been coveting for years fell into her lap. But she didn't get happiness. It can't be easy knowing that she helped drive Katica to her death and Lovro married her because he needed her help with the children and the store."

The three of them were quiet for a moment, Giuliana contemplating the idea of a life so full of loss that contentment was unachievable.

"What I want to know," Ueli said, "is what role Friedli played in all this. I can see why you still suspect him more than Schweizer. I agree that Friedli was probably the one who followed Katica up those stairs. But why? Was he trying to stop her from killing herself? If so, why not wake up the Kellenbergers? Was he trying to hurt her? Then why didn't *she* wake them up?"

"Exactly," said Renzo. "I don't understand it, either. Everything I've learned from the Horvats supports the idea of suicide, but I can't stop suspecting Friedli of having *something* to do with it. I can't let it go. He's—" Renzo broke off, and Giuliana had the feeling he'd wanted to use the word evil. "I'm sure he's lying. But I had to release him yesterday morning. I failed to come up with any reason to keep him."

Giuliana watched Renzo lean back in his chair, shaking his head. "I can't remember the last time I felt so indecisive—no, so conflicted. There's no real evidence—just people's memories, and half the time, they could still be lying. It was sheer luck, really, that I was able to see Katica's note and that Lovro was forced to tell me the full story because Zora and Goran confronted him and Ivana. As for Friedli, I have no proof of anything. I was hoping the narcotics team would come up with something illegal stored in that wine cellar, but the dogs didn't find a thing. That means there's nothing I can hold over him, and he knows it."

"What about his job?" Ueli asked. "Can you threaten him with losing it—?"

Renzo shook his head. "Since the minister learned about the smuggled cigarettes, she can't wait to get rid of him, and I'm pretty sure a member of the parish council has joined her crusade. It's only a matter of time—and, believe me, I approve wholeheartedly."

The three of them were quiet, listening to the summer noises of the neighborhood—a basketball bouncing on the pavement, crows cawing, small children calling out and laughing.

Giuliana stared at the geraniums on her balcony. She was trying to articulate something, working it around in her head. "I keep thinking about the Horvat case in relation to Werner Allemann's death," she said at last. "On the surface, we have Ruth Seiler poisoning her husband and Katica Horvat jumping off a tower. A murder and a suicide. But if you look at it another way, Ruth only carried out her husband's wishes, allowing him the death she believed he wanted, while Ivana, Lovro, Schweizer, and maybe in some way Friedli all share responsibility for Katica's death."

Elbow on the table, Renzo rested his chin on his fist. "I see what you're saying," he told Giuliana. "But there's still so much we don't know about both cases."

"I guess I'm thinking about the limitations of the law," Giuliana continued. "We can't bring Ivana to trial for inciting Katica to kill herself because, despite that note, there's no clear evidence of causality. And we *have* to try Ruth for killing her husband because she didn't follow the rules we have in place to protect vulnerable people. Even in Switzerland, with the most liberal assisted suicide laws in the world, we don't have a way to handle a case like Werner and Ruth's. And we don't have a law against hounding someone to death, either."

"Maybe the law can't take these nuances into account, but the judges can," said Ueli. "If they're good enough at what they do, they can read between the lines, learn the family histories, hear the emotions behind the testimonies, and think about what it all means. I'm convinced a system like ours, where judges decide cases as well as provide sentences, is better than a trial by jury."

Giuliana had seen judges deal brilliantly with witnesses and make excellent decisions, but she'd also seen lazy, sloppy judges. As for juries, her main knowledge of them was from movies, where they almost never made good decisions. But that was usually part of what the movie was about, so it didn't count as proof that they didn't work. "I hope Ruth Seiler gets one of those sensitive judges you're describing," she said. "I'd like her to receive a suspended sentence, but we'll see what happens." Renzo's face was distant. "What's still bothering you, Renzo?"

"Friedli. I hate the fact that my gut is yelling that he's to blame somehow, but I can't prove it. I feel so unsatisfied. I just—I don't see justice in this anywhere."

"Sometimes there is no justice," Giuliana said. "We're just lucky if we get some answers."

"Answers," Renzo echoed dismissively, raising his eyes to the sky and spreading out his palms. "There are no answers either! I *still* don't know if Katica's death was murder or suicide."

"Yeah," said Giuliana. "But at least Goran found out that he's his father's son, thank God. Zora got proof of how much Lovro loves her, even if she isn't his daughter by blood, and she can contact this man in the Netherlands if she wants to. Lovro and Ivana might stop keeping so many secrets from each other. Although, who knows what's going to happen after all these revelations? Maybe he'll leave her."

"No," said Ueli decisively. "From what Renzo's told us, I think Lovro values loyalty too much. Poor Ivana. The first man she wants to marry is killed horribly during the war, and the second runs off with her friend right after she's been raped. It's hard to blame Ivana for turning on Katica."

"*You* can be kind about her." Giuliana poured more wine into her empty glass. "But when I think of her coming to Bern to wreck Katica's marriage, I'm happy to continue disliking her."

She noticed Renzo wasn't paying attention to this exchange. It turned out he was still tallying the few results that his frustrating investigation *had* accomplished. "Denis got to tell Zora and me how terrible he has felt about not waking up his grandparents the night Katica died. That's been weighing on him for fifteen years. And I got to tell *him* that Katica had a key to the doors of the Münster *and* the tower, so he doesn't have to wonder if he left any of them unlocked. Plus, as I said, Friedli's almost sure to get fired as sexton." He shook his head. "Not enough, but . . ."

Ueli added his own contribution. "It also sounds as if Denis and Zora have found each other again. That might not have happened if you hadn't started looking into things. It's not exactly an answer, but it ought to cheer you up."

"It does," Renzo said, smiling broadly at last. "They make a striking pair."

"I bet Grossenbacher would love to hear what you've found out, Renzo," Giuliana said. "Maybe he'd have some advice about how to get Friedli to talk."

"I promised I'd fill him in when I finished the case. I wanted to go by and take him a present anyway, after all his help. I'm glad you reminded me." Renzo smiled at Giuliana in what was almost, but not quite, his old way. He picked up his empty glass and poured in a small splash of wine. Then he held it up to Giuliana and Ueli. "To answers," he said and raised his eyebrows at Ueli. "That should be easy for a journalist to toast to. Certainly easier than truth."

Ueli gave an exaggerated groan and touched Renzo's glass with his. "Don't get me started on Truth with a capital T. But yes, I'll toast to answers."

Giuliana and Renzo clinked glasses, too. "To answers," she said, as the two of them briefly locked eyes. "In police work, journalism, and relationships."

"Speaking of relationships," said Renzo, "it's time for me to switch with Fränzi. She has a big date tonight, she told me."

Ueli looked at him with sympathy. "Rubbing your nose in it, is she?"

Renzo shrugged and stood up. "I brought it on myself. Sometimes that's hard to remember, and I get an attack of self-pity, which is revolting. Then I think about how great it is spending every other week with my kids without Fränzi there telling me what a terrible husband and father I am."

"You are neither of those things!" Giuliana felt a familiar surge of anger at the way Fränzi undermined Renzo.

The three of them made their way to the front door, and Ueli shook hands with Renzo. "Come for dinner next time. With your children if you like. Our two would be glad to keep them entertained." He headed off to the living room with a last wave.

Giuliana opened the front door, and she and Renzo stood in the doorway.

"Thanks for jumping to my defense," he said. "But Fränzi was right, at least in part. I did turn out to be a bad husband—for her. No black and white in all this."

"I know," she said softly. "I appreciated your telling me about Mädi."

"Thank you for understanding," he said. "I can't . . . I can't begin to say how grateful I am that you're . . . making this easy. Well, not easy, because it isn't, believe me, but less painful."

Remember what Renzo just said about attacks of self-pity, she told herself sternly, though her chest was tight. She smiled at Renzo's beautiful face—that was never hard to do. "So, did you and Mädi go out?"

"Not yet. But I'm working on it."

And with Renzo working on getting Mädi into bed, what chance did she have? *I might be the only person who's ever turned him down. And I did it over and over for an entire year.* The thought didn't make her happy or proud of her fidelity. But it had been the right thing to do.

They clasped hands and once again gave each other three very correct cheek kisses.

"I think Mädi's terrific, both at her job and personally," Giuliana said. He met her eyes again. "Thank you," he repeated. "For everything." She only nodded this time before closing the door. As she headed toward the living room, she felt something lift inside her. Ueli looked up from his computer and smiled at her—a smile with no regrets or apologies in it, just pleasure in her company on a perfect summer evening.

She smiled back, then walked behind him, put her arms around him, and laid her cheek on the top of his head. He took one of her hands in his and squeezed it. She thought about the Horvats and felt lucky.

39
Before

Fifteen years earlier
Berner Münster, Tuesday, November 23, four in the morning

Katica sat in the place where she always sat when she came to the Münster to pray: the second pew from the front, on the left facing the altar. In spite of all her months with Ben, she still didn't think of the church the way he did, east and west doors, north and south aisles. To her, it was front and back, left and right.

Oh Ben. What is my life going to be like without you?

What life? she reminded herself. *Your life is done.*

But she didn't know yet what that meant. That was why she was sitting here, thinking and praying, trying to decide where to go, what steps to take—although she shouldn't, she *mustn't* be here when Ben came back. He'd assume she'd changed her mind, and it was cruel to give him hope. Which meant she had to leave. But she had no place to go, not if she wanted to live, not even if she wanted to die. What on earth was she going to do?

Right now, all she could picture was Lovro's face as he'd called her filthy names, whispering them, despite his rage, so he wouldn't wake the children.

He knew about her and Ben. He knew! It was unbearable, the shame of it. It made her feel like . . . like a used tissue scrunched in a ball that should be thrown away. Yes, she deserved to be thrown away. Ivana had said it: she was a wicked, selfish woman. She'd known that finishing things with Ben would hurt. But finding out that Lovro knew had been worse, much worse. She'd moved toward him in bed the night before, but he'd turned away from her. No wonder. Her body had repelled him like something foul.

And Goran! Now that Lovro knew about Ben, did he think that Ben was Goran's father? Well, the truth was—God forgive her—it was possible. They'd been careful with the condoms. Well, most of the time. But it could have happened, a pregnancy. She didn't know.

There was a noise, and she looked up to see that man staring at her, the one who took care of the church. His name was Klaus, but she never called him that. She couldn't stand him—never talked to him at all if she could avoid it—and she knew he couldn't stand her either. After the first time she'd left Zora here, he'd told her it wasn't allowed, but she'd ignored him. What right did he have to keep anyone out of a church? The second time he'd told her, he hadn't been so holy; he'd called Zora a dirty Yugo brat. And then Zora made friends with Denis, and they met Denis's grandparents, who were important people. After that, the man couldn't do anything to keep Zora out of the church. But this only made him more of a threat, so she'd told Zora to avoid him, never to go into his office, never to be alone with him. But there was no way to stop him from staring like he was doing now.

To hell with him. She leaned her forehead against the pew in front of her so she couldn't see him. She whispered the Act of Contrition over and over until she felt calm enough to add a Hail Mary and an Our Father. "Deliver us from evil," she mumbled. *But I'm the one who's evil*, she thought with despair. *How can I be delivered from myself?*

I have to leave the Münster. If only she weren't so tired. She'd barely slept since that awful party. When she and Ivana had spoken since— only on the phone because Ivana wouldn't meet with her—her child-hood friend had pounded the words into her like nails: sinner, adulteress, whore. Your life isn't worth living, Ivana had told her. Maybe that wasn't exactly what she'd said, but it was what she'd meant. In the letter Katica wrote to answer Ivana's accusations, she'd agreed that she was worthless. But now, after all that Lovro had said to her, how could she go without telling him goodbye, without a letter or even a thank you, a final embrace? She'd managed to persuade herself that leaving him and the children sleeping was the best thing for them. But to walk away with him staring after her, knowing that his last words to her had been to tell her she was a monster . . . No! He'd been full of fury, but he wasn't like that, not at all, and his words would haunt him. All those things he'd said to her and the way he'd shaken her and bruised her would torment him forever. She couldn't leave him to suffer like that.

At least Ivana wouldn't let him suffer alone. He'd never marry her, of course, but he'd need her, and she'd help him. Jelena had warned her that Ivana had come to Bern to steal her husband, but Lovro wasn't like Jelena's husband, who had silly affairs and made a fool of himself. No, Ivana had been lonely, and Katica had persuaded Lovro to accept her presence in their lives as a friend. Perhaps if Katica hadn't fallen in love again or gotten pregnant, it might have worked. But she, Katica, had destroyed everything with her longing for Ben and her discontent with the good life she had. And then to be rewarded for her infidelity with a beautiful baby boy. That had infuriated Ivana, perhaps more than anything. But Ivana hadn't caused the disaster. She'd only witnessed it.

She thought again of Jelena. Maybe *that's* where she should go. Jelena cared about her; on the night of that terrible party, Jelena had wanted to stay and help. But she was beyond help now, wasn't she? Besides, how long could she stay with Jelena? A few days, a week, a month? That was no solution. Her first idea had been to return to Croatia with Zora. But she wasn't close to her sisters anymore, and, besides, Zora was Swiss now. A Swiss girl, a city girl. She wouldn't want to live in a sad little village in Istria. Besides, the only money Katica had was the last two hundred francs in her pocket. Not the bank card on their joint account. Not if she was leaving Lovro. And she wasn't going to get far with two hundred francs.

She heard the sound of footsteps and looked up, horrified that she'd let Ben find her still here.

But it wasn't Ben, it was him again, that wicked man, standing at the end of her pew. "I got a text from the van driver. He's going to be late, so I've told Ben not to come back in here. He's going to be outside for at least twenty more minutes."

She was so relieved to know she still had time to leave that it didn't occur to her to wonder why the man was being helpful, telling her Ben's schedule. She nodded curtly at him and turned back to the altar.

The man shuffled quickly along the pew behind her, dropped onto the seat, and leaned forward as if he were about to say something to her. Instead, he put his right arm around her neck, his forearm squeezing hard against her throat. He unzipped her puffy jacket with his left hand, then shoved the hand into her jeans, under her panties, and down to her crotch. He grabbed and squeezed her vulva, then seized one of her labia between his thumb and forefinger and pinched her viciously hard. He cut off her scream of pain with his forearm, pressing on her windpipe until she could only just breathe.

"No noise. Twenty minutes is more than enough time to do what I've been wanting to do to you for over a year now, you cunt." His right hand was twisting itself in her hair until her scalp burned. "And if you tell anyone, just think what I can do to that little girl of yours." He pulled his other hand out of her pants to grab her left breast through her sweater. He groaned into her ear, panting out a string of words she'd never heard before. Then he squeezed and twisted her nipple as his right hand jerked down on the hank of hair it was holding. She screamed again, and it came out as a croak. He tightened his arm on her throat and moaned at the sound of her pain.

She was so frightened she couldn't think; she felt urine running down her legs and into her winter boots. *Oh God, oh God, oh God.*

But God did nothing, and the man stood and started to drag her over the back of the pew toward him, using the arm wrapped around her throat to pull her, the fingers of his other hand still clawing into her breast. With her head yanked back, she could see his face upside down, looming over her, and she was terrified he would sink his teeth into her, maybe even bite a piece out of her. Nothing seemed impossible in this nightmare, nothing.

Instead, he leaned down and spat on her. "I've always wanted to spit on a Yugo," he said, laughing. The back of the pew was digging into her spine. She wriggled and kicked, but her feet skidded uselessly on the wood of the bench.

As he dragged her, the fleshy part of his forearm shifted up from her throat until it was on her chin. She opened her mouth and bit him as hard as she could.

He bellowed, and as she felt his grip slacken, she squirmed and fought with all her strength. Then she was free of his arms, and, half scooting, half crawling, she made it out of the pew and raced to the back of the church, toward the huge front doors that led to the Münsterplatz where Ben was waiting.

"Ben," she screamed, "Ben!"

The west end of the church was dark, but she could see the doors, and she fumbled for the Münster key that was always on the ring with her house keys in her pocket. Then she saw that the massive double doors in front of her were bolted with heavy bolts.

She could hear the man walking slowly down the aisle toward her, not hurrying, chuckling to himself. "You've given me a great idea, running down here. I think I'll fuck you in the minister's office, right across her desk. Won't be the first time I've used it that way. Or would that be too comfortable for you?"

Rage flooded in and drowned her terror, and in the moment of clarity that followed, she thought of the tower door, the one off the shop. The shop doors would be locked, but her key worked for the most important doors in the nave and choir—she knew that from Ben. Like a flash, she was in, locking the shop behind her. The door to the tower in the corner was up a few stairs. She opened that, too, and locked it behind her as well. That man had more keys than she did, but at least she could slow him down.

She started up the spiral staircase.

It had been fewer than seven weeks since Goran's birth, so she wasn't fit. Still, she was good at stairs—she ran up and down stairs between the apartment and the basement, fetching stock all day long. *You can do this*, she told herself, *run!*

She could see almost nothing, and each triangular stone step narrowed to a sliver at the center of the staircase. She grabbed the outer banister and forced herself upward, round and round, past narrow windows where pinpricks of light from the city below shone onto the walls, past the two bell chambers.

She heard the door at the foot of the tower bang open and heavy footsteps begin to follow her up. She tried to put more speed into her aching legs. Her breast throbbed where that man had bruised it, her scalp stung, and her damp jeans chafed at her thighs. Her milk started to leak, and her shirt clung to her stickily. But the Kellenbergers' apartment was up here. If she could make it and he was still following, she'd wake them up.

When she stepped onto the balcony, she was attacked by the wind. It roared around her ears, snatching her breath away and making it impossible to hear anything at all. The Kellenbergers were asleep in there. She only had to scream to wake them up. But would they hear?

She crossed her arms against the fierce wind and stepped hurriedly along one side of the rectangular space and across the balcony to the spiral staircase that went up to the next level. She moved just inside the tiny chamber where the second set of stairs began, and, hidden, she waited to see what would happen. Her breath was coming in gasps and moans, and she fought to get it under control. From her hiding place, she couldn't see the man, nor, because of the wind, would she be able to hear him. But because of her hiding place, he wouldn't be able to see her dark figure silhouetted against the city lights, either. All she could do was wait and pray that he didn't search for her for very long.

She had visited the Kellenbergers twice in their apartment, so she knew which window opened into Hans-Peter and Ursula's bedroom, and it was on the other side of the tower from where the man was coming up, which meant she ought to be able to get to it, bang on the shutter, and yell without having to pass the opening to the main staircase and the man. She was about to run round to the window when suddenly he was there, coming out of the stairwell—he was so close she could hear him despite the wind, panting heavily and shuffling his feet. Then she could hear nothing more. Perhaps that meant he had turned the other way onto the balcony, away from where she was hiding. Now he might circle around and come at her from the other direction. She crouched down until she was sitting on a step, arms braced on either side of her body, eyes straining. If his figure appeared before her in the narrow stairwell doorway, she was ready to kick him as hard as she could and then race past him to the Kellenbergers' window.

She trembled with the strain of waiting to be attacked. But the man didn't come. He must be waiting, too. She knew she should stay here for as long as it took the family in the apartment to wake up, when she'd be safe, but the tension was too much to bear. Slowly, she inched out of her hiding place and peered around the staircase doorway. Seeing no one shadowed against the light of the city's streetlamps, she moved along the inner wall and risked a look around the corner—no one there either. Another few minutes, step by careful step, and she'd circled the Kellenbergers' entire apartment and found the gallery empty. But her terror didn't leave her until she checked the stairwell where she'd hidden to make sure that the man hadn't taken her place there, waiting for her in her own tiny sanctuary. With a sigh of relief, she decided he was gone—and then froze again when it came to her that he could be standing in wait on either of the sets of stairs leading back down to the nave. In the staircase, he'd truly have her trapped.

Driven by fear, thinking only of getting further away from him, she climbed to the higher balcony, more slowly now but still afraid that he might give up his wait and come after her. She looked back at the curving stairs that kept her from seeing more than a few steps behind her. How would she even know if he was following?

On the second balcony, it was even windier, noisier, colder. She knew there was a storeroom inside the eight-sided tower, and she tried the door desperately, but it was locked, and this time, her key didn't fit. This balcony, so high above the city, had breast-high stone balustrades, and the floor was covered with some kind of perforated metal sheeting over the stone to keep people from slipping. When she'd been here with Ben to watch the sunset, they'd... No, no. She wouldn't think about Ben.

Katica sat down on the metal-covered stone, her back against the least windy side of the tower. She drew up her legs and wrapped her arms around her knees. Bending her head over her hunched body, she smelled the urine on her jeans. So much had happened to her over the past week; so many dreadful things had been said. But at that moment, stinking of piss was the worst thing of all, the final mark of shame. She cried then—sobbed and wailed into the wind.

After the crying passed, she was calm.

She stood and walked to the side of the tower that looked down on the Münsterplatz, and she hooked the toes of her boots into the chicken wire that was meant to keep people from climbing the balustrade. With a few careful steps up, her waist was level with the top of the wall, and she could see down to Ben, pacing back and forth between the Münster and the Moses fountain, smoking a cigarette. God in heaven, he was still there. Did that mean fewer than twenty minutes had passed since that man had attacked her? It seemed impossible, but Ben was still there, waiting for the van.

Her phone rang, and she let it ring until it stopped. Then she climbed down and took it from her pocket. Lovro. It was almost five in the morning, and Lovro had called her.

No, she wouldn't call him back, even though she loved him. Not the way she'd loved Zora's father, Bram. That had been a craving she'd thought she'd never feel again until Ben walked into the shop, and she couldn't stop looking at him, couldn't keep away from him. But for more than ten years, she and Lovro had shared a life: working together in the shop, raising Zora, eating at the same table, sleeping in the same bed, making love, mourning her miscarriages, laughing and planning, teasing and arguing.

She stared at her phone and then wrote, "I love you" to Lovro. After that, she walked to the other side of the tower and stood, looking out at where the city was darkest. She waited until she was sure the message had been sent and then threw her telephone as far as she could into the night. No more calls. After a moment's thought, she threw her keys after her phone. She didn't want Ben to get into trouble for giving her a key to the church doors.

Now that she knew what she had to do, she wanted it done right away.

She went back to where she'd been before, climbed until her knees were on top of the balcony, and crouched there. Ben was still in the square, but she wiped him from her mind and filled it with Zora, only Zora. Ivana and Lovro would look after Goran. He had barely known Katica and wouldn't miss her, but Zora would suffer.

Yes, she would suffer, but eventually, she would forget her mother, and that was the way it should be. Her strong and beautiful daughter would grow up to have a good life and learn not to miss a mother who'd been a slut, a waste of breath. Zora deserved someone better than she was, and Lovro loved Zora like his own. He would take care of her.

Zora, my heart, my darling girl, you will be all right without me.

At that moment, she believed it was true.

Still kneeling, she said a Hail Mary out loud, the wind whipping away her words, and then she spread her arms, launched herself into the air, and fell.

40
Epilogue

Two months later
The Münster Park, Saturday afternoon, August 24

Renzo sat at one of the little bistro tables on the edge of the Pläfe and watched Zora and Denis walk toward him along a gravel path, the Münster tower soaring over them. He smiled to see how the two of them, arms around each other's waists, also soared over the people they passed. They were close enough to his table now that he could see them grinning at him, two benevolent blue-eyed giants.

When he'd phoned Zora to set up this meeting, Denis had been with her, so she'd put Renzo on speakerphone. The couple had been somewhere outdoors, and Zora told Renzo she was teaching Denis about flowers. When Renzo asked her where they were, she laughed and told him they were in her secret garden. Renzo had no idea what she'd meant.

After a hug from Zora and a handshake from Denis, Renzo took their orders and got in line to buy three iced coffees with milk. As he waited, he thought about Mädi, whom he was seeing for dinner that night, their third date since the Indian takeout at his house. The last two times had been at restaurants, but tonight they'd be at her new apartment in Breitenrain, where she'd moved the week before. Renzo hoped Mädi also liked gardening because, as a housewarming present, he'd bought her a plant—well, a tree, really, a large bonsai. He had great hopes for the evening with Mädi, and he was so lost in contemplating them that the woman taking orders had to ask him twice what he wanted.

At last, with the three coffees on a tray, he walked back to the table under the trees. He'd decided to bring Zora and Denis up to date on his case. Not that it was *his* case anymore. He still did some work on the Seiler case, though, now and then. He'd been the one to find evidence of the KESB threat among the files on Tamara's lawyer's computer. Tamara had been scared into silence by Rosmarie filing a criminal charge against her for attempting to blackmail her stepmother, and Sebastian faded out of the case. It looked increasingly likely that Ruth would be tried for manslaughter and receive a suspended sentence. That was what Giuliana hoped for, and he was glad for her.

With the coffees distributed, Renzo took his place under the trees and said, "I want to talk some more about your mother's death today, Zora, because I feel it's important to keep your family informed. I'm starting with the two of you; then I'll go by the Golden Goat and discuss things with your father and stepmother and Goran on Monday."

Zora was frowning at him. "What's new, Renzo? Have you decided Majka was murdered after all?" She sounded almost hopeful, and Renzo knew why and also knew that he'd have to disappoint her.

"No, not that. I haven't come up with any evidence of homicide, and I'm almost sure no one ever will. I still have strong suspicions that the sexton, Klaus Friedli, had something to do with her death, though. According to your mother's lover, Ben Schweizer, Katica was alone with Friedli in the Münster for at least twenty minutes before she died, and I believe him. I'm convinced Friedli was the man you saw standing outside your window that night, Denis. But I'll never be able to prove it."

"Klaus Friedli," Denis breathed, and Renzo waited a hopeful moment in case the younger man said, "Exactly! It *was* Friedli I saw. I realize that now." But Denis just stared at him. "As a child, I hated Friedli because he hated me, but I never imagined—"

Zora put a hand on Denis's arm as she set her half-empty glass down. "The sexton! You know, my mother told me never to be alone with him. She said if he ever tried to get me to go anywhere with him or even came close to me when I was by myself, I should grab my book bag and run away. She said I should go into the Münster shop and stay there or come outside here to the Pläfe. Then I met Denis and his family, and she didn't seem so worried after that."

Renzo opened his mouth to ask why she'd never said anything about this before. Then he realized he'd never discussed Friedli with her. She'd been a child, after all. More silence and secrets. Well, this one was his fault. Not that her mother's fear of the sexton was evidence of anything specific, but if he'd known about it sooner, maybe he would have asked Friedli some additional questions.

"I don't know what happened, and I don't have any way to find out," he said wearily. "But I've learned something at last that . . . well, it will allow me to make sure that Friedli goes to trial. I feel quite sure he'll end up in prison, even if I can't arrest him for anything he did to your mother."

"What did he do?" asked Zora and Denis, almost in one voice, which made them giggle. Renzo didn't laugh back.

"I told two people who care a lot about the Münster that I suspected Friedli of having something to do with your mother's death. One is the Pfarrerin, Selena Zehnder, who's a very smart and principled woman, and the other is a retired lawyer. He's the person on the parish council who's responsible for everyone that works at the Münster, both employees and volunteers. Neither of them had any trust in Friedli, so they started checking up on him. They discovered that over the past five years, he has hired nine cleaning women for the Münster, all foreign-born and several of them recent immigrants, which makes them particularly vulnerable. Four of them quit before their probation period was over—one of them after only a day. None of the others have stayed a year; the woman who's working there right now, a Somali, has been in her job for five months."

The two of them seemed to guess from his face where this was going. Zora put a hand over her mouth, and Denis asked, "Are the rest . . . are they alive? Are they okay?"

"Alive, thank God, but not okay. A team specializing in violent crimes against women tracked them down—all but one of them, because she's gone back to Brazil. And thanks to what we were told by those former cleaners, plus the Somali woman who's still at the Münster, we've been able to arrest him for rape with violence, physical and sexual abuse, and sexual harassment. Over the past five years, he abused all eight of the women we talked to. Two of them were brutally attacked. None of them went to the police. He always threatened to hurt someone close to them, especially their children or grandchildren, if they said anything."

Tears were running down Zora's cheeks. "My mother . . ." she choked out. Then she stopped, her fist pressed tightly against her mouth. Denis pulled his chair closer to hers and put his arms around her. There was silence for a moment. Finally, Zora pulled herself together and asked, in a low voice, "Do you think he raped her? Do you think he killed her because she was going to tell someone?"

Renzo answered immediately, keeping his voice low as well. "The forensic evidence showed no signs that she'd been raped just before she died. But I don't know what he did to her, Zora. I just don't know. I—and other people, too, the best the Kantonspolizei has—are going to try to get the truth out of him, but I have to tell you that I don't think he'll say a word. He's not the kind of criminal who confesses. Still, there's no doubt about what he's done to these other women. They don't know each other, and they were interviewed separately, yet their stories are almost identical. He ought to be convicted and sentenced to years in prison. I know that doesn't answer your questions. And I know it's not justice for your mother. But I hope it gives you something. A sort of closure."

Zora leaned against Denis. "I don't know how I feel about this except . . . horrified." She brushed away tears. "Knowing that Friedli probably made Majka suffer before she died is unbearable. Still, everything I learn about her death is useful to me in some way."

Denis kissed her hair, and Renzo was glad he'd told the news to both of them at once. For a while, the three of them sat in silence, swirling the ice cubes in their glasses.

Renzo looked up into the leaves over his head. As it so often did in the second half of August, the weather was beginning to turn toward fall. It wasn't a dramatic change, not yet, but although the sun felt warm, Renzo could sense the shift happening. Mostly he felt it in the morning when he got up very early and hurried to the gym, or after sunset when the warmth no longer lingered in the air. Now there was something in the quality of the light that told him summer was ending.

Zora broke the silence. "About three weeks ago, I talked with my father." She said the word with no hesitation or uncertainty, which made Renzo dare to hope that finding out about the Dutch soldier had not changed Zora's relationship with Lovro in any meaningful way. "Now, when it's just the two of us, he's finally able to talk to me about my mother, and it means . . . the world to me." She stopped again, perhaps to get a grip on her emotions. "I asked him to tell me more about what she was like when they were together, more about their marriage—nothing important, just everyday stuff. And I asked him more about the night she died, too."

Renzo was willing to bet that had taken courage. But he already knew Zora was a fighter, didn't he?

"He wanted me to know that after he shook my mother and . . . and called her a whore, he calmed down and started to worry about her. In the end, he phoned her. She didn't answer his call, but a minute later, she sent him a text. It was 'I love you.' He told me how much those words have meant to him all these years—that she wanted him to know that before she died."

Renzo smiled but didn't speak. The police had never found Katica's phone. Was the story true? He didn't know, but it made Zora happy, so maybe its truth didn't matter.

"Come on," Zora said suddenly. "Denis and I want to show you something." The three of them stood and walked along the parapet, glancing down at the Matte and the Aare far below until the wall turned toward the western end of the Münster. They turned, too, and followed the wall another ten feet. Then Zora said, "Look down."

Below him was a steep, high-walled garden climbing up the hill from the Matte to the buildings along the edge of the Münsterplatz. The terraced land was filled with rows of plants. He could identify grape vines, but he didn't know what any of the other things were. Just below him, there was a kind of lean-to shed up against the Pläfe wall; two-thirds of the way up the slope was another small building, this one modern.

"That's our garden," Denis said, "and Zora has the key. It's called the Stiftsgarten. It isn't really a secret. Other people have keys, too. But we can use it whenever we want because we work on the plants. Do you want to come and help us harvest the grapes—when it's time, I mean?"

Renzo knew he must have seen the garden before, but he had never noticed it, and he was touched by the invitation. He found himself wanting to know what was going to happen to Denis and Zora and hoped this could be the beginning of a friendship with them. He'd never picked a grape in his life—he wasn't sure he'd ever watered a plant, either, at least not since childhood. Nevertheless, he said, "I'd love that. Send me an email letting me know when, and I'll come if I can. If it's during a week with my kids, can I bring them?"

"Of course," Zora said. "There'll be tons of kids there."

The three of them gazed down at Zora's garden. Then Zora turned away, Denis put his arm around her again, and Renzo joined them. Together they walked toward the west end of the Münster and the tower, bathed in sunlight.

Acknowledgments

The Berner Münster is a real place, along with the cobblestoned Münsterplatz at its main entrance and the Münsterplattform, a park on the church's south side. Every person in this book, however, is fictional, and so are all the events that take place. I want to emphasize that the real sexton working at the Münster, who talked to me about his job and took me around the church, is a conscientious and honorable man, not a criminal. I'll be very sorry if my story causes pain to anyone who works or worships at the Berner Münster since the people connected to it with whom I spoke while researching this book were, without exception, warm and helpful. I thank them for their support.

Nathan Winter, the glass artist in *Splintered Justice* who trained Denis Kellenberger, is also a fictional character. Still, I couldn't have created him and accurately described his work if I hadn't met Daniel Stettler, a real master of the art and craft of making glass. Daniel welcomed me into his studio, described how he learned his profession, and showed me some of the many amazing things he does with glass. He also let me climb a scaffold with him in the Münster and observe his meticulous work on a window containing fifteenth-century stained glass panels. I am very grateful to him for sharing his passion for making and restoring glass.

As for the scaffold I climbed with him, I was never in danger of falling. Still, Denis's crash to the Münster floor was inspired by my perch high above the ground that day.

As usual, I asked friends and family to read earlier drafts of my book, and I got useful feedback, some of which led to significant changes. I am greatly touched by these people's willingness to spend hours reading and commenting on my manuscripts. My primary helpers were Gabriele Berger, Giuliana Berset-Brignoli, Betsy Draine, Karen Fifer Ferry, Donna Goepfert, Bob Hays, Darlene Hays, Natasha Hays, Dale Herron, Melina Hiralal, Pia Flobecker Malmquist, Thomas Malmquist, Joanne Manthe, George Morrison, Clare O'Dea, Catherine Puglisi, Julia Reid, Isabel Roditi, Michelle Stucker, and Peter Stucker. Thank you, my dears. In addition, Karen Fifer Ferry and Julia Reid gave the book a final polish when it was in the copyediting stage. This was a huge help!

Among my readers, I have to single out Gaby Berger, who found time to answer questions and critique this manuscript despite her demanding work for the Bern Cantonal Police. Then there is Clare O'Dea. Because she is an excellent writer, thoughtful critic, fellow expatriate, and close friend, Clare is someone I count on for good advice. This time, she also gave me information about assisted suicide, which she has researched for her own fiction. Like my first three Polizei Bern novels, *Splintered Justice* also benefited enormously from the input of Kathryn Jane Price Robinson, a brilliant editor and lovely person.

I am fortunate to have Rene Sears as my new editor at Seventh Street Books. Her appreciation for this fourth book and our comfortable collaboration are a blessing. I also sincerely thank the Seventh Street Books team, especially Ashley Calvano, Meghan Kilduff, and Wiley Saichek. Their hard work and support make my writing life easier and happier. Thanks, too, to Paula Guran for my beautiful book cover. Finally, I want to express my gratitude to all of you who have written via my website or in a review to say how much you enjoy the Polizei Bern books. Your praise warms my heart, and your reviews help to sell my books!